VOYAGE OF
INNOCENCE

By the same author

The Frozen Lake

ELIZABETH EDMONDSON

Voyage of Innocence

HarperCollins*Publishers*

This novel is a work of fiction. The names, characters and incidents portrayed in it are the work of the author's imagination. Any resemblance to actual persons, living or dead, is entirely coincidental.

HarperCollins*Publishers*
77–85 Fulham Palace Road,
Hammersmith, London W6 8JB

www.harpercollins.co.uk

Published by HarperCollinsPublishers 2005
1 3 5 7 9 8 6 4 2

A catalogue record for this book
is available from the British Library

ISBN 0 00 718487 5

Typeset in Sabon by Palimpsest Book Production Limited,
Polmont, Stirlingshire

Printed and bound in Great Britain by
Clays Limited, St Ives plc

For Jean Buchanan
a friend indeed

PROLOGUE

OCTOBER 1938

'Sir, it's an emergency.'

The officer of the watch tried again, speaking more loudly and urgently. 'Sir, Captain, sir, please wake up. It's an emergency.'

Reginald Sherston, Captain of the SS *Gloriana*, passenger vessel bound for India, lifted his grizzled head from his starched white pillow.

His eyes opened, the faded blue eyes of a man who had been at sea since he was a boy of fourteen. They looked at the first officer, a capable man, not given to fuss, and across to where his steward was hovering, his uniform in his hand.

'Tell me about it, Mr Longbourne.'

Minutes later, Captain Sherston was on the bridge.

The officers in their white uniforms went quietly about their duties, the man at the wheel, locked on its course, was alert. They were all intent on what the first officer and captain were saying.

The ship sailed on through the waters of the Red Sea. Above them the sky blazed with the brilliant stars that were the gift of ocean travel, and were reflected in the inky, gentle swell. The throb of the engines was steady, reassuring.

'This Mrs Hotspur, a passenger to Bombay, she went ashore at Port Said?'

'Yes, sir. For the day.'

'Did she go on one of the tours? To the pyramids?'

'No, sir. She went ashore with friends.'

'But came back on board.'

'As far as we know, sir. Her re-embarkation card was handed in.'

'And her stewardess says her bed wasn't slept in last night? Who is the stewardess?'

'Pigeon, sir.'

'She didn't report it?'

'It happens, sir, that a woman might . . .' the first officer looked at Captain Sherston's Presbyterian face, and he swallowed, '. . . spend the night elsewhere, sir.'

'The dining room stewards say she didn't take breakfast, lunch or dinner today?'

'That's correct sir.'

'And this ten-year-old boy, Peter Messenger, says he saw her standing by the rail on C-deck at about nine o'clock, one hour and ten minutes after we sailed from Port Said?'

'Yes, sir.'

'Tell me about Mrs Hotspur.'

The first officer consulted his notes. 'Mrs Verity Hotspur. A widow, I understand. A very charming lady, and a cousin of Lady Claudia Vere, who is also aboard – she joined at Lisbon. It was Lady Claudia who raised the alarm.'

'Lady Claudia Vere. So this missing passenger, Lady Claudia's cousin, will turn out to be connected to all kinds of important people?'

'Bound to be, sir.'

Captain Sherston let out a long sigh. 'Emergency procedures for man overboard, Mr Longbourne.'

'Yes, sir.'

Then when the orders had been given, the first officer asked, 'Not much chance for her, is there?'

'None whatever. If she missed the propellers, the sharks will have got her. If not, she'll have drowned.'

PART ONE

SEPTEMBER 1938

ONE

Verity came out on deck into one of those pale autumn days that hovers between rain and sunshine; a breath of wind rippling the still waters of the harbour warned that summer was yielding to autumn.

Despite the light wool jacket she wore, she shivered, both from the chill in the air which heralded the approach of winter, and from an inner cold of fear. Fear for the times, with the shadow of war looming over the country she was leaving; fear for herself. She was no longer afraid of war itself, since there was nothing she could do to prevent or prepare for that. What made her afraid? Her nightmares? Klaus, and his successor, that flat-faced man with no discernible personality? Her future, her brother's fate?

All of those.

Gulls drifted in the sky above her and bobbed on the oily waters far below, their eerie mews a counterpoint to the whistles and hoots of tugs and the flotilla of other vessels going to and fro in the busy harbour. Vee sniffed the salty air, the dockland tang of tar and sea and smoke, and it brought a bitter taste to her mouth. The vast area of Tilbury Docks, alive with the bustle and activity of one of the busiest ports in the world, held no appeal for her; she longed for the boat to leave, for the line of water between the ship and the quay to widen and become an arm's length, a fifty-yard gap, for the land to fade into the distance, for there to be nothing but green-grey waves and foam and sky.

By some trick of the breeze, voices floated up to her from the quayside, the words reaching her ears with extraordinary clarity. A cheerful woman's voice: 'I say, isn't that Mrs Verity Hotspur up there? Looking fearfully smart? In the red hat!'

'Who's Mrs Hotspur when she's at home?

'She's a society lady, a widow, her husband . . .' the words were lost on the wind, then were clear again. 'I expect she's off to Egypt, for the winter.'

'Running away somewhere safe, more like,' said a morose nasal voice. 'Wish I could do the same.'

'Come on, Jimmie,' said the cheerful voice, 'got to fight for your country, you know. Anyhow, who says there's going to be a war? Let's look on the bright side.'

'They're all running away. One law for the rich and another for the rest of us.'

Running away. Dear God, if only they knew what she was running away from. War? It was laughable. Inevitable, but irrelevant and nothing to do with why she was standing on the top deck of the SS *Gloriana*, soon – not soon enough – to be setting off on a voyage to India.

She rested her arms on the teak rail. On board ship was an orderly world, where wood and brass were polished to a gleaming, reflective finish. It was a world run by bells and routine and people who knew their duty. Where lascars rose before dawn to scrub down and dry the decks to immaculate perfection before foot of passenger or officer stepped on them. Where meals were provided on the dot of the appointed hour, where the distance travelled was noted at precisely twelve o'clock each day.

It was, nonetheless, a more changeable world than the one she was leaving. As the *Gloriana* made her steady way across the sea, the stars would move imperceptibly out of their customary places, until, one day, they would be different stars, the stars of the southern skies, and the ship would have sailed out of Europe and into the Indian Ocean.

New skies, a new country, but an old life. She wished that this voyage marked a clean break in her life, one of those turning points when the door shut on the old and you stepped out into the beginning of something completely new.

How often in life did that happen? When you were born, of course. When you learned to walk, although no one ever remembered, at least not consciously, what a difference that made to a life: the first steps, the first taste of independence. School, perhaps, was another new start; for her, going away to boarding school had marked the end of her childhood. And the biggest step – no, stride – of all, when she'd taken the train from Yorkshire to university.

12

Where, even while she was still an undergraduate, a new, adult life had begun. Like a nun hearing the call of God and taking up her vocation, that was how she had seen it. How wrong she had been, how dewy-eyed and naive and angry and full of herself and so sure of what was right.

And because of listening to that deceitful inner voice and giving in to her anger, she was here now. On board the SS *Gloriana*, sailing at another's bidding, full of fear and hatred, uncertain whether she could possibly do what was asked of her, knowing that she didn't want to. And the price of failure?

A life.

She looked down the steep sides of the great liner, down over three more railings and decks and then rows of portholes, down to the quay, where the wind stirred scraps of paper and litter on the quayside. Down there, pieces on a chessboard, people were milling around as the moment of sailing drew near.

The last few passengers hurried out of the customs house, checking passports and boarding cards. Porters with trolleys laden to improbable heights with towers of luggage, each suitcase and box and trunk labelled with stickers: P & O; SS *Gloriana*; initials, a large capital letter in a circle, B for Brown, J for Jones, S for Smith; destination labels for Lisbon, Port Said, Bombay; Wanted on Voyage. The Not-Wanted-on-Voyage luggage had all been taken away to the hold, to sit in staid rows until the port of disembarkation; she wished she could wrap herself up and pass the time among the lumber in the darkness of the hold. That was where she belonged, among the rats and the detritus, not here in the comfort and luxury of first class.

'Rats leaving the sinking ship, that's what they are,' said the nasal voice. Vee looked towards the great hawsers stretching to the capstans on the quay, holding the vessel tightly in place; she had heard that rats did indeed know when a ship was going to founder, when something was amiss, and would be seen streaming down the ropes and on to land. No, there were no rats. She was the rat, in that man's eyes. She and all the other passengers.

'Watch out for Sam and don't be so uncharitable.'

That was the cheerful-sounding woman who had recognized her; who had no doubt seen her photo in *Tatler*, or in the more scurrilous papers when . . . No, she wasn't going to think about that.

13

Vee narrowed her eyes, trying to identify who, of all those standing so far down there, had called her a rat. It was that man in the shabby mac, with a hat that had seen better days. Beside him stood a perky young woman, wearing a coat too thin even for this weather. She had a look of dogged good humour on her face; her hair, escaping from a velvet hat that had been brushed to raise a fading pile, was blonde and brassy. She wore too much lipstick, but she had a personality, a confidence about her. Vee envied her. She felt that whoever she was, Miss Velvet Hat had a better, less complicated life than her own. She probably slept soundly and dreamlessly at night, and woke with a curiosity and excitement about the day to come, even though she no doubt had to work hard for a meagre living, never had quite enough to eat and little hope of a better future.

'Sam's not running away, Jimmie. He's got a job to do out there, same as you and me have here.'

'I didn't say Sam was running away, and I don't suppose the rest of them going tourist class are either. Ordinary people they are, like Sam and you and me. No,' with a contemptuous gesture up at the deck where Vee was standing, 'it's that lot up there get my goat. All those first-class passengers, hoity-toity, not lifting a finger to do anything for themselves. Seven-course meals and dancing every night, and not a care in the world, and get out of England, quick, before the Nazi bombs come raining down and they might get hurt.'

'Like I said, maybe there isn't going to be a war.'

'Like the sun isn't going to rise tomorrow. Those toffs all know there's going to be a war. If they can't scarper to America, then they think they can hide away in some warm spot where life isn't going to change, and they can have their servants and their whiskies and let other people be blown to pieces. It makes me sick.'

'Everything makes you sick, Jimmie.'

'I know who that Mrs Hotspur is.' Jimmie's voice was indignant. 'It was all in the paper when her husband died, fishy business, that, if you ask me.'

Vee was following the swooping, soaring flight of a gull with her eyes, but she saw nothing. She was looking inwards, at another scene, a bloodstained study. Klaus's words, from that day in Paris, came creeping into her mind, 'We have arranged for certain things to happen.'

Certain things? No, it was impossible. Why should they have done that? And then, if they were responsible, then how safe was she? In

14

London, here, anywhere? Words drifted into her head. Don't put a foot wrong, always do as they say, they've no forgiveness in their souls. You don't want to come to a gory end . . .

There was a smell of fish in her nostrils, fish and seaweed, the smell of the beach when the tide turns and goes out, revealing the debris that lies beneath the sea.

'Look, there's Sam waving.' Her face beaming, the young woman in the velvet hat pulled off the red scarf she was wearing round her throat and flapped it towards the other end of the ship, where the tourist-class passengers were coming out on deck to wave their good-byes and watch their native land fade into the distance.

She was looking up at Vee again and, for a moment, their eyes met. Then the woman turned back to the man in the shabby mac. Once again the words reached Vee. 'Scandal wherever she goes, she's often in *Tatler*, and her cousin, Lady Claudia Vere, oh, she's lovely, blonde hair and huge blue eyes. Her picture's always in the society magazines.'

'Yes, and she's got a noble brother who's stark staring bonkers and will swing from the nearest lamp-post come the revolution.'

'Oh, you and your revolution. I tell you, there isn't going to be any Bolshevik revolution, and the sooner you realize it, the happier you'll be. Then you can get on with life instead of moaning about it.'

Vee turned away, dismayed as the girl's words struck home. She pitied Jimmie and his illusions. Probably, even before the year was out, he would be in uniform, at close quarters with his brothers to a degree that would make him long for less comradeship, and without a minute in the day to ponder on the rights of men or the oppression of the workers.

There was a greater sense of urgency on the quay below; a car arrived and its doors flung open even before the brakes were on, three men got out, a porter came hurrying to unstrap cases from the boot, an official with a clipboard and a frown ushered them towards the customs shed, pulling out a watch as he did so.

Vee stiffened, her eyes fixed on a tall, dark man in a grey suit standing beside a wicker basket. She couldn't put a name to him, she had never been introduced to him, but she had seen him before, several times, always as a shadowy, lurking figure. A watcher. In the park, when she and Klaus . . . And outside her flat. A man with a bony face. Not distinctive, and yet his features were etched on her

15

mind. He wore the kind of clothes that would never stand out in a crowd, he was a blender.

Panic set in. If he were coming on board, it could mean only one thing.

She must get off. This was a hideous mistake. She would get off the boat right now, this very minute, never mind her luggage, never mind anything. She would take the train to London, and then to Scotland, to Ireland, anywhere . . .

She couldn't. Despair swept over her.

But was he embarking for the voyage? He was making no move towards the ship. Instead, his eyes were scanning the decks, resolutely and systematically. She stepped back and tucked herself behind a metal buttress. The watcher's eyes paused, moved on, came back. Only his eyes weren't on her. His hand rose in casual acknowledgement, then he turned abruptly, and was lost in the crowd of onlookers.

He hadn't been looking for her. Who then? Someone on the deck below, over to the left. She hung over the rail; all she could see were hats; everyone was looking down at the quay or over to where the tugs were manoeuvring into position.

She ran along the deck, pushing past other passengers, and almost tumbled down the steep gangway to the deck below. It was teeming with people, some sombre, tearful, even; others cheerful. Which of them had the man been looking for? She caught a glimpse of a man who looked just like Joel. It couldn't be, of course, Joel was the last man to leave his college and set sail just before the start of term.

Some of her fellow passengers recognized her, there were whispers and curious glances. But not one of them was the right kind of person; none of them could be an associate of the man on the quay.

A cheer went up from the quayside, paper streamers rained down from the decks and the gangways were trundled aside. Answering cries and shouts floated down from the decks, there was a burst of steam, a whistle and then a blast from the SS *Gloriana*'s funnel, an oddly lightweight sound in comparison to the bass notes of the tugs. A band was playing, bunting flapped and a strand fell loose, swooping down into the sea.

Inch by inch, the boat glided away from her mooring. There was a foot of murky water, a yard, fifty yards. Then the *Gloriana*, attended by her acolyte tugs, was sailing serenely down the grey stretches of the Thames, moving slowly past warehouses and wharves. People in small boats waved, more hooters and horns and whistles sounded; the voyage had begun.

Vee stayed at her post, watching without attention as they sailed past cargo boats, unkempt and tubby and rusty, holds gaping, crates and laden nets being swung down into their bowels on winches. Business, purpose, activity.

Lucky, lucky people.

Unlucky her?

The moment of self-pity passed before it had begun. It wasn't a question of luck. It was a matter of taking the wrong decisions, in acting out of anger and temper and folly, and of one disastrous mistake, a well-meaning mistake, leading to another and another and another until here she was, where she had no wish to be, acting and living like a puppet, with strings pulled by a puppet master who had no more interest in her or her rage or wretchedness than if she had indeed been a painted marionette.

If only . . .

The if only's went back a long way, she knew that. If only her sister Daisy hadn't died. If only Grandfather hadn't been such a tyrant. If only . . .

Her life might have taken a very different path. If she could have those years back, be given a magical chance to live them again, the one place she wouldn't be was here, on this boat.

There they were again, the terrible thoughts that rattled round and round in her head. She'd need a sleeping tablet tonight, to bring her at least an hour or two of the heavy and dreamless sleep that she craved. For that brief space of time, no dreams broke through the pharmaceutical veil of her white tablets: take one at bedtime.

She was profoundly grateful to a medical friend for prescribing them.

'You're a fool, Vee,' he'd said. 'They aren't any kind of an answer, and if your own doctor won't give them to you, he's probably right.'

'Darling, he's simply too old-fashioned. The only reason I sleep badly, according to him, is because I'm a young woman without husband or children, not fulfilling my *raison d'être*, do you see?'

'He can't blame you for being a widow.'

'He can blame me for being a well-off young widow who, after a decent interval, hasn't remarried. That's an affront to the natural order of things, almost as bad as someone like Cynthia Lovelace going off to live in a cottage in Wales with her burly woman friend who teaches PE at Grandpont, or the unfeminine types who choose to go to university and have a career instead of sacrificing their virginity and independence on Hymen's altar to an eligible and suitable young man. So, no, he won't give me sleeping pills.'

Vee's thoughts flitted to Cousin Mildred, who had her own means of dealing with the strains and stresses of life, 'Do try some, dear child, there's nothing like it.'

There were bound to be people she knew on board, several of them with Mildred's habit. Most of them from the ranks of the idle rich, not people going out to do a job of work like the unknown Sam with his friends Jimmie and Velvet Hat waving him goodbye from the quayside. Egypt? India? Their week's holiday would be spent hiking in Wales or at a b. & b. in Weymouth; they wouldn't have the luxury of weeks and months of leisurely travel in warmer climates, with expensive substances to change their spirits and mood if they felt the need.

Oh, yes, there would be friends and acquaintances on the *Gloriana*, people going to winter in the Egyptian sun, and it was the time of year when mamas with daughters who hadn't taken during the season, or during several seasons, chose to go on pilgrimage, to set off for foreign shores where the heat and the inward-looking British communities might produce the elusive mate not found in the ballrooms of Mayfair or the country houses of Shropshire and Gloucestershire.

Vee went slowly down the wide, mirrored staircase that linked the upper and lower decks. She attracted a good deal of attention; the junior officer on his way to the radio room with a sheaf of telegrams; the florist going the other way with an armful of flowers; the lady's maid hurrying to the beauty salon to acquire some essential forgotten item; passengers, anxious to find their cabins; all of them noticed to some degree the particular allure that Vee had. Some noticed with only a fraction of their attention, some admired, some envied.

Vee herself was oblivious both to her surroundings and her fellow human beings. Her ability to attract the attention – and the affections and desires, it had to be said – of those around her was an old story, and one that no longer interested her.

A stewardess was hovering at the end of her corridor. 'Mrs Hotspur? Cabin sixty-seven? It's on the left, I'll show you. Are you travelling with your maid?'

18

She was not. A smile, a *douceur*, and this ungainly but kindly-looking woman would be her slave for the voyage. A maid! That was the last person she needed on this journey.

It was a single cabin, spacious for a liner, with a dressing table and neatly fitted cupboards and drawers, an outside cabin, with a rectangular window looking out on to a secluded deck. No strollers or nosy-joes were allowed along this stretch of deck, this was a reserved area for the lucky occupants of cabins sixty-five to seventy-seven. Her luggage was already in the cabin, strapped and labelled with a large round H for Hotspur, First Class passenger to Bombay.

She sat down at the dressing table, and took off her scarlet hat, laying it carelessly down on the glass top. The stewardess, hovering in the doorway, came forward and took it. Vee smiled at her. 'What's your name?'

'Pigeon, madam.'

'Thank you, Pigeon.'

'Shall I unpack for you now, madam?'

'Later, if you don't mind.'

Still Pigeon lingered. 'We were expecting a Mr Howard to have this cabin.'

'Mine was a late booking, a cancellation.'

It had been a risk, leaving it so late, but the clerk at the shipping line had murmured confidentially that there was usually a cabin available at the last minute. It didn't trouble the company, because there was always a waiting list, especially for a vessel like the SS *Gloriana*, and at this time of year.

A smile, a note, and Mrs Hotspur moved to the top of the waiting list. What had happened to Mr Howard? she wondered for an idle moment. An elderly gentleman, struck down with apoplexy? A prosperous businessman with urgent business to attend to, that prevented him from sailing? A man of substance, undoubtedly, to travel in this type of cabin. A young man in disgrace, being sent out to the East by a distressed family? Did young men still get sent out to India to keep them out of harm's way? What if her parents had sent Hugh out to India? No, she wasn't going to think about Hugh. The list of people and things she didn't want to think about was alarmingly long. Back to Mr Howard. 'I dare say he was a family man, escaping to a new life,' she said out loud.

'I beg your pardon, madam?' said a startled Pigeon.

Vee laughed. 'Oh, nothing. I was just thinking aloud.' She got up, smoothing out the wrinkles from her slim-fitting skirt. 'I'm going to look around, so you can see to my things while I'm gone. There's a wine-coloured dress in that big suitcase, the one on its side. That'll do for this evening.'

'Best go and see the purser about your place in the dining room, madam,' said Pigeon as she made a dive for the suitcase. 'You'll want to be at a good table at the second sitting.'

One look at Mrs Hotspur, a fashionable woman and a real lady, you could see that at a glance, thought Pigeon as she held out her hands for the keys, and the purser would be delighted for her to sit wherever she wanted. Which wouldn't be at the captain's table, if she, Pigeon were any judge of a passenger. Too dull for such a smart and lively lady. She was sure she'd seen her picture in the *Tatler* more than once. It pleased her, she much preferred upper-class passengers to some of the riff-raff you got on board these days.

TWO

Peter Messenger loved ocean liners with all the enthusiasm of his ten years. He loved catching the boat train and arriving at the docks where the great sleek white liners were moored with unbelievably huge cables stretching far up into the bows. He loved the oily briny smell and the gulls and the gloomy customs shed and the piles of trunks, all labelled and waiting to be trundled up into the ship, some to disappear into the hold, that mysterious place where the Not Wanted on Voyage went, or to appear in your cabin, waiting to be unpacked and then stowed away by the baggage steward until the end of the voyage, three weeks in the future.

The first time he'd been on a boat, he'd been overwhelmed by the size of it, by the notion that anything that big could sail without sinking. This time, he'd led the way up the gangway with jaunty steps, ahead of his stepmother, Lally, with that Miss Tyrell bringing up the rear.

Miss Tyrell was the one blot on his happiness. What had possessed his mother to bring her?

'Darling, I'm not bringing her. She's on her way out to India in any case, to look after her brother and her nephews and nieces. Her sister-in-law died recently, so sad, a tropical disease she said.'

Peter wished Miss Tyrell could be struck down by a tropical disease, right now, before they were even on board. 'She's a nanny.'

'Not any more, and she's coming to look after me as much as you. My clothes and so on. I shan't be taking a maid, your father says an English maid is always a nuisance in India, they don't adapt. Miss Tyrell will be very helpful, and you'll grow to like her.'

21

'I'm far too old for a nanny.'

'You're not too old to need some extra looking after, you've been so ill, darling. It'll make me feel much happier when I'm not there to know that Miss Tyrell has you under her eye.'

'Why won't you be there?'

'Well, there's a social life on board ship, you know that. Bridge and games, and then dancing and so on in the evenings. I don't want to have to worry about you all the time.'

'I can look after myself.'

'Of course you can. You're the man of the family while Daddy isn't here, but even so, we'll be glad of Miss Tyrell. I don't think she's a fusser. She seems very practical and down-to-earth.'

Lally kept her own doubts to herself. Miss Tyrell had, although she wouldn't say so to Peter, been wished on her. Claudia's sister-in-law had telephoned her.

'Mrs Messenger? My name is Monica Sake. We met once, in London, when you were staying with Claudia, but I don't expect you to remember me.'

'Oh, of course . . .'

'I hear from Agnes that you're going out to India.'

Lally's heart sank, as it always did when her mother-in-law was mentioned.

'On the *Gloriana*.'

'Yes.'

'Then I'd like you to take our old nanny with you.'

Visions of some decrepit family retainer sprang to Lally's astonished mind. 'Oh, no, really, I don't think –' And why was their old nanny going out to India in any case?

'We're desolated to lose her, she's the best nanny imaginable, been with the family since she was a nursery maid, she was my husband's nanny. And Claudia's of course, she was nanny to all of them.'

Monica Sake was Lucius's wife, that was it; she was the Countess of Sake. And the nanny Lady Sake wanted to foist on her had looked after Claudia, and Lucius, whom Claudia and Vee said was – what was the word they used? Bonkers.

Monica's voice was quacking away. 'We've tried to persuade her to stay. However, her brother's wife died a little while ago, some foreign illness, and Nanny Tyrell feels she owes it to her brother to go and keep house for him. It isn't a particularly convenient time for us, she was due to go to Henrietta and take care of the baby. But I suppose she must be allowed to do what she thinks best.'

Lally began to warm towards this unknown Miss Tyrell.

'She wants to work her passage out. She's a thrifty soul. I heard you'd be taking your stepson – sickly, isn't he, and so not yet up to school? She'll be perfect, she can take the boy off your hands. You won't want to be bothered with a boy that age when you're on board. Or are you taking your own nanny?'

'Well, no.'

'Or your maid?'

'No.'

'She can do that for you as well. She's extremely competent, she'll be a great help to you. That's settled then.'

And it was, to Lally's dismay. She still hadn't told Henry that she was bringing Peter with her, and she hoped that news about the sickly boy didn't reach her husband through the letters that his officious family wrote to him whenever they had an idle moment. Fortunately, Henry rarely read private letters; she suspected the only ones he looked at with any attention were the ones from her, and she took care to keep them brief.

'Official correspondence is enough for any man,' he would say, opening a long screed from his mother, flicking through the pages and crumpling the letter into a ball before tossing it into the waste-paper basket.

This wasn't Miss Tyrell's first voyage. She'd crossed the Atlantic more than once, had accompanied the Veres out to Hong Kong – now, there was a strange country – and had spent six months in Bombay. She liked India. She liked the heat and the people and the energy, although the shocking poverty and the skinny animals made her uncomfortable.

She was pleased for the chance to work her passage rather than pay for it herself. For one thing, it meant she would be travelling first class, which was what she was accustomed to. If she'd had to pay, it would have been tourist class, and a shared cabin down in the bowels of the ship, and not at all the kind of company she was used to. She wasn't sure about this Mrs Messenger, though. Lady Sake had spoken of her in the pitying tone her employers used about half-wits, cripples and social outsiders.

'Of course Harry is absolutely one of us, the Messengers go back for ever, but Lally, as they call her, I believe her name is actually Lavender, is not. She's American, well that's another world, don't you think? Headstrong, I'd say, by the look of her, but then you'd need strength of character to cope with Harry, I never knew a man with so much energy. Her father's a politician, from Chicago of all places. He was a doctor before he went into the Senate, Irish, of course, her name was Fitzpatrick. And she's Catholic. Will that bother you, Nanny?'

Having no religious convictions of her own, merely subscribing to the conventional Anglicanism of her employers, Miss Tyrell said no, in the tone of voice that made Lady Sake feel for a moment that she had committed a solecism by even mentioning religion.

'I do hope you don't suffer from seasickness, Miss Tyrell. It can be very bad in the Bay of Biscay at that time of year.'

Seasick? Not her. As the SS *Gloriana* sailed into what her crew called a dirty night, her stomach was perfectly in order. She gave Peter a dose of tonic, though, just in case there should be any inclination to collywobbles, as she called any kind of stomach upset, and it would help to keep him regular, so important when a child was convalescent. Peter was the nervy sort, you could see that, although that might be due to his having been so ill. And Mrs Messenger? Miss Tyrell felt sorry for her. She didn't care to see a young woman with those tired eyes and that look of haunted care to her. The child had been in danger, yes, but he was better now, and he was a stepson, not one of her own. Perhaps that was the problem. But here she was, on her way back to India, to be reunited with her husband. This was a time for happiness, not for fretting.

And not a good sailor by the look of her.

'Run along, Peter, Mummy's not feeling very well and isn't in the mood for your chatter.'

'I was only telling her about some people she knows on board, that's all.' It wasn't for Miss Tyrell to keep him away from his mother. Then he understood. 'She's seasick,' he said with scorn.

THREE

Perdita Richardson looked around her narrow cabin. She liked the round porthole, it had a distinctly nautical air that was pleasing; if you were going to be shunted off on a sea voyage, then you might as well feel you were on board a ship, and not merely in some floating hotel. She'd seen her friend Tish and her new husband off last year after their wedding. They'd had a stateroom on the *Queen Mary* – they'd been going to spend their honeymoon with her husband's family in New England – and Perdita had been disappointed to see how ordinary it was. Plush, but it could have been a hotel anywhere.

This, however, was unquestionably shipshape; fitted lockers beneath the bunk, everything in its place. She took off the shapeless brown felt hat she'd crammed on her head for want of anything better being immediately to hand, and gave her hair a vigorous ruffle. Curly and unmanageable, she kept it in place when she could be bothered with a fearsome array of pins and fixative. Usually, she left it in its natural state; that was one good thing about being a student of music, appearances went for very little. Most of her fellow students at the Royal Academy of Music were young and hard-up and had minds above mundane items of clothing or the nice arrangement of hair.

She'd tried cutting her thick curls short, but in her opinion it made her look like one of the woolly sheep that chewed the grass around her home in Westmoreland, and there was some hope of elegance, just every now and then, if you had hair long enough to be pinned up. She rummaged in her bag for a hairbrush and tugged it through the disorder. It made little difference to her appearance, but she felt she had made an effort.

Not evening dress the first night out, everyone knew that. So she'd wear – what? Despite the small cabin and the untidy hair, Perdita was far from being a poor student, or a poor anything. Her family were wealthy and she had money of her own; she could buy all the clothes she wanted, but found it difficult to find much ready-made that fitted her tall, rangy frame, and had a dislike of the fussing around at the dressmakers, as she put it. So her clothes were an odd collection of what she'd found that fitted her, including some pairs of men's slacks, which she found comfortable and which fitted her long legs. No one made anything of them at college, but now, throwing open the lid of her suitcase, she did wonder whether they were quite right for a sea voyage.

I expect lots of people will be frightfully posh, she said to herself. Well, they'll have to be satisfied with their own poshness, how I look can't affect them at all. She took out a favourite green dress, gave it a shake, and opened the narrow cupboard to find a coat hanger.

A woman in uniform appeared at the door as though by magic. Small and shrewish, she cast a disapproving look at Perdita's open suitcase and stepped inside the cabin, making Perdita retreat until she had her back against the washbasin, the green dress held in front of her like a shield.

'I'll unpack for you, miss. I'm your stewardess. My name's Merkin.'

'Oh, thank you. Only, I can do it myself.'

Merkin paid no attention. 'You go along to the dining room and put your name down for the second sitting. Not the first, mind, that's for kiddies and people who don't care for the social side. My passengers always take the second sitting.'

Such was Merkin's moral force that Perdita found herself outside her cabin and following the arrows guiding her to G-deck.

'Boat drill half an hour after we sail, miss,' Merkin called after her. 'You're muster station twenty-three, and you'll need to have your lifejacket with you.'

Boat drill? Lifejacket? This was Perdita's first voyage, and she was mystified. Not to worry, someone would explain it to her, and say where she had to be and what she had to do. People always were keen to put you on the right path, especially when it came to anything as institutional-sounding as boat drill. Like fire drill at school, only not shinning down ladders in the dead of night and usually in the rain, it was to be hoped.

A sudden tiredness swept over her, irritating her with her weakness. She was completely well, they all said she was fully recovered, only needed time to get her strength back. Hence the voyage, a round trip to India, with a month or so staying with friends in Delhi; it would do her the world of good, the doctors had assured her. She hadn't been interested, wasn't interested in going on a voyage, had never wanted to go to India, they were her grandfather's friends in Delhi, not her friends, she didn't want to stay with a lot of strangers, and in what she knew would be a very strange country.

Only Grandpapa had been so keen on the idea, and he hadn't been well himself, and she hated to disappoint him; it would be churlish and unkind to refuse his generous offer of a ticket and all expenses paid.

Not for the first time, she wondered if he was so urgent for her to go, not because of her recent illness, but because of the coming war. If war broke out soon, she could be stuck for the duration in India. Which might suit Grandpapa, but didn't suit her at all. What music was there for her in India? Besides, if there was a war, she wanted to be where she belonged, in England, not away from all the bombs and terror on some distant verandah. The last war had gone on for four years; she couldn't imagine not seeing Westmoreland for four whole years.

No, to be fair, Grandpapa would have sent her to America if he were concerned for her safety and wanted her out of England in time of war. He must think that the war he was so sure was on its way wasn't going to start for a few months yet.

Her friends weren't much interested in talk of war, but those who talked about it mostly reckoned that it was necessary to do something about Hitler and the Nazis. Others, cynical arrivals from Austria and Germany, Jewish refugees with music in their souls that made the English students sigh and give up hope, said that Britain and France wouldn't fight for Czechoslovakia or for anyone else, it was all just words. Hitler got what he wanted, always would get what he wanted, and what he didn't want was to fight England.

Perdita's mind turned to the here and now, and to her music. The first thing she had to do was find a piano. There were several on board; that was one thing she had insisted on. 'Grandpapa, I can't go if I can't work. I'm hopelessly out of practice, and more weeks with no playing will just be a disaster. If I can work on the voyages

27

out and back, and if your friends have a piano, something at least halfway decent, I'll be able to practise there.' Weren't things like pianos liable to be eaten by giant ants or inclined to warp and go out of tune for ever in the moist heat of the unimaginable east?

The friends did indeed have a piano, a good one, they had assured her in a courteous letter. So possibly not yet eaten by ants. And Grandpapa had spoken to the chairman of the shipping line, an old chum, needless to say, and had been assured that Perdita would be able to practise in one of the lounges whenever she wanted.

Perdita knew about practice and doing it whenever you wanted. That meant, when no one else was around; well, that was all right with her. She was an early waker, distressingly so since she'd been ill, so if she could get a couple of hours in first thing, no one would be about to bother her or to be bothered by an hour of scales and arpeggios. The dining room forgotten, she set off on a piano hunt.

FOUR

Vee held the white, round box in her hand, hesitating. She lifted the lid, and shook two pills on to her palm.

Recently, these pills had begun to have a strange effect on her, in some mysterious way causing her to relive, in the utmost clarity, scenes from her life. Not truly dreams, for there was nothing in the sequences that rolled through her mind that hadn't happened. The past was simply playing over again, as though she were watching a film.

When she woke, tired and thick-headed, for she always had alcohol to help the sleeping pills work, she could remember only a little of these waking dreams, the re-enactments of her former life, but the memories and images they left in her mind disturbed her profoundly throughout the ensuing day, until the evening came, and her mind cleared, and she could numb herself once more with a drink and companionship. She never drank to excess. She couldn't risk losing control, the alcohol was merely a crutch, not a wiper-out of the emotions and dilemmas she longed to be free of.

She had been tempted, over the last few months, to try some of Mildred's remedy for keeping the world at bay, but it wasn't for her, she didn't want a sense of heightened excitement, she had that on her own account. What she wanted was the cessation of feeling, then she could be happy.

Better to relive scenes of her past than to be caught in more nightmares.

She sat down and brushed her hair, long firm strokes to soothe her fears away. Then she climbed into bed, between stiff sheets, smelling of ironing and starch. She left the light on, a glowing blue night-light. Like on a train, she thought drowsily, as the pills began to take effect. Sweet dreams, she muttered to herself, as her eyelids closed. Sweet dreams, or bitter dreams, to match her thoughts.

Tonight, she was back in the Deanery. She was eighteen years old, she knew that, because there was a birthday just past, and a card on the fireplace of her room, wishing her a happy birthday from Hugh. He'd drawn a caricature of her and her cat, a brilliant sketch, both the cat and the chair it was on decorated with bows. Hugh was as gifted with his pen as he was with words.

She was sure that it wasn't going to work. It was worth a try, it was always worth a try, but she, and the mistresses at school, and Hugh, who had been as encouraging as he knew how, had all known that Grandfather would forbid her to go to university.

'No chance of a scholarship, Vee, I suppose?' Hugh asked her as they sat, legs outstretched, on the white window seat in their sitting room on the top floor. The window was open, although the day was cold, since they were enjoying an illicit cigarette. Smoking, like alcohol, was banned in the Deanery.

'There's a chap I know at the House, he gets two hundred and fifty a year. Twice what his father earns, actually.'

'What does his father do?' Vee asked.

'He's a carpenter, I think.'

'Only Daddy isn't a carpenter, unfortunately, so I doubt if I count as a deserving case.'

'Should have had Jesus for a father,' said Hugh irreverently. 'After all, God the Father, one substance with the Son, so . . . All right, I'm not really being frivolous, I'm trying to help.'

'Irreligious rather than frivolous, don't you think?' She tapped the ash from the end of her cigarette carefully on to the outside ledge of the window. 'Women's colleges aren't rich, and the scholarship girls are all poor.'

'You'll be poor, if Daddy and Grandfather cut off your allowance.'

'It isn't the same. Besides, you have to be brilliant to get a major scholarship, as well as being deserving, and I'm neither.'

'True. Joel Ibbotson is brilliant, no doubt about it.'

It was all very well for Hugh, but however compassionate he was, his was a different situation. He was a man, he didn't have to earn

30

or justify or sweat for his place at university. It was the next natural thing for him.

'Whereas for me, the next natural thing is getting married and starting a family.'

'I pity the poor husband,' said Hugh, tossing the butt of cigarette out of the window.

'You are an ass, Hugh, now we'll have to go down and find it before the gardener does.'

The gardener, a dour ancient of even more puritanical inclinations than the Dean, deeply disapproved of smoking, and had been known to harangue tourists with a stream of Old Testament prophecy about where those who smoked would end up.

Hugh slid to his feet. 'Lord, yes, what a bore, but anything not to get a lecture about going from one smoking pit to another.'

Vee got up and linked arms with him. 'Or Daddy being distressed and asking himself where he went wrong with us.'

Hugh looked at Vee with affection. He was barely half a head taller than her, short for a man. They were very alike, obviously brother and sister in physique and colouring, and with the same direct gaze in their dark eyes.

'He did go wrong, in a very big way, I fear, but smoking is the least of it.'

Hugh wasn't there when their grandfather arrived to discuss Vee's future. 'Lucky for me I'll be back in Oxford when he comes,' he'd said. 'You know how scenes upset me.'

Unfortunately, scenes didn't upset Grandfather.

With the easy movement of dreams, she was no longer in her austere, bare-floored bedroom, but in the drawing room, large and sombre; Victorian in furniture and colour, and even smell.

It was a Monday. Family conferences always happened on a Monday. Grandfather never came to the Deanery at the weekend, because on the Saturday the Dean would be polishing his sermon, and on Sunday, Grandfather's absence from divine service would be noticed.

Unlike many a child of the clergy, Vee never longed to escape Sunday services. The time spent in the great gloomy, chilly Minster: Matins and Evensong, and sometimes Holy Communion as well, gave her hours of peace. Sometimes she thought it was a God-given peace, could almost feel herself wrapped in the arms of a loving God; at other times a harsher realism told her it was simply that it was possible

31

to be alone in church in a way that you couldn't at home. The Dean never questioned his children's faith. Even though he had lost all his trust in a beneficent and watchful God, he hoped by one means or another that his beliefs would return, and, meanwhile, his remaining children were going to be brought up in godly ways.

They were both a disappointment to him, Vee knew that perfectly well. Hugh was an aesthete from birth, a fey, babbling infant who had grown into a brilliant twister and spinner of words. His time at school had not been celebrated, as the Dean's had, by success at sport, and the grim establishment he was sent to at thirteen, his father's old school, had neither time nor liking for any boy who was different, who wasn't obsessed with sport, who was in any way unchristian.

Hugh had survived, as Vee had survived her own bleak, northern boarding school. In fact, for most of the time, she was happier at school than at home, although in the holidays there had always been Hugh to escape with, to share jokes and enjoy the excitement of a modern world beckoning from outside the Deanery walls.

Grandfather, when he arrived late on Sunday evening, was in one of his jolly moods. Vee's heart sank as she gave him a dutiful kiss, allowed him to pinch her cheek – how she hated that, and put his stick in the hall stand.

Grandfather in a jolly mood meant he had a scheme, something that pleased him, and she had a presentiment that it was to do with her – that was why he had come, she was sure of it, from the hints her mother had let drop, clothes for her, now that she was growing up, not much scope for a young lady in York . . .

She had already broached the subject of What next? with her father. When she told him her plans, striving to sound natural even while her hands were held so tightly together that her nails dug into her skin, he'd simply looked through her in that way he had.

'Oh, I doubt if that will be possible, my dear. Your mother would hardly like it.'

The truth was, her mother wouldn't care what she did, as long as she did it somewhere else. Vee knew that her mother was dreading her leaving school and spending days and weeks and months at the Deanery. Almost as much as she herself was dreading it.

'Besides,' her father went on, 'there is the question of money.'

'Hugh's paid for.'

Which was a stupid thing to say. Hugh was a man, it was different for Hugh.

'Your grandfather's paying for Hugh at Oxford, not me. You'll have to ask him.'

She knew what the answer would be.

Now they were all in the drawing room. Grandfather, his large and magnificent head under a mane of splendid white hair, sitting erect in the Dean's chair. The Dean standing awkwardly by the fireplace, not looking at Vee, and Mummy, sitting on a slender upright chair, her tapestry in her hand, fingers searching among her wools for a colour match. Like one of the fates at work, Vee thought with a sudden feeling of resentment. Spinning and weaving and cutting, and what choice or say did any of the lives represented by those slender threads have in their fates?

Vee perched herself on the edge of the heavy-footed sofa.

'Eighteen, now,' said her grandfather genially. 'A grown-up lass. Time to go out into the world. You're looking forward to leaving school, I feel sure.'

Vee said nothing.

'So we need to settle what you're going to do next. You can't hang around at home, getting under your mother's feet and taking up with some stiff-necked young curate, that would never do.'

The Dean stirred uneasily and gave the fire an unnecessary stir with the poker.

Vee took a deep breath. 'I know what I want to do when I leave school, Grandfather.'

'You do?' His face became more watchful. 'Out with it, then.'

'I want to go to university. I sat the exams, at school, and I've been accepted. At Oxford.' She swallowed, and ploughed on. 'For the new academic year that starts in October.'

The silence was palpable. The Dean looked down at the floor, her mother stitched resolutely on. Grandfather's face was reddening alarmingly.

'And I thought that perhaps I could spend six months abroad before I went up. I'm going to study modern languages, you see, and I'd like—'

Vee moved her head from side to side in a vain attempt to avert the explosion of wrath, the deadly missiles of her grandfather's anger as they rained about her. She always hated to be shouted at, and even

33

her mother's cold reserve and chilly indifference was a thousand times better than this terrible rage.

Alarmed, the Dean rang for the maid, ordered a brandy, and the maid, after a frightened glance at the thunderous countenance of the bellowing Jacob Trenchard, scuttled away for the restorative.

It would take more than a brandy to soothe Grandfather. His contempt poured over Vee in an abusive torrent, the stupidity of all women, the wickedness of any university to open its doors to women, the incredible folly and wilfulness she had shown in going about her selfish, pointless schemes with no thought for family or her place in the world.

'Have you wasted my money on education, so that you can turn into some dreadful bluestocking? Why, they won't even give women degrees at Cambridge, because they know the whole thing's a sham. Women's brains aren't designed for academic study, just as they aren't designed for business or politics or any of the other spheres they try to meddle in these days.'

Her grandfather's hatred and fear of women streamed out of him. Even Vee's mother looked up from her needlework with a doubtful glance, but she wasn't going to defend her daughter.

He hated educated women? Dear God, if only he knew how much she hated and despised him. 'Daddy, please,' said Vee desperately.

She should have known better than to expect any support from that direction.

'My dear, it's folly, and the school should never have encouraged you or allowed you to think of such a thing. I shall have something very sharp to say to your headmistress there, in fact, I shall write to the governors. They have no right to put such notions into an impressionable young head. Your grandfather and your mother and I will decide what's best for you, and you should know that.'

'What's best for you, not what's best for me.'

Vee had prayed she wouldn't cry, she mustn't show any weakness in front of Grandfather. Now she was white hot with rage of her own, and she had no tears to shed.

Grandfather sipped his brandy, calmed down, and proceeded as though she had never spoken, as though he hadn't said the terrible things about her, about women.

'Your mother's place is here, a man in your father's position needs a wife to help him. So we can't ask her to go to London with you.'

'I don't want to go to London.'

He went on as though she hadn't spoken. 'Her sister, your Aunt Lettice, is bringing out Claudia this next season, and she's agreed that you shall do the season together.'

Vee stared at him. 'Do the season? In London? Me? Are you mad?'

Not all her arguments or pleading could avert her doom. Grandfather held the purse strings, and her father was too weak and too poor to stand up against his domineering sire – why should he, over this, when he hadn't gone against the paternal wishes ever in his whole life? As for her mother, London was a long way away, and Vee would be out of her sight, which was all she cared about. She had suggested a year – two years, even – in Switzerland, for Vee to work up her languages and that kind of thing, but she had been over-ruled.

'Waste of time and money,' Grandfather had said. 'Let her be a debutante, then she'll meet the right kind of young man and marry. Young women can't marry too young these days, it's the only thing that keeps them out of mischief. Let Vee find a husband a bit older than herself, that works best. Mind you, I don't want her getting attached to any layabout young aristocrat. I don't have any time for that kind of thing, and I shan't part with a penny unless I approve of the man. She can pick someone who's got a career ahead of him, of good family, she is your daughter, Anne, and the cousin of an earl, she's no reason to go feeling grateful for any fly-by-night who grabs her in a taxi and wants to whisk her to the altar four weeks later.'

'You're to go to London and do the season and be grateful for it,' were her grandfather's parting words.

He was gothic, as gothic as the Minster, as gothic as Daddy's encrusted beliefs.

'I'm very displeased at the way you've behaved, Vee. I shan't forget it.'

And I, vowed Vee, shan't ever forget the way you've behaved, and one of these days I'll get my own back.

She was a modern, and they could make her go to London, but they couldn't make her marry any man against her will. Which meant, any man at all, for the last thing Vee wanted was to move from the authority of her grandfather to be under the thumb of a husband.

'Ring for the maid, Vee, your grandfather . . .'

*   *   *

Vee wrenched herself awake, to find herself bathed in sweat and hardly able to breathe. There was a tap at the door and Pigeon peered round it. 'You rang, madam. Are you ill?'

'I didn't ring,' Vee said, but knew that she had no idea what she might or might not have done in the grip of that haunting memory.

Pigeon advanced into the room. She was wearing her uniform; did she sleep in it? Vee wondered.

'Is it seasickness, madam? Shall I fetch a basin?'

'No, I'm not sick. It was a bad dream, a nightmare.'

'If you're sure. That's why I'm up, so many of my ladies have succumbed.'

'Go away!' Vee said, under her breath.

'Can I fetch you anything?' Pigeon asked.

'No, thank you,' said Vee, with an attempt at a smile. 'I'll be fine now. I'll just have a drink of water, please.'

Pigeon poured out half a glass from the carafe that had been sliding up and down on the shelf beside the bed. The water slopped to and fro, mimicking the roll of the liner, Vee timed her swallows and gulped it down. 'Thank you, Pigeon. I hope you manage to get some sleep yourself.'

Typical, Vee thought wearily. Pigeon was a working woman, who probably put in a twelve-hour day, and she had to stay up to pander to the needs of the wealthy passengers who'd probably never done a day's, let alone a night's work in their pampered lives. It was all so unfair, she'd always said it wasn't fair. It was that nursery cry of 'It isn't fair' that had, in the end, brought all her troubles upon her.

FIVE

The next morning, the passengers on board the *Gloriana* awoke to lowering grey skies and an increasing wind. The waves were dark and menacing, with foam from their breaking crests sent whipping across the surface by the angry wind.

'In for a bit of a blow,' a cheerful young officer with a cherubic face remarked to Vee as he met her at the door to the dining saloon. 'Won't be too full in there, I don't expect.'

He was right. Even allowing for those passengers who were having breakfast trays brought to their rooms, there was only a thin scattering of people in the huge dining room. Down in the bowels of G-deck, it had brilliant cut mirrors mimicking windows; the bronze-flecked pillars and rows and rows of empty tables, set with white napery, were reflected and multiplied, giving the room a vast and surreal appearance.

Vee, after a restless, unhappy night, didn't feel like eating anything; she stared at the menu printed on crisp white card. Juice, porridge, eggs, bacon, sausages, mushrooms, omelette . . . the list went on and on.

She ordered coffee.

'Aren't you going to eat anything?' asked the other occupant of the table. 'Are you feeling queasy because of the boat? It's amazing how it rolls, one minute there's nothing but sky to be seen, and then it's down, down, and walls of grey sea. Dramatic, I call it.'

Vee had hardly noticed her fellow diners the previous evening. Overcome with tiredness and despair, she had gone through the motions of meeting and greeting the strangers at the table, the men and women with whom she would share all her meals for the next two and a half weeks, without noticing much about them; thankful that the watcher on the quay wasn't there. After all, he could have boarded at the last minute, when she'd been down in her cabin.

This child, for she was hardly more, must have been one of them. Bony, lanky, gawky, a young lady who had still to stretch her wings. Yet, now Vee was paying attention, an interesting face. She would be a beauty one day. And, come to think of it, where had she seen her before? It wasn't a face you'd forget.

'I'm having the lot,' the girl said. The waiter arrived with a heaped plateful of bacon, eggs, sausage, two little triangles of fried bread, a tomato, mushrooms and a ring of apple. 'Perfect. And then lashings of toast and butter and marmalade. Heaven. I haven't been hungry for ages, and I can't believe I suddenly just want to eat and eat. It's the sea air. I say, there aren't many people about this morning.'

Vee sat back as the steward poured her a cup of coffee.

'They're affected by the motion of the ship, miss,' the steward said, with a grin. 'We won't see most of them until we've passed through the Bay.'

Perdita swallowed a mouthful of sausage. 'Bay?'

'Bay of Biscay, miss. Terrible place for storms, especially this time of the year, and the equinoctial gales are severe this year. Even some of the old hands among the passengers are complaining. Still, things are tricky back home and I reckon a storm or two will seem like nothing compared to what's coming, so they're better off where they are.'

Perdita watched him go. 'Awfully clever the way he keeps his balance. I suppose, if there are going to be real storms, that's why they've put up these little wooden things around the table. To stop everything sliding to the floor. Do you suffer from seasickness? I don't think I can do, not feeling as hungry as I am. I've never been on this kind of a voyage before, only sailing boats and steam yachts, that kind of thing. It's been blowy, and it never bothered me, so I suppose I'll be all right.'

'York Minster,' Vee said suddenly.

'What?' Perdita looked up from her plate. 'What about York Minster?'

'That's where I've seen you before. Just before Christmas, 1936. The carol service, for the Yorkshire Ladies' College. It was held in the cathedral every year.'

*　　　*　　　*

'Don't forget you're due in the Minster at twelve-thirty for the rehearsal,' Mummy called after Vee.

'I won't.' She wrapped a muffler tightly about her throat, and pulled on fur-lined leather gloves. Under her warm tweed coat she was wearing a woollen suit over vest and jumper; how cold it was in Yorkshire, and it would be icy, as usual, inside the cathedral. No power of God or man could warm that cavernous interior.

She crossed the yard where two stonemasons were surveying a large block of limestone with ropes looped round it, ready to be hoisted up to some distant place above one of the great flying buttresses. Keeping the cathedral in a state of even moderate repair was a year-round task. The masons recognised her, the Dean's daughter, and touched their caps as she went past.

Vee pushed open the door and went in. Mary Becket and Mrs Lancaster were in the flower room, snipping and cutting and sorting a pile of Christmas foliage. They looked up and called out a greeting; they had known her since she was a little girl, running in and out of the cathedral and the stone yard, fascinated by the Minster's immense size, the glowing colours of the windows, the stone statues of the kings of England, the carvings and effigies on the silent tombs, the memorial slabs underfoot, the crypt, with the stream running far below. How odd to build over a stream, she always thought. One of the masons, bent from years of labour, told her that it was because streams were sacred for the old folk, and that was where they put shrines, and then, when the Christians came, they built their churches in the same places.

She'd told her father about that, and he'd frowned and said that was pagan nonsense and she shouldn't gossip with the masons, they had a job to do.

She believed the mason, though. It was obvious the building went back a long time – there were Roman walls under there as well, the vergers had told her, in answer to her questions. And once, they said, the whole cathedral would have been painted and gilded in reds and golds and blues. It was hard to believe, when you saw the austere Protestant stone soaring up into the tower and along the great nave.

'Idolatrous,' her father said, dismissively, when she said how wonderful it must have looked, glowing with colour. With the cynical eyes of her grown-up self, she saw it all as part of a centuries-long endeavour – a very successful one – to dazzle and oppress the lower classes; to keep them in awe of their betters, fearful of this life and doubtful of the next, to allow them a glimpse of a more glorious world while teaching them their place in this one.

The sound of a choir reached her ears. 'Are the boys practising?' she asked Mary Becket, who came past with an armful of greenery.

'They aren't the choristers,' said Mary Becket scornfully. 'It's girls, an end of term service.' She gave a sniff, and went back to beating a stiff sprig of holly into submission.

Vee slipped into the side aisle of the choir and walked towards the transept, treading softly because of the service in progress. She caught a glimpse of a sea of grey hats, familiar hats, with the purple initials – YLC – embroidered above a purple grosgrain riband. A uniform that was utterly familiar to her. This was her old school, Yorkshire Ladies' College, in its habitual act of carols and collective worship at the end of the Christmas term.

A senior girl was reading the lesson. 'And when they were come into the house, they saw the young child . . .'

The carol service came to an end with the thundering chords of 'Hark the Herald Angels'. The congregation knelt for final prayers, and Vee noticed a tall man in a tweed coat who had ignored this ritual and was edging his way along the row of seats. Eager to escape, probably. No, he was heading up towards the choir, engulfed in a swelling crowd of schoolgirls in their grey uniforms, he was searching for someone. There, he'd spotted her, a lanky girl coming out of the choir, a surplice draped over her arm.

'Perdita,' he called out. She was his sister, that was evident; with those bones, she'd grow out of her plainness and be a beauty by her twenties.

The habitual sound of the upper classes let out of church sang about Vee's ears: greetings, enquiries, exclamations, farewells. The congregation moved like a sluggish river out of the great west doors, until only a few lingerers were left: a girl, the choir prefect, checking the hampers containing the choir gowns, a chubby, pink-cheeked girl dashing back in to retrieve a glove, a mistress stopping to talk to a verger.

'You were in the choir, and a young man had come to meet you.'

'That's right. Goodness, how clever of you to remember me, I don't have a very distinctive face. That was my brother Edwin.'

40

'I was at Yorkshire Ladies',' Vee said, helping herself to more coffee and reaching out, without thinking, for a piece of toast. 'You're Perdita Richardson. I was Verity Trenchard then, and when I was in the sixth form, you were a first-former, all round cheeks and pigtails.'

'Not round cheeks,' said Perdita. 'I've never had round cheeks. I grant you the pigtails, though. What a coincidence. Did you hate it there? Lots of people did.'

'Did you?'

'Not really, home was pretty ghastly a lot of the time, and so I didn't mind too much.'

Vee laughed. 'Snap! I couldn't wait to get back to school after the holidays. Although it was rather awful there. I minded the cold most, in winter, that window open five inches rule.'

'I took the nail out of the window in my bit of the dorm,' Perdita said. 'Or rather, loosened it, so matron wouldn't find out. Then after lights out, I'd close it. Only I had to wake up before she came clumping round and whip it up again.'

'Did you never get caught?'

'No, never,' said Perdita with pride. 'With my family, you had to do things for yourself and do them discreetly. I had – well, have, only I don't see her any more – a ferocious grandmother. More or less everything I did was wrong, so I learned cunning.'

Vee took another piece of toast. Cunning? No, she hadn't learned cunning from her family, she had simply learned to be self-contained, to pretend that all was well, that she was a member of a normal loving family. Reserve was natural and native to her parents' generation and class, no one need ever know that the reserve and cool well-bredness was more than skin deep, that beneath the unruffled surface there were no depths of affection or feeling of any kind: nothing but indifference and dislike, at least for their daughter.

Perdita finished her substantial breakfast, wiped her mouth, gave a satisfied sigh and stood up. 'That was wonderful,' she said to the hovering steward. 'Goodbye for now, Mrs . . . I say, I am sorry, I don't know your name. It isn't Trenchard any more, is it?'

'Hotspur. I'm Mrs Hotspur.'

'I'm glad we're at the same table, Mrs Hotspur. Anyhow, I must push off, I've got to practise.'

'Nice to see a young lady enjoying her food,' said the steward. 'Is there anything else I can get for you, madam?'

41

'No, thank you,' said Vee. She lit a cigarette and sat there, gazing out over the almost empty dining room, a field of white linen and silver cutlery, flowers at every table – where did they get flowers when they were further out at sea? She had no idea, she realized, of how a ship like this functioned. She knew it had a gymnasium, and a swimming pool – that was a joke in this weather – and a beauty salon and library. And the crew and several hundred passengers, all having to be fed and laundered for days on end. She watched the smoke from her cigarette drifting away. It must be interesting, working on board. She asked the steward.

'I love it, madam. Wouldn't consider any other job. I've always worked the lines, every since I was a nipper and took my first voyage as a page. My dad's in the business, too, he's on the Liverpool–New York run, White Star. He's in the engine room, he never did stewarding. He wanted me to sign on with White Star, but I said, No, it's the old Peninsular and Orient Line for me, Dad. I prefer the East, you see, I always had a yen for the East.'

He deftly collected the coffee pot and her empty plate, swaying with a dancer's ease as the ship began another of its wallowing rolls. 'Course, it'll all change if there's war. They used the liners for troop carriers in the last war. My dad served in a mine sweeper, four years, and never a scratch. Then the first day he was back on the liners, a bolt worked loose and broke his toe. Isn't that typical of life?'

He went on his nimble way, and Vee, getting up, discovered that she was a good deal less steady on her feet than when she had come into the dining room. Presumably the blow was getting stronger. She would go to the library, she decided. Find a book, something to while away the hours and take her mind off Hugh, and the man with the bony face, and everything else – the many many things that haunted her waking and sleeping hours and which she longed to drive out of her head, if only for a few merciful moments.

Vee walked along endless corridors, down steep flights of stairs, past linen rooms, the sweet smell of fresh linen wafting out. She met no one on her way, bar a hurrying steward. It was eerie, the emptiness of the ship. She reached the corridor where her cabin was and walked past the row of shut doors, counting them off, fifty-nine, sixty, sixty-one. She stopped abruptly outside number sixty-two, a few yards from her own cabin, number sixty-seven.

The door to sixty-seven was slightly ajar, and someone was in there.

The corridor stretched away, deserted, no cleaners to be seen. Who was in her cabin?

Vee, her nerves tingling, made herself walk silently to the door. Then, with sudden vigour, she pulled the door wide open. 'What . . . ?' she began.

Pigeon looked round, surprise on her face. 'I'm just tidying away your things from last night,' she said, shutting a cupboard door with a neat click. 'I can't linger, I've got that many of my ladies poorly.'

'Thank you,' Vee said, her back to the door.

'I've left the passenger list on the table, madam,' the stewardess said. 'I expect you'll want to look through and see if you've friends on board. My ladies are always surprised, it never fails, there are always people they know on board, and didn't expect to see. "Oh, look," they say, "I had no idea that the so-and-sos were going out to Egypt." It always makes me laugh, how amazed they are.'

She whisked out of the cabin, and Vee sat down in the armchair, her heart still thudding. She was irked by the fright Pigeon had given her, irked by feeling so jumpy, constantly looking over her shoulder and starting at shadows. She should have guessed at once that it would be the stewardess in her cabin, about her duties.

She took her cigarette case from her handbag. She was smoking too many cigarettes in an attempt to soothe her nerves. She took one out, lit it, then picked up the typewritten list. There was Perdita Richardson's name. An unusual girl. Might prove a bore, but she didn't think so. How old was she? Probably seventeen or eighteen, if she'd left school, but no more.

Vee closed her eyes, overcome with a sudden terrible longing to be seventeen again. At seventeen, she'd been uneasy, perpetually hurt by her mother's dislike of her, but still full of hope, with life a white and shining canvas, a tablet of possibilities. A daubed and messy canvas now; what part of her life had she not made a mess of, whom of her family and friends had she not in some way hurt or distressed or betrayed, or even, God help her, destroyed?

She wondered for a moment if she were going mad, for this bizarre image to float into her mind, but decided, regretfully almost, that there was no escape that way. She turned her attention back to the list.

The name jumped out at her, as though it had been printed in bright red letters.

Messenger, Mrs Henry, and beneath that, Messenger, Peter.

For a moment, pure joy flooded through her. Lally was on the boat. Lally, her incomparable friend. And she'd brought Peter. Had Harry relented? Had the boy had a relapse, was he not well enough to go back to school? She must find Lally immediately, what was the number of her cabin?

Then reality struck, and her sense of pleasure and excitement evaporated.

Lally, her friend. Yes, that was exactly what Lally was, but she, Vee, was no friend of Lally's. Not after what she had done, what she was planning to do. If Lally knew, or even suspected . . . How could she ever face Lally again?

Lally didn't know, surely she couldn't have kept so calm and serene, if she'd had the least idea.

No, Lally didn't know, and for Vee, it must remain one of those grim secrets that couldn't be told. Even though at times she felt that to confess to Lally, to tell her friend what she had done, would be such a relief.

But, even if Lally didn't know – and Vee had tried desperately to be discreet, flaunting instead her other liaisons before a scandalized world – then how could it be kept a secret from her in Delhi?

Had Klaus known that Lally was going out to India on the *Gloriana*? It was so obvious, so natural, after all, that she would go out to join her husband. She would have gone with him when he was first posted to Delhi, if Peter hadn't still been ill.

No, Klaus hadn't known. He'd told Vee that Lally was staying in England until the boy was safely settled back at school, that she would wait until after Christmas before going out to India.

Lally herself, in the one, unsatisfactory conversation they'd had – a hurried phone call, with Vee pretending she was in a rush, would telephone her back – had said nothing about sailing to India. Vee hadn't telephoned again, of course, what could she possibly say to Lally, one of her closest friends, whom she had so utterly betrayed?

What could she say to her now, face to face?

Her eyes skittered on down the list.

Joel Ibbotson.

So it had been Joel she'd seen on deck. Joel, for heaven's sake! What could he be doing on board the *Gloriana*? Had the watching man been on the lookout for Joel? Impossible, the very idea of Joel

44

getting mixed up with that lot brought a smile to her lips. She'd be fascinated to find out why Joel, wrapped up in mathematics and college life, should be going to India. When had she last seen him? Berlin, 1936. And of course, Yorkshire last year, for the funeral. Another blink, another memory to be refused admittance to her mind. Keep to the present, keep to the here and now.

Another name leaped out at her: M. Q. Sebert, Esq.

Marcus, on board? How odd, had the BBC come to its collective senses and sacked him?

It was a ghost ship, that day. Peter was everywhere, exploring, questioning, bothering the staff, who took it in patient good humour, with so few passengers about, they had time to listen to his endless questions. Only the cabin stewards and stewardesses and the doctor and nursing sister who staffed the tiny hospital were kept busy as the dark grey of sky and sea turned imperceptibly to twilight and night.

Vee spent most of the day in the library, alone and undisturbed, reading *War and Peace*, grateful for the chance to spend some hours in a different world entirely, her own problems shut out by the far away and long ago world of Napoleon and Imperial Russia. History, however complicated, seemed to make sense in a way that the contemporary world – at least, her contemporary world – didn't.

A waiter brought her coffee, she went to the cafe for a light lunch, taking Tolstoy with her, then back to the library, soft lights lit over the desks, the potted plants somehow fixed in position, how did they keep upright with the incessant roll of the ship? It was only a momentary thought, then she was once again in Moscow, in the thick of war, following in Pierre's questioning footsteps, caught up in the sweep of history.

Would some profound novelist in years to come pen an epic of her time in a book like *War and Peace*, a novelist with a brooding mind and a sense of the power of history, writing about Hitler and the Czechoslovakia that wasn't worth a war, and Stalin and weak, unworthy Chamberlain, and an island people who clutched at any straw of peace, but who would fight like terriers when war came knocking uninvited at the door?

SIX

The *Gloriana* hummed and throbbed as it ploughed its way through the storm. On the bridge, the duty officers were relaxed, quiet in the dog hours, used to the sea and her wild ways.

In their cabins, passengers slept soundly or tossed and turned, or clutched stomachs agonized by spasms of seasickness. In the great kitchens, the first staff were coming on duty, the bakers ready to bake the bread and rolls and brioches for breakfast.

'Half as much as usual,' the head baker said. 'Most of this lot won't be eating anything for the next day or so.'

'They'll make up for it when the sea calms down and they get their appetites back.'

Perdita was awake, relaxed but wide awake. She was still prone to sudden bursts of heat, a relic of her days of fever, the doctors had told her, and they always woke her. Soon, she would drop off to sleep again, and those last two or three hours of sleep were the best she had. In her mind, her fingers played Bach, the intricate patterns soothing her brain in time to the sound of the ship's engines.

On D-deck, Marcus Sebert came to and eased himself groggily out of his bunk. The floor came up to meet him, and he passed out, contentedly, on the linoleum floor of his cabin.

The chill roused him an hour later, and he staggered to his feet, imagining for a moment he was in the studio at the BBC; why was everything sliding up and down, had war broken out and the Germans bombed Broadcasting House, had there been an earthquake?

This wasn't the BBC, he wasn't at work, he was at sea, on a

goddamned liner. Was he staggering, or was it the damned boat? It didn't matter. His eyes fell on one of the bottles of champagne he had brought with him. Champagne was good for seasickness, not that he was prone to seasickness, but you couldn't be too careful. He eased the cork out of the bottle, and cursed as the wine frothed over him, spattering his shirt. A glass? He looked around his untidy cabin, then decided, as he slid across the floor, that a glass was unnecessary. He carefully climbed back into his berth, dribbling the wine into his mouth from the bottle.

Let the wind roar and the waves lash against the boat. 'And we jolly sailor boys were up and up aloft,' he sang to himself. Jolly sailor boys, jolly good idea. He could go and find one right now, 'Below, below, below. Bugger the landlubbers!'

Perhaps he couldn't. Perhaps he'd just have another drink and wait for the storm to blow itself out. How many days to Lisbon? Another two, three? That wasn't a problem, he'd stayed drunk for a week at a time before now. Alcohol and sleep, the cure for all life's little difficulties. Blot it out, sink into oblivion, no need to worry about anything in the world.

One deck up, Joel Ibbotson sat glumly looking into the bowl the steward had thoughtfully provided and wishing he were back in the tranquil surroundings of his Oxford college.

'There's running hot and cold in the basin, sir. I'll be back to see if there's anything you need.'

'I suppose these liners don't generally sink?'

The steward was shocked. 'They do not.'

'*Titanic* did.'

'That was in the past, sir. And she hit an iceberg.'

'Any icebergs out there now?'

'Hardly, sir.'

'Pity,' said Joel, his face growing rapidly paler. 'A great pity. I just want the ship to sink to the bottom of the sea as quickly as possible, so we can get it all over with.'

'I see you like your little joke, sir.'

47

SEVEN

Lally lay in her bunk, wishing she'd never set foot on the *Gloriana*, that Harry had never been posted to India, that she'd never been born.

Peter offered advice, before being shooed away by Miss Tyrell. 'Look at the horizon, and then you won't feel sick any more.'

There was no horizon to look at.

None of her transatlantic voyages, stormy though some of them had been, had prepared her for the Bay of Biscay in this kind of weather.

Pigeon was kindly, but brisk, she'd seen it all before.

'Have you ever been seasick, Pigeon?' Lally asked, reluctantly sipping from a glass of ginger water that the stewardess had brought her.

'It's not my place to be seasick. If you can keep a little of this down, you'll feel much better.'

Liar, Lally said to herself, as nausea swept over her. A few minutes later, she began to think that Pigeon might be right.

'You try and get some sleep now, madam,' Pigeon said. 'Don't worry about the little boy, Miss Tyrell is looking after him.'

Thank God for Monica, thank God for Miss Tyrell. It would be much worse to lie there, helpless, if she knew that Peter was running free about the ship. Miss Tyrell would keep an eye on him, and she didn't seem so authoritarian as to drive him to rebellious folly.

Lally didn't sleep, but she dropped into a drowsy state, eyes closed, trying not to anticipate any of the sudden lurches that were even worse than the steady heaving and rolling of the ship.

Claudia was never seasick, Miss Tyrell had told her. She'd had Claudia from a month old, wild as a monkey, that girl, determined to do things her way even before she could utter a word. Never wanted a vest on, like catching an eel with your bare hands, trying to pull a vest over her head. Headstrong then, and headstrong to this day, from all she heard. Yet at bottom there wasn't much wrong with her that a few shocks and a bit of growing up wouldn't put right. Independent-minded, that was Lady Claudia.

Lally wasn't so sure; to her Claudia's political views smacked of more than mere wildness and a determination to hold contrary views. And independent-minded? Miss Tyrell wouldn't say that if she'd seen Claudia hanging on Petrus's every word.

'Ah, that John Petrus, now, there's a wily fellow.'

Surely Miss Tyrell hadn't been nanny to him as well.

'No, and I'm thankful for it. But when you're a nanny in London, you get to know the other nannies, and their charges. Mr Petrus and Lady Geraldine, she's the eldest of the Vere sisters, they're much of an age. We use to wheel the prams together in the park, and then the children went to the same parties. Mind you, Mr Petrus wasn't the same background as the Veres. His father was very rich, some kind of a financier. He had a good nanny, though, in Nanny Fortan. We were old friends.'

Lally wondered where Peter was.

'Upstairs, drawing, a Miss Richardson, as nice a young lady as you could hope to meet, although I don't care for the way she dresses, is keeping an eye on him. He likes her, and she won't let him get into any mischief. I said I wanted to see how you were, and she at once offered to stay with him.'

'Drawing? With the boat doing these wild plunges?'

'He's seeing which way the crayons go. Abstract art, Miss Richardson said. It's making them laugh. I like to hear youngsters laugh. You didn't hear Mr Petrus, who we were speaking of just now, you didn't often hear him laughing. He was a serious, self-centred child. Ready smile, and a lot of charm, I don't care for a child with charm. Still, it got him what he wanted, most of the time. I always felt you couldn't trust that boy. Now, of course, he's an important man, advises the government, so Lady Sake tells me, Ministers of the Crown hang on his every word.'

She paused, and Lally opened her eyes for a brief moment, watched a towel on its hook sway through a hundred and eighty degrees and shut them quickly.

'More fool, they,' Miss Tyrell finished. 'The child is father to the man, I've always believed that. I've seen enough of my charges and their friends grow up to know I'm right about that. There are those you can trust, and those you'd be unwise to believe a word they say, five or fifty.'

'You'd trust Claudia.'

'Oh, yes.'

'Not Mr Petrus, though.'

'Never trust a man who looks you straight in the eyes. Either he's hiding something, or he wants you to believe he's sincere and interested in you. Either way, take care. Now, I'll just take this glass away, you don't want it sliding about.'

The door shut behind her with a soft click. She lifted a hand to push away a strand of hair from her face. Peter said she looked green; well, she felt green.

Claudia didn't suffer from seasickness, Miss Tyrell said.

Lucky Claudia.

Wild as a monkey? Lally's mind wandered back through the tossing of the boat, to the day she first met Claudia. Maybe remembering times when she was on dry land would make her less aware of the endless rise and fall of the ship, and the constant sound, creaking and shifting and the crash of waves breaking against the sides.

Oxford, 1932, and the motion of the ship seemed to alter into the steady rhythm of an English train. Tuppence three farthings, tuppence three farthings. American trains, how did they sound? She couldn't remember, it was quite a while since she'd travelled on a train in her native land. Nothing as old world and romantic as tuppence three farthings, though.

English money was still a mystery to her in those days, fresh from America, used to the simplicity of a hundred cents to the dollar. A pound divided by twenty shillings and each shilling divided into twelve pennies, and then each in half for a ha'penny, which she had wanted to call a halfpenny, and fourths for a farthing. There was a ship on the copper ha'penny coin, no, she wasn't going to think about ships. The farthing, concentrate on the farthing, with that cute little bird on it. What was it, a wren?

She'd pitied the kids in school when she first wrestled with change. However did they learn to do any math except adding and subtracting and dividing their odd currency?

The train journey hadn't taken long, from Paddington, London, to Oxford. An hour and ten minutes. The train had been full. Mostly with students, just to see them milling about the platform had given her a thrill. There'd been another woman in her compartment, a young woman in spectacles, who'd opened a fat and serious-looking book even before the train had started.

Lally squinted at the spine. P. Vergili Maronis Opera. Latin. Unquestionably a student.

Pale eyes looked at Lally through the round spectacles. She held the book up so that Lally could see it more clearly.

Lally laughed. 'I was snooping, I guess. I'm always curious to see what people are reading. Vergil's impressive.'

A long, considering stare. 'You're American?'

'Yes.'

'Tourist, I suppose.'

'No, I'm going to college in Oxford.'

'College? Do you mean the university?'

'Yes, Grace College.'

That earned her a longer, more appraising look. 'I'm at LMH.'

LMH? What was that?

'Lady Margaret Hall. Another women's college.' The pale eyes swivelled up to the luggage rack. 'Is that a musical instrument?'

Lally nodded. 'I play French horn.'

That got a look of pure astonishment. 'The French horn? A brass instrument?'

'Yes. Is that so strange?'

'It is in England. Women don't generally play brass instruments in England. Piano, violin, cello, harp, flute. Not the French horn.'

'Then they'll welcome me into the college orchestra.'

The young woman gave a kind of harrumph and returned ostentatiously to her text.

Lally sat back and gazed out of the window, loving the still green countryside that was sliding past: villages with churches, a big house on a hillside, hedged fields, a line of elms on a ridge . . . The train gave a shriek and dived into a tunnel, smoke drifting past the darkened window, then out into the sunshine.

'Did England look like this in Jane Austen's day?' Lally asked the Latinist opposite her.

'I don't read novels.'

'Your loss,' Lally said equably. Now they were on the outskirts of a town, rattling past streets of identical terraced houses, built of red brick. Some of the houses were so close to the line you could see into the windows. A woman ironing, a boy on a swing in a tiny garden, a man sitting in a chair, reading a newspaper.

'Is this Oxford?'

'Reading.'

'What's that building that looks like a fortress?'

A quick flick of the pale eyes from the page to the scene outside the window.

'Reading Gaol.'

'Reading Gaol!' Entranced, Lally twisted to try to catch a better view. 'Where Oscar Wilde wrote *The Ballad of Reading Gaol*. Did they really imprison him in there?'

'I don't read poetry.'

'Vergil is poetry.'

'I don't read English poetry.'

Lally was of too sanguine a temperament to feel dampened by this contempt for England's great writers. She'd just landed up in the company of a dull girl, the students wouldn't all be like her. Or maybe they would at – what was it? LMH – but not at Grace.

Lally looked at her wristwatch. Not so long now. Wasn't Oxford the next station?

This time there was no doubt about it. There were the spires, the dreaming spires, unmistakable, serene against the cloudless blue sky.

'I don't suppose you read Matthew Arnold,' she said to her fellow passenger, who had got up from her seat and was pulling down a battered canvas suitcase with brown leather corners. '"Home of lost causes, and forsaken beliefs, and unpopular names, and impossible loyalties!" That's what he said about Oxford.'

'No.'

Lally was tempted to say a quick prayer to St Jude for this woman, who was so clearly a lost cause, but the train was slowing down and she had her luggage to think about.

Then it was down on to the platform, even more full of jostling people than Paddington. Lally stood wide-eyed, holding her French horn in one hand and a suitcase in the other. She must go to the baggage van, make sure her trunk was taken off.

'Porter, miss?'

She pointed out her trunk and boxes in the van.

'You go over the footbridge, miss, I'll bring this lot across.'

So many of these people seemed to know each other, they were calling out greetings and news. Even the girl from LMH had joined up with an acquaintance and was engaged in earnest conversation a few feet in front of her. Then out into the crowded station forecourt. There was her porter.

'A taxi, miss?'

'Yes, please. I guess I'll have to wait a while.'

'This lot will soon be gone,' the porter said comfortably, leaning on the handle of his trolley.

Out of the corner of her eye, Lally saw a gleaming automobile draw up. A blonde got out and came towards her, very assured, very well dressed, followed by a slighter, darker girl in a tweed coat.

'Are you for Grace?'

And that, thought Lally, rolling over and reaching out for a basin, was Claudia. And there, behind her cousin, was Vee, looking faintly surprised. There was no question in her mind as to whose the car was. Elegant, expensively-dressed Claudia, in that cloud of scent she always wore, was clearly at home in the sleek Daimler. Whereas Vee, all eyes and her hair caught in a scrawny bun at the back of her unflattering felt hat, looked rather as though she'd been kidnapped. With English Oxfords on her feet, brogues, very well polished, you could tell she came from a good home; such sensible shoes, so worthy and practical compared to Claudia's crocodile high heels.

Even then, Vee gave nothing away. She watched, and listened, but what was going on behind those intelligent eyes? That was for Vee to know, although Lally had come to wonder just how well Vee did know herself. Did any of them? Did anyone, ever? Probably not, which might be one of God's mercies when you came to think about it. Yet she'd got to know Claudia and Vee, and they her, better than she could possibly have imagined at that first meeting.

The workings of fate, that had brought them together, at that place, at that time. There they were, the three Graces.

She slept for a while, then woke feeling more seasick than ever. She could feel her hair damp and clammy at the side of her face; would this dreadful rolling and plunging never stop?

It was worse with her eyes open, and she closed them again. The stewardess came in, and persuaded her to sip more ginger cordial. Lally hated the taste of ginger, but Pigeon was right, it did soothe her stomach, if only a little.

Why were those early days at Grace so much on her mind?

She was back in the quad, the biggest open space inside the college. There was a single tree, in the centre, a plane tree, and the square grassed area, in which the tree was set, was intersected by diagonal tarmac paths.

Claudia was there, on her bicycle. Or, more accurately, off her bicycle. She'd decided to buy a bicycle and learn to ride it that very afternoon.

'It'll take more time than that,' Miss Harbottle said, in her most authoritative voice. 'Your sort always thinks you can do anything at once.'

'My sort usually can,' said Claudia, picking herself up and launching herself off again.

'And the quad isn't the place to learn,' Harbottle shouted after her. 'Bicycles aren't allowed, as you very well know.'

'It's the perfect place to learn,' Vee said. 'Only think of the chaos she'd cause if she went on a road.'

Alfred Gore appeared through the arch at the south side of the quad, tall and lanky and amused. You could tell, even then, that he had eyes for no one but Vee, until a loud yell from Claudia, who had ridden with wild abandon into the tree, distracted him. He sauntered over and hauled her to her feet, then righted the cycle.

'Good thing you hadn't got up any speed,' he said. 'I'll hold on to the back of the saddle, and you concentrate on getting your balance. OK?'

Claudia nodded, and they were off, Alfred running beside her, holding the bicycle steady.

Claudia was right, her sort usually could. Instinct, balance and confidence were what made her so different from Miss Harbottle. And Vee, watching and laughing? Observant, self-controlled, quite different from her cousin.

Lally half opened her eyes. Were they so different, after all? Hadn't they both thrown themselves, heart and soul, into causes? In both cases, with disastrous results, and with who knew what repercussions to come?

Vee was blessed with a clear mind, but hadn't used it. Claudia had the gift of intuition, but was blind about herself.

Moderation in all things, Lally said aloud.

'You're fretting,' said Miss Tyrell. 'I have a sleeping draught for you. You will feel better for a sleep.'

'I've been dreaming. Of the past,' Lally said, not wanting to swallow what Miss Tyrell was holding to her mouth.

'This will put a stop to that,' Miss Tyrell said, with unassailable nursery authority.

Lally doubted if the draught would stay down long enough to do any good, but she was too weak to resist.

'I remember the last Commem,' she said in a thread of a voice. 'At Christ Church. The grandest of all the balls that summer. I didn't know what a Commem Ball was when I started at Oxford. It has a language all its own. They have May Balls in Cambridge and Commemoration Balls at Oxford. Only they don't hold them in May, I always thought that was kind of strange.'

She stopped talking, holding her breath so that her stomach would settle. Keep talking, don't think about the boat or the queasiness. 'That was where I met my husband. At a ball. No, at a dinner party before the ball. At the Oronsays. Do you know the Oronsays, Miss Tyrell? They have a big house in Oxford, set in spectacular grounds. It was June, you know, and the French windows were open, and the scents and sounds of summer came drifting in above the smoke and the talk. The smell of newly mown grass and jasmine, and bees, buzzing in a tub of snapdragons just outside the windows. And a woodpecker, tap, tap, tap. Midsummer, with a huge full moon. Magic in the air, and music, and love. Just like a movie.

'They were all there, all my Oxford friends. I was going back to America, as soon as term was over. My passage was already booked. On the *Normandie*. So I wanted a chance to say goodbye to the friends I'd made while I was at Oxford.

'I didn't tell Vee or Claudia, but just set about persuading the ones who had gone down to come back for the ball. Alfred, have you come across the Gores?'

'That'll be Almeric Gore's younger son. He was at Eton with one of Claudia's brothers, always stirring up trouble, a hothead, but no harm in him. He writes for the papers, now.'

'Yes, so there was Alfred, and Giles and Hugh, Verity's brother, who'd gone down the previous year. He was the tricky one to get hold of, given that he was wandering about Europe, but friends at the American Embassy tracked him down for me and delivered the invitation. People who were still at Oxford, like Joel and Marcus, weren't a problem. And I asked Sarah Blumenthal, from Grace, for although she and Claudia didn't get along too well, I liked her, and we'd played a lot of music together.'

Another silence. 'I wonder where Sarah is now. We've rather lost touch, she married and went to Germany. I don't think Germany is a good place for her.'

'Not with a name like that, not these days, not with the way those Nazis are carrying on,' Miss Tyrell said. She pronounced it 'Nasties.'

'Sarah married, I don't remember her married name. Then Ruth Oronsay got wind of my plans, and invited my party to dinner before the ball at their Oxford house. Sir Iain had been at the House, you see. That's another one of those Oxford things you have to learn, like Brasenose being BNC, and Teddy Hall, not St Edmund Hall. Aedes Christi, Christ's House, that's why they call Christ Church college the House. Sir Iain had made up a party of his own contemporaries, so Ruth said, Let's all dine and go to the ball together.'

The memories flashed before Lally's eyes, like stills from a film.

Vee's face full of delight when she saw Alfred was there. What was it with the two of them? Everyone else could see they were crazy about each other, but seemingly they couldn't.

Alfred in tails, looking completely at ease in the Oronsays' magnificent drawing room, Vee teasing him about it: 'Where did you get those, do you own a set, now you've joined the world of the grown-ups? They're hardly the ones you borrowed from your tutor, he wouldn't be so unwise as to lend them again, surely.'

Alfred looking down at himself without enthusiasm: 'They belong to my elder brother. I always forget how damned uncomfortable this kit is, I feel as though I'm being throttled.'

Vee smiling at him: 'You look very good in them. You and your brother must be much of a size.'

Claudia, drifting past in a haze of blue, champagne glass in her hand: 'Does he know you've borrowed them?'

Alfred, laughing, asking if that was guesswork or the famous Vere insight. 'As it happens, I thought it easier not to ask.'

'What if he has a dance tonight?'

'I dare say he has a spare set. Or he can take a leaf out of my book, and go in flannels.'

Marcus, in an outrageous gold-threaded waistcoat, sliding through the guests, giving Alfred a kiss: 'Lovely to see you.'

'Don't kiss me, Marcus, it's bad for my reputation as a hard-hitting journalist. The reason for the tails, Vee, is that Ruth issued an ultimatum re dressing, and I rather wanted to come. I need a little frivolity in my hectic and serious life.'

A heavy sweetness and brilliance from the roses massed in silver bowls around the room. More colour from the women's long dresses, set off by the austerity of the men's evening clothes. Sir Iain and a nephew flamboyant in their tartan kilts. An army officer in black and red.

Marcus noticing the officer: 'Who's the handsome soldier?'

Henry Messenger, darling Harry, dashing and full of life. Joel, watching him watching me, his face stricken, then glowering.

John Petrus, appearing suddenly, like the demon in the pantomime. Complimenting Claudia and Vee on their looks. A blue glance from Claudia at him, then her eyes fixed on her shoes; how did Petrus so often manage to wipe out Claudia's gaiety and sense of humour, just by being there?

Vee seeing Hugh across the room, her face lighting up: 'Hugh! Oh, Hugh, I'd no idea you were coming! I didn't know you were back in England.'

Hugh, almost gaunt, looking rather tense, accepting a glass of champagne from a hovering footman: 'Couldn't miss this, not after a three-line whip from Lally. I only got back this morning, and I've been a bit rushed.'

'You're looking frightfully thin.'

'Got a tummy bug that laid me low for a while. Thought my number was up, actually, but a local witch woman looked after me and fed me on foul messes and herby brews; I had to get better, simply to get away from her. Ah, Alfred, good to see you.'

The dinner table, gleaming and glittering with silver and crystal and white and gold porcelain. Shimmering reflections of faces and jewels in the silver epergnes filled with more flowers.

Wonderful food, the buzz of conversation, a sense of pleasure almost tangible.

Ruth Oronsay, addressing her younger guests with sudden seriousness: 'Youth is a precious time, which vanishes quickly and absolutely. And for your generation, going out into a difficult world, it is doubly precious. You may be called upon to bear terrible responsibilities, just as your fathers were, and then you will look back to this evening and remember the joy of dancing a June night away. Memories of music and light and laughter stay with us all the days of our life; they are the gift that youth bestows upon maturity.'

Prescient, Lally said to herself now. A touch of the Claudias.

Sir Iain on his feet, glass in hand, footmen stepping forward to fill glasses, the guests pushing back their chairs and rising to their feet, the younger people light-hearted and amused by the touch of solemnity.

Sir Iain lifting his glass for the King. Adding another toast, with a smile for his wife. 'Youth.'

Ruth Oronsay collecting up the ladies and leading the way to the drawing room. No one lingering over coffee and exquisite hand-made chocolates. Guests streaming out of the house and into the waiting motors, the women sweeping their long skirts out of the way of the men's gleaming patent shoes. The cars setting off through the wrought iron gates on the way to the ball.

Lally dozed, then accepted some more ginger cordial, it did seem to be working, then slept, and woke feeling almost human.

Miss Tyrell was in the cabin, folding clothes.

'I hope I didn't wake you, Mrs Messenger. You're a better colour, that's a good sign.'

'I'm feeling better.' Lally yawned and stretched. 'Perhaps you can run me a bath. I don't suppose they have showers on board, do they?'

No, they didn't, of course not. And maybe the bath could wait a little while, it was soothing just to lie there.

'So you were up at Oxford with Mrs Hotspur, were you?' Miss Tyrell said. 'Peter was talking about her, but I didn't pay much attention, what a talker that boy is! Miss Trenchard as was, Verity Trenchard, but they always called her Vee.'

'Do you know her? Oh, you would, of course, I was forgetting she's Lady Claudia's cousin.'

'As it happens, I had charge of her for a brief while. I was nanny at the Deanery the summer of 1926.' She wrapped a piece of tissue paper around a cashmere jumper and tucked in the edges with deft hands. 'My word, that was a bad time for the family.'

'So you looked after Vee – Mrs Hotspur?'

Miss Tyrell had the remote look of one gazing into the past. 'There were three Trenchard children.'

'Three? But I thought . . .'

'There was the boy, Hugh, he was away at his public school at the time. Then there was Verity, who was twelve, too old to need a nanny. My charge was little Daisy, five years old, and the apple of her parents' eye. They adored her, and they were heartbroken when she died.'

'Died?' Lally was appalled. 'I had no idea! I never knew that Vee had a sister.'

'Diphtheria, there was a lot of it about that year. They blamed Verity for it; they said Daisy must have caught it from her, but since both girls went down with it within days of one another, I had my doubts. There were several cases in the city, Daisy might have picked it up anywhere. Verity was very ill, hers was the life they despaired of, not the little one, but then Daisy took a turn for the worse and died, while Verity recovered. Mrs Trenchard had what you might call a breakdown. Nerves.'

'I'm not surprised.' Lally closed her eyes, remembering the frightening days of Peter's illness. 'How dreadful for her.'

'The one I pitied was Verity. She was the one who suffered most in my opinion. Oh yes, her parents grieved, how do you ever get over such a loss? But to my way of thinking they had two other young lives left to them, and those were the ones who mattered. There was Verity, still very weak after her illness, and then Hugh came home from school, once the whole place had been cleaned and disinfected.'

'It must have been a terrible shock to him, to lose his sister.'

'It was, of course, but he had a head on him, that boy. All the servants went on and on about Daisy, saying she was an angelic child, too good for this world and all that kind of sentimental nonsense. I had my own opinion of her, you get to know about children when you do my job, and you watch them grow up. I heard Hugh say to Vee, as they called her, that it was sad about Daisy, but he reckoned that she'd have grown up to be an unpleasant person; if you were sly and deceitful at five, he said, what hope was there of your growing up into a decent human being?'

'Hugh said that?' Lally wasn't surprised. 'Yes, I can believe it. Hugh never goes in for self-deception, he is the most clear-headed man.'

'Of course, not being a very nice child has nothing to do with the gift of life, and if we only survived on our deserts, then where would most of us be? However, to the parents, to the Dean and his wife, Daisy was their lodestar; perfection itself. A tragedy like that can work in two ways, it pulls a family together or splits them apart. There was no question which it was in that household. The family was already divided, and if I hadn't known it from the moment I stepped inside the front door, I'd have known it when I heard with my own ears Mrs Trenchard say that she wished Verity had been the one to go, why had Daisy been taken from her, and Verity left behind.'

Lally stared at Miss Tyrell. 'She said that, about her own daughter?'

Miss Tyrell nodded. 'I'll put away these warmer clothes, you won't be wanting them now.' She opened a cupboard door. 'What's more,' she went on, 'she said it in Verity's hearing, and that's a thing I could never forgive her for. She had no time for that girl, none at all, and Verity thin and wretched after being so ill, and so distressed about Daisy.'

'What about Vee's father?'

'The Dean was too troubled in his conscience to take any notice of what was going on around him. He lost his faith, you see, the night that Daisy died. For all the rest of the time I was there, he'd walk up and down, up and down, in his study at night, talking out loud. I thought he was writing his sermon, or talking to someone else. Then I thought he might be talking to God. Praying. Only he wasn't. He was arguing with himself. Wrestling with darkness. And the darkness won. It usually does.'

'Did he think to give up his position, leave the church?'

'You're Catholic, aren't you? Yes, I heard it said that Mr Henry had married a Roman Catholic. So perhaps you don't understand about the Church of England. Most of the clergy don't believe in what they teach or say to start with, or if they do, the gloss soon wears off. Now, Dean Trenchard was different. He was truly a religious man, a man of faith. That's why it was so terrible when he lost his faith. It was the centre of his life, well, Daisy and God were. He lost one and then the other. But he went on, did his job at the cathedral same as before. No one noticed any difference, I shouldn't think.'

Lally was shaking her head. 'Oh, poor Verity. What an appalling thing to happen to her. And at that age, when a girl's so vulnerable. I had no idea, she's never spoken about it. Did her father really not care about her?'

'No, I don't think he ever gave her a thought.' Miss Tyrell shook out a twill skirt. 'This with a light jumper will be just right for when you're up and about and want to go on deck.'

'What happened in the Deanery after that?'

'I stayed on for a few weeks, helping to care for Mrs Trenchard and for Verity. Then I left in the autumn. They were sending Verity away to school, Mrs Trenchard didn't want her in the house, if you ask me.'

'I can't believe it,' Lally said. 'How could a mother treat her daughter in such a cruel way? And why did Vee never say a word about Daisy? Nor Hugh, if it comes to that.'

'Being an American, perhaps you don't understand that English people like the Trenchards are brought up not to talk about their personal problems and griefs. Mr Messenger must be just the same. It's not considered good manners to do so, although in my opinion, bottling things up can go too far, and it can lead to a lot of trouble that would never come about if people had opened their mouths and said how they felt about this or that.'

Miss Tyrell was right about that; it was squeezing blood out of a stone to get Harry to talk about anything to do with his emotions – or anyone else's.

'And, looking back,' Miss Tyrell said, 'I don't think it was just Daisy. I don't believe Mrs Trenchard ever liked Verity. Sometimes that happens. Mrs Trenchard herself is a reserved woman, cold you could say, but who knows, perhaps her own mother didn't have much time for her when she was a little girl. It wasn't the same with Hugh, she was quite different with Hugh.'

'That must have made it even worse for Vee.'

'I thought, when she was getting better, that Verity was as cold as her mother, that she didn't feel anything very strongly. Some children are like that, they live on the surface and take life as it comes.'

'Oh, that isn't true of Vee!'

'No. It was her way of defending herself, shutting it all away inside, so no one thought she cared as much as she did, not about Daisy, nor how much her mother disliked her. Heartless, the servants said she was. But she did care. She felt Daisy's death keenly, and she was devastated by her mother's remark. I know, because I saw her face before the shutters came down.'

'Did Hugh know about what his mother said?'

'Perhaps Verity told him; they were very close, those two. I think

Daisy's death and the way their parents reacted to it had a long-lasting effect on both Hugh and Verity. It wasn't a secret, it wasn't hushed up or anything, everyone in the family knew about it, but Hugh and Verity entered into what you might call a conspiracy of silence.'

'Claudia knew about Daisy, then. And she never said a word.'

'Why should she? It happened a while ago, and the two families don't see much of each other. I doubt if Claudia ever thinks about it. If Hugh and Verity don't talk about it, why should she?'

EIGHT

Vee hesitated that night. If she took her pills, then the night brought the past back to her, memories she didn't want. If she didn't take the pills, then the dark hours of the night were a torment, an endless hour of the wolf with beasties and ghoulies coming out of the woodwork to fill her tired mind.

Exhausted in mind, body and spirit, she decided not to take her customary pills, trusting to the roll of the boat and her fatigue to bring her sleep. In an odd way, she found the huge motions of the vessel soothing, like being rocked in an immense cradle. Lulled, she slept for a few hours.

Until the nightmare began. It wasn't a nightmare at first, in fact it was a gentle dream, of a summer's afternoon, a memory of a drive, with Lally and Piers Forster. Kind, clever Piers, who had wanted to marry her; but this was before he proposed. They were going to Stratford, to see a Shakespeare play. Lally, the passionate Shakespearean, was sitting beside Piers, talking about *Macbeth*, they were going to see *Macbeth*. Some rational part of her mind, still wakeful, told her that was odd, reminding her that she had never seen *Macbeth* at Stratford, not with Piers or Lally.

The tranquil summer landscape blurred and dissolved, and they were in the theatre, taking their seats. The clarity and detail of the dream was extraordinary, the numbers on the velvet seats, the shape and feel of the programme, Piers's head tilted towards Lally as she made a comment on one of the actors, with the smile she remembered so well.

The house lights dimmed, the curtain rose, the theatre vanished, and Vee was standing on the upper steps of a stone spiral staircase in a Scottish castle, with the wind howling and whistling through the tower. A huge raven perched on the wide ledge of an arrow slit, its cold eye fixed on her. Pressed against the wall was Macbeth, blood dripping from his hands, his face, the dagger in his hand. Words whirled about her head, desperate words of violence and torment and pain.

Macbeth had murdered Duncan, whom had she murdered? She had a bloody dagger in her hand as well, and she was overwhelmed with anguish, with the knowledge that she had struck a fatal blow and sent a soul into eternity, irretrievably lost, beyond her reach, a deed that could never be undone, guilt that couldn't be assuaged or borne.

She struggled into wakefulness, overwhelmed by fear and panic and remorse, and unsure for a while where she was, in the darkness, with the creaking of the boat and the swaying motion and the sound of the sea. She switched on the light above her bunk, heavy-eyed and tired, but with no intention of letting herself go back to sleep, not until grey dawn sent its half-light filtering into the cabin, and the day brought its sense of normality and relief.

She didn't feel sleepy, anyhow. Her mind was clear and sharp, all sleep driven away by the anguish of her dream.

Had Pigeon locked the door behind her? It appeared to be slightly open. An invitation to anyone walking by . . . Vee wasn't thinking of visitors with amorous intent, she was afraid of quite a different kind of caller. She slid out of bed, and, holding on to the table as the ship paused for a moment at the height of a roll before plunging back the other way, reached out for the door and locked it. She had been wearing an eye-mask, which had ridden up on to her forehead; now she pulled it off and tossed it on to the bed.

Where had Pigeon put the notebook that Claudia had given her?

'Voyages can be a most dreadful bore, Vee, plenty of time to write the story of your life.'

Vee had thanked her and had dutifully packed the journal together with a bottle of ink and her fountain pen. She had done so mechanically, with no intention of writing a word. Now she was desperate to find them, they must be there somewhere.

Here they were, in a drawer with her hankies, stowed away in a stupid place by Pigeon.

She cleared the table in front of the mirror of books, packets of cigarettes, magazines and a jar of cream and took out the bottle of ink and the leather-backed notebook, and sat down. Then she unscrewed the barrel of the fountain pen and dunked it in the pot of ink, squeezing the filler and watching the dark liquid being drawn up; she'd loved fountain pens ever since she was a girl.

It was a good pen, it suited the paper. Now all she had to do was to write.

My life, she said to herself, doodling the figure of an angel on the receipt for the ink. Who was she writing this for? For posterity? For her family? For Henry? To explain herself to an astonished world?

Or for protection. No diaries, no written records, never commit anything to paper, no letters, nothing that anyone could ever find that would reveal a scrap of information about your private life, that was the rule. Only, if she put it down in writing, with all the details, then if anything did happen to her—

She winced as she thought of the great propellers and the foaming water around them, and that ghoulish little boy of Henry's, so like his father to look at, telling her with enthusiasm how anything that got in the way of propellers would be sliced up and the ship would barely register a judder in its deepest workings, nothing that anyone would ever notice.

'Even if you managed to keep clear of the propellers, if you went overboard, then you still wouldn't drown,' he'd added. 'It's the sharks who get you first, long before you drown.'

She wasn't going to think about it. She was deliberately keeping clear of the decks, of the rails, where once her delight on board ship was to stand for hours at the rails, looking down into the shifting colours and movement of the sea, green and foaming, or darkest blue, or even, as so often in the Atlantic, grey and forbidding.

'Mummy will die one day,' he'd said, his face suddenly troubled. 'Everybody will. They get old, like people do, and then they're gone. That's everyone, even Mummy and Daddy.'

She'd consoled him. 'Mummy and Daddy won't die for years and years, not until you're grown up and have children of your own to worry about.'

'If there's a war, and Daddy goes to fight the Germans, then he could be killed.'

What could you say to that, except that it was the truth?

'Sometimes, very important soldiers, like your daddy, don't get sent out to fight. They're too valuable to lose, so they stay at Headquarters and make sure things are done properly.'

'Not Daddy. He isn't a coward, he won't want a desk job, not if there's a real war.'

Probably not.

She was writing it for herself. So that, if anything happened to her – and she thought again of those great, relentless propellers – someone might read it, and say: 'I understand.'

Perhaps Alfred was in her mind at that moment, although she wouldn't admit it to herself. Of all the people she knew who deserved an explanation, Alfred was the one whose opinion she most cared about. Although she hoped that Lally, if she ever came to read it, might think of her with compassion rather than hatred. It would take a saint to be so forgiving, but then Lally was a remarkable woman.

And Claudia? Claudia was out of the same mould as herself, although their fanaticism had taken different directions, it was, at root, the same. A burning desire for a cause greater than oneself. Perhaps her cousin Lucius's madness came from his mother's side, after all, and not from those generations of lunatic earls, perhaps folly was in her blood, and in Claudia's.

There was no excuse there for what she had done.

Well, she would write it down. As her dream had shown her, her life over the last few years would come pouring out in a wave of painfully sharp memories, given half the chance. Those would fill her mind, while her pen could trace the mere bones of her life during those eventful and mistaken years.

PART TWO

1932

ONE

Vee hadn't seen Claudia for five or six years. In those days, her cousin had been a fair, chubby, awkward creature with a mouthful of ironwork and protuberant pug-dog eyes – although those were of an intense and dazzling blue that caused pangs of envy in Vee's breast. In comparison, she felt that her own almost black eyes, an inheritance from her French grandmother, were dull and commonplace.

Vee's train from York had got into Oxford railway station half an hour ago, and she had crossed from the up platform to the other side, to wait for the train from London. The down platform at three o'clock on that bright October afternoon was almost deserted. A porter leaned against his trolley, squinting into the slanting sunlight as he watched for the arrival of the 1.49 express from London. The station cat was sunning itself in feline abandon on the meagre flowerbed at the end of the platform. A passenger in a trilby and a green mackintosh waited beside a battered suitcase.

She walked along the platform to the chocolate machine and put in a penny for a Nestlé bar. She unwrapped it, took a bite, then put the remains of the chocolate into her coat pocket. She wasn't hungry. What she was, she realized, feeling the butterflies in her tummy, was nervous. Nervous about coming to Oxford, nervous about meeting new people, nervous about the work, fearing that everyone else would turn out to be much cleverer than she was. They, and her tutors, would despise such stupidity and wonder how she had ever managed to get a place at the university.

And what a miracle it seemed that she was here at all, after the flat refusal of her grandfather to let her go to university. It was thanks

71

to Claudia that she was here, it was Claudia who had announced to her own astonished and disapproving family that no, she wasn't going to become a debutante, she wasn't going to stay in London and do the season.

The day that the letter from Aunt Lettice breaking this piece of news came had been a red-letter day for Vee, if a wretched disappointment for her parents.

'I don't know what your grandfather will say,' her father said.

Vee knew exactly what he would say, and she didn't care. If she weren't going to London, then, she said, she'd just have to hang around at home. No, thank you, Mummy, no Swiss finishing school for her, she'd feel out of place with all those rich girls.

'You must speak to your father,' Mrs Trenchard said to her husband. 'Perhaps, in the circumstances, a year or two at university . . .'

He must let me go, Vee said to herself. She went to the Minster and knelt and prayed and prayed, feeling that it was somehow wrong to pray so desperately for oneself, but if God didn't help her, who would?

'In the end, she should do what she wants,' she overheard her mother say to her father. 'It isn't as if she were a beauty, or had any special talent. A season would have done her good, she might have caught some young man's eye, but I can't ask Lettice to present her if Claudia isn't going to be a debutante. We both have daughters who are a disappointment to us. Only Lettice is fortunate, she has the other girls.'

Daisy hung in the air.

Vee didn't care about her mother's dismissal of her looks and gifts. Let them think there was no better alternative. Claudia wrote to her. 'What a lark that we both want to do the same thing. I've talked Mummy round, so it's going to be all right, I can go. And I should think that once your old snob of a grandfather knows you can't do the season, he'll have to let you go to Oxford.'

Not without a tremendous argument and more dreadful scenes, he hadn't. In the end, he washed his hands of her, furious that his daughter-in-law's grand connections should have come to nothing. 'She'd better stay in York with you, Anne, there'll be dances and so on here. You must know everybody who matters.'

'I think you'd better go to Oxford,' her mother said to her.

'I can't. I can't afford it on my allowance. Not the fees and every-thing.'

'I'll pay.'

'You?'

'I have a little money of my own. And don't feel you have to come back home for all the holidays,' she went on. 'You young people like to spend time abroad. Or with your friends. Like Hugh does.'

'Hugh has a generous allowance.'

'I'm sure Grandfather will come round in the end. Now he knows the season isn't a possibility. After all, most of the young men who go to all the London parties and dances are at one of the universi-ties. You'll meet plenty of eligible men at Oxford, I'm sure.' She paused, searching for words. 'I gather Claudia is very smart and extravagant. When your grandfather finds out, he won't want you to be short of money and not be able to keep up with her.'

Which seemed pretty unlikely to Vee, since smart and Yorkshire school and Deanery hardly went together.

'Of course, he won't give you as much as he gives Hugh, young men are always more expensive at university.'

Her mother agreed to pay her first term's fees, and Hugh made Daddy give her a small allowance.

'Mummy's right,' he said. 'Grandfather will see sense in the end. If Oxford's OK for Claudia, why should it be so wrong for Vee? I'll drop a few hints when next I see him.'

Vee was too warm in her thick winter coat. When she'd left York that morning there had been frost on the tracks, and she was grateful for her wool coat and gloves and scarf. Now they seemed out of place and uncomfortable.

A bell clanged, and the signal at the far end of the platform clat-tered down. The porter stood up and straightened his cap. More porters began to trundle their trolleys across the line. Even the station cat woke up and flicked her tail round herself.

The track hummed, then Vee heard the train, the shrill sound of a whistle, a cloud of smoke in the distance. With a roar and a grinding of brakes, the engine was alongside her, then past, coming to a snorting, squealing halt almost at the end of the platform.

Gone was the tranquil peace of a few minutes before. Heads

appeared at windows all along the train, doors were flung open, people poured on to the platform.

She felt a sudden panic. Would she recognize Claudia – or would Claudia recognize her? When they last saw one another, they'd been schoolgirls, clumsy and at that awkward age, neither children nor adults. Pupae, in fact. Had Claudia turned into a radiant butterfly, or a dreary moth? Had she grown much? She'd been shorter than Vee then, and Vee had always been small for her age.

Her eyes darted here and there among the faces in the sea of humanity. Youthful humanity, she noticed, which lifted her spirits; young men and women of her own age. More men than women, which she supposed was only natural – inevitable, if they had parents and a grandfather like hers. The men were casually dressed in tweeds and flannels, and had an astonishing array of bags and suitcases and golf clubs hung over shoulders and held in masculine hands. They greeted one another with loud good humour and waves and claps on the back. A group of them clustered around the luggage van as bicycles were wheeled down the ramp.

However would she find Claudia in this throng? She heard a shriek in her ear and whipped around to come face to face with her cousin.

It was as well Vee hadn't changed that much in the intervening years, for she would never have recognized her. How could this willowy, exquisitely groomed creature be her dumpy, toothy cousin? Her smile was immaculate now, and those blue eyes were huge and ravishing.

'Good gracious,' Vee said. 'I'd never have known you.'

'Well, I'd have known you, with that discontented look on your face and that air that northerners have when they come south.'

'Air? What do you mean?'

'Oh, a tinge of hay bales and beer and clogs, you know.' Claudia glanced down at Vee's overnight case. 'Is this all you've got? What a mêlée! Are they all university people?'

'My trunk came on ahead. I was looking out for you, I never saw you get off the train.'

'I wasn't on it. I came in the motor car, I had too much luggage to come on the train.'

'I didn't have any choice. Can you imagine anyone offering to drive me from York?'

'Doesn't Hugh have a car?'

'He can't even drive.'

Claudia glanced up and down the platform. 'You didn't travel down together on the train, though, not unless he's got the gift of invisibility.'

'He came up last week. Some work to catch up on, he said, but I think he just wanted to get away from the Deanery.'

'Could be an advantage having a brother up at the same time as you. He'll have heaps of men friends for you to meet.'

That made Vee laugh. 'You'll get to meet all the men you want, I feel sure.'

'No, it's going to be like a convent, being at a women's college, don't you think so? We go this way, the car's over at the other side of the station. Oh, Vee, aren't you happy? Aren't you just brimming over with being here?'

Vee thought about it as they went up the steps and across the footbridge. 'I don't feel it's real yet.'

'I know what you mean. Pinch yourself, and you'll wake up in the usual old bed. I've been saying to myself all the way here, I've made it, I've done it, it's happening, and nobody can stop me now.'

They went down the steps to the other platform, and out on the north side, where a gleaming motorcar was waiting, a liveried chauffeur in attendance. Vee had forgotten just how rich her Vere cousins were.

'Do you remember Jenks?' Claudia said with a wave of her hand towards the chauffeur. 'My ally, aren't you Jenks?' and she gave him an enormous wink before pushing Vee into the car.

Vee sat down on the sumptuous leather seat and stared at Claudia, who had produced a ridiculously long cigarette holder and was fixing a cigarette into it. 'I shan't offer you one, coz, because I know that coming as you do from the Deanery, you won't touch drink or tobacco.'

'I do smoke, as it happens, and I'd love a cigarette.'

'We'll have to get you a holder, nothing less chic than stubs with lipstick all over them.'

'I'm not wearing any lipstick.'

'That's too obvious, but you'll have to start. I'm not going to become known as the one with the dowdy cousin, I assure you.'

The car purred down to the Botley Road and turned under the railway bridge. The main entrance to the station was thronged with students and taxis and porters and luggage.

'Stop, Jenks,' Claudia said suddenly, and even before the car halted, she had the door open and was hurtling through the crowd towards the taxi rank.

What was she up to? Vee dived out of the car after her cousin, who had gone up to where an astonishingly beautiful girl was standing amid a helpful crowd of young men.

'Are you for Grace?' Claudia asked.

'Why, yes, as it happens, but how . . .' She spoke with an accent. American, Vee thought.

'Is this your luggage?' Claudia was asking.

'Yes, it is.'

'We can't take the trunk, but that doesn't matter.' Claudia beckoned to a porter. 'This trunk needs to be delivered.'

'Of course, miss. Where to?'

'Grace College. When will that be?'

'Later this afternoon.'

'That's all right, but don't make it too late.'

'Name, miss?' the porter asked the American girl.

'Fitzpatrick.'

He brought out a stub of chalk and scrawled her name and the word Grace on the trunk. He called out to a colleague standing nearby, 'Joe, this is for one of the hen houses. Grace.'

Claudia pushed Miss Fitzpatrick towards the car, which was causing something of a traffic jam. 'Hop in, before a policeman arrives to harangue Jenks.'

Vee got in after them, knocking her shin against a strangely-shaped black case.

'I'm sorry, that's in the way,' the American said, leaning down to move it.

'What on earth is it?' asked Vee.

'My French horn. Why did that guy back there say my trunk was for one of the hen houses?' said Miss Fitzpatrick.

'It must be what they call the women's colleges,' Claudia said. 'A lot of people haven't got used to having women at the university.'

Miss Fitzpatrick held out a hand. She was wearing exquisite kid gloves, Vee noticed. 'I'm Lavender Fitzpatrick, only I get called Lally.'

'If you say Lavender, no one will call you anything else,' Claudia said. 'I'm Claudia Vere, and this is my cousin Verity Trenchard. Known as Vee.'

76

'I prefer Lally. It'll make me feel more at home. Say, how did you know I was going to Grace? Are you freshmen there, too?'

'Intuition,' said Claudia. 'One of my more useful talents. I think they call us Freshers at Oxford, at least they do the men. Where are you from, what are you reading?'

Lally looked puzzled, Vee could see she was about to reach into her bag for a book or magazine.

'She means, what are you studying?' Vee said.

'Oh, what course am I taking? English Language and Literature. And I'm from Chicago.'

'Where the gangsters are?' Vee asked.

'Yes, but we try to avoid them as much as possible. What are you taking . . . reading, I mean?'

'Modern Languages,' Vee said. 'French as my main language.'

'I'm reading Greats,' Claudia said. 'Greek and Latin. It's a four-year course, you see, so more annoying to my family.'

'Annoying?' Lally said.

'Even now, my dear brother is stamping up and down in his ancestral hall, incensed that I've made it to the university. He doesn't approve of education for women.'

'My father isn't too keen on the idea, either,' said Lally.

'And Vee's grandfather, who rules the roost in her family, will never forgive me for turning my back on being a debutante and coming to Oxford. You see, he'd planned for Vee to do the season with me. Only when it turned out I was coming here, he more or less had to let Vee come too.'

Lally laughed. 'My grandmother was at Oxford, she was one of the first girls at Grace College, back in the nineties. So she wanted me to come, and so did I, and in the end Pa agreed, although he still thinks a good American women's college would have been much better. We had quite a few arguments about it, before Grandma and I got our way.'

Vee's own battle had been such a bitter one, she'd imagined, for no good reason, that other people didn't have to fight so hard for what they wanted. Yet here were Claudia and Lally agreeing that their families didn't want them to be at Oxford.

'I may switch to another school, though,' Claudia was saying. 'Greats is hard work.'

Vee was looking out of the window. There was a clarity to the air that day, a clarity that she later came to realize was unusual in Oxford. Perhaps it was in her eyes, and not outside at all, but everything seemed sharply delineated: the cobbled streets, the newspaper vendor on a corner shouting out the headlines, a college servant in a bowler hat stepping through the wide open doors of an ancient college.

The motor drew up in front of the arched gateway into Grace College, causing various vans and cars to brake abruptly and a man pushing a handcart to call out a few unsavoury epithets as Jenks got out of the car and came round to open the rear door.

The lodge was chilly and brightly lit. A gnome of a man stood behind a polished wooden counter as the three of them came in. He flicked his eyes up from the ledger in front of him. Names? Trenchard, Vere, Fitzpatrick. He made three careful ticks on a list and turned round to where a row of keys hung on numbered hooks. 'Quite a coincidence you arriving together, since your rooms are next to one another. Sign here, please, Miss Trenchard. Now you, Miss Fitzpatrick. Miss Vere.'

Claudia took the book and signed it with a flourish. 'It's Lady Claudia, actually. Where do we go?'

That earned her a sharp look and a sniff. 'A scout will show you to your rooms. Do you have any luggage with you? Big luggage. A trunk, for instance, I have no record of any trunk under your name, Miss Fitzpatrick,' he said, emphasizing the 'miss'.

'It's coming up from the station.'

'It makes more work for us when you young ladies don't send your boxes and trunks on in advance.'

'That would be difficult, since it came across the Atlantic on the boat with me.'

'Young ladies from abroad always cause problems for us.'

They started with Claudia's room, number seventy-three, on the second floor. Lally was seventy-four, just across the corridor, and Vee was seventy-five, next door to Claudia.

Claudia unlocked the varnished wooden door. A card with her name on it was already slotted into a little brass holder: Lady Claudia Vere. She opened the door and Vee and Lally peered past her into the room. Claudia put down her crocodile handbag on the top of the bookcase, edged round the trunk that took up most of the available space in the centre of the room and surveyed her new domain.

A narrow bed, a small chest of drawers, a wardrobe, and a desk made up the furniture. There was a tiny grate in the fireplace in one corner, with a gas ring set beside it on green tiles.

'I'd call this a cell, myself. Lord knows how I'll fit everything in.' She turned to the scout who had come with them to show them the way. 'Are all the rooms this size?'

'First years are put in the smaller rooms, miss.'

'Are your rooms the same?' she said to Vee and Lally. She bounded across the corridor to inspect them. 'Yes, they are.'

'Kind of cosy,' said Lally.

'Kind of cramped,' said Claudia.

Vee didn't care. 'They can put me in a broom cupboard, if they like. I'm here. And that's a miracle, and nothing can spoil it.'

Claudia was dangling her keys on one finger. 'The scout's vanished,' she said, irritated. 'Where do we ring for her?'

'I don't think we do,' Vee said.

'I need her to unpack my trunk.'

There was a pause, and then Lally said, 'I'm not sure it works like that. I guess we do our own unpacking.'

Claudia stared at her. 'How? Bowler packed it for me, it'll take me hours to get everything out, and then what do I do with it?'

'Bowler?' Vee said.

'My maid.'

'Didn't you unpack your trunk at school?'

'No, of course not. Matron and the school maids saw to all that.'

'We had to do our own at Yorkshire Ladies'.'

'Pass over those keys,' said Lally, kneeling beside the trunk. 'Vee and I will show you what to do.'

TWO

Vee would never forget the first night in hall, for Freshers' Dinner. It was a handsome panelled room with the high table for the dons set on a raised area at one end and three long tables in the main part of the hall for the undergraduates.

The noise of all those women's voices startled Lally; Claudia and Vee were used to it.

'Just like school,' remarked Claudia, raising her voice to be heard above the din.

A tall girl in a scholar's gown stood and said a Latin grace, and the maids rushed to and fro serving the food. Claudia said it was dreadful; Vee would have eaten a plate of raw turnips that evening, and not noticed it.

When the plates were cleared away and coffee had been served, a wiry woman, grey hair pulled back in a severe bun, rose from her seat. She waited for the buzz of conversation to die down, and said a few more words in Latin. Then she swept sharp eyes over the assembled undergraduates.

'The Mistress of Grace,' Vee's neighbour hissed in her ear. 'Dr Margerison, the biologist.'

'This picture that hangs behind me is a striking portrait of our founder, Dame Eleanor Grace,' Dr Margerison began.

'Grim old party,' Claudia said, *sotto voce*.

Actually, she looked to Vee as though she had a twinkle in her eye, unlike the rest of the biddies pinned on the wall around the hall. Was that what brains and education did to you, turned you austere and disapproving and thin-lipped? The fact that most of them were dressed in the clothes of the last century didn't help, of course, high-necked, sombre clothes, or academic dress. Dame Eleanor, in her portrait, appeared to be wearing a pith helmet.

'Why the camel?' Lally whispered to Claudia. She shrugged, but Dr Margerison soon enlightened her.

'Dame Eleanor was a pioneer. She was eminent in her field of Egyptology and all her life had a passion for the education of women. That is why, when she came into a fortune, after the untimely death of her only brother, she used her inheritance to found and endow this college.

'You who are here today, starting out on a new life as members of this great university, are the cream of your generation. Gifted with intelligence and the capacity for hard work, you have become part of a centuries-old tradition of learning and scholarship.

'Here at Grace, we expect the young women who come to us to display the same characteristics as our founder: intelligence, diligence, intrepidity, persistence in the face of adversity, combined with a sense of duty, honour and love of country. And to this love of country, we hope that you add love of this university and of this college and that none of you throughout your lives will do anything to bring the institutions that have nourished you into disrepute.

'We live in restless, difficult times. Young people today are keenly aware of the world they live in, and the rights and wrongs existing within our society. We encourage compassion and concern for those less privileged than ourselves; you will find many ways in which you can contribute to the good of others while you are here.

'We expect, however, that your energies will be first and foremost directed to your studies, the *raison d'être* of your presence here, so that when you go down, neither you nor your tutors feel that you have wasted your time here.

'We are a college founded on Christian principles, and Evening Prayers, held at six p.m. in the chapel, are compulsory for all undergraduates; this is an opportunity for us to come together as a community and the time when notices concerning the college are given out.'

She paused for a moment, her cool eyes sweeping over the faces looking up at her.

'I and the Fellows of our college welcome you to Grace. We hope, and expect, that you will make the best possible use of your time here, and go forth into the world more complete human beings as a result of what you will learn and experience at this university.'

Vee pulled back the sheets and got into bed. The mattress was lumpy and the sheets were starched into discomfort; she'd had worse at school. Goodbye Verity, the Dean's daughter, she said to herself as she pummelled her pillow into submission. Hello Miss Trenchard, undergraduate of the University of Oxford.

There was a volley of knocks on the wall and Claudia's voice came through, muffled but comprehensible. 'For God's sake, I think they've stuffed my mattress with a dead donkey.'

'Goodnight,' Vee called back. And from the other side of the corridor came an echoing goodnight from Lally.

THREE

They had a mentor at Grace, the three of them. She was a second-year scientist, called Miss Harbottle. Big-boned and with dark eyebrows that gave her a brooding appearance, she informed Claudia, almost before she'd introduced herself, that she was a Socialist and didn't believe in titles, nor in any aspect of the aristocracy. The sooner the House of Lords was abolished, the better, she added, giving Claudia a frosty look.

Presumably Miss Harbottle didn't know about Claudia's brother, Lucius, but Vee thought he certainly made a strong case for immediate abolition of the Lords. Claudia took no offence at Miss Harbottle's hectoring manner, merely saying that she knew many people who felt the same way.

'But while we're waiting for the revolution, can you tell us all those things we need to know?'

Miss Harbottle sniffed. 'There's a notice in your room with all the college rules. About signing out and in and all that kind of thing. What you'll be fined for, or sent down if it's bad enough. Men.' She said the word as though she were speaking of black beetles. 'There are strict rules about men in the college. You may never entertain a man privately in your rooms, for instance.'

'It would be difficult, given the size of the rooms and the bed,' Claudia said with a straight face.

Lally was laughing; Miss Harbottle looked vexed.

Lally quelled her laughter. 'Tell us about this Freshers' Fair.'

'That's tomorrow afternoon. It's where you join University clubs and societies, or sign up for sporting activities. Only, please remember that we at Grace prefer to concentrate first and foremost on our academic work. Most first years go, though. It's held in Schools.'

'Schools?' Lally asked. 'What are they?'

'Schools is the building in the High, on the corner of Merton Street. Lectures are held there, and it's where you'll take all your exams.'

Lally had a map of Oxford in her hand. 'Here?'

'Yes. In the morning, there's Matriculation. There's another notice about that.'

'I read it,' said Lally. 'Subfusc clothing? Dark skirt and boots, white shirt and tie and cap and gown? Are the boots obligatory?'

'It means shoes as well. And for dark, read black, please, including stockings. The Dean likes the women from Grace to look well-turned out and all the same.'

Their purchase of gowns and caps took place amid much hilarity. Lally was surprised to find she didn't get to wear a mortarboard. She looked doubtfully at the soft, square-topped cap that she was handed.

'It's mediaeval, miss,' the assistant said.

'I believe you,' said Claudia, perching hers on top of her blonde waves and peering at herself in the tiny mirror that was all the shop afforded. 'It suits you best, Vee, I think you have the right kind of face for it. Like that portrait of Richard III, dark and introspective and waiting for the Renaissance to come along and liven things up a bit.'

Freshers' Fair was awash with noisy masculinity. Men talking in loud voices, men on the stands shouting to be heard, male bodies pressing against one another and thrusting to get through the knot of under-graduates clustered round the popular stands. There was only a sprinkling of women, and most of them looked rather alarmed to find themselves among so many men.

'There's a peculiar smell in here,' Lally said, wrinkling her elegant nose.

'Men,' Claudia said instantly. 'I bet Hugh's school smelt like this, didn't it, Vee? It's when they're all together, there's always a pong. And some of them here don't wash that much, if you ask me. Don't worry, you'll get accustomed to it.'

Vee wasn't worrying about the smell. Her eyes were scanning the tables and placards and banners proclaiming various activities: some sporting, some erudite, some absurd, like the Tiddlywinks Soc. 'I'm sure most of these clubs and societies don't welcome women,' she said to Lally, who had her startled look again.

'Too right,' said a man wearing cricketing flannels and blazer, who was sitting at a nearby table. 'This is what the university's all about, sport and having a good time, and you female undergraduates come butting in, wanting to work and take life seriously, it's a crashing bore.'

'I play baseball back home,' Lally said, ignoring the cricketing fan. 'Do you suppose there's a baseball club?'

A burst of song rose from the other side of the room.

Lally cupped her hand to her ear. 'That sounds fun. I like to sing.'

'Gilbert and Sullivan, and I bet they don't take women members, either,' said Claudia. 'They'll get singers for the female roles up from London.'

Lally went over to investigate a stand where they were singing madrigals and came back to report that was men only, too. 'Imagine, they have men singing alto and soprano, did you ever hear anything like it? When there are women around.'

'They think it's traditional, I expect,' Vee said. Her attention had been caught by a lanky individual in a faded pair of flannel trousers, held up at the waist by a frayed tie. On his top half, he wore a grubby fawn jumper. 'Join now, join now, equal shares for everyone, that's our motto,' he was bellowing through a megaphone, drowning out the frail sound of the madrigal group.

He was an arresting figure, with dark hair that fell forward from an untidy parting to be pushed back with an impatient hand, a hand with long, muscular fingers, a strong hand. He radiated energy, but there was a quirkiness to his mouth that suggested the intensity was alleviated by a sense of humour.

'R-A-P-M-O-C,' Claudia read out the sign propped on the table. 'Rapmoc? What on earth's that?'

The young man lowered his megaphone. 'Rational and Political Men Only Club.'

'There you are,' Vee said. 'You asked, and he's told you, if you're any the wiser for knowing.'

'Good Lord, it's Alfred Gore, isn't it?' said Claudia. 'My mother's your godmother, only you never come to see her, so perhaps you aren't aware of it. You were at Eton with my brother Jerry. Stop brandishing that megaphone and tell us why you don't want women in your club.'

'Who are you?'

'Claudia Vere.'

'I suppose you are,' he said, after giving her a hard stare. 'You've got Jerry's eyes, all you Veres have those very blue eyes. Anyhow, don't take any notice of the club name, we welcome people of all sexes. Or none. Come along and drink beer and talk serious politics. Thursday evening in the Arnold Room at Balliol.'

'What a bore that sounds,' Claudia said.

Vee had seen Hugh on the other side of the room. 'Hello, Hugh!' she called out, standing on tiptoe, and waving a handful of leaflets. 'Over here.'

Hugh surged through the crowd, followed by a tall, fair man with a handsome face. 'Vee, this is Giles Hotspur, we were at Repton together, and we share a set. My sister Verity, only we call her Vee. Hello, Alfred, no good shouting your wares, however much you yell and make a noise, it won't add up to a sensible argument. Don't go near that organization, Vee,' he said, waving towards Alfred, who had started work again with his megaphone.

'Why not?'

'Because it's the Communist outfit. They aren't allowed to be the Communist Society or club or whatever, the proctors won't have it. You'll be in deep trouble with your Dean if you attend a meeting and get busted. Red faces, never mind red politics. That's why they call themselves that idiotic name. It's Com Par backwards, you see. Bags, there, is a Marxist.'

'Bags?' said Claudia.

'It's all he wears. Hasn't got a suit as far as anyone knows. Always goes about in disreputable bags and a ghastly pullover.'

'Is he very hard up?' Vee asked. 'Surely, if he went to Eton . . .'

'His people have got plenty of money, but since he took up the Cause, he likes to identify with the working masses who don't have many changes of clothes. Solidarity, you see.'

Vee only had a vague idea of what a Marxist was. Both at school and at home, it was a word that wasn't mentioned, and when she'd asked a question at either place, she had quickly been silenced. 'Are all Communists Marxists?'

'The most extreme are, and since they're all extreme, yes, you could say Marxists and Communists are one and the same. However, we'll all be Communists and Marxists soon, it's quite the coming fashion. I bet membership of RAPMOC is growing fast.'

Vee was shocked; where she came from, at school and at the Deanery,

Communists were Bolshevists, and there was no question but that Bolshevism was the work of the devil.

Alfred was looking at Vee with a quizzical expression in his eyes. 'Do you know that nearly a quarter of the working population are unemployed? Do you have any idea how difficult it is for an unemployed worker to keep body and soul together, let alone his family fed and housed? The working man can't take much more, and when he rises up to throw off the chains of capitalism, then you'll see what the word revolution means.'

'Is Communism really the answer?' asked Lally. 'Matters are pretty dire in the States, but I don't think anyone's predicting a blood-red revolution. I guess if Roosevelt gets elected, he'll do his best for the working man.'

'With the Depression you've got over there? You don't know what you're talking about,' Alfred waved his megaphone in the air. 'Come to our next meeting, then you might begin to understand what politics really is, all you women have your heads in the sand.'

'Thank you for the kind invitation,' said Lally, 'but I think I'll pass.' And to Claudia and Vee: 'I'm going to go sign up for the Bach Choir. They surely have to have women in that.'

'Not necessarily,' said Claudia. 'They probably prefer little boys.'

A thought occurred to Vee. 'Hugh, what are you doing here? You aren't a Fresher.'

'I'm manning the Poetry Society stand. Better hop back to it, in fact. Care to join?'

'Are women allowed to be members?'

'Of course you are,' he said, suddenly cross. 'All these misogynist groups here, they're out of touch with the times.'

She put her name down, although she didn't think she'd go to any of the meetings or readings. She'd leave the poetry to Hugh. She signed up for the Literary Society and the French Club, avoided the blandishments of the Women's Hockey squad – she'd had enough hockey at school to last a lifetime – and looked around for the others. Lally was chatting to compatriots at the Anglo-American Society stand, and Vee went over to join her.

'Isn't your pop standing in November?' said a rangy, clean-cut man who looked as though he, at least, took a bath every day.

'He is.'

'Come on over on election night. There'll be a party for all us Americans, there's quite a crowd of us here at the moment, and we shall get the results by wireless as they come in.'

'Sounds fun,' said Lally.

'Standing?' said Claudia, who'd appeared beside them.

'For the Senate,' said Lally.

'I thought you said your father was a doctor,' Vee said.

'Yes, but he's very politically minded. Hates what's happening in our country with the Depression and everything. He's running for office so that he can make a difference.'

Vee became aware that someone was hovering behind them. She turned round and came face to face with a man who looked like a cherub. He was gazing at Lally.

'What a lovely, lovely woman,' he breathed. He laid a hand on her arm. 'I say, may I paint you? Oh, please say yes. Everyone loves to be painted by me.'

Alfred, who had abandoned his megaphone for a moment, paused on his way back to the RAPMOC stand; he was carrying a glass of water in his hand. Yelling about the injustices of society gave you a thirst, Vee supposed.

'This is Marcus,' he said, waving his free hand towards the cherub. 'A Balliol man, an artist.'

'Can you study art at Oxford?' Lally asked.

'Law,' said Marcus, in his soft voice. 'I'm reading law because I have to, but I paint because I love to. What beauty!' he went on, looking at Lally again. 'That exquisite colour of hair – it is natural, I do hope?' he added, anxiously.

'Perfectly,' said Lally, who seemed happy to take Marcus in her stride.

'Neither red nor brown, and together with a cream complexion, not a freckle in sight, so fortunate, because often that colouring is so sadly marred by freckles, the effect is ravishing. Slightly aquiline nose, hazel eyes, no, golden eyes, long neck, slim as a willow. I shall paint you as Artemis, with a bow in your hand. Please say you'll come. Not to my room, if that offends your maidenly sensibilities. It can be at the Ruskin, if you prefer, I work there as well. And bring your friends, bring a chaperone. Not that you aren't perfectly safe, I never touch women, Alfred will vouch for me.'

'Oh, pipe down, Marcus, and leave the girl alone,' said Alfred. He drank his water and dumped the glass on the nearest stand. He gave Vee a direct look. 'Give RAPMOC a go, Miss Trenchard. It might change your life.'

'Are you a Christian?' boomed a voice from across the way. 'Join OICCU, and spend worthwhile time in the company of your fellow Christians.'

'One for you, Vee,' said Claudia.

'Perhaps,' she said, feeling suddenly guilty that she was so disinclined to have anything to do with the Christian Union.

Why, Vee wondered, as they left Schools clutching handfuls of leaflets, did Christians dress so badly? Why was she so dowdy in comparison to the dashing Claudia and stylish Lally? It was partly a matter of money, but even so . . .

'It's interesting, the way the men dress,' she said, as they set off down the High.

'Several distinct groups,' agreed Claudia. 'Tweedy squire-ish ones.'

'Fops,' Vee said. 'Did you see that one in a floppy bow tie and that big hat?'

'He looked kind of cute,' Lally said.

'Better than those grubby ones in duffel coats,' said Claudia. 'What is it about duffel coats?'

'Then there are the don't-cares, like your friend Alfred Gore,' Vee said.

'Don't you believe it,' said Claudia. 'I'm a cynic when it comes to people who look as though they have minds above clothes. I think Alfred's outfit is just as artfully put together as the bow tie and the hat. Men!' she added with affectionate scorn.

Alfred took a few minutes' break from his megaphoning and wandered over to talk to Hugh. 'Which college is your sister at?'

'Grace,' said Hugh, scribbling on a card and filing it away. 'So's Claudia, but you know her. She's a cousin of ours. Don't know anything about the American one. My word, she's a looker.'

Alfred raised his eyebrows. 'Giles might hear you.'

'Anyone may hear my opinion, she's quite lovely. Claudia's grown into a minx, by the look of her.'

'The Veres are all mad,' said Alfred. 'Lovely eyes.'

'Claudia? A bit intense for me.'

'No, Vee has lovely dark eyes.'

Hugh considered this. 'Does she? I've never thought about it.'

Alfred went back to his stand and his megaphone.

FOUR

A few days later, Vee found a note from Hugh in her pigeonhole in the Lodge. 'Hugh's invited us to tea,' she said, flourishing a sketch of the three of them.

Claudia was sifting through a handful of her own letters. She had more post than anyone else in their year, most of which she tossed into the bin without a second glance. She twitched the note out of Vee's hand, looked at it, and laughed. 'Wicked likenesses, what a devil the man is! Four o'clock at Christ Church. Peckwater 3.4. Do you suppose the divine Giles will be there? If so, I'm definitely on. What about you, Lally?'

'Does he mean for all of us to go?' asked Lally.

'The picture tells its own story,' Vee said, 'and, besides, it's addressed to the three of us.' She handed Lally the envelope, addressed in Hugh's elegant script: The Three Graces, c/o Miss V Trenchard.

'He should be more specific, and name names,' said Claudia. 'He might get any three, such as Miss Harbottle, or that girl in the third year who's so passionate about Moral Rearmament.'

'It's what he and Giles call us,' Vee said.

'I take it as a compliment.'

'It might suit you and Lally, but hardly me,' Vee said, feeling that with her dull Yorkshire clothes, and washed-out winter face, the soubriquet could only count as a courtesy. It irked her, the difference between how Lally and she looked. Lally wore no make-up, but her wonderful colouring and complexion put her in another league from Vee. As for Claudia, she never went out without make-up, which earned her the disapproval of quite half the college.

'God prefers us to look the way He made us,' one sanctimonious second-year told her in Hall.

'Did He tell you so? Then why does He allow make-up to be made or sold?'

'Make-up is the work of Satan.'

'I'll look out for the name when next I buy a lipstick,' Claudia promised.

'I'll meet you at Christ Church, but it won't be until a little later,' said Lally, 'I've got a choir rehearsal until four.'

'We'll stop off and buy a cake,' Claudia said as she and Vee set off at a quarter to four. 'Just to be sure of our welcome.'

They went into Fullers, busy with women in hats having tea. 'I hope Hugh hasn't invited that dreary man from the next staircase up,' Vee said 'What kind of cake shall we buy?'

'Walnut, I think,' said Claudia. 'All men love walnut cake.'

They watched the cake being put in a box. The assistant made a loop with the ribbon and passed it to Vee while Claudia paid. 'No, put your purse away, Vee, this is my treat.'

Claudia was well aware that her cousin had to watch every penny, and she managed to be generous in a casually kind way that made it impossible to refuse.

'Which dreary man?' she asked as they went out of the shop and into Cornmarket.

'Jonathan somebody. Short and pink and hates women.'

'A Repton man, what do you expect from your northern waste-lands? You're all years behind the times there. Anyhow, most of the men here hate women, haven't you noticed?'

'No, I haven't. I know a lot wish women had never been admitted to the university, but that's simply unthinking prejudice. Why should they hate us?'

'It's what men do, when women trespass on their territory. Except for those that are queer, some of them get on quite well with women.'

'Queer? Odd, you mean, men who are eccentric?'

Claudia stopped and turned to look at her companion. 'Vee! Queer. You know, men who go to bed with other men. Like at their schools.'

Vee was taken aback. 'Men who go to bed with men?'

'Yes, of course.' She gave Vee a quick, concerned look. 'Do you mean you didn't know? What did you think they do at school, all those boys cooped up together? They get the habit there, and when they come on here, or go to Cambridge, they just carry on.'

'Well, there's nothing wrong with sharing a bed.'

'My pet, when I say go to bed together, I don't mean they doss down for a sound night's sleep. It's for sex, for heaven's sake.'

'I don't believe it.'

Vee's upbringing had been sheltered, but she still felt she had a reasonable grasp of the facts of life. Books, a chatty maid and earnest discussions with her more sophisticated friends at school had sorted it out for her – or so she thought. Of course, it was a taboo subject for her parents, as it was for most of their generation. More out of embarrassment than principle, she thought.

'I expect your mother was going to tell you about men on the eve of your wedding,' said Claudia. 'And she wouldn't think to mention about men's other tastes. Perhaps she doesn't know, I'm sure my mother's a terrific innocent about that kind of thing.'

What about Hugh? He'd been to public school. Only Hugh never talked about sex or love or anything like that.

'Maybe there are men like that, but Hugh isn't, what did you call it? Queer. He's perfectly normal.'

'My pet, of course he's queer, everyone knows that. He's had a tremendous thing going with Giles, why do you think they share a set?'

'Most of the men share sets. It's how they room at men's colleges. They're old friends, from school.'

'Yes, and some are friends, and then there are those for whom two bedrooms aren't really necessary.' Claudia took Vee's arm, and drew her out of the way of an angry student on a bicycle. He swept past them, ringing his bell in violent disdain. 'You can't tell me you didn't know.'

Vee felt as though the world had just opened and spat her out. Hugh in bed with another man, for sex? It was inconceivable. 'And disgusting, I don't know how you can say such things, Claudia.'

'They don't find it disgusting at all, they like it, or they wouldn't go to bed together.'

'I don't know how you can bring yourself to say such things.' Vee broke away from Claudia, desperate to escape from these awful revelations, and plunged into the traffic, causing a delivery van to stop with a squeal of brakes and a stout woman cyclist to swerve and nearly come off.

'Vee, I'm sorry,' Claudia called after her. 'Honestly, I'd never have said anything if I thought you didn't know about Hugh and Giles. I mean it's as obvious as the nose on your face.'

Tears were pricking Vee's eyes as she whirled round to shout at Claudia. 'Not to me it isn't.'

Claudia caught up with her. 'That's because you've led such a sheltered life in the Deanery, didn't the girls at school talk about it?'

Vee had bitten her lip in her agitation, so hard that she'd drawn blood. She dabbed at her mouth with the back of her glove.

Claudia put a hand out to touch her cousin's stiff shoulders, but Vee shrugged her roughly off.

'Well, it's as well I've enlightened you. You'd have found out sooner or later. Ignorance and innocence aren't the same, and ignorance can get you into terrible scrapes.'

The glory had gone out of the day, and Vee stalked through the lodge at Christ Church with her head held high and her stomach churning. She walked unseeing past the Custodians in their habitual bowler hats, and almost ran across Tom Quad, wanting to get away from Claudia. Past the great Wren Library, unnoticed, even in the beauty of the reflected late-afternoon light. She dashed over to Staircase Three, but there she stopped.

She didn't want to see Hugh. Not after what Claudia had said. To do that – what exactly – with Giles? No, Claudia was making it up. It was one of these fancies she'd picked up from her strange London life. Her brother was potty, who was to say that Claudia didn't have a loony streak as well? Vee wasn't going to believe her, and that was that.

The outer door, that they had learned to call an oak, was open. Inside, Hugh was stretched out on a sofa in front of the blazing fire, a pipe in his mouth, fanning himself with a copy of the *Spectator*. He leaped to his feet, and came over to give Vee a hug.

She shrank away from him, hating herself for doing so. This was Hugh, her brother, not some monster conjured up by Claudia, damn her.

'What's up, old thing?' he said. 'You look as though you've seen a ghost. If you thought you did, don't worry, it's probably just Bartlett, my tutor, he's been dead for centuries, only no one's noticed yet. Giles, buck up over there and yell for Tewson to bring tea.'

Tall, exquisite Giles. She stared at him, her mind still unable to cope with Claudia's bombshell.

No, Claudia had got it all wrong, at least about her brother. Perhaps one or two men might be like that; all right, she could accept that. Although she hadn't said so to Claudia, there had been talk at school about Oscar Wilde. And what did men do, two of them? She drew back from these uncomfortable anatomical thoughts and went over to the window.

The quad outside was half in shadow, half glowing in the autumn sunlight. That was like her, she thought, she'd been walking in the sun, and now the shadows had caught up with her. Unreal shadows, things of the darkness of the night and restless dreams, and no more substance in them than such phantasms had. Curse Claudia, for even suggesting such a thing.

Giles came over to her with a cup of tea, and as he went back to the table, Vee saw him touch Hugh lightly on the shoulder. Hugh turned and smiled at him, a smile of such sweetness and affection that there could be no doubt at all about the intimacy that existed between the two men.

The cup and saucer slipped through her fingers; the delicate porcelain smashed in pink and white chips on the dark wooden floor, tea splashed on to the carpet.

'I'm so sorry,' she said mechanically. 'How clumsy of me.'

'The Dresden is wasted on you, Vee,' said Hugh. 'It'll be an enamel mug next time. Tewson, we've had a spillage, come and see to it, would you? Giles, pour out another cup for Vee, and this time, for heaven's sake hold on to it. Have a biscuit, that'll soothe your nerves, I never saw you so on edge. That's what education does to a girl, I see how right all the misogynists are.'

This Hugh was almost a stranger to her. The brother she'd grown up with at the Deanery seemed to have vanished, to be replaced by this new person, a person she knew nothing about. Was this the brother she had confided in, moaned about their parents to, shared jokes with, laughed with when he did his merciless drawings of York notables, the brother who laughed when she did an imitation of the senior clergy wresting the tall palms from each other's grasp on Palm Sunday, in an effort not to have to carry the small and weedy ones?

The memories crowded into her head, a jumble of images and voices.

That was the brother of her childhood, of the Deanery, of times that had gone. Here, in front of her was the man, with his own life, his own feelings – and his own attachments. To Giles.

94

'I'm sorry,' she said, putting down the fresh cup with a bang. 'I think I'm going to be sick.'

'Not in here,' said Giles. 'Down the stairs, turn right before you get to the door. Claudia, do you want to go with her, to hold her head?'

'No,' said Claudia. 'Leave her alone, she's just had a bit of a shock, that's all,'

'Oh?' said Hugh, enquiringly.

'Nothing you two need to know about,' said Claudia.

As Vee stumbled down the stairs towards the lavatory she heard Claudia talking.

'Are you going to cut the cake? Is anyone else coming to tea? I feel like meeting some new people.'

'I hope John Petrus may drop in,' Hugh said. 'Brilliant man, Fellow of Balliol, and . . .'

Vee heard nothing more.

FIVE

Vee was having tutorials that term with Dr Nettleton at Christ Church. She never knew whether he'd be there or not, as he was apt to take off for weekends in France and not get back until Tuesday morning; her tutorial was at eleven-thirty on Mondays. His rooms were in Canterbury quad, and that Monday she climbed the three flights of stairs to discover a note on the door. He was away, would Miss Trenchard please come on Thursday at five.

Which left her with time to kill, and official permission to be in Christ Church before the witching hour of one o'clock. She wandered into Peck and was hailed from the window by Hugh. 'Hi, intruder,' he called down. 'Your nose is pink, is it cold? Who let you in?'

'I'd a tutorial with Nettleton, but he's away.'

Giles joined him at the window. 'Rogering his French mistress, I expect,' Vee heard him say. 'Come on up,' he called down to her.

Rogering? What did that mean? Vee went up to Hugh's room, to find a man in a black jacket barring her way. 'You can't come in here, miss,' he said in a lugubrious voice. 'No visitors to the college before one p.m., and certainly no members of the female sex on my staircase.'

'Give over, Tewson,' Hugh called out. 'That's not a member of the female sex, it's my sister. Turn your mind to more important matters.' He flapped a book towards the windows, where dust motes were dancing in the beams of sunlight. 'Dust, Tewson, look at that. You need to dust, not fuss about my sister.'

'Dust is in the air, I can't deal with dust until it hits the ground or the table and how can I dust a room that's in the state you two young gentlemen leave it, with piles of papers and books everywhere? Of course there's going to be dust.'

'Books go with the life of an undergraduate, Tewson,' said Giles, heaving himself up on to the window seat and stretching out his grey flannelled legs. He had a small telescope in one hand, and he lifted it to his left eye and gazed out over the quad.

'I'll be with you in two ticks,' said Hugh, from his desk. 'Just let me finish this article.'

'Hillier is still asleep,' Giles reported. 'Leaves his curtains pulled back so that the light wakes him, but there he is, fast asleep.'

'That Mr Hillier, his scout can't do anything with him, sleeps like he's the proverbial log,' Tewson said. 'Mr Hotchkiss, as has that staircase, he bangs on the door, but to no purpose. Mr Hillier may leave his curtains open, like you say, sir, but the oak's shut, nothing gets through to him. Mr Hotchkiss has complained to the Censor again and again, how can he do his job and wake someone up who doesn't want to wake? It's hard enough clearing up after some of you young gents; if you carry on like this at home, I can't think that you've got any staff left.'

He hitched up his grey striped trousers and gave a sniff. 'Not but what at least you have staff at home, not like that Mr Ibbotson, you can tell his family doesn't keep anyone above a tweeny.'

'Mr Ibbotson's father is a carpenter,' said Hugh. He threw down a copy of the *New Statesman*. 'God, what rubbish these fellows write. And don't you think the less of him for that, Tewson, you dreadful old snob. Joel is brilliant, far brainier than any of us, he'll probably end up Chancellor of the Exchequer.'

'Time was when nobody who wasn't a gentleman came to the House,' said Tewson.

'Ah, just you wait,' said Hugh, tapping his magazine with his fingers. 'Soon, come the revolution, all the aristos will be swinging from that lamp-post out there, and you'll have to change your view, too, Tewson, pretty smartly, or you'll be had up for being a member of the petty bourgeoisie. It's the workers who'll call the tune in the years to come.'

'Workers! What do you know about workers?' Tewson flipped his duster at the motes and stalked out, bearing the tray of dirty crocks in front of him like a trophy. He shut the door with a defiant click.

'You shouldn't tease him,' Giles said. 'Look, the Angelus must be about to ring, there's old Horsley just coming out of the library. Punctual to the minute, off to his rooms for the first port of the day.'

'He has one at breakfast,' Hugh said.

'Port? At breakfast? Surely not.'

'Whisky. Gives him stamina, he says. Sets him up for the day, purely medicinal. Do you remember, Vee, one of the vergers at the Minster had the same habit, only it was the communion wine? He helped himself to a snifter every morning when he opened up. Passed out in evensong while the choir was singing *Wachet auf* one Sunday afternoon. Flat on his face.'

Vee did remember, how could she forget such a glorious event?

'Let's drive out into the country, find a place to have lunch, Vee,' Hugh suggested.

Did that include Giles? Vee wondered. Then, 'You can't drive.'

'Oh, but I can.'

'You don't have a car.'

'I use Bungy's. I do his prose compositions, he lends me his car. A perfect quid pro quo.'

'When did you learn to drive? How?'

'Last year, and there's nothing to it. You get in the car, screech a few gears, and you're away.'

Giles put his telescope down. 'Don't, Vee, is my advice. Hugh turns into a fiend behind the wheel, and he's the worst driver I know.'

'I can't lunch, anyhow. I must get back to Grace. Claudia's bought a bicycle, and we're going to teach her how to ride it.'

'Good God. Will it be a private affair, or will spectators be admitted?'

'Only helpers, and you aren't that. You merely want to laugh.'

'I should like to see our cousin at a disadvantage for once.'

Vee and Lally had both acquired bicycles in the first week of term, Vee an ancient black boneshaker from the pound, and Lally a rather more respectable model from a third-year who'd broken her leg and said she was never getting on a bike again.

Claudia was at first scornful of this primitive means of transport, and then envious. 'Can I have a go?' she asked Lally.

'Can you ride a bike?'

'I never have, but it looks easy enough.' Claudia hauled herself into the saddle and thirty seconds later, she and the bike were in the lily pond in the centre of the quad.

'Easy, huh?' said Lally, looking resignedly at her twisted wheel. 'Get your own bike, and we'll teach you how to ride it.'

Claudia had continued to walk everywhere, and then had given in. 'A man from the bicycle shop is bringing it around this afternoon,' she'd announced at breakfast.

It was new and shiny, and Lally shook her head when she saw it. 'It'll get stolen, the first time you leave it propped up against a lamp-post.'

'I'll put a spell on it,' Claudia said. 'Anyhow, it isn't going to get pinched. I see Jenks strapping it on the back of the car when we come down for the last time.'

SIX

They didn't take their bicycles when they went to Balliol for John Petrus's party, not in those clothes.

Vee was surprised to get an invitation. 'I've never met him.'

'He's a don at Balliol,' Claudia said, her voice careless, her face alert. 'Fearfully clever, and very good-looking. He knows Hugh quite well, and he wants to meet you and Lally.'

Vee returned to the invitation. What did one wear to a don's cocktail party?

'Not tweeds,' Lally and Claudia said together. Vee's bristly Yorkshire tweeds, built to last, were a standing joke. Practical and warm they might be, but they were no more than a distant relation to the lovely American tweed that Lally wore, or Claudia's even prettier and much softer ones, and Vee knew which she preferred.

'Petrus is the most terrific dandy, frightfully dashing for a university fellow,' Claudia said. 'Such a shame that we don't fit into each other's clothes, Vee, and Lally's far too tall for hers to be any use to you.'

'I wouldn't mind being able to wear your clothes, but I don't think you'd want to borrow any of mine, even if you could fit into them,' Vee said. 'Not your style.' She minded very much about how old-fashioned and frumpish most of her wardrobe was, but she wasn't going to let Claudia know that.

'No, I wouldn't, although those tweeds do have a certain bizarre character to them.'

In the end, Vee wore her green moiré frock for Petrus's party. She'd thought it very elegant when she bought it in Leeds, but she knew she'd win no prizes for smartness with Claudia and Lally there. It shrieked 'provincial' beside their clothes: from Paris in Claudia's case, and New York in Lally's.

Claudia wore a grey silk dress, cut on the bias, which made her look like a Norse goddess out for a good time. Lally's frock was a cocktail in apricot silk, a demanding colour that suited her hair and eyes.

They set off to Balliol, Vee feeling countrified and dowdy in her thick coat. Claudia had a fur wrap, needless to say, and looked fearfully glamorous.

They arrived at the lodge at the same moment as Alfred Gore. His vitality swept over them as he waved the porter aside. 'I'll take the ladies up to Mr Petrus's rooms,' he said, and set off across the quad, brandishing a large black umbrella.

He guided them to a dark entrance and up three stone steps. Inside, it was dark, with a kind of stuffy dampness in the air and a strong smell of urine.

'It is a bit whiffy,' said Alfred. 'All the same, these Balliol men, they don't know the meaning of the word drains, they're far too clever to bother their heads about details like properly functioning lavs. We're on the third floor, I'm afraid,' he went on, bounding ahead up the stairs, then waiting on the landing for them to catch up. 'In we go.'

Vee was used to crushes, since the York clergy liked to gather together in small spaces with their wives and families, but her first impression was that she had never seen so many people crammed into one room. It was a large room, with three sash windows set in bays, a large fireplace, and a closed door, which must lead to a bedroom. There was a huge rolltop desk, pushed into a corner and stacked with papers. A grand piano took up a lot of space at the end of the room; its lid was down and it was draped in green baize, which was just as well, given the glasses set down on it.

Alfred eased his way through the mass of chattering, smoking people until he came within reach of Petrus. Being taller than most of those there, he could look over their heads and catch the attention of their host. 'Petrus!' he cried. 'Refugees from Grace.'

'Hello,' said Claudia, fixing Petrus with her most dazzling blue look.

He was a slender man, quite tall, with very pale fair hair combed back from his forehead. He had a mouth that Vee found slightly disturbing, but the most remarkable thing about him were his dark grey eyes, watchful, clever, penetrating eyes.

'Claudia, my dear, how lovely to see you.' He gave her a brushing kiss on one cheek and then on the other, and made a little bow to Lally. 'Our American visitor, I assume. Miss Fitzpatrick, isn't it? I had the pleasure of meeting your father when last I was in Chicago. I'm sure he will win a seat in the Senate, and then we may expect great things from him.' His eyes moved to Vee. 'Ah, the Yorkshire cousin. Hugh Trenchard's sister, I believe. Good evening Miss Trenchard. You honour us this evening.'

Vee could feel a flush creeping over her face. Was he being ironic? She was infuriated to find herself both flustered and overwhelmed by this man. He wasn't handsome in any film-star kind of way, but he made the other men around look diminished. Except for Alfred, who had his own energetic personality wrapped around him like a cloak.

As for clothes, the two men couldn't have looked more different. Alfred was wearing an appalling pair of grey flannel trousers, held up with an Eton tie, she noticed, and his usual shabby pullover. Petrus, in contrast, was wearing an immaculately tailored suit and a dashingly embroidered waistcoat.

'Call her Vee, everybody does,' said Claudia, manoeuvring so that she stood beside her host. 'This looks as though it's going to be a lively party.'

Vee had no desire to stand there with Petrus's sardonic eye upon her, so she edged backwards and slid towards the window.

At first glance, although much more eccentric or dowdy or casual in their dress, she would have said the guests were the same as at any other party; people who knew one another extremely well and probably met each other every day, and who therefore had lots to talk and gossip about.

Then her ears tuned in to the conversation. No, this wasn't the desultory chitchat of York parties. Arguments were raging all about her; people were giving their opinions with an intensity and at a volume that was never found in the drawing rooms of Yorkshire. They were discussing politics. Or international trade. Or the rights of the workers.

'You look out of it, Vee.' Alfred was beside her. 'You have to muscle in and start talking at the top of your voice, it's the only way.'

'I might, only everyone's talking about things I know absolutely nothing of.'

'Let me enlighten you. That stout fellow there, with the rather regrettable moustache, is Evans, of Jesus. He's an economist, was a Marshallian and is now a complete Keynesian. He's arguing with Joel, the red-headed man. Have you met Joel? He's a friend of your brother's, so I thought you might have. Joel knows all about economics from the mathematical point of view. He's a Marxist, so he and Evans will never see eye to eye on anything. They're talking about capital, very dull, unless it happens to be your subject.'

'It isn't,' she said. Capital was one of her grandfather's favourite subjects and, as far as she knew, was what you had tied up in bonds or stocks or shares, if you were lucky enough to possess any.

'Over there, that vehement chappie with the wavy hair, do you see him?'

She nodded. You could hardly miss him.

'He's another Marxist, but his field is art. He's supposed to be reading modern languages, but all he's interested in is art. He has a great many theories about art and is gaining himself quite a reputation.'

Vee was impressed. Art theory, Marxism, words pouring from him. This was the true intellectual life. 'He seems very passionate about what he's saying.'

'Lives, eats and sleeps it, despair of his tutors.'

'Does he paint, like Marcus?'

'Good God, no. He's keen on the theory of art. Critics, you know, very rarely have any ability in the field they criticize. If they had, they'd be composing or painting or whatever on their own accounts. Now, behind him, do you see that tall, older man, the gaunt chappie?'

'The one who looks like his own skeleton?'

'Don't you have a way with words! Exactly so. He's the Regius professor of Greek, and he's got some very outré views on ancient history, quite setting the faculty by the ears. He'd never have been appointed if they'd had any idea what he was going to get up to. Regius Professors aren't expected to rock any boats. He's writing a history of Periclean Athens. With particular attention to the sexuality of its population and the beauty of Greek youth, if I know anything about it.'

'What?'

Alfred laughed at her evident astonishment.

'He's a pederast, duckie, of the most shameless kind.'

'Pederast?'

Now it was Alfred's turn to look astonished. 'Lawks,' he said, embarrassed. 'You don't mean to tell me – I'm sorry, it never occurred to me.'

'What's a pederast?'

A wide-shouldered man with short cropped hair and very well-tailored trousers whirled round on them, and Vee saw to her amazement that it wasn't a man, but a woman, a mannish woman, with a monocle, a vivid red mouth and a dramatically long tortoiseshell cigarette holder held casually between her fingers.

She narrowed her eyes as she looked Vee up and down, then drew on her cigarette and blew lazy rings of smoke that floated into the already smoky air. 'Pederast?' she said in a penetrating voice that rang through the room. 'Who's this neophyte who wants to know about pederasts? Little boys, young woman. Grown men who like little boys' bottoms, very rude and quite illegal. As practised at all the best public schools.'

With which devastating summary, she turned back to her companion.

'It's not funny,' Vee said, crimson to her ears.

'You shouldn't have asked,' said Alfred, laughing even more heartily. 'Lord, won't Oxford dine out on that one?'

Vee was mortified – mortified at her gaffe, and even more mortified by Alfred's finding her ignorance so amusing. How was it that other people knew about these things, and she didn't? Claudia would have known, naturally, and probably Lally did as well.

And what about the woman with the monocle, dressed like a man? No, she didn't want to know any more about her, and she certainly wasn't going to ask Alfred.

At that moment, Vee almost regretted being at Oxford. Intellectuals? If this was what coming to study at an ancient and venerable university was about, she wanted none of it. She'd visualized a world of pure scholarship, of mental rapture, of age-old libraries and peaceful quads, of serious-minded people lost in thought and philosophic reflection, with a few inspired modernists to leaven the whole.

Not this tightly-packed collection of noisy people with a distaste for the norms of her world, which made her feel an outsider.

Alfred, who'd been talking to a willowy man on his other side, gave her an encouraging smile. 'Wishing you hadn't come?'

She nodded.

'Rampant bourgeoisie, for all they talk Marxism and communism. If you want real people, you want to get among the working classes. That's where you'll find integrity and honesty, not here in this stuffy haunt of would-be thinkers, nor at ghastly London parties.'

'I don't know anything about London parties, I've never been to any.'

He downed his wine at a gulp. 'You need to meet some of the people who haven't had any of the chances that you and Hugh have had.'

'Or you,' she said, looking pointedly at the tie round his waist.

'Touché,' he said, 'but I can't help where my people sent me to school. There are people in cities up and down the country who put in a hard, long day's work and then, in the evening go to adult education institutes or the extra-mural departments at universities in order to get an education. They weren't born with a silver spoon in their mouths, like you and me, and they're all the better for it, what they achieve, they've done for themselves.'

Vee felt under attack. 'I know I'm lucky to be here. And never mind silver spoons, if my grandfather had had his way, I certainly wouldn't be here, or at an adult education college, because he disapproves of women's education.'

'Attagirl,' said Alfred. 'Finish up that fizz and we'll get another glass to toast your future as a bluestocking.'

She was feeling slightly light-headed after drinking the first glass so quickly, but Alfred had darted away before she could stop him.

It would be a while before Alfred came back with another glass of wine for her, by the look of it; he had paused to join in an argument about the dole with Evans, and had dumped the glasses so that he could gesticulate with greater enthusiasm.

With Alfred gone, Vee was marooned. Claudia was in a little group around Petrus. Flirting. Where was Lally? Sitting on a window seat beneath one of the graceful windows, talking to the mathematician with the flaming red hair, Joel Ibbotson. He was clearly bowled over by Lally, and she, always good with the tongue-tied, was drawing him out in the kindest way. Hadn't Hugh told Vee about him? Yes, he was the carpenter's son, the one Hugh said was quite brilliant.

Lally liked Joel; she liked his nervous vitality, and the way his greenish eyes lit up when he started to talk about running.

'Is it just a hobby?' she asked. 'Or do you do it seriously?'

'Hobby? Oh, you mean to keep fit. No, I run to win.'

'What kind of running? The hundred yards, mile, longer?'

'Actually, it's hurdles, the four hundred yards hurdles.'

'That's some tough race.'

A gap opened, and Joel sat down beside Lally. In no time at all, he was telling her about his childhood, growing up in the East End of London, finding out how clever he was, and then how fast he could run, what it was like to be a Jew in England, the son of a grateful immigrant from Poland, why he was a mathematician. When he launched into an impassioned description of Planck's Constant, he lost her, but she laughed at him and said she'd like to come and watch him race.

'Would you? Would you really?' And then, as one offering a great treat. 'Come and watch me train. I'm at the track nearly every afternoon. On the Iffley Road, do you know the university sports ground?'

'I'd like that. Do they hold race meetings there?'

'Sometimes.' Then, in a burst of eagerness, 'I'm hoping to have a crack at getting into the Olympic team, for 1936. They're to be held in Berlin.'

'Hello, Verity.'

It was Marcus, drunk by the look of him. He gave Vee a moist kiss upon each cheek, and waved his empty glass at Lally. 'The divine Miss Fitzpatrick, how one rejoices to see such beauty. Now, you don't take offence at that, I see, so glad about that, I can't abide a jealous woman. You'll never be able to hold a candle to Lally, but you have charm and allure. Which count for a good deal in this wicked world.'

Nobody had ever said Vee had either allure or charm, and it pleased her. 'Lally has allure and charm as well as beauty.'

'Not in the same way,' Marcus said. 'And I shall never call you Vee, Vee is too prosaic and short a name for you, you have a complexity to you that is very interesting to a student of the human face and psyche, such as I am.'

'Call me whatever you like.'

'There is a sweetness to the name Verity, signifying as it does, truth. Are you a truthful woman, Verity?'

He was absurd, but she couldn't help liking him. 'I hope so,' she said with a laugh.

'Ah, don't mock truth. So few people ever tell the truth. Even fewer are truthful in any way, either to others, or to themselves. Are you a religious woman, Verity? There is a kind of lingering feeling of Puritanism about your name and your personality. And something, perhaps of the fanaticism of the Puritan.'

'My father's the Dean of York.'

'Very estimable, no doubt, but that doesn't answer my question, or perhaps it does, one feels sure that a daughter of the Deanery is likely to be off religion entirely. Now, I am very high church, and that annoys all my family and friends, which is great fun.'

'Incense and unnatural services,' Vee said, under her breath.

'What did you say?'

'Sorry, that was rude. It's what the Precentor at York used to say about his high church colleagues. Worshipping the host, was what I think he meant by unnatural.'

'I shall do a painting of a maiden worshipping at the altar of Truth, in your honour.'

'Thank you,' she said, wondering in what style he painted. Perhaps it would be all cubes and spikes, or blobs. Or maybe more like Burne Jones, pretty and old-fashioned. Maybe Lally knew.

'You look lost, O truthful truth.'

'Not really. But I think I might edge my way through to the door.'

'On no account. Shortly, the crowd will thin, the duller among us will depart, and we shall have music and song.'

'What?'

'That piano is more than mere ornament, nothing in Petrus's rooms is without a use or purpose.'

'I've got an essay . . .'

He lifted his hands in horror. 'Sweet Verity, on no account become a bluestocking, I simply can't do with serious university women. Heed my advice, take nothing seriously at Oxford, especially not yourself. Follow the example of your delightful cousin Claudia.'

He swung round. 'Look at her vamping Petrus. Now, entrancing though this conversation is, I must go and say *Salve* to the Archangel, why should Claudia be allowed to monopolize the divine being?'

'Archangel?'

'Petrus, sweet Verity.' And he was gone, as abruptly as he'd come.

107

'What a peculiar man,' Vee said to Alfred, who'd returned to her side.

'Marcus? He's a bit of an ass, but not as much of one as he makes out.'

'He called Petrus the Archangel.'

'Did he? There's a reason for that.'

'But you aren't going to tell me what it is.'

'Not in this company, no.'

A voice was calling his name. 'Come on, Alfred, time to tinkle the ivories. Joel, where's Joel?'

Marcus was right. The older guests were drifting away, many of them still deep in discussion as they went down the stairs. The atmosphere was changing before their eyes.

'Like a scene shift in the theatre,' Lally said. The main lights went out, and a scout was switching on smaller lamps around the room, which gave out a softer glow. Another scout was clearing the glasses off the piano and on to a tray. Alfred swept off the baize and bundled it into a corner. Then he raised the lid of the piano, pulled out a piano stool and began to adjust it with vigorous hands.

'I didn't know that Alfred played the piano,' Vee said to Hugh.

'Very well, as it happens. Joel's a musician, too.'

'Clarinettist,' said Lally, with appreciation, as she watched Joel take out his clarinet and begin to put it together. 'He didn't tell me about that.'

There was a commotion at the door, and Evans the economist, who had left with the others, reappeared, holding a double bass above his head. A tall stool appeared, Joel sucked at his reed, Alfred played a chord, they tuned, and then they were off.

'Do you like jazz?' Marcus was standing close behind Vee.

'I've never heard much, but I like this.'

Lally was rapt. 'They're very, very good,' she whispered to Vee, tapping her feet to the rhythm.

Petrus and Claudia were dancing, a stylish pair.

Vee looked around the smoky, merry room. She liked the music. She liked watching the musicians, especially Alfred, who dominated the big piano with practised ease.

She was, after all, happy. Simply and purely happy. This was a moment to capture, the music, the gaiety, the informality. This was an evening she would remember, she knew it with certainty. There were not so many happy times in her life that she was going to forget this one.

SEVEN

Alfred said he'd see Vee back to Grace. 'It's on my way.' He was striding along, and she had to make little skips to keep up with him. He didn't seem to notice. 'You asked why Petrus is an Archangel. There's a society here in Oxford known as the Angels. Not the sort you see at Freshers' Fair, it's a private one. Secret, some people say. It's been going for decades, people like Matthew Arnold belonged to it, and I believe Pusey and Newman were members before they turned to religion proper.'

'Can anyone join?'

'Meaning women? Certainly not, but most men can't, either. You have to be invited. One of the existing members puts your name forward, and if you're elected, then you're tapped.'

'Tapped?'

'On the shoulder. It's supposed to be a great honour.'

'Is it a dining club, full of rowdies?'

'Not at all, although the drink flows freely. Members give papers and then there's a discussion. Debate, really.'

'About what?'

'Could be anything. Right is wrong. If not, why not. Rather Red than Blue.'

'Clever things.'

'You mean clever-clever. Yes, you could say that. Only with Petrus as chairman – that's why Marcus called him the Archangel, by the way – it's all very political at the moment. Fascists arguing with Marxists, Communists laying into Socialists.'

'What's Petrus?'

'Politically? A good question. One would say he's to the right of centre, but he's a slippery soul, intellectually speaking.'

'And are you a member?'

'I was, but I don't go now. It's all talk and no do, and rather too right-wing for me.'

Right-wing to Alfred meant pink to anyone else, Vee couldn't help thinking. But, slightly tipsy as she was, Vee could read the Keep Off sign, and forebore to ask any more about the society, although she would have liked to. A secret society run by Petrus sounded intriguing.

'Are you supposed to spill the beans about the Angels?'

'Definitely not, so don't pass it on.'

'Is Hugh an Angel?'

'Yes.'

'Giles?'

'Where Hugh is, there is Giles.'

'I know,' Vee said, almost to herself. Her happiness was beginning to evaporate.

Alfred paused, gave her a keen look and said nothing. Then his expression changed.

Vee opened her mouth to speak, but he put his finger to his lips and drew her into a shadow.

'Progs,' he breathed into her ear.

Progs? What was he talking about?

'Proctors. University proctors. On the prowl to catch undergraduates out after hours.'

Vee realized with a jolt that she had no idea what time it was. She had a pass until ten, but it must be later than that.

'Ten past eleven,' Alfred said, when she tugged at his sleeve and pointed to his watch.

'Oh, no.' The Lodge at Grace was locked at eleven. If she'd got back between ten and half past, she'd have been fined half a crown. Between half past ten and eleven, and it would be five shillings and a wigging from the Dean.

After eleven? Dear God, what did you do after eleven?

'Never mind the lodge, it's the Bulldogs you have to watch out for,' said Giles. He almost dragged her around the corner and down the narrow lane that ran down the side of Grace. 'Buck up, or they'll catch us.'

The Proctor, in a black gown and white tie, patrolled the streets of Oxford every evening, accompanied by two burly university officials in bowler hats – the Bulldogs. Town and gown kept an uneasy truce, as far as authority went, but the university liked to control its own. Vee knew that getting back to college after hours was a gating offence. Being nabbed by the Proctors in the company of a member of the opposite sex would make matters much worse.

'Handy bush, here,' said Alfred. 'And I'm going to love you and leave you. I can draw them off, I think, and if they do catch up with you, you'll be in less trouble if you're on your own. Here, take this, it's starting to rain.'

He thrust the umbrella into her hand, and took to his heels. There was a shout from the end of the lane, and a Bulldog ran past in steady pursuit.

The bush, Vee discovered, was already occupied. 'Lally! What are you doing here? You left ages before me.'

'I did, but I got chatting to Joel, he has a friend with rooms just across from Petrus. We're going to set up a wind quintet.'

'Wind quintet?'

'Music. He knows a flautist, and Sarah plays the oboe. Bassoonists are harder to come by, but we'll find one.'

All this made no sense to Vee, but she was unashamedly relieved to find that she wasn't the only one back late.

'What do we do now?' she whispered to Lally.

'Climb in.'

'Where?'

'I haven't a clue, I've never done it, but I guess that if we wait a while, Claudia will show us how.'

Lally was prophetic. Less than ten minutes later, they saw Claudia strolling along the lane as if she owned it, and had a perfect right to be out in the streets of Oxford at that hour.

Lally called out to her, softly, 'Claudia.'

Claudia stopped and looked up and down the street.

'Over here.'

'What, are you locked out?' she said, joining them.

'Yes. Where do we climb in?'

'Along here.' She looked doubtfully at Vee. 'Bit of a haul for you, being a midget, but we'll manage.'

'Over those spikes?' said Vee.

''Fraid so. Clamber on the wall here, then hold on to that branch, it helps you balance.'

'That's neat,' said Lally admiringly, as with a few swift movements Claudia was over the spikes and safe on the flat roof beyond.

'All that gym at school,' Vee said. 'Who'd ever think it would come in useful?'

Her own ascent was a good deal more of a scramble, with Lally giving her a heave from below, and Claudia tugging from the other side. But she managed it, and then Lally joined them without difficulty.

Claudia was at the window that looked out on to the roof. The curtains were drawn, but there was a chink of light shining out.

'She's shut the window, damn her,' said Claudia.

'Can't you knock on it or rattle it?' Vee asked.

'I don't want to make too much noise, the Dean has unnaturally keen hearing.' Claudia tapped on a window pane.

There was no response.

'This is Sarah's room, right?' Lally asked.

'Yes.'

'Can't we try another window?'

'The next two windows along are the one on the staircase, which is always locked, and a don's room, only used for teaching, and also locked. The only other way in is round the other side, and it's very tricky, especially in the rain. Over that high wall by the library, and there's broken glass on top of the wall.'

It was now setting in to rain in earnest. Lally had thrown up the umbrella on to the roof before making her own ascent. She picked it up and opened it. 'This is handy.'

'It's Alfred's,' said Vee, joining Lally and Claudia under its protection.

'Very gallant, to give up his brolly,' said Claudia.

'He's taken with Vee,' Lally said.

'What, because he lent me an umbrella?' said Vee. 'I'd call it good manners.'

'Sarah's in the bath,' Claudia said. 'If she's in there with a book, we could have a long wait.'

'How do you know she's in the bath?'

Claudia shrugged, and adjusted herself into a more comfortable position, with her back leaning against the brick wall. 'I just see her in the bath.'

'But you don't see the book?' Lally asked.

'No.'

'Sarah does tend to read in the bath,' Vee said. 'I noticed a soggy book on her towel the other day.'

'There's a light on in the lodge,' Lally said, peering out from the shelter of the umbrella.

'That's the troll looking through the books to see who has and hasn't signed in.'

Vee and Lally stared at each other. 'If our initials aren't in the book, then we're sunk, even if we do get in,' Vee said.

'Your initials will be in the book,' Claudia said carelessly. 'Sarah does it for me; if you weren't signed in, she'll have done it for you as well.'

'You shouldn't call him a troll,' Lally said, with unusual asperity. 'He's a perfectly sweet man when you get to know him. He has a wife called Mary and seven children.'

'Seven gnomes, then,' said Claudia.

'He is gnome-like,' Vee said. 'It's the way he hunches over, and those sharp eyes looking up at you. And being rather small, he isn't even as tall as I am. How do you know about his family?'

'We got talking,' said Lally.

'He doesn't like his job,' Claudia said, after a few minutes when they had just listened to the steady patter of the rain on the umbrella and the drip of a nearby gutter.

Vee had been thinking about Alfred. 'What?' And then, 'Who doesn't like his job?'

'The troll. He wanted to join the police force, but he's too short.'

'There, you've been talking to him as well,' Lally said.

'No. I see a constable's helmet on his head, that's all. Seven children! Seven gnomes, do you think?'

'Sometimes, unprepossessing parents have very good-looking children,' Vee said. 'But I can't imagine being one of seven.'

'I am,' said Lally. 'I can't imagine not having six brothers and sisters.'

'Older or younger?' said Claudia.

'I'm right in the middle. Three older, three younger.'

'You're the peacekeeper,' said Claudia, making a statement rather than asking a question.

'That's about it,' said Lally. 'Can you see into your own heart and mind the way you get flashes about other people?'

'Now you come to mention it, I don't think I do.' Claudia seemed struck by this. 'Which is a pity really, since I'm much more interested in what I want and what's going to happen to me than I am in the troll and his lost dreams. Ah, I hear sounds within.' She leaned forward and tapped on the window again.

The curtain twitched, they saw Sarah's face looking owlishly out at them, and then the wonderful sound of the window opening.

'Three of you,' said Sarah, tightening the belt on her pink dressing gown. 'All wet, and dripping on my rug. It's too much.'

'Thank you,' said Lally and Vee.

Claudia gave Sarah a wink. 'Fetching turban,' she said, gesturing at the towel wrapped around Sarah's head.

Vee looked from one to the other. 'Do you know, without your specs and with your hair out of sight, you could be Claudia's sister?'

'Oh, thanks a bundle,' said Sarah, reaching for her spectacles and putting them on. 'I suppose you realize your frocks are ruined?'

Vee tumbled into bed and fell asleep at once, to dream about Petrus and Hugh and Marcus taking part in a satanic cult meeting. In the usual dream-like fashion, this turned into a session of the music club in the common room at her school, with the headmistress wearing a pair of horns set in her rigid grey curls, and announcing that a new world order had arisen, to be called the Company of Saints, which only those who spoke German might join.

Vee woke the next morning feeling disoriented, and then laughed at the strangeness of the dream. It left an unpleasant aftertaste, a thread of unease lurking in her brain for the rest of the day.

EIGHT

Vee knocked on the door of Claudia's room.

Silence.

She tried the handle. It turned, and the door opened. Within, the room was dark, with only the cracks of light around the curtains showing that it was daylight, and the sun was shining, and it was nearly ten o'clock.

'Claudia!'

The hump in the bed made a convulsive movement, and a pair of baleful eyes blinked out at Vee.

'What is it?'

'It's Sunday morning, and it's past ten. You've missed breakfast.'

'To hell with breakfast,' said Claudia and pulled the blanket back over her head.

Vee made for the window, stepping round the clothes strewn across the floor. She tripped over a high-heeled sandal, steadied herself, and dragged back the curtains. Sunshine streamed into the room. 'Time to get up.'

'To hell with getting up,' said Claudia, struggling into an upright position and pushing the hair out of her eyes. 'I feel awful.'

'You drank too much last night.'

'I was sick.'

'I'm not surprised.'

'I climbed in.'

'Sarah told me.'

'Just go away and let me get back to sleep.'

'It's Sunday. We need to leave in less than half an hour.'

115

'What for?'

'Church.'

Claudia sank back into her crumpled bed. 'There speaks the daughter of the Deanery. I'm damned if I go to church.'

'Damned if you don't.' To Vee, Sunday mornings and church were inseparable. The morning rituals a reassurance, calm in a turbulent world.

'I don't believe in God, so why should I go to church?'

'Oh, come on, Claudia. That's the kind of thing you say when you're fourteen.'

'I did say it when I was fourteen, and I meant it. I meant it then, and I mean it now.'

'So why do you go to church when you're at home?'

'Because I get to wear smart clothes and show off a new hat, and all my friends are there, and it's fun. It isn't fun here. They preach those sermons that sound like a very boring lecture in the philosophy school, and all the dons' wives are there looking as though they bought their clothes at the jumble sale, and nobody stands and chats afterwards. No, I'm not going to church today, or next Sunday, or any Sunday while I'm in Oxford. I'll make-up for it when I go home, if you're worried about my immortal soul.'

'But, Claudia—'

'Just go away.'

Vee went back to her room for her gown and picked up her leather-bound prayer book, a confirmation present from her father. She went down the back stairs, in a hurry now, as the clock was striking the three quarters.

Lally was sitting on the small, uncomfortable sofa by the dining hall, wearing a flat hat that would have made nine out of ten women look frightful, but which gave her the air of a Botticelli angel, complete with halo. She was holding a flat handbag and a white prayer book.

'Are you coming to church?' Vee asked. 'I'm going to hear the university sermon at St Mary's.'

'I'm going to Sung Mass at Blackfriars.'

Blackfriars? It took Vee a moment to understand what she meant. 'You're Catholic?'

Lally grinned. 'Yup.'

Vee felt a fool. She had what she realized was an ungrounded belief that most Americans were Episcopalians, which was their way of saying Anglican. Or if not, didn't they belong to churches called the First Congregational and things like that? Vague memories of the Pilgrim Fathers and severe men in black hats and white collars hovered at the back of Vee's mind.

'Why are you Catholic?' Vee said abruptly. 'Oh, I'm sorry, that's rude.'

'Aren't there Catholics where you come from? There are quite a few in England, you know, and Yorkshire's produced its fair share of martyrs.'

'Martyrs?'

'The blessed Oliver Plunkett, for example.'

'Are all your family Catholics?'

'We're Irish Americans, so it would be surprising if we weren't. At least, my father's family are Irish. My mother is half Irish, but a hundred per cent Catholic. Dad couldn't have married her if she weren't.'

Lally glanced at her slender gold wristwatch, and stood up.

'Time to go.'

'Were you waiting there for someone?' Vee asked, keeping step with her.

'No, just thinking.'

Lally was a very peaceful person. Not dull or placid, but she had an inner calm that Vee envied.

They reached the church of St Mary the Virgin, Lally looked up to the tower; they had gone up it in their first week at Oxford, to look out over the city.

'It's odd to think it all started here, isn't it? Of course, we were all Catholics then, there was no such thing as a Protestant.'

'I suppose not,' said Vee. 'I'll see you later.' Her conversation with Lally had made her feel uncomfortable, and she was relieved when she heard Alfred's voice behind her.

'Hello, are you going in?'

'Have you come for the service? I didn't know you were a church-goer.'

'I am on occasion.'

'It's very full,' whispered Vee, as they squeezed themselves in at the end of a pew.

'That's because Dr Graham is preaching. He always gets a good turnout. Wonderful voice, should have been an actor. Now, ssh, there's the introit.'

The music wound to a satisfying conclusion, and the clergy processed in, preceded by a row of shining-haired boys in red and white.

For some reason the familiar words didn't have their usual soothing, mesmeric effect on Vee. Alfred, motionless beside her, seemed to pay no attention to them at all, his eyes were fixed on the patterns of light the sun made on the stained-glass windows.

It was time for the sermon. The portly, stately figure ascended the pulpit. He had a shock of white hair that stood out about his stern, craggy face. He hitched his gown further up on to his shoulders, rustled his notes, looked around the congregation for a long moment and then launched into an intricately worked out argument about the duty each individual Christian had to create and maintain peace in the world, and how those who increased the power of the state were returning the civilized world to pagan disorder.

His voice was powerful and melodious; Vee could see why Alfred had said he should have been an actor.

'Aren't you taking communion?' Vee asked Alfred, as he remained seated.

He shook his head.

Vee's mind wasn't on the sacrament; she took the wafer and wine with only half her mind, and had to be nudged by her neighbour to get to her feet and go back to her place.

Alfred was sitting there, reading the front of the prayer book. He glanced at her as she slipped to her knees and buried her head in her hands.

'Why do you come, if you don't take communion?' she asked as she sat back in the pew.

'Because I'm not a Christian,' he whispered back. 'I come to survey the enemy, and this morning to listen to old Graham sounding off about the fascists.'

The service came to an end, the blessing was given, and the congregation straggled out into the pale sunlight.

'Let's walk across the meadows and have lunch at the Perch,' Alfred said.

'I've signed in for lunch in hall.'

'So?'

'They don't like it if you don't show up. The Dean says it upsets the servants.'

'That's the difference between a man's college and a woman's college.

118

My college couldn't give a damn about the servants. If slavery were still legal, they'd buy a posse of those and never give them a day off or any wages, that would be perfect. Whereas, at a woman's college, the dons believe that the servants are people, that they have feelings, and must have some consideration taken of them. Therefore, women's colleges point the way to the future, they are in the vanguard of the revolution.'

Revolution? 'Grace is the least revolutionary place in the world, even more staid and traditional than my boarding school. They'd say the servants must know their places, that's hardly revolutionary.'

'True. And none of it will matter in a few years in any case, because there won't be any servants. Or masters. No us and them.'

Vee laughed. 'I can't see the dons liking that.'

'Several of your dons will be swinging from the lampposts,' said Alfred, his face growing severe. 'Your Miss Rooke, for instance, the woman's a menace.'

'The philosophy don?'

'She belongs in the middle ages. Did you hear what she said to one of your fellow undergraduates?'

'Which one?'

'Jane Marshop.'

Vee shook her head. 'I don't think I know her.'

'Second year. Brilliant. County scholar. Poor as the proverbial, daughter of a docker. Miss Rooke said she had no business being at the university, that her sort weren't welcome here. Not the right kind for Oxford, she should have gone to redbrick, or better still, the technical college. Presumably before marrying some drunken representative of the lower classes and spending the rest of her life as one of the underserving poor in a Liverpool slum.'

'You sound awfully serious, Alfred. What's got into you?'

'Oh, just impatience, Vee. I want all this to end, and to end now, or next weekend, not years down the line.'

'All what?'

Alfred waved a hand in a sweeping gesture that took in the church and All Souls, as well as the rest of the High. 'All of this. The privilege, the backward ways, the unfairness of it all.'

'You want to do away with the university?'

Alfred's voice was bitter. 'Yes, the university and everything it stands for. Tear it apart, brick by brick, and then rebuild it as an

119

institution that serves the people, and is no longer an engine for their oppression.'

Vee could see a tall, slender figure coming towards them; two tall slender figures. One was Lally, and the other was a Jesuit priest.

'Here's Lally.'

'Keeping company with another of the forces of oppression,' muttered Alfred. 'Good morning, Lally.'

Lally smiled at Alfred, and Vee felt sure she'd heard what Alfred said, and was amused by it. 'Father Ferguson, this is . . .'

'Good morning, Hamish,' said Alfred.

'You know each other?' said Lally, glancing from one face to the other.

'We were at school together,' said Alfred.

Father Ferguson laughed. He was a remarkably handsome man, Vee noticed; his black soutane suited him.

'Alfred used to try and fight my battles for me. He was very pugnacious.'

'I didn't fight any of your battles,' Alfred said. 'When it came to fighting, you didn't need any help. He was the school boxing champion,' he explained to Vee and Lally. 'Only very much senior to me, and quite a tough. Only he came in for a lot of abuse on account of his being a left-footer.'

'Left-footer?' said Lally.

'Roman Catholic, like you, Lally. Eton wasn't a happy home for Catholics. Catholic boys go to Ampleforth or Downside or other priest-ridden establishments like that. I can't think why your people ever sent you to Eton, Hamish.'

'My mother was Catholic, but my father, who was an Etonian, wasn't.'

'Why did you try to fight his battles?' Lally asked.

'Because I didn't like the way he got baited for being RC. Same with the Jews, they had a hell of a time. Ah, well, come the revolution, Eton will be no more. It'll become a rest home for worn-out miners, I expect.'

Father Ferguson laughed. 'Still breathing fire, I see,' he said.

'Are you going back to college?' Vee asked Lally.

'No, I'm lunching at the Chaplaincy.'

'I've invited Vee out to the Perch,' Alfred said, 'but she's afraid the servants in hall will be upset if she isn't there to tuck into the unspeakable fatty mutton and soggy roast potatoes they are about to dish up.'

'How do you know what's for lunch at Grace?' asked Lally.

'It's a guess. After all, your college food is notoriously bad. You'll do much better among your fellow Catholics, the church has always known how to do itself well, isn't that so, Hamish?'

Father Ferguson pursed his lips. 'We'd better be on our way, Lally.' He gave a little bow to Vee, nodded at Alfred and, touching Lally on the elbow, led her away.

Alfred watched them go. 'Devilish attractive man, wouldn't you say? He'll get into trouble if he spends too much time with the gorgeous Lally.'

'Oh, come off it, Alfred. What's wrong with that?'

'He's a celibate, remember. Or supposed to be, although I could tell you stories about Catholic priests . . .'

'I don't want to hear them,' said Vee. 'Anyhow, Father Ferguson is safe with Lally. She's as good as gold.'

'She is, too,' said Alfred. 'A rare woman, indeed. Unlike Claudia, Lally's rival in the beauty stakes, but a laggard when it comes to goodness of Lally's kind.'

'Lally doesn't see herself as a rival to anyone.'

'Lally is so lovely that she makes people turn and stare at her in the street, in case you hadn't noticed. Now, Claudia is very glamorous, but she can't do that, warpaint or no warpaint.'

'I wouldn't know.'

'You, now, you don't turn heads in the street, but you've got what neither Claudia nor Lally have.'

'What's that? A figure like a boy? Thank you very much.'

Alfred linked his arm through hers. 'No. Beckoning power, charm, whatever you want to call it. That's the really powerful stuff, you know.'

'Don't be silly.' Charm, indeed. It didn't seem to have any effect on Alfred, his tone was entirely that of the detached observer.

What had happened to her lovely Sunday-morning glow, the feeling of ease and yes, happiness, that hung about her after church? A happiness she had always valued, even if it never lasted long. The memory of listening to her parents' desultory Sunday-lunch conversations, conducted as though they were strangers on a train, should have made her glad to be in Oxford, but instead it depressed her, and she felt restless and discontented.

'Were you ever a serious churchgoer?' she asked Alfred.

'Serious as in not laughing at the stupidity and brutality of it all? Or serious in the sense that I swallowed all the nonsense and went dutifully to the services to have my soul uplifted and cleansed? I gave up on God when I was about twelve, duckie. It just didn't add up. Hanging about, waiting for God to fix everything that's wrong with the world hasn't worked in endless centuries, so why should it work now? No, if there ever was anyone up there, he's long since been given his cards and been thrown on the heavenly scrapheap. Face it, Vee, we're on our own here, in this life, and there certainly isn't another one. So it's up to us to do what we can to make the lot of the wretched on this earth better than it was when we were born.'

NINE

Next Sunday, Vee didn't even try to wake Claudia. Her cousin had climbed in at half past five in the morning, Sarah Blumenthal had indignantly reported in Hall, at breakfast. 'Reeking of drink. The college is going to find out, and she'll be sent down.'

'They won't find out if you don't squeal,' Vee said.

Sarah gave her a withering look. 'Have I ever? But I tell you, next year I'm going to have a room in the attics, with no possibilities whatsoever for anyone to climb in.'

'Kate Witham came in through the kitchens last night,' said a mousey historian. 'She landed in a huge tub of eggs in water which had been left just underneath the window.'

There was silence at the table.

'Eggs in water?'

'Yes, ready to scramble for breakfast.'

Sarah looked at the egg in front of her and pushed the plate to one side.

'So, they water the eggs,' said the historian, reaching for Sarah's plate. 'So what? If you aren't going to finish that, I'll have it.'

'Has Lally been in to breakfast?' Sarah asked. 'She's got the Langham commentary on Beowulf, and I must finish my essay today.'

'Catholics don't breakfast on Sundays,' said a plump girl at the end of the table. 'They have to fast.' With a contemptuous look at Sarah: 'You wouldn't know about that, of course.'

'I have no need to fast, I'm naturally slim,' Sarah said. She took another piece of toast and began to spread it thickly with butter.

'Some Anglicans also fast, if they're going to take communion,'

Vee said, not liking the undercurrents, which she didn't quite understand.

'It's barbaric,' said the historian. 'If we had a proper education system, no one would have any of this religious rubbish left in their heads by the time they were ten.' She pushed back her chair. 'While the devout head for the sermon, I'm going to the library.'

This week, Vee had decided to go to St Cross, a mediaeval church tucked away at the end of Holywell Street.

The smell hit her as she went in through the porch. Stone and polish and dusty books and old surplices. The church was dark and cold, despite a wheezing stove in the corner, but that was nothing to Vee. Religion had always been a cold experience. It was beyond the wit of man to heat the enormous space of the Minster in York, which was bitterly cold for most of the winter and barely tolerable for all but a few weeks in the year. Vee had often sat there with the chill of ages rising through her feet. Like Socrates and hemlock, she thought as she pushed the hassock into position and slipped to her knees to say a prayer, almost without thinking.

Her hands, encased in soft leather gloves, were tightly clenched; she looked at them as though they belonged to a stranger. She finished and got up from her knees, giving her coat a quick dust down, it didn't seem that the cleaners at St Cross were very thorough. She sat back in the pew, and waited for the sense of calm and expectation to gather her into its grasp.

Nothing.

A sense of alarm was rising in her. Suddenly, this was all wrong, the familiar had become unfamiliar, and she had the sensation of being in a place where she didn't belong. The words of the bidding prayer ricocheted off the ancient walls, buzzed and rang in her head. The hymns came to her as though reproduced on a cracked and wrongly-paced gramophone recording. When the time came to go up to the altar and take communion, she felt as though her legs were made of lead. The wine on her tongue made her gag, the wafer hung in her mouth. She almost stumbled back to her seat. Eat and drink in memory of . . .

The thought came to her of Lally, actually eating the body of Christ, the flesh and blood.

She was going to throw up. She was going to be sick here, in the pew.

She rammed a gloved hand against her mouth, and, with a gesture of apology, pushed past the other worshippers in the pew; she had to get out of the church and into the fresh air.

Outside, the frosty air caught in her lungs. Dizzy, fighting the waves of sickness, she leaned back against the wall. Her unseeing eyes flickered over the bicycles leaning against the railings, the moss-covered path. From inside the church came the rousing sounds of the final hymn, waves of sound that came and went.

The words and music might as well be messages from another planet for all they meant to her.

She was ill. Perhaps it was the scrambled egg, something on Kate's shoes.

No, it wasn't that. Vee headed for the lych gate, she had to get away from the church, off sanctified land, out into the other world, where words had meaning and sounds were clear.

She'd lost her faith. That was what had happened to her.

No, that was impossible. She was going down with the flu, or maybe her monthly was coming early, that often made her moody and down in the dumps.

She wasn't down in the dumps. She felt sick and exhilarated at the same time. What did it mean, not to believe in God? If that's what it was, she would surely be left with a void, an emptiness where there had been security and ritual and relief; what was there that could ever fill the space?

What if God really didn't exist? What if the God she had believed in all those years had been nothing but a figment of her imagination? A made-up deity, resembling a loving father, who looked like a loving grandfather, and whose love was greater than any real father or grandfather could possibly give you, which wasn't, she thought with sudden misery, a lot.

Was stopping believing in God like killing your father? She didn't want to kill her father, but she'd more than once found herself wishing her grandfather were dead. One day, she'd always told herself, he wouldn't be there any longer, angry and authoritative and tyrannical, belittling her father and laying down the law to her and her mother, and believing that money was the answer to everything.

The God of the Old Testament was tyrannical all right, and, now she came to think of it, the prophets were probably a bunch of men just like her grandfather.

Was this what happened to her father when he lost his faith?

If he hadn't lost his faith, would she have found any succour or comfort in the church for these last few years? Wasn't it that the church had become a place where her father was the alien, and she was the beloved daughter that made it such a blessed experience? For, if your own father didn't love you, didn't want you, then with what joy did you fall into the arms of another, greater Father, who was, so you were taught, love incarnate.

Where had the comfort and the love and the peace gone? Was she suffering from nerves? Was this really a spiritual experience, was she being tested in some bizarre way?

She walked faster, eager to put more distance between herself and St Cross.

I shall never go to a service again. The words rang in her head. It's over. Finished. Religion is nothing. It's a fraud. It has no answers.

Alfred's impassioned words rang in her ears. 'Religion is the opiate of the masses.' He was quoting, of course. Quoting Karl Marx. What else had he said? We can't hang around waiting for the kingdom of heaven to arrive while millions of people are groaning under the yoke of tyranny.

The Russians had thrown out religion, hadn't they? That was what made people like her parents and all the good clergy and citizens of York tighten their mouths and shake their heads whenever Communism was mentioned; that was one of the few things about which her parents and grandfather truly agreed. Reds. Bolsheviks. A threat to all right-minded people. What had happened in Russia, her grandfather said, was an overthrow of all order, a collective madness.

To her father, it was the work of the devil come amongst us.

Only, of course, Anglican clergymen didn't believe in the devil. Not any more. What did they believe in? The royal family. The government. The rich man in his castle and the poor man at his gate.

Alfred had sung that to her, the words of the childish hymn sang in her ears, 'All things bright and beautiful . . .'

It was all a lie. It was all a gigantic fraud.

The billowing black clouds that had been threatening rain suddenly parted and a shaft of sunlight spilled on to the pavement in front of her. A sense of rip-roaring joy that she was quite unused to almost overwhelmed her. She felt light-headed, but not in the way she had back there in the tomb-like atmosphere of the church.

126

She was free. There was no heaven and no hell, except that which men made. She didn't have to pray, there was no one and nothing to pray to. The whole thing was a trick, a make-believe of light and sound and chanting that deceived and lulled the mind into a sheep-like state of submission.

Not her, not any more.

She began to run. She ran down Longwall and into the Broad. Where would Alfred be? In his rooms? She must find him, tell him what had happened, it couldn't wait.

His college wouldn't be open, not yet. But he might be in the King's Arms, they would be serving coffee at this time of the morning and she knew he often went there for a late breakfast. She arrived panting at the door of the hostelry and plunged in. She knew that her hat was askew, that her hair was untidy; people stared. They think I'm mad, she thought exultantly. She wanted to shout out, I don't believe in God.

There was Alfred, rising to his feet, looking surprised.

'Vee! Why aren't you in church, this is Sunday morning, remember, and here you are, looking like a wild woman.'

'I am a wild woman! Buy me a drink, Alfred. I'm an atheist.'

Alfred looked at her, his mouth quivering. Then he broke into laughter. 'Vee, you are a card.'

'I'm free.'

'No, duckie, not yet. But you will be, we will all be free.' He pushed his way through to the bar. 'Half a pint of mild and bitter, please.'

'Alfred, I hate beer.'

TEN

That night, Vee had a dream. She was standing outside a church, a huge building, many times the size of the Minster. The façade rose far above her, a cliff of faith, the spires in the clouds. Before her was a great wooden door, bolted and barred. She moved forward to the smaller door set within it, and gave it a push. It didn't move. She grasped the great iron ring of a handle and tried to turn it. Even as she did so there was a rattle of chains, which materialized across the surface of the door.

She fell back, and woke in a sweat, the sound of chains rattling in her ears. A beam of moonlight crept between the curtains and cast a silvery line across her floor. She got up and went to the window. After a stormy day, the sky had cleared. Pale stars prickled the sky, outshone by a majestic full moon. The trees and river bank were full of eerie shadows, and the water of the Cherwell gleamed palely, shadowing into inkiness where overhanging boughs cut off the brilliant moonshine.

Vee felt drawn out of herself as she gazed at the moon, her heart thudding. Today had been a rebirth. Today was her real birth. Leaving home, starting here in Oxford, that hadn't been a new life. What had happened today was the beginning of a new life, and one that held all kinds of undreamed-of possibilities. Her fingers tingled, not with cold, although the room was chilly, but with excitement.

'Didn't you sleep well last night?' Lally asked as she took a seat beside her at breakfast. 'You have shadows under your eyes.'

'I sat up and watched the moon.'

'The moon?'

'It was full. Didn't you notice?'

Lally spread butter on her toast, and then helped herself to marmalade. 'Can you imagine I lived all those years without ever tasting English marmalade? When I go back to the States I'm going to carry jars and jars of it back with me.' She took a mouthful of toast. 'I don't care for moonlight. I find it unsettling. Oh, there's Claudia.' She waved to her, pointing to an empty seat.

Claudia, bright-eyed and very soignée in a pewter-grey suit, came to join them. 'Good morning. Pass the milk, please, Vee.'

'You look smart,' said Vee. 'Is this to impress your tutor?'

'I'm not going to my tutorial, I've swapped. I'm off to London.'

'London? Why?'

'To lunch with Oswald Mosley, no less.'

There was silence at the table, as the other breakfasters' conversation died down.

'The British Fascist man? Claudia, why?'

'Oh, he's a chum of my stepfather's, a fearfully attractive man. Only it won't just be me and him, unfortunately.'

'Doesn't he have a wife?' said Lally. 'I'm sure I saw her picture in the *Tatler* a while back.'

'Oh, Cimmie Mosley. What's that to do with it? Tom Mosley's a terrific rake, always has been.'

'I thought you said Oswald Mosley,' said Miss Harbottle, stiff with disapproval at Claudia's loose talk.

'He's called Tom by everyone who knows him. Anyhow, it's a big affair, at the Café Royale, to celebrate the new party he's formed.'

Sarah frowned from the other end of the table. 'If you support the British Fascists you're even more of a fool than I thought you were,' she said, tossing her napkin down on the table. 'They're nothing but a mob.'

'You won't say that in a year's time when they have millions of supporters, just like in Italy and Germany. It's the future, Sarah, only you're too backward-looking to recognize it.'

'Not my future,' Sarah said.

'Have you got Dean's permission to go to London?' Lally asked.

Claudia shrugged. 'I'll be back in time for Hall, no one will know I've gone.'

Vee watched her leave. Further along the table, Sarah shook her head. 'She needs to be psychoanalysed or something, she has no idea what she's getting mixed up with.'

129

'It's all her posh friends,' said Miss Harbottle. 'They're the sort who back a man like Mosley.'

'At least Mosley cares about the unemployed,' said Vee, Alfred's indignant words springing to her lips. 'Don't you know that a quarter of the workforce are out of work, and that's not including women or agricultural workers? Someone has to do something about it.'

There was an uncomfortable silence, broken only by a clatter of dishes from the kitchens.

'Yes, duckie, but don't deceive yourself that Mosley's the one to do it,' Alfred said later, when they were sitting on a bench outside the Radcliffe Camera, watching the pigeons strutting about on the cobbles. 'He's a demagogue, and a dangerous man. The last thing this country needs is a dose of fascism.'

'Of course not, according to you,' said Vee. 'According to you, what every country on earth needs is a dose of communism.'

'Quite right, and communists and fascists are opposites.' Alfred took out a packet of Woodbines and offered one to Vee.

'No, thanks. I don't know why you smoke those ghastly things.'

'Mosley and his crowd will kit themselves out in uniforms, with boots, just like the Italians he so much admires, that'll be the next thing. Then they'll start attacking the Jews.'

'Why not, everyone else does?' said Vee, remembering the look on Sarah's face in Hall.

'Jews don't suffer oppression in the Soviet Union. No one cares if they're Jews or not, as long as they're working for the Revolution. For the workers, nationality and religion and patriotism have no meaning.'

Alfred, Vee said inwardly, if you truly believe that, you'll believe anything.

ELEVEN

Vee went back to Yorkshire when the university term ended, to spend Christmas with her parents. Hugh, lucky man, was off to Switzerland for the winter sports. Christmas was always dreary at the Deanery, and this year, when the words of the Christmas message carried none of the glory that they used to, the hours she spent in the Minster were simply cold and boring, the carols were lies sung to a good tune.

Claudia wanted Vee to spend the whole vac in London, but Vee felt she ought to go north. Once there, she wished she hadn't bothered. Daddy was wrapped up in church affairs as usual, and she could see that Mummy wouldn't have minded whether she was there or not. So she telephoned Claudia to ask if she could come sooner than planned. 'Before New Year, would that be all right?'

Vee didn't tell Claudia why she was keen to be away from York at the New Year, which was that the first of January was Daisy's birthday. That was why Christmas was such a gloomy time at the Deanery, and every year, on New Year's Day, Vee and her parents visited Daisy's grave. Vee hated it, and she knew her parents would much prefer to go and mourn on their own.

Claudia met Vee at King's Cross. She had a dog in the back of the motor car, a bull terrier with melting eyes. 'It's Mummy's dog, she's called Euphemia. She adores going in the car, doesn't she, Jenks?'

Euphemia settled herself down with a snort of contentment, resting her face on Vee's shoes.

'She's pleased to see you,' said Claudia. 'So am I.'

Vee bent down to fondle Euphemia's ears. It made her feel warm inside, to be welcomed by both cousin and dog.

'It's so fortunate that I'm the fourth daughter,' said Claudia as she ran up the steps of the elegant eighteenth-century house, discreet behind handsome railings. 'Kimber,' she said to the portly butler who opened the door. 'This is my cousin, Miss Trenchard. Do you remember her? She came here once, years ago.'

The butler took Euphemia's leash and inclined his head in Vee's direction. 'I remember you well, miss. Welcome to London. I trust you left the Dean and Mrs Trenchard in good health? It's a while since we've seen Mrs Trenchard, but the Dean was here earlier in the year.'

'Yes, thank you, they're very well,' said Vee.

'I hope you have a pleasant stay in London.'

'Pleasant, nothing!' said Claudia. 'She's going to have a sumptuous time, Kimber, we'll make sure of that. Come on, Vee, we'll find Mummy, then when that's over with we'll have to make plans.'

She led the way at a brisk pace across the hall and up the wide, handsome stairs. Vee hurried after her, and put out a hand to stop her cousin as they reached the first landing. 'Why lucky to be the fourth, Claudia?'

Claudia was the youngest of her family, and had three older sisters as well as two brothers. Claudia's father, the late earl, had died when she was little, in a hunting accident. Her mother, Vee's Aunt Lettice, then married Vernon Saxony, an important Treasury official with so stinging a tongue that even the Prime Minister was afraid of him, according to Claudia.

'As to being the fourth,' Claudia said, 'it means Mummy's kind of run out of puff. My sisters have all been married off, as you know, to rich and well-bred husbands. But Mummy had to do three seasons on the trot, and really, she's not a sociable bird at all. What she most likes to do is sit in the attic and paint for hours on end.'

'Goodness, I didn't realize she was that keen. From what my mother said, I thought she dabbled.'

'She's not a professional, of course, Vernon would never stand for that. But you might say she's semi-professional. She does illustrations for children's books, although not under her own name. Doing the season was a nuisance and exhausting for her, since the mothers have to stay up until three every morning, and there's only the same dull other mothers to talk to, night after night. It quite wore her out, and that's partly why she stood up for me when I said I was going to

Oxford. Vernon wasn't keen, but after all, he isn't my father, and I've got my own money, so in the end, he had to give in. And when I'm at home, like now, Mummy doesn't feel obliged to escort me anywhere; instead, she foists me off on Cousin Mildred. Do you remember her?'

Vee shook her head, bemused by her flow of words.

'Mummy's first cousin, so Aunt Anne's as well. She's a fearful snob, very big in society, you know the kind of thing. Only her mind's always somewhere else, so one can do what one likes, and she never notices. She's so grand that her consequence covers up any little slips those under her care may make.'

Slips? Vee didn't know what to make of all this. Then it struck her how funny it was, and she began to laugh.

Claudia had reached the top of the next flight of stairs. 'What's funny?'

'Only, what would Mummy say if she knew that Aunt Lettice wasn't really keen to be a chaperone?'

'And that you're going to be left to the tender mercies of me and racy old Cousin Mildred? Best if she doesn't know. I consider it a kindness to one's parents not to let them ever find out anything that might distress them. Mummy, here's Vee.'

Aunt Lettice was much as Vee remembered her, the waxing moon to her mother's waning one, ebullient and with a heap of silvery hair piled on her head, and eyes that had the wrinkles of a naturally cheerful disposition about them.

She embraced Vee; it was like being hugged by a friendly goose, Vee thought, as she disentangled herself from a piece of wire that protruded from her aunt's painting smock.

'Sit down, darling, you must be exhausted after your journey. How I hate those trains to and from the north, only at least you're coming instead of going up there, which is always so very depressing, the chimneys and the blackness of the houses and the rain, so lowering to the spirits. Claudia, ring for tea, Vee must be starving.'

'I had lunch on the train.'

'That was hours ago. Now, tell me how your dear mother is, and your father, too. And is wicked Hugh at home? No, of course not, he's gone skiing with chums, hasn't he? I hear such amusing stories about him.'

Vee dutifully passed on the messages from her parents. Her mother wrote regular letters to her sister; much of Mummy's time was spent at her writing table, penning endless letters to relatives, friends and acquaintances. Aunt Lettice was probably better informed about what was happening in Yorkshire than Vee was.

'Well, darling, it's quite lovely to have you. I dare say it's dreadfully dull for you up there, nothing ever happens in York, I'm sure of it, and hardly much fun for a girl. We'll make sure you have a wonderful time in London. Claudia will see to it that you do, she already has a host of invitations for you.'

Claudia, Vee soon discovered, saw to practically everything. She swept Vee off to a large bedroom on the second floor. 'My bedroom is up here, and you can use my sitting room. I thought you'd prefer it to one of the guest rooms on the first floor. The ancients live down there, so it's more fun up here, and you won't mind sharing a bathroom.'

The Deanery was comfortable enough downstairs, but Mrs Trenchard had austere views about what was suitable for young people, and Hugh and Vee's bedrooms had always been spartan. 'Heavenly,' Vee said, looking round at the polished furniture, chintz curtains, thick carpet, comfortable chair and large bed, not to mention a good fire burning in the grate.

'Bowler – she's my maid – will look after you as well, is that all right? Now, I must go and change, I'm dining out. I didn't bother with an invitation for you, because it's not so frightfully interesting, and I thought you'd be tired after that awful journey from York.'

She flew out of the room, only to thrust her head round the door seconds later. 'Don't fret, there's bags going on, even after Christmas. I know all the best parties and places to go. Pity we haven't had time to sort out what we need to do about your clothes and things, but we can be up bright and early tomorrow to go shopping. See you in the morning.'

Vee heard Claudia come in. The noise of doors opening and shutting stirred her from a deep sleep – the bed was wonderfully comfortable – and she rolled over to switch on the bedside light. Half past three. Not much chance of the threatened bright and early start, then.

She was wrong. At seven-thirty, Claudia, wrapped in a dazzling Chinese silk dressing gown came yawning into her room, accompanied by the maid with the early-morning tea, and plopped herself on her bed. 'Bring mine in here, Bowler,' she said.

Claudia was brimming with plans for the day, and it seemed impossible to Vee that so much could be crammed into a single day. Hair, dressmaker, off-the-peg, beautician, lunch, shoes, tea at Gunter's with some friends, a private view, dinner, dance.

'That's nothing,' said Claudia. 'Just wait until the summer, when the days really get full.'

Vee was longing to have her hair cut short; neither Claudia nor Lally nor anyone else but dowds and church mice had long hair, but there'd been no question of having it cut in York. Mummy, Daddy and the hairdresser would all have pronounced against it, and if she'd got her way, she'd probably have come out of Vivienne's Hairdressing Salon with the same cut as the Archbishop.

'Short hair?' Claudia said. 'What a good idea. Bowler, ring Jacques and tell him he has to fit my cousin in.'

Here in London, of course, it was all quite, quite different. The hairdresser, French vowels perfectly placed over Cockney ones, stalked round her, crouched, swished her hair this way and that, grasped her chin and examined her profile and finally declared that the Parisian look, gamine, you understand, would be perfect for mademoiselle.

'I look like a boy,' Vee said, gazing, astonished, at her reflection in the mirror, not sure whether to be horrified or delighted.

'Very fashionable,' said Claudia. 'You're so lucky, that minute waist and slim hips, you'll look astounding in the right clothes.'

It was fortunate that Grandfather, brought up to the starting line by Hugh, as her brother put it, had now come up handsomely with an allowance.

'He didn't like the idea of me figuring as the poor relation from the provinces,' Vee told Claudia.

He'd had a go at his daughter-in-law, too: 'None of this Cinderella nonsense, Anne. You're to give her some of your jewels, whatever's suitable for a girl of her age. You never wear any of them except those pearls you've always got round your neck.'

'What did Aunt Anne say?'

'Oh, that her pearls suited her, but that I could have my grandmother's set, and she looked out a few other pieces as well.'

Claudia was loud in her condemnation. 'Heavens, you don't want to wear those. They're the kind of thing dutiful daughters wear at home in the morning when they're doing the flowers. Which you won't be, life's far too much fun to worry about flowers, and Mummy leaves all that to the housekeeper. No, what you need is some really up-to-date jewellery, I know just the place.'

The shop did have some wonderful things, but the prices made Vee stare.

'An investment, I promise you,' said Claudia, and when she got home, she telephoned Vee's grandfather. Vee listened with bated breath, as though her grandfather's temper might fly down the instrument and destroy Claudia.

Not a bit of it, and Vee listened, stunned, as her cousin said, 'Very well, those three I told you about, and they're to send the bill to you.'

'There you are,' Claudia said to Vee as she put the receiver down with a triumphant click.

'I'd never have asked him,' Vee said. She wasn't entirely sure that she wanted to accept anything from Grandfather, only how else could she manage the rest of her time at Oxford? 'I didn't really want to ask him for anything.'

'You don't have to, I did.'

Claudia was frank in her relief that she and her cousin were physical opposites. 'If you'd been your sister – what was her name, the one who died and went to heaven?'

'Daisy.'

'What a name, well, she was fair and blue-eyed, wasn't she? Much better that you're dark and slim and svelte and can cultivate enormous chic.'

Chic? It seemed unlikely.

A good time to Claudia meant never spending more than half an hour at any party or dance that bored her, and frequenting many of the nightclubs that were expressly forbidden to well brought-up girls.

'Won't your parents find out?'

'Not if I don't let on. Word gets about, but it won't go any further than Cousin Mildred, and she's too busy playing cards and sniffing cocaine to worry what I'm up to.'

'Don't your parents know what she's like?'

Claudia shrugged. 'They prefer not to. Like most people, it's much easier for them only to see what they want to see. I told you, Mummy steers clear of the party types, and Vernon's too busy saving the economy. And Mildred's very smart, very rich, very well-connected.

They'd never have let my sisters near her, but now it's my turn, they think I'll be the same as my sisters.'

'Were they like you?'

'Not in the least. Dismally well-behaved, all three of them. Lord, I go down on my knees night and morning and give thanks that they were so good and decorous, for it's made my life so much easier.'

Vee's conscience was pricked by the money her new look cost. Part of her revelled in the frocks Claudia made her buy, for day wear and evening, far more sophisticated than anything she'd ever worn.

'Definitely chic for you, Vee. You're not the sort to look good in upholstered clothes. Buy that rich plum one, and the silver one as well, and you must have that black chiffon cocktail; yes, I know you've never worn black, but that's got to change. They're sleek and beautifully cut, the kind of frocks that men think you can buy anywhere for a few shillings, but which in reality cost a fortune. Less is more, but less also costs more.'

Coats, suits for spring wear, shoes, handbags. 'And your underwear, Vee, I can't believe what you wear under those tweeds! Into the rubbish with every stitch of it, you'll have to start from scratch.'

Yet part of her was filled with a sense of guilt. Not for nothing had she grown up in an austere household. Much as she longed to throw off all the shackles of her years in York, she was still appalled by the extravagance she saw all around her.

'Care about the unemployed?' said Claudia. 'Of course I do, my sweet, when I think about them, which is practically never. You see, we're doing our bit, though it might not seem like it. Vernon explained it all to me, at such tedious length, I can't tell you.'

Vernon Saxony's home life seemed to consist of sitting in his large study doing more of the work he did at his office. He had considerable private means, Claudia told Vee. 'Of course, we couldn't possibly live like this if he had to live on his government salary.'

'Vernon says that if we don't buy and consume and employ people, which people like us do like mad, especially during the season, then everything would be much worse, as more people would be out of work. We've all got to spend like anything, those of us who can, I mean, the more the better. Are you going to buy that ravishing frock we saw in Daniela's? Too smart for words.'

Gradually Vee's scruples vanished, as though that part of her had grown numb. She lived in the moment, gave no thought to tomorrow, nor to yesterday, and deliberately refused to let herself be upset by the thin, hungry faces which were as evident in London as they were in her native Yorkshire.

1933

ONE

John Petrus was in London a lot that vacation, and it was clear that Claudia was seeing a good deal of him. She talked about him all the time. 'Petrus is an authority on Germany,' Claudia told Vee. 'He's spent masses of time there, goodness, you should hear him talk about it, Armageddon isn't in it. He's sure there's going to be some great upheaval in Germany and that it will all end in war.'

'I thought the Germans were even more hard-up and unemployed than we are; I don't suppose they could ever afford to go to war again.'

'Oh, everywhere's depressed, no one has any money, but Petrus thinks the Germans have a kind of energy about them, and that in five years or less, Germany will be the dynamo of Europe.'

Vee never gave a thought to the Germans, now, or as they might be in five years' time. To her, they were the bad men of the Great War, the Hun, the unspeakable, and though she supposed they were now perfectly ordinary people, she didn't particularly want to have anything to do with them.

'I'm going to get my German up and switch to modern languages, like you,' Claudia said. 'Much more useful these days than classics, I find I'm not in the least interested in all those long-gone poets and philosophers. Modernity, that's the thing.'

Petrus was very keen on Germany, Vee reminded herself. Claudia's conversation was sprinkled, these days, with Petrus says, and Petrus told me, and Petrus believes. He seemed to have cast a spell over Claudia. How? Vee didn't care even to think about Petrus, who both fascinated and repelled her. She told herself he was simply too grown-up for her, too clever; unlike her cousin, she was out of her depth in his dazzling company.

By the time the vac was nearing its end, Vee found herself growing bored with the social round. Parties went by in a blur. Girls with high, affected laughs, men with sweaty hands pawing her in taxis, stupid conversations, tired scandals, aching feet where clumsy partners had trodden on her, all sense of gaiety and fun had fled.

After one tussle in a taxi, when she'd fended off a particularly tiresome young man, all eager eyes and questing hands, insisting that she wanted to sleep with him, she'd told Claudia how she hated being mauled, so much so that she'd forgotten herself and slapped the wretched man's face, thus convincing him that she was in earnest and not merely being coy.

Despite her Deanery-bred caution, she had done her share of kissing. This was far from being the first man to make a serious pass at her, but their embraces had always left her unmoved. 'I'm frigid, I think,' she said to Claudia.

'That wouldn't be surprising, with your upbringing, I know a lovely little Viennese Jew, a whizz at psychoanalysis, you'd better fix yourself up for a few sessions.'

'No, thank you, I don't want to enjoy being kissed by men who bore me.'

'There is that,' agreed Claudia. 'You'll just have to find yourself someone wildly exciting and give it a go with him. It will be quite, quite different, I promise you.'

Which made her wonder just what kind of kissing Claudia did with Petrus, for no one else gave her voice that caressing tone.

Claudia wasn't always the liveliest of companions; she had something on her mind, but she wasn't saying what it was. Vee did wonder if she'd been sampling Cousin Mildred's substances; it hadn't taken her long to understand that many a London hostess and not a few of the younger smart set fuelled themselves on drugs and alcohol. But no, Claudia wasn't twitchy, and her eyes weren't odd, no huge pupils such as Vee had noticed in Cousin Mildred, among others.

Grandfather sent enquiries via her mother as to where she was going, whom she was meeting, meaning, she knew, had she met a nice young man, in which case she'd presumably chuck Oxford and rush to the altar.

Aunt Lettice had periodic fits of worry when Mummy's letters arrived, fretting that she wasn't doing her duty by her niece by making sure she met plenty of eligible young men.

Claudia came to Vee's rescue. 'Leave her alone, Mummy, Vee's got bags of allure and sex appeal, all the young men flock, tell Aunt Anne so, that'll shut her up.'

'Don't speak like that of your aunt,' said Aunt Lettice, suddenly sharp. 'And Anne would be horrified if I said any such thing. Besides, is there any truth in what you say?'

Which wasn't very flattering to Vee, but she could see her aunt's point of view.

Claudia lay back on the sofa and closed her eyes, sending out a stream of smoke rings from her cigarette. She always seemed to be smoking these days.

'Quite a lot, actually. Vee has a host of admirers, far more than me. She has a touch of the femme fatale about her, especially now she's grown so smart, and that boyish look drives the men wild. It's because they all fell in love with boys while they were at school, I suppose.'

'Claudia, you are not to say these things. If your stepfather were to hear you—'

'He won't, he's never here, haven't you noticed?' She sat up and yawned. 'Lord, how bored I am. What time is it, Vee? Time for lunch? No? Let's have a cocktail to keep our spirits up.'

'I can't think what's come over Claudia,' Aunt Lettice said crossly when Claudia had gone out for the afternoon.

Vee could, it hadn't really been so difficult to work out why Claudia was out of sorts. Petrus was away. He'd gone to America, and Claudia was missing him. But she could hardly say, Claudia thinks she's in love with an Oxford don.

'He's going to be away for weeks,' said Claudia dolefully. 'It's not the same when he's not around. Don't you think he's marvellous?'

Vee didn't. She found him sinister, and the more so as she got to know him better. She had the impression that what one saw was a brilliantly conceived public persona, and that there was an entirely different man behind the mask. He had a sister, Lily, who drifted in and out of their life in London, appearing mostly at the grandest parties with a very rich, handsome and dim-witted German aristo-crat in tow, whom everyone said she was going to marry.

'None of you knows the real Petrus,' Lily said. 'No one except me, and I'm not telling.'

'It's all something to do with the Anglo-German Fellowship, whatever that is,' Claudia said in a discontented voice, as she sat on the end of Vee's bed in a floating robe, filing her nails. 'They want to bring the Americans in on it, I can't imagine why. I think I'll go to Berlin this summer, Petrus is going to be there, Lily told me, conferring with all his German friends. That's all a fearful bore, but one gathers the nightlife is good.'

'Claudia, you can't! Uncle Vernon will never let you go.'

'He will, because I'll say I'm going to stay with some frightfully stuffy cousins he has over there; luckily for me, his half-sister married a German. By the time he finds out I'm not there at all, it'll be too late and I'll be back.'

'There'll be the most frightful row when he finds out.'

'I'll worry about that when it happens.'

It was one of Claudia's more endearing characteristics, that she believed in not meeting trouble until trouble met you. 'Live for the day, is my motto,' she'd say to Vee. 'Pay attention to Horace, "Tomorrow do thy worst, for I have lived today." He's the only poet I'll regret when I give up classics. So sensible, and witty, too. Mostly poets just go on about things one couldn't care less about. What are you going to do come the summer, in the long vac? Are you going to feel obliged to go back to York? You know you can come here whenever you like, Mummy said so. She approves of you, and she enjoys your company.'

Vee felt touched by this. Catch her own mother saying she liked her company.

'Not Yorkshire, thank goodness. I always go to France in the summer, to stay with Grandmère.'

'Sooner you than me, I can't stand the old witch.'

'She's not in the least like a witch.'

'Yes she is. Not the crone in a pointy hat sort, but the slinky, suck-your-blood kind of witch.'

Vee wasn't going to argue with Claudia. She loved being in France, eating delicious food, lying in the sun, reading and reading and reading, and listening to Grandmère and her friends talking about life and art. And this year, she'd buy some lovely French clothes. Grandmère despaired of the way she looked; how surprised she'd be at the new her.

Aunt Lettice bade her a most affectionate farewell when they went back to Oxford, on one of those sleety, desolate January days when it seemed that winter would last for ever. Jenks was at the wheel of the car, Kimber had supervised the stowing of the luggage, and Vee realized with a pang that she felt this London house, where she had spent such a short time, was more of a home to her than the Deanery.

'It's been lovely having you,' Aunt Lettice said, giving her one of her soft hugs. 'I'm only sorry you didn't find a young man to fall in love with, it's such fun being in love at your age. You've seen quite a lot of Alfred Gore, haven't you?'

In fact, Vee had seen Alfred twice. He came to deliver a Christmas present for his godmother – a week after Christmas day, which was typical Alfred – and, to her surprise, one for her. 'It's a book, by Aldous Huxley: *Brave New World*,' he told her.

She could see that for herself, since he hadn't wrapped it.

'Just published. Read it, Vee, it's an important book.'

Vee did read it; she couldn't say she enjoyed it, but it did make her think, as she told Alfred when he came round one snowy afternoon and carried her off to the British Museum.

'To look at the Assyrian kings,' he said. 'I always do that when I want to regain a sense of proportion. Then we'll have tea and a bun in Museum Street.'

He'd been full of talk about something that scientists had done at a Cambridge laboratory. 'They've split the atom,' he said.

'I read a paragraph about it in *The Times*.'

'It's going to change the world, Vee.'

Alfred and his enthusiasms.

'Can you imagine Alfred having the time or energy to be in love with anyone?' she said to her aunt. 'And I'm not in love with him, I hardly know him. He talks all the time, but it's always politics and books and what's going on in the world, never about himself. So how can one get to know him?'

'Alfred lives for causes,' Aunt Lettice said. 'He'll find out what life's really about, one of these days.' She looked a trifle wistful. 'There's no one that Claudia cares for, I suppose? She so secretive about her life, she never confides in me.'

'I don't think so,' Vee said untruthfully, hoping that Claudia's open adoration of Petrus wouldn't come to her parents' ears. It was a mercy that her uncle and aunt chose not to mingle in the more social side of London life. Cousin Mildred might spill the beans, but although

Lettice was happy to use her services as chaperone, she didn't like her cousin, and wouldn't go out of her way to have any contact with her.

Was Claudia falling in love with Petrus, not just hero-worshipping him? Even to Vee's inexperienced sense of fitness, he seemed an improbable suitor. She couldn't see her uncle taking to him. When she tentatively asked who his people were, Claudia dismissed the question with an airy wave. 'People, just like everyone else. What does it matter who his people are?'

That was a change of tune from Claudia, who might flout the rules, but who had an acute social sense of who was and wasn't acceptable. It seemed to Vee that Petrus, despite an impeccable upper-class accent, might not come from the same drawer as an earl's daughter. Did it matter? Not to her, it was really nothing to do with her, except that she didn't want Claudia to get hurt.

'Petrus has no time for class distinctions,' said Claudia, an eager light in her big blue eyes. 'He says it's all my arse.'

Jenks's shoulders were rigid.

'He says what?' Vee said.

'Mummy's waving, Vee, buck up and look sorry to go.'

TWO

The Hilary term of 1933 was chilly and rather an anticlimax after the exhilaration of the first term. Lally caught a dreadful cold and coughed through her exams, which worried her dreadfully. 'So anti-social, hacking away, and smelling of those revolting pastilles.'

Claudia looked tired, the dark rings under her eyes making her eyes look even more intensely blue, and Vee thought, slightly mad. She was bad-tempered as well, snapping at Lally. 'You're hardly the only one with a bad chest, half the people taking exams seem to do nothing but cough and sniff.'

Vee found the cold and the damp easier to bear; years of boarding in a school on the Yorkshire moors had made her hardy. But she found the grey skies depressing, and was glad when exams were over and it was the last week of term.

'One's second term is never much fun,' Alfred said, as he helped Jenks to strap Claudia's hatbox on to the luggage rack. 'Wait until Trinity, when the sun shines and there's punting and swimming . . .'

'Don't be ridiculous, Alfred,' said Claudia. 'Swimming in May? And I don't think the sun is ever going to shine again.'

There was no question of Vee going back to York for the Easter vacation. Her parents were going on a cruise to the Norwegian fjords as soon as Easter week was over, and her mother said, in a detached way, that with Easter being such a busy time, perhaps Vee would prefer to be in London. Aunt Lettice, on the other hand, had written her a letter full of welcoming noises, and Claudia took it for granted that she would be there.

Lally was invited, as well. She could have gone back to America, but she suffered from seasickness and had found the winter Atlantic crossings more than she'd bargained for. 'It's different in the summer, the sea may be calmer, and in any case I have three months to get over the horror of the voyage out to the States.'

Lally was an intrepid explorer of London. Vee went with her a few times, but the sights that enchanted Lally didn't interest her. Claudia was out and about on her own pursuits, and Vee felt rather at a loose end. Six week vacations, were, she decided, too long. Then, one day, she saw an advertisement in the Underground, for art classes.

Vee had gone with Lally to some of her sessions with Marcus, although, as he'd so truly said, a chaperone wasn't necessary. She found the whole business of drawing and painting fascinating, and so, on an impulse, she signed up for a life-drawing class at the Marylebone Institute. It would do her good to try something entirely new, even if she did turn out to be hopeless at it. Drawing from the nude was not encouraged at Yorkshire Ladies', and it gave her a kick to think how her father would disapprove of her doing any such thing.

So, it turned out, did Alfred, whom she met outside Baker Street Tube station after her class, he'd telephoned and said there was a film she should see. He would take her.

'Waste of time, all that kind of art you're doing,' he grumbled, when they came out of the cinema, having sat through what seemed to Vee to be a very tedious film about the meaning of life. Fred Astaire and Ginger Rogers were more her kind of film, she nearly told him, but then stood self-accused of frivolity.

'Art has to serve the people, or it's nothing.'

This was a novel idea to Vee. 'Why should art do any such thing?'

'Because everything has to serve the people. Art's remote from them, do you see the working man spending his free time in the picture gallery, looking at a lot of art done for rich patrons? No, you don't. It's remote from his experience, it doesn't speak to him. It's designed not to, it's all about exclusion. Artists have to become the mouthpieces of the proletariat, they must learn to express nothing but the will of the many, all this individualism has to go.'

'I don't think many people in my class are going to be serving anyone,' she said. 'I certainly shan't, I find it awfully difficult to do what they want, and Mr Fingle, who teaches us, comes round and lets his half-glasses slide down his nose and looks at what I'm doing,

148

and sighs, and mutters oh dear, oh dear, and then goes on to someone else. There's one girl who's good and very keen, but she wants to do illustrations for greetings cards. Maybe that's serving the people, everybody buys those.'

Another explosion from Alfred. 'You simply don't understand. As if the working man, who hasn't got enough money to buy food or put boots on his children's feet buys birthday or Christmas cards. You come with me next Wednesday, there's a meeting down in the East End, that'll show you what I'm talking about.'

Vee was about to turn this invitation away with a laugh, but she hesitated. Why not? Apart from anything, she liked being with Alfred. She liked his energy and his taut mind and the strength of his opinions.

'All right then. Where shall we meet?'

'I can come to Rochester Street and pick you up. Don't let your Uncle Vernon know, though, for the Lord's sake.'

'Why not? Aunt Lettice won't mind.'

'No, but that stiff-necked husband of hers desperately disapproves of me and all my kind, he says I've gone to the bad. He's going to be front of the queue for the lamppost, come the revolution, no question.'

'All right, I'll meet you outside the National Gallery.'

Vee walked alongside Alfred as he threaded his way through a series of mean streets. They went past great warehouses and along dingy streets smelling of refuse, where the clanks and thumps of machinery rang out from the upper floors.

'Sweatshops,' said Alfred. 'You'll know about harsh labour conditions, with your family background.'

She heard the irony in his voice, and flushed. He'd sounded off more than once about Grandfather, and how he represented all that was worst in the capitalist class.

'Is he any worse than your grandfather?' she asked. Not that she wanted to defend her grandfather, who liked nothing better than grinding the faces of the poor, but Alfred's self-righteousness was irksome; after all, Aunt Lettice had told her that Alfred came from a land-owning family in the Midlands.

'Oh, my lot are almost as bad, but at least they work the land, and there's some honour in that. Although they'll have to give it up,

149

we must have common ownership of land. And the pile my brother lives in, which is large enough for about a dozen families to live in comfort, that'll belong to the people as well. It should be turned into a rest home for exhausted workers. Or pulled down, why should the proceeds of workers go to keep up a house that stands for everything that's oppressed them for centuries?'

'You can't mean that!'

'I can and do.' Alfred stopped under the weedy glow of a gas lamp. He took her by the shoulders, looking her straight in the eyes. 'I do mean it, Vee. Every word. I'm deadly serious. The world can't go on like this, can't you see that? You can't have millions of workers living the most awful lives, while the plutocrats get fatter and richer by the day.'

He looked down at her, and, for a heart-stopping moment, she thought he was going to kiss her.

Alfred's hands dropped from her shoulders. 'Come on,' he said. 'We can't be late.'

They walked silently through narrow streets of squalid houses, where ragamuffin children were playing.

'They're barefoot,' Vee exclaimed.

'What?' said Alfred, slowing down for a moment. 'Oh, the children. Most of the men who live here are dockers, and how much work do you think there is at the docks right now? Do you know what they get on the dole? Twenty-one shillings. That's to feed a family of maybe four or five. Where do you think the money for boots is going to come from? Do you know how much the average . . .'

Vee's mind shut off as the torrent of statistics poured over her. 'Shut up about all that. What about these children, here, what do they do in winter?'

'Get chilblains. And bronchitis and pneumonia and TB and all the other things that go with poverty.'

And that very morning, she'd paid ten guineas for a new frock, without giving it a moment's thought.

At the end of the next street, light was streaming out on to the pavement, and people were hurrying through a red-painted door.

'Hurry up,' said Alfred. 'We're late, I think they've already begun.'

They squeezed into the back of the packed room. The air was stale, with the smell of cheap cigarettes mixing with an aroma of boiled

150

cabbage and general unwashedness. Vee shifted uncomfortably on the crowded bench where Alfred had plonked her down.

'It's James Klugman speaking tonight,' Alfred hissed in her ear. 'He's from Cambridge. He'll have his work cut out, because the Party hates types like him, intellectuals. Although that is beginning to change. Now, ssh.'

Which was a bit much, when she hadn't said a word, she thought, trying to find space for her feet.

She could sense the hostility among the audience, and to begin with, Klugman was heckled. 'We don't need your sort to tell us about the revolution,' called out a burly man from the front row. 'You're not one of us.'

'Shut up,' called someone else. 'Let him speak,' shouted another.

'Bloody toffs,' came a mutter from beside Vee; she wasn't sure whether he was referring to the three men on the platform, or to her and Alfred.

Afterwards, Vee couldn't remember much of what Klugman had said. Too many words, just like Alfred, and her mind was still on those children playing in the gutter without shoes on their feet.

When she did catch his argument, she disagreed with him. Were the middle classes the demons Klugman made them out to be? She might be heartless and extravagant, but there was nothing demonic about her. Besides, she didn't want any living creatures to be swept away in rivers of blood. And while the Soviet Union might now be a paradise for the worker, that was in Russia, and doubtless if you'd been a serf, owned body and soul by cruel landowners, anything would justify throwing off the yoke.

But in England? Never.

Alfred was annoyed by her reaction. 'It's people like you who hold the movement back,' he said gloomily. 'You're young and have a conscience, at least I thought you had, and you're energetic and educated. Yet you're content to let things drift, to go on as they are, and somehow it'll all go right again, the shipyards and the steelworks will open up, men will be back in work, and everything will be just as it always has.'

'Isn't that the way it usually works?'

'In the past, maybe. Not any more.'

Whatever Alfred said, Vee wasn't convinced that a communist revolution was ever going to sweep through the towns and cities of England, and still less convinced that if it did so, it would be a good thing.

But yes, she would help in a practical way, if there were anything useful she could do. She cared about those children without shoes, whereas she didn't really give a fig for the downfall of capitalism.

Yet at the back of her mind were those reports of what the papers were calling the night of the long knives. Hitler, it seemed, had a terse way with his rivals and enemies. Communism versus capitalism left her cold. Communism versus fascism might be a different matter.

Alfred stopped, his face delighted. 'You will? Oh that's terrific. You'll love the comrades, and they'll love you.'

THREE

It was too near the end of the vacation for Vee to be swept up in any of Alfred's schemes, and the memory of the thin, ragged children faded as Trinity term began. Trees were greening, blossom billowed about the streets of North Oxford, exams were over, and finals were two long years away. The weather was kind, with enough sunny days for punting and picnics and tennis and long lazy afternoons on the lawns of Grace.

Vee spent many happy hours in the Parks, stretched out beside her books, sniffing the quintessential smell of newly-cut grass, listening to the ritualistic sound of a cricket match while she read Verlaine and Baudelaire.

Hugh was a keen cricketer, and so was Alfred, who could have had his Blue, so they said, if he hadn't been erratic in attendance at practice.

'I love cricket, Vee,' he'd say, flinging himself down on the grass and flipping off the top of a bottle of beer. 'Only it's an indulgence, what chance does a miner have to spend his afternoons whacking a ball around on velvet grass?'

Why always miners? Why not hat makers or match girls? she wondered.

It was the season of parties and dances and balls.

And, in Germany, the season of the burning of books.

That was in another country, and nothing to do with her, Vee told herself, quelling the sensation of fear that began to prickle deep inside her. Germany had been a mess, everyone agreed on that. What could she do to halt the rise of Hitler and fascism? Could she really be a judge of what was going on in a foreign country on the other side of the Channel?

153

But in her heart of hearts, she didn't need Alfred to tell her that the new secret police force, called the Gestapo, and Hitler's Stormtroopers, were bringing fear to the cities and towns and villages of Germany.

'If I were a German Jew, I'd be out of there,' Marcus said.

'If you were Jewish, you'd think you were German first and Jewish second, and wait for things to get better,' Joel said.

'They won't,' said Marcus, yanking off his cream pullover. 'Watch me bowl that swine Jenkins out with my first ball.'

Which he did, and the slow ripple of applause, a sound she would always associate with that summer, drifted over the grass.

Some of the smaller college dances were more fun than the main Commem Balls. Trinity had had a Commem the year before, which had been a great success, and they decided to throw a Queen of the May Ball to celebrate the first of May. It was held on the thirty-first of April, so that revellers would be awake at dawn to hear the choristers sing from Magdalen tower on May morning.

Lally had been asked by the ball organisers to come as the Queen of the May, and Marcus took up the idea with vast enthusiasm, designing a dress that would, he told her, make everyone stare.

It did; it was a fairy-tale dress of cream and green chiffon, with tendrils of spring flowers wound into it. It flowed and fluttered around Lally as she walked, and the effect when she danced was magical.

'Ever thought of becoming a dress designer, Marcus?' Hugh asked him. 'You'd make a fortune.'

There was a maypole, which caused much merriment later on, when some tipsy men attempted to weave the ribbons in the approved way, and ended up in a tangled heap at the foot of the pole.

Vee's party dined together before the ball. They were ten: Lally, attracting a lot of attention in her stunning frock, Claudia, Hugh and Giles, still inseparable, Marcus, Joel, who couldn't take his eyes off Lally, Sarah from Grace, and a pretty cousin of Giles's from London, called Posy. And Alfred.

Alfred was the great surprise. Not only was he there, but he was dressed, for once, perfectly correctly; it was the first time Vee had ever seen him out of his flannels.

'Where did he get tails?' she asked Hugh. 'Don't tell me he's got a wardrobe of decent clothes that none of us knew about.'

'His tutor lent them. I told him he had to come, because we were

154

a man short when Giles wanted to ask Posy. She's just been jilted by the fellow she was going to marry, he ran off with a chorus girl, and she's been a bit miserable. Giles is very kind about things like that, and he thought coming up to Oxford for a weekend might cheer her up and take her mind off it.'

'Even so, I'd have expected Alfred to point out there were dozens of men you could ask to make-up the party.'

'Oh, Alfred's an obliging sort, despite his sharp tongue and violent views. He's going to be a writer, he says, words that'll sear the paper and make everyone sit up and pay attention. Actually, he seemed quite keen on the idea of the dance, even when I told him tails or not at all, went meekly off to ask old Vale for the kit.'

Vee danced first with Joel, sleek from his smoothed down hair to his gleaming pumps, and a very good dancer. Only he kept turning to look at Lally, who was twirling around the floor with Giles, and laughing a good deal.

'Doesn't she dance well?' Joel murmured into her ear as he manoeuvred them closer to the other couple. 'It comes of being musical, I suppose. Are you coming to our concert next week?'

'The quintet? Yes, I am. I've never heard a wind quintet.'

'You'll enjoy it. It's a shame Lally can't play in the orchestra, but the brass players hate the thought of a woman sitting among them.'

'How ridiculous. If she plays well enough, then why not? We had a girl at school who played the trumpet brilliantly.'

Joel's mind was back on Lally and her partner. 'Damn Giles for grabbing her for the first dance.'

'Jealous?' she said, in a moment of temper.

'Of Giles? Come off it. Lally will dance the next one with me, or I'll know the reason why,' he said, performing a quick combination of steps that took her mind off everything except trying to keep up with him.

Claudia was dancing with Alfred, and she had a pleased expression on her face that Vee could see was a mask for discontent. Surely she didn't find Alfred boring. He had a caustic wit and a way with words, and had been in very good form at dinner; not a word about politics.

Actually, Vee could take a good guess at why Claudia looked like that, and it was nothing to do with Alfred. Her cousin had been hoping that Petrus was going to be at the dance, and the light had quite gone out of her when she'd bumped into Lily, who told her that her brother had gone up north and wouldn't be back in time for the dance.

'He doesn't much go in for this kind of thing,' Lily said. 'He doesn't know what he's missing, I just love to dance.'

Champagne, and more champagne. Vee danced with Giles, and he disarmed the hostility she still felt towards him on Hugh's account, by being funny and rude about everyone else on the floor. He was keen to talk about Hugh when he was a little boy. 'I knew him at school, but we came more or less fully-fledged there, at thirteen. I can't imagine what he was like as a child.

'Quiet and turned in on himself, mostly. You had to be, at home. We lost a sister, and after that, everything was very gloomy, and when the parents saw us, they just thought about our sister, the one who died.'

'Good Lord, Hugh never mentioned that he had another sister. He talks about you, sometimes.'

'Daisy died when she was very little.'

He gave her a keen look. 'You or Hugh didn't smother her or push her down the stairs in a fit of sibling rivalry or anything like that?'

Vee was appalled. 'Of course not! She was ill, and died.'

'The other does happen, you know, even in the best-regulated families. But her spirit lives on, dominating your lives? Bet you were glad to get away.'

For a moment Vee was overcome with melancholy, at the thought of Daisy and her parents. Then Giles began to talk about Yorkshire, where his family came from, and she began to enjoy herself again. It was impossible not to be cheered by dancing and laughter and the energy flowing around her. Fun had never been a feature of life at the Deanery, and to be honest, she hadn't found the parties and dances she'd gone to in London as enjoyable as the Oxford ones.

'Oh, mostly those London dos are stuffy affairs,' said Giles. 'I never go to them if I can help it, although aunts and things are always trying to rope one in, they're always desperate for men. When I go up to London, I like to have a good time.'

'How do you do that?'

There was a moment's hesitation before he replied, 'Clubs and things.'

At three in the morning, Vee found herself sitting with Claudia, while Alfred fetched ices.

'Lord, I am hot,' said Claudia, fanning herself.

156

It was becoming very sultry; Vee smelt thunder in the air. 'I hope it doesn't rain or brew up into a storm, I want to go in a punt.'

'Count me out,' said Claudia, putting up her hand to smother a yawn. 'This is all rather a bore. I should have known that it was a mistake to come to anything Hugh had set up. Now look at us, stranded; there's Joel wrapped up in Lally, Hugh and Giles have disappeared, what a surprise, Marcus is drunk, Posy and Sarah have joined up with that noisy lot from Univ, which leaves the two of us with ghastly Alfred, who laughs at one.'

It wasn't like Claudia to sound so petulant. 'What on earth's wrong?' Vee asked.

'The mask slips from time to time,' said Claudia. 'This is a bore because we can't get away from it, except to toddle back to our beds, like good little girls. I wonder if anyone's planning to drive up to London. The night's young.'

Vee knew that reckless look. 'If you go up to town now, there's not a chance of your getting back by the time the scout arrives in the morning. I know you bribe her, but that's no use tomorrow, because the head scout's coming round on an inspection foray.'

'Oh, to hell with it.' Claudia stubbed out her cigarette, and flipped it out of her holder, grinding it into the grass with a slender heel. 'It's all too stupid.'

Vee wasn't sure how she came to be in a punt, at dawn, with Alfred. Not a soft and radiant dawn, but a threatening sky, full of strange grey-greenish light. Alfred was lying in the bottom of the punt, the pole held in his hand and drifting along behind it. She was paddling in an effort to keep the punt from lodging itself yet again in the bank. No one else seemed to be on the river, which was odd, surely punting at dawn was de rigueur on the first of May.

Alfred was quoting poetry, in ringing tones. He had a deep and resonant voice, with a hint of laughter in it, and if Vee hadn't been so cross, she might have been impressed.

> 'Hail bounteous May that dost inspire
> Mirth and youth and warm desire . . .'

He fell silent, his eyes closed. Then he opened them again and looked at her from beneath heavy lids. 'Hugh would place that

157

instantly, but I can see you don't know it. "Song On May Morning" Milton. One of our greatest and most sensuous poets. Sex and Satan, a heady combination.'

Another silence.

'He was a Puritan. Passionate for Cromwell, then he wrote the *Areopagitica*, the greatest polemic ever penned on behalf of freedom of the written word. I wonder if it's been translated into German. I wonder if Hitler has ever read it.'

Alfred was drunk. Very drunk. He was cradling an empty bottle of champagne, crooning to it and occasionally giving it a kiss before lapsing into silence and, it seemed, sleep.

'For God's sake wake up and do your share of this,' Vee yelled at him. Her dress was ruined, stains of food and wine and green slime from the river marking its skirts and a bigger stain near the waist, where she'd vainly tried to rub out the consequences of someone throwing up over her. Alfred? She didn't remember. Was she drunk? She thought not. If she had been, a chilly dawn on the river and the likelihood of both Alfred and her drowning had rendered her sober again. She gave him a shove with the pole end of the paddle.

At this, he gave a galvanic start, staggered to all fours, then to his knees, then, with a final great effort, upright. He wavered there for a moment, and fell headlong into the murky morning waters of the Cherwell.

'Drown, then,' she shouted, furious. 'I'm not jumping in to rescue you.'

Alfred didn't need rescuing. The cold water had an immediate effect, and he swam splashily round the punt a few times, dipping his head under and then surfacing to shake it like some small wet dog.

She began to laugh. 'Whoever you borrowed your clothes from is going to be furious.'

Alfred raised a soggy arm, adorned with a trail of weed.

'My tutor. All part of his pastoral obligation, don't you think? Help me back into the boat, for God's sake, don't just stand there laughing.'

The punt rocked violently as Alfred heaved himself back in. He plucked a damp feather from his shirt front and presented it to her.

'Are you calling me a coward?' she said.

She remembered her mother telling her – with some approval – about officious women, during the war, handing feathers to men who weren't in uniform.

Alfred looked down at the feather. 'It's a black feather, not a white one. From a raven's wing. The colour of your hair, Vee. A feather of omen. With this feather, I can see into the future.'

'I'd rather you didn't. I'd much rather you took the paddle and we got back to the landing stage.' Alfred had let go of the pole, and it had drifted away down river. 'I think it's going to thunder.'

As she spoke, the sky lit up and there was a resounding crash. A pair of ducks scooted across the water in front of them and dived into the shelter of the bank. The sky darkened still further, and huge drops of rain began to fall.

'Here, give me that paddle,' said Alfred. 'May I offer you my coat?'

'Don't be silly, your coat's sopping wet.'

'So it is. Well, no one can say I'm not the soul of chivalry. I offer it, that will be noted down by the recording angel in his little black book.'

'Why black?'

'Because he writes with a black quill pen, don't you see angels all in black and gold? This feather is one of his rejects, that's why it's potent.' He tucked the limp thing into his buttonhole. 'Now the voice of prophecy is come upon me. I see revolution spreading over this dismal land, I see the oppressed rising to overwhelm the unjust and a new dawn of freedom and equality bursting over the playing fields of Eton.'

'If you see that, you must be even drunker than I thought.'

To her surprise, Alfred grew suddenly serious. 'I fear you're right, but by God, shouldn't I like to see it happen. Rivers of blood on Agar's Field.'

'Oh, do shut up about your rivers of blood. It's so boring.' She shouted the last word so loudly that it could be heard above the crack of thunder that accompanied it.

'It will come. Maybe not this year, nor next year, but it will come. It's the future, we've lived through the birth of an entirely new era in the history of the world, and its spread is as inevitable as, oh, the spread of writing or printing.'

'You honestly think people in this country are going to rise up and shoot the king and queen and the princes and princesses? You're mad.'

'Put them in a boat and let them sail away for a year and a day. No, stay, I have a better idea. Put them down the mines. Together with the House of Lords and every landowner in the kingdom. And all the priests and bishops, too.'

'Do steer better than that. My father's a dean, and I can't see him at the coalface, thank you.'

'He'll have no choice. The rich will be poor, the same as everyone else, and the rule of the proletariat will begin.'

Vee was feeling cold and annoyed, and if Alfred was going to start on the proletariat, she would be tempted to push him back into the river. She might care about children without shoes, and want to do something about it, but what use were these grandiloquent rantings?

'Why do you men drink so much?'

'To numb our feelings, to shut out the pale cloud of reality, to leave a warm glow that otherwise would be lacking in our lives.'

'If you're so keen on the proletariat, why are you at Oxford and not out earning a living?'

'The revolution needs its intellectuals.'

'Oh, give me that paddle. I've no patience with you.'

They had a brief tussle over possession of the paddle, but Alfred, who was much stronger than his drunken state suggested, wrested it away from her. He sat back and pushed a damp lock of hair out of his eyes.

'With your hair all wet,' he said, 'you look like a boy. I'm glad you aren't, though,' he added cryptically.

After they'd scrambled ashore and were walking along the path in the pounding rain, Alfred made a grab at her and drew her into the bushes. 'Kiss me,' he said.

She didn't want to kiss him at all. She was wet and cold and cross, and yet she felt a sense of relief; she had had a disturbing suspicion that Alfred might be another one who liked men better than women. And his kiss was surprising, wet, but only from rain and river water, and pleasant. Light at first, it became more passionate and urgent, making her spine tingle in a way that was quite new to her.

Was Alfred wildly exciting? No, he wasn't. He was odd and altogether slightly alarming. She pushed him away. 'I'm cold and wet, and all I want to do is get back to Grace and have a hot bath.'

They walked back from the river in the rain, Alfred, seemingly perfectly happy, humming snatches of Italian songs to himself. Vee was filled with irritation and hostility towards him. Had Alfred actually wanted to kiss her? She doubted it. He would have kissed any woman who had been in the punt with him, Claudia, Lally or Posy, damn him.

FOUR

That summer, Vee went to France, Lally back home to the States, and Claudia dashed from London to the country, from Cowes to Le Touquet, and from the moors to Berlin.

Vee loved Grandmère's mellow, eighteenth-century house in the Loire. It had traditional shutters and a formal garden that led into a grassy meadow beside the river. She slept and ate delicious food and spoke nothing but French.

She knew all the families in the village, the permanent residents and those who fled the heat of Paris to spend the summer months in the country, by the river. This had always been a separate part of her life, set apart from her Yorkshire existence. Now Oxford, the college, the work, her friends, seemed as remote as York and school had done.

She travelled back to England by train, meeting Claudia in Paris and shopping for clothes. Then it was train and boat to Dover, where Jenks was waiting on the quay to drive them back to London. Lally was already there, still pale after a bad crossing, and then they were off back to Oxford for the start of a new academic year.

Vee was in the JCR at Grace when she opened the invitation. It was a thick cream card, with embossed black calligraphy. One Lancelot Bray was inviting one Ronald Trenchard to dine as a guest of the Bradley and Brocklehurst Society, New College, Oxford.

How very peculiar. Ronald was her father's name, but how had this come to her? It had been forwarded under cover, the original envelope was indeed addressed to R Trenchard Esq, Jesus College.

She turned it over and read a scrawled message on the back. 'Your brother Hugh will be attending.'

Hugh? This had to be a practical joke.

Claudia strolled into the JCR. 'What's that, Vee, an invitation? Is there one for me, is it something exciting?'

'I doubt it, just some nonsense.' Vee made as though to toss the card and the two envelopes into the fire, but Claudia leaned over and took the card from her.

'Nothing of the sort, I'd call it an honour.' Claudia said primly. Her eyes flickered to where Hermione Harbottle was steadily eating her way through a plateful of digestive biscuits, her ears flapping as always. 'Lovely-sounding invitation, Vee, to dine and meet some interesting people. What will you wear?'

Then, once outside the JCR, Claudia gave way to a fit of laughter. 'If only the Harbottle knew what we were up to.'

'We aren't up to anything.'

'Oh, yes, this is the most terrific joke. I fixed it, you see. Petrus and Hugh thought it was a splendid idea.'

'Claudia—'

'Do you know about Lancelot? No? He's the most woman-hating don that ever walked these hallowed lanes. He can't abide the female sex, he speaks of us as though we were a step below cockroaches in the chain of being. He spends all his spare time campaigning for women's colleges to be closed, or at least not allowed to be part of the university. He's queer as a coot of course, that's half his problem, but there's some kind of complex as well, that Austrian psychoanalyst explained it all too me, his mother or nanny smacked him on his potty or didn't or something. Goodness, what a lark. Now, where are we going to get you some evening clothes? You can't wear Hugh's, he's too tall. And they've got to fit well, or it'll give the game away, Lancelot's got a keen eye for the set of a coat.'

Vee shook her head. How could she possibly dress up and deceive a roomful of men? 'If Hugh's there, I'd catch his eye and get the giggles.'

'Hugh will have to be severe, and keep his eyes on the table. I know, Geoffrey Goodwin's brother is about your height and build; he's still at school and isn't really growing yet, but he'll have evening clothes. Leave the sartorial side to me. Pen a formal reply to the invitation, and I'll tell Petrus that you're on.'

162

'Will Petrus be there?'

'Oh, yes.'

Claudia hadn't mentioned Petrus much recently, and Vee had hoped he might have dropped out of her cousin's orbit; Claudia was a great dropper of men, losing interest and then ignoring them entirely. But there was that in her voice when Claudia said his name that made Vee doubt it was the case with Petrus.

They met Alfred coming out of a second-hand bookshop, and Claudia told him about the dinner party.

'If you've got time to waste on all that kind of thing,' he said sniffily. Then he grinned. 'I've been invited too. What a joke when old Lancelot learns how he's been tricked. You'll have to have your hair barbered properly, though, Vee. I'll take you to my chap in the High, he'll give you the right look.'

'Oh, no, you don't. I'll make it more boyish myself, thank you. I'm not having any barber leaving me looking a perfect fright for weeks to come.'

'Vanity, vanity.'

'Have you ever done any theatricals?' Claudia asked, surveying Vee's hair with a critical eye. It was extraordinary how boyish she looked. 'You're a good mimic, but are you going to get stage-fright?'

'I used to act at school,' Vee said. 'But being slight and not very tall, I usually played women's parts, they gave the male roles to beefier types.'

Claudia held up a silk scarf. 'Take off your blouse and slip, and let's flatten you.'

Not that Vee needed much flattening, with her slim figure and small breasts. 'Hold up your arms, that's right, now go round and round. I'll pin it at the back. Not too tight? OK, now the shirt.'

Vee pulled on the stiff-fronted white shirt, crackling with starch, and stood while Claudia did the studs for her.

'Be careful, you're strangling me. However do men manage to breathe in these collars?' She stepped into the black trousers and twisted round to admire the silk stripe down the legs.

'Perfect,' said Claudia.

They were in Hugh's bedroom, Claudia having pointed out that it would be impossible for Vee to walk through Grace in a man's evening clothes.

'Harbottle would be bound to put her head out of her door in that annoying way she has, and exclaim and ask if you were going to a fancy-dress party.'

'And to warn me that if I continue to put my social life above my work, I'll end up with a poor third.'

'Do up the braces,' Claudia said. 'I'll call Hugh for the tie.'

'Amazing,' said Hugh. 'You're a useless brother, though, if you haven't learned to do your tie yet.'

A few deft movements and it was done. Vee strutted up and down in Hugh's sitting room feeling very masculine, while the others laughed at her.

'Stride a bit more,' said Alfred, who was lounging in Hugh's armchair and smoking a disgusting pipe. 'If you look prissy, Lancelot won't be able to keep his hands off you, and then there'll be the devil to pay.'

'What if he unmasks me there and then?' Vee asked 'Will I be hustled down the staircase and across the quad and thrown out on to the cobbles?'

'He won't be doing any unmasking,' said Alfred. 'By the time we get to the fish, he'll already be worse for wear, and his eyesight isn't too brilliant anyhow. He's too vain to wear spectacles, thinks it makes him look old.'

'Who else is going to be there?' Vee wanted to know.

'The usual crowd,' said Hugh. 'We shall be ten. Alfred, Petrus, Vee, Lancelot himself, of course, then there's Giles – God knows where he's got to, he was supposed to be here at seven, swotting for his first again, I suppose. Marcus is coming, and Pigot-Brown from Magdalen, they're in on the joke, and du Bossey and Quinlan, who aren't, but they won't notice, they don't know what a woman is.'

Claudia gave Vee a quick, knowing glance. Her cousin was thinking about Hugh, she was sure; she still hadn't come to terms with him and Giles. It was a pity she couldn't just accept people as they were. Hugh was the same Hugh, whether he went to bed with Giles or a townie slut or a girl from LMH.

Vee knew this perfectly well. Alfred had said very much the same thing, and indeed, she and Hugh were back on something like their old, easy terms. Only, dressing up as a man made her wonder just where boundaries lay between men and women and men and men, or even women and women. Sapphics, Miss Harbottle called them – romanticising her pash on an angelically fair fourth-year, Claudia said, with scorn.

Vee rejected these troubling thoughts and concentrated on the evening ahead. Curiosity was getting the better of her. She'd never been in a convivial gathering of men like this before. Seminars where she was the only female present were different, although not entirely, given that quite half the tutors made a point of ignoring her, often addressing the group simply as 'Gentlemen'.

Now she was being given the opportunity to be on the inside, a fly on the wall, observing an alien species in their natural habitat. Or would the fact that most of them knew she was a woman mean that they wouldn't behave as they normally would?

She'd asked Alfred what men talked about when they were together.

'Depends on the men. If they're sport mad, then that's what they talk about, ad nauseam, and very tedious it is, too. Then there are the club bores who drone on about people you've never met and don't want to meet. Mostly though, it's gossip.'

'Gossip?' That did surprise her. 'I thought gossip was a woman's vice.'

'What's vicious about it? Gossip makes the world go round, and among the idle classes, who have nothing better to fill their empty heads, it occupies a good deal of their waking hours.'

'Gossip about what?'

'Who's in, who's out, who's sleeping with whom, who's broken up with whom, what happened at old Codgers the other evening and did you hear that Reggie lost all his money at Monte last week?'

'While women go on about clothes and how expensive silk stockings are and how ghastly Deirdre looked at the Groves' party, and why does Winifred paint her face so thick unless it's to hide the cracks.'

'You get that too. George is getting fat, Jamie's trousers are too short, does he wash them . . .'

'I shan't be able to join in, shall I? Not knowing whom they're gossiping about.'

'They may gossip a bit, but in this sort of company, it'll mostly be politics. It's inevitable if Petrus is at the table. Besides, politics and detective stories are all anyone ever talks about at Oxford dinner parties these days. It used to be art and culture and Bloomsbury ideals, but now Marxism's the hot topic, I'm glad to say. I don't think the London establishment has any idea how red the universities have become.'

'Cambridge, too?'

'Yes, more so than us. They boast that there isn't a first-year man who isn't communist by the beginning of Trinity term, but that's just Cambridge swank. They think we're less forward-thinking and up-to-date than they are, we're supposed to be more poetic than practical, but even they admit it's hotting up over here.'

'I can't talk about Marx, I've never read a word of him.'

'Don't worry, nor have most people. Just look serious and nod your head. After a glass or two, they're only interested in their own opinions, you'll find. A couple of them are very anti-Marxist, which makes for lively arguments. Du Bossey, for instance, is so far to the right he's falling off the edge of the world, Bray himself is pure fascist, Giles is right-wing but ready to listen to reason, Hugh – well, you might know what Hugh thinks, no one else does, since he keeps his own counsel most of the time. Marcus will join in whichever side of any argument he feels like at the time. Pigot-Brown believes in World Government . . . Yes, it should be a lively occasion.'

Alfred and Hugh had neglected to warn Vee what a glass or two meant. Cocktails were followed by a different wine for every course. She sipped her claret cautiously, then saw that Marcus was raising his eyebrows at her, and making tutting noises with his little red mouth. Men don't sip, she told herself, and began to drink her wine glass for glass with her neighbour.

It all went beautifully. Lancelot Bray, a tall man with a thin but soft mouth and very white hands greeted her with exquisite courtesy and what she recognized as a lascivious eye. He was out of luck this evening, even if he didn't know it. He wanted to have Vee on his right when they went in to dinner, but adroit staff work by Alfred and Hugh saw her seated further away from him. The table was a large round one, and she was thankful to be out of Lancelot Bray's direct line of vision. She didn't want to trust to Hugh's assurances of his being as blind as a bat; her host's eyes might be short-sighted, but they were alarmingly intelligent.

Quinlan, sitting next to her, sounded her out on various subjects, and frightened her by asking if she knew Jenkins, a chum of his at Jesus. 'Third-year man reading forestry. Got a chance of a seat in the Eight.'

Hugh came to her rescue, asking her to put him right about a story

166

he was relating about the Archbishop of York, and Quinlan, drinking steadily, apparently forgot about Mr Jenkins.

The conversation became heated. They were talking about E M Forster and whether it was better to betray friend or country. 'That's one for the Angels,' Giles said to Petrus, who merely smiled and looked a little bored at the intense and not very coherent burst of patriotism flowing from Pigot-Brown. Then Lancelot Bray broke in, his voice rather louder than anyone else's, holding the floor with his lecturing tones.

'If you want patriotism, go to Germany. You'll back me up on that, Petrus, you hang around with all those Prussians at the embassy. They really care about their country. It's been hauled in the dust, and they're determined to rise again, and more power to them. They know where the trouble lies, they've got the measure of all those damn Jews, and they've got discipline. And they've no time for all this left-wing spiel that's trotted out in the common rooms of this university.'

'The Germans want to keep women in their place, too,' said du Bossey. 'Kitchen, church and raising children. None of this education business over there.'

Bray frowned at the mention of women, but played the gracious host and let it pass. Alfred, outraged, began to attack du Bossey, asking him if he had any notion how dangerous fascism was. 'Hitler's going to be the biggest menace in a hundred years,' he asserted.

'Fascism's no more dangerous than your stupid Marxism, old boy,' said du Bossey. 'It's nothing to me, we mathematicians don't go in for politics, we've got real problems to solve.'

Vee drank some more wine and kept her mouth shut. When asked in aggressive tones by Quinlan what her politics were, she said austerely that she had none. 'I don't have time for politics, I'm concentrating on my work.'

'What are you reading?' came the reply.

'Modern languages,' and before any queries about tutors and papers followed, she began to talk to Petrus about seventeenth-century French playwrights, a subject on which he was surprisingly knowledgeable.

'Being an economist doesn't mean I'm uncultured,' he said, reading her expression accurately. She felt flustered and said weakly that she knew he spoke German.

'German is very useful for me professionally, but French literature is closer to my heart,' he said suavely.

167

She laughed, remembering to adjust her voice downwards. Not that anyone was paying her the slightest attention. They were all, except for Petrus, engaged in heated discussion, Fascists hurling abuse at the Marxists, and Bray vainly trying to restore some calm to the table.

All the good mood of the earlier part of the evening had vanished. The port went round in near silence; where was the gossip and camaraderie Alfred had promised? If this was how men really were when they got together, give her a group of women any day, they might be catty, but they usually kept their sense of humour.

FIVE

The party broke up early, and they spilled out into the quad, Quinlan and du Bossey ostentatiously separating from the others as soon as they got to the lodge.

'You were very silent this evening, Hugh,' commented Petrus, as they waited for Alfred to light a cigarette.

It was true, now that he mentioned it. Hugh had taken hardly any part in the conversation or arguments.

'I'm like Vee, here,' he said. 'I don't go in for noisy and pointless discussions. The facts speak for themselves, why should I waste my breath trying to convince other people to share what I know to be the truth. Come on, Vee, I'd better get you back to your lodgings, and Giles to Christ Church; he's roaring drunk, by the way – that silence is alcohol, not reflection. In a while, he'll wake up and start lashing out at whoever's nearest, so best get him back before then. If we get stopped by the proctors, sing out that you're Mr Jenkins of Jesus.'

'It's not on your way,' said Petrus. 'I have to call in at Queen's to pick up some papers from the lodge. I'll escort Vee. If she doesn't mind?'

Which was how Vee came to be walking beside Petrus, light-headed, her wariness of him dispersed in a haze of alcohol; he might have been an old friend that she was quite at ease with.

'I'm drunk,' she said. 'I've never had so much wine in my life. He didn't guess, did he?'

'Not the faintest suspicion. He'll be so angry when he finds out how he's been duped.'

'You're going to tell him?'

'Good Lord, no, where's the subtlety in that? No, I shall mention it in the strictest confidence to one or two gabby fellows, and then stand back and watch.'

'You'll have to let me know how he reacts.'

'My dear, I can tell you that now. He'll exclaim that it isn't true, and pout, and sulk, and then he'll accuse, and then he'll try to tear a strip off Hugh, which will do him no good at all ... All rather childish, but it passes the time.' He looked down at Vee, with those compelling eyes which she had thought sinister, but which now seemed to be kind and good-humoured. 'I think a stroll in the fresh air might clear your head. After all, the night is young.'

He had a key to the Meadows. It was eerie to walk along the empty broad walk. They came to the Isis and turned to walk beside the river. The moon was up, turning Petrus's hair even paler and sending silvery ripples across the black surface of the water. A coot scuttled across to the other bank. In the distance, she could hear the sharp bark of a fox. She felt dreamlike, as though her feet weren't really walking on the ground, as though, if she stretched out a hand and touched a bush, or bent to pick up a stone, the apparently real world would dissolve about her.

Petrus talked on, amusing, flattering her opinions, laughing at her and with her when she ventured a joke. Why had she been afraid of him, why had she thought him alarming and dangerous? Goodness, it was easy to see now what Claudia found so attractive about him. She stumbled on a tussock of grass, and he held her up with a strong hand. Then he tucked her arm under his. 'We can take a short-cut back to Grace through here,' he said. 'On the other hand, you might care to come back to my rooms for a nightcap.'

That brought her out of her reverie. 'It's too late,' she said. 'No women after nine, unless it's for a meeting.'

'Ah, but you aren't a woman tonight. Why don't we see if we can slip you in past the porter? It would be amusing.'

It appealed to her, this sudden acquisition of new, male territory. The porter, who had been listening to the wireless, didn't give her a second look, merely called out a 'Good evening, sir' to Petrus, and then they were walking across to Petrus's staircase.

Was this where Claudia came? How did she get in and out, no chance of her passing as a man?

The staircase was in semi-darkness. She could just see the name board with its sliding panels indicating whether the occupants of each room were in or out.

'Aren't you going to slide it across to show that you're in?' she asked.

'I don't think so,' he said, leading the way up the stairs. From behind a closed door came the sounds of voices and laughter.

'Here we are,' he said, stopping outside his door. He had a key already in his hand, and he inserted it into the lock of the outer door. He pushed open the inner one, and waited for her to go in. Then he shut both doors. She stood in the dark while he crossed to a table and switched on a lamp. There was a slight scent in the air, an elusive whisper of familiar fragrance, but she couldn't place it.

Panic struck her. What was she doing here? Was she mad?

'I think I'd better go,' she said. 'I'd better get back to Grace.' The light was muted, but Vee was sure that Petrus could see she was shaking.

'In a minute,' he said, coming towards her. He took hold of her chin and turned her to look at him. 'Such a pretty boy,' he murmured, and then he was kissing her, urgently and firmly.

So this was seduction, she said to herself, as his fingers ran down her stiff shirt front, pulling at the studs. He gave a mocking laugh when he found the silk scarf; it wasn't terribly comfortable, she was glad to be rid of it. There was an urgency to his embraces that was beginning to frighten her, and he was much stronger than she had realized. Now she really should resist, she must stop this, she had to go. This was going too far, and yet, what the hell . . .

Afterwards, she asked herself whether curiosity rather than lust had got the better of her, and she thought that was probably the case. She'd wondered what it would be like to make love with a man, although could you call it making love when there was nothing between you beyond his desire, his exclamation of delight and lechery at man turning into woman?

'So very sexy, you dressed as a man, you should wear these clothes more often,' he murmured into her ear as he slipped the braces from her shoulders and began, with exploring fingers, to unbutton the flies of her trousers.

The act of love left her uncomfortable and unmoved.

Petrus, restored to his normal cool self, told her it was often so.

171

'It was your first time, I hadn't realized. It takes a while to become accustomed to making love. Ecstasy for me, but unfamiliar for you. Easier and more pleasurable next time, I assure you.'

One thing she was sure of, there wasn't going to be a next time, at least not with Petrus. She vanished into the night like a creature from a Gothic novel, and, she decided, back in Grace where she ran a forbidden bath and washed and scrubbed her body as though to punish it, a Gothic novel was where Petrus belonged. Claudia was welcome to him.

It was only when she got back to her room, shivering, searching for a clean pair of pyjamas, that the memory of the scent in Petrus's rooms made sense, its origin coming to her. It was Claudia's scent, of course. The merest trace of it, light as a wisp of smoke, but a scent such as that lingered, which was why Claudia paid so many guineas for the tiniest phial of it.

Of course, Claudia was sleeping with Petrus, was probably his mistress, no casual bout of sex behind a locked door, never to be repeated, for Claudia. And presumably making love with Petrus meant something to her cousin.

Whereas, to Vee it left her with no more than a sense of distaste, a certain embarrassment and a relief that that was one aspect of life she need no longer be curious about. She hadn't enjoyed it, wouldn't have described it as lovemaking – where did love come into it? It hadn't exactly disgusted her; rather, it had left her numb, but with a glimmer of understanding that if you had any passion for a man, the whole act might be quite different.

With Alfred, for instance.

At that she sat up and switched the bedside light on again. Alfred, indeed. Alfred with his drunken kisses in the rain, a man who valued communism and a good argument far above any woman. Bother Alfred.

Think of Claudia, rather. Feeling flooded back into her now, but the feeling wasn't to do with Petrus, or with Alfred. It was guilt, guilt at her betrayal of Claudia. How could she have been so stupid as not to remember that Claudia was in love with Petrus, physically, emotionally entangled with him? And Petrus had taken her, Claudia's cousin and probably her closest friend, to bed.

Did that mean that he didn't regard their relationship in anything like the same way as Claudia did? Didn't he care for Claudia? Was there nothing serious in that relationship as far as he was concerned?

172

There was no question of his being in love with Vee. The opportunity had arisen, for some reason her presence in men's clothes had aroused him, that was all there was to it. So, if that was how it was with her, then it was likely to be the same with other women.

Poor Claudia. No wonder she looked so jaded, no wonder she showed no interest in other men, Claudia, who had always played the field until Petrus came on the scene.

Damn Petrus. There were dozens of men with loose morals and twitchy sex organs in London, she'd done some avoiding herself, but others hadn't, and then the tales of conquests and scandalous, delighted gossip did the rounds.

She went hot and cold at the thought: Petrus mentioning in passing that he had gone to bed with her. Word might get back to Claudia, as word did in their small world where everybody knew everybody else.

Damn it. Why hadn't she turned round at the door and left? Why hadn't she stayed in the quad, said goodnight, gone on her way? Petrus would have shrugged his shoulders and that would have been the end of it. It wouldn't have changed what he felt – or didn't feel about Claudia, not a jot. But it would have left Vee out of it, untouched by Petrus's messy games, unassailed by this ghastly guilt that pricked her eyes and filled her with self-hatred.

Despite the bath, she felt grubby. She went to the basin and washed her face again.

Internal grubbiness, she told herself. The sort that can't be washed away. Words from the Bible came into her mind and hammered at her brain, 'Washed their robes and made them white in the blood of the Lamb. The Lamb of God who takest away the sins of world . . . the blood of the Lamb that washes away the sins of the world.'

Sins of the world, indeed. It was her sins that she wanted washed away. She buried her damp face in a towel before rubbing it dry with painful vigour.

What could she do to put things right?

Nothing. Nothing at all.

She climbed back into bed and dragged the eiderdown up to her eyes, shutting out the light, the room, life.

Where Claudia found her, fast asleep, hours later.

'Wake up, what on earth are you doing asleep with the light on. I want to hear about last night. Were you found out? What did Petrus say?'

173

Vee dragged her head above the covers, blinking in the light as Claudia ruthlessly pulled the eiderdown right off the bed. 'You're steaming in there. And look at your face, I know what that is, barber's rash.'

'What?' Vee said, still half asleep. 'That's what men get.'

'Men get it, and it's what I call it when one's cheek gets roughed up by a man who hasn't shaved. Who made a dive at you, then? Bet it was someone fair, blond men don't think they need to shave in the evening, they imagine no one notices their pale five o'clock shadow. Only women do, of course.'

Vee was coming to her senses now, and the whole sickening business of the last twenty-four hours came rushing back to her. Blond? Petrus? She felt her cheek. 'It is a bit sore,' she said, trying to sound sleepy and unconcerned.

'Who was it?' There was a moment of suspicion in Claudia's voice.

'Giles, fooling about.'

'Oh, Giles.'

Claudia lost interest in the rash burning on Vee's face. 'Who else was there? Did Lancelot Bray have any idea who you were?'

'No,' Vee said, and gave a violent yawn. 'Men are terribly dull when they're all together. Much bitchier than women, too.'

'That's what Petrus says, only I never believed him. Not having but the one sane brother, and him so secretive that he wouldn't dream of giving his little sister the low-down on club or table talk, I don't know about these things. You've had Hugh to tell you all about it, so I suppose it wasn't such a surprise.'

'It was pretty boring, really,' Vee said, struggling to a half-sitting position. 'What time is it?'

'Half past eight.'

Vee groaned. 'I've got a lecture at nine, throw me my dressing gown.' She padded over to the wardrobe, and took out a skirt. The evening clothes were strewn across a chair; it made her shudder to see them. She didn't want to be reminded again of how the evening had ended.

'You'd better bundle those away,' Claudia said. 'You don't want the scout to find them.'

1934

ONE

At the end of that term, Vee greeted Jenks as an old friend and was rolled back to the Veres' house as though she belonged. Her parents had made desultory noises about her going north for Christmas. Although perhaps she would rather go to Switzerland with Hugh?

Snow and ice held no appeal for Vee. She was relieved to be in London, and moved by the warmth of her welcome from Aunt Lettice, 'You're one of the family, Vee, darling.'

Once in London, though, she felt restless and discontented. She didn't feel inclined to tackle any of the reading she had to do, and the social round bored her, with its vacuous gossip, back-biting and desperate search for novelty and stimulation for jaded appetites.

So she went back to the studio to paint and try her hand at throwing pots, not with any great success. She enjoyed it, though, the feel of the wet clay and the moment of stillness when a pot centred and formed into a shape within her hands. The art filled an emptiness, at least for a while.

The Institute was shut over Christmas and the New Year, but in early January, when it reopened, she was on the doorstep. Painting drove everything else out of her mind, she had discovered, and she used it like a drug, to stop the nagging thoughts that plagued her, memories of her childhood and of Daisy, of the barefoot children, of the afternoons she spent working for the comrades, addressing envelopes, of Petrus.

On the first day back, two hours at her easel made her happy. What didn't make her happy was the knowledge that she was going out that evening.

She didn't want to dine with the Oronsays, who were in London for the Christmas season, nor, in fact to dine anywhere. A sandwich in the snack bar with some of her fellow students in the little café they went to near the Institute would have been perfect for her, but she'd accepted the invitation, and it would be rude to cry off at the last minute. At least there was always a crowd at the Oronsays' London parties; she wouldn't have to sparkle or do more than make the usual inane small talk.

She went into the ladies' lav to get the last of the paint off her hands and to change. It was a grim place, painted in institutional cream, with black-and-white tiles and a very dim light bulb casting more murk than light. She dressed, and made up her face as best she could in the gloom, with the help of a mirror speckled with brown patches where the silvering had worn off. A fellow student came in and eyed her with what she felt sure was scorn. She tried to convince herself that it was surprise, not scorn, smoothed the skirts of her dress into place and left the cloakroom, her evening shoes clicking on the austere stone floor, along the bare corridors and out through the gates to flag down a taxi.

From one world to another, she said to herself as the butler opened a door into a fairyland of crystal lights, and she went to greet Ruth Oronsay, who was holding court at the entrance to their lovely drawing room. The Oronsays were a glittering couple; Sir Iain, a Scot of ancient lineage, Ruth, rich and intelligent and amusing and Jewish. They had a huge house in Oxford, where Ruth held a fellowship in chemistry, and spent the vacations in this large and glamorous apartment in London. Vee liked them both, and the company was always lively; her gloom and reluctance to be sociable dropped from her as Ruth kissed her on both cheeks and a footman came forward with a cocktail.

'Far too many Jews here tonight,' Claudia whispered in her ear. Vee frowned, Ruth was close to them, standing beside a man with an interesting, clever face, who was wearing a monocle.

Had Ruth heard what Claudia said? Vee was filled with sudden irritation at the way Claudia was behaving. It was rude, and unkind, and not really like Claudia.

'This is Piers Forster, an old, old friend,' Ruth said.

Mr Forster must have heard Claudia's words, because he gave her a hard look as Ruth went off to talk to some newcomers. 'Do you object to Jews?' he said.

Claudia had the grace to blush.

'No point in being shamefaced, I don't think one's views are worth having if they can't be stated aloud. Are you a Mosleyite, perhaps, Lady Claudia? It is Lady Claudia Vere, isn't it? I know your brother.'

From the expression on his face, Vee guessed that the brother in question was Lucius, the earl, and she was amused to see Claudia take a step back at this direct attack. 'I am one of Mosley's admirers as it happens,' she said.

'Mosley's a fool,' the man said pleasantly. 'Throwing away a political career for a will-o'-the-wisp. Madness.'

'He'll come to power after the next election. History is on his side.'

'Nonsense. Arrant nonsense. History will sweep on its way leaving him high and dry.' He turned away from Claudia as though dismissing her and smiled at Vee. 'Do you share your cousin's views, Miss Trenchard?'

How did he know they were cousins?

'You make a striking pair. I've been out of England for more than a year, and you were both pointed out to me on my return. I am acquainted with Vernon Saxony – your uncle, I assume?'

Claudia had drifted away, a discontented figure looking about for someone to talk to. Looking for Petrus; he was a close friend of Sir Iain's and might well be there. He was the last person Vee wanted to see, but for Claudia it would clearly be a wasted evening if he weren't there.

'Am I a Mosleyite? No, I'm not any kind of a fascist.'

'You aren't bowled over by men in black boots, then.'

Was he being ironic, or just trying to provoke her?

'Politics are too serious for fancy dress.'

She wanted a cigarette, and looked around for the silver boxes that Ruth always provided for her guests.

'Allow me,' Piers Forster said, pulling out a slender case and flipping it open. She took out her holder, tucked the cigarette in its end and waited for him to light it.

'Why have you been out of England, Mr Forster?'

'My family owns properties in various Godforsaken parts of the world, and I've been beating the bounds, as it were.'

'Godforsaken?'

'Australia, you know, and parts of India and Argentina.'

'So now you're back in England, what do you do?'

'Go back to the country, heave a sigh of relief that I don't have to go abroad for years, with any luck, and ruralize.'

'You don't look like a ruralizer.'

'Like Horace, I am both a town and country mouse. I have a flat in London so that I can spend as much time here as I want.'

'What do you do in London?'

'I go to concerts, I'm very fond of music. Also to the play as much as I can. Exhibitions. All the kind of thing one doesn't get in the country.'

Dinner was announced, Vee was sitting some way away from her new acquaintance, and she promptly forgot all about him, content to eat the sumptuous meal the Oronsays always provided and make small talk with her neighbours, a retired admiral, full of nautical bonhomie, and a poet who only wanted to talk about himself.

Afterwards, when the men joined the ladies in the drawing room, Piers Forster came over to her, and they talked about modern French writers, just the distraction Vee needed so that she didn't have to think about Claudia's bored, unhappy face.

Her cousin was sitting on one of the great brocade sofas, twiddling with a piece of tassel and returning monosyllabic answers to the man beside her. Petrus hadn't appeared. Vee had overheard Claudia asking Ruth Oronsay about him and being told that he had been due to come, but some pressure of work had kept him in Oxford.

'Such a busy man, I hardly know how he finds time to attend any social functions, but he does. They say he's going to get married soon, have you heard?'

Claudia went pale. 'Married? Who to?'

The man beside her broke into the conversation, glad to have something to say. 'No, no, Ruth. It's Lily Petrus who's getting engaged, not her brother.'

'Lily? Oh, that ethereal creature, one doesn't see much of her in town. Who's she marrying?'

'Prince something *von und zu* something. I don't remember his name.'

Ruth Oronsay put her head on one side. 'A German.'

'A Prussian, I believe. Petrus knows a lot of Germans, he's doing very sound work over there, he's regarded as the man on their economy, you know.'

'I don't care for modern Germany,' said Ruth Oronsay, and went to join another group of her guests.

Claudia's face was alight with relief. Vee saw her say something to her neighbour in a low voice; he looked over to Ruth Oronsay, and laughed.

Claudia was going too far with her Mosleyites and anti-Semitism. And she should keep her opinions to herself, here of all places.

Vee said as much, in the taxi going home.

'I don't give a fig about Ruth, she's so rich she doesn't need me to like her. I only go because Iain's such an old friend, I can't think why he married her. Well, I can, for her money of course.'

'It seems to me that he's devoted to her.'

'Do you think so? Petrus thinks very highly of Iain, but he never talks much about Ruth. All the rich Jews are taking over everything, even our old families. It's appalling. I saw you flirting with Piers, what a stuffed shirt he is. I didn't know he was back in England. What did you talk about? I always find him dreadfully stiff, and he thinks I'm a fool.'

'Cocteau,' she said. 'And Picasso.'

'Oh, Lord, Vee, how too shatteringly dismal. You'll fulfil your mother's worst fears if you talk about French books and art in London drawing rooms, and never get a husband. You'd better marry Piers, he's very well off and has a lovely house, Kent, I think. Then you can talk French culture all day long.'

Vee wasn't amused. 'I'm not marrying anyone, least of all a man I met five minutes ago. I have other things going on in my life, remember, like getting my degree.'

The next day a dozen roses arrived, together with a courteous note from Piers, inviting Vee to the theatre.

'Told you so,' said Claudia, admiring the flowers. 'Mummy, Vee's made a new conquest.'

Aunt Lettice told Claudia not to be so vulgar and asked who had sent the roses. 'Piers Forster? How very nice. That man has the most perfect manners of anyone I know. You could do worse, Vee, my dear.'

'I hardly know him. But the roses are lovely.'

TWO

Alfred turned out to know Piers quite well. 'He's quite sound,' he said tolerantly. 'He'll never set the world on fire, but his heart's in the right place and he treats his tenants uncommonly well. He's been involved in social housing, done a lot of good work locally, I gather.'

'So he won't be a candidate for the lamppost come the revolution?'

'Oh, he'll have to go, along with the rest of them. Being kind to a few families doesn't take away the fact that your ancestors have been busy grinding the faces of the poor for the last few centuries.'

'I'm going to the play with him.'

'You'll enjoy that, he's good company, if a trifle dry.'

For a moment, Vee wanted to lash out at Alfred. He'd never invited her to the theatre or to anything except meetings, or a cup of coffee after an exhausting afternoon's work stuffing pamphlets into envelopes or, even worse and more exhausting, helping another girl deliver the envelopes.

'Saves on postage,' they said in the office. 'They're grouped into areas, so it isn't too much walking.'

Walking, she noticed, like so many of the more repetitive and boring tasks, was women's work.

She went to the theatre, to see *Pygmalion*, an unusual choice, and she told Piers so.

'Did you want to go and see the latest drawing-room comedy?'

'Not at all. This was much more interesting.'

'Perhaps you would like to go to some Shakespeare.'

After that, he drifted in and out of her life, inviting her to hear a concert given at the Queen's Hall, or a play, and even coming to

Oxford, to take her and Lally, a keen Shakespearian, to the new theatre at Stratford-upon-Avon.

He was restful company, without being dull. Lally liked him, and she was a good judge of people. Sound was the word Alfred had used, and yes, he was sound. There was nothing extreme about him, but he didn't think or talk in clichés. He was very grown up, Vee concluded, no older than many other of her friends and acquaintances, but just grown up.

They dined in good restaurants, never anywhere wildly fashionable, but places where the food was excellent and the surroundings comfortable and conducive to conversation.

In April, he invited Claudia and Vee down to his house in the country for a Friday to Monday.

'He's joking, of course,' Claudia said, tossing the invitation into the waste-paper basket. 'He loathes me, we're absolute deadlies, and why would I want to go and yawn my way through a weekend in the depths of nowhere?'

Unexpectedly, Aunt Lettice and Uncle Vernon put their respective feet down.

'Vee will be glad of your company,' said Aunt Lettice, who was feeling very hopeful about Piers, or so Claudia said, and she had written a guarded letter to York about him. 'If only Claudia could find a more promising suitor than Geoffrey Goodwin,' she said to Vee. 'I don't think he's the sort to make her a good husband, he isn't lively enough for her.'

Vee was embarrassed, she hated to deceive her aunt, but she knew perfectly well that there was no question of Claudia and Geoffrey getting married. Geoffrey wasn't the marrying sort, like Giles, and Claudia had taken him on as escort to distract attention from her affair with Petrus. For his part, it did his reputation good to be seen around with the dashing Lady Claudia.

'We can't marry while we're at Oxford, the college won't allow it,' Vee said. That had the virtue of truth, even if it evaded the issue.

'Oh, as for that ... Look at that slip of a girl, Lily Petrus, in *Country Life* this week, looking far too fragile to carry the immense name that will be hers once she's married.'

'You're to go,' Claudia's stepfather said to her. 'I don't want to hear another word. Do you good to get out of London. You're looking peaky, you'll benefit from country air, and Forster's got a nice place there. Ask him to invite that Goodwin fellow for you. And let's not hear any more about Lily whatshername, please, Lettice. I wouldn't let you marry a man like that, Claudia, he's the sort we fought the last war against.'

Claudia opened her mouth to make a hot reply, but Vee's frantic gestures and the warning look in her mother's eye stopped her, and she shrugged. 'I dare say Lily fell in love with him, that can happen to anyone. He's a friend of her brother's, Petrus has known him for ever.'

'And that's another man I'd rather you didn't see too much of,' said Vernon as he headed back into his study. 'He's causing quite a stir in the Foreign Office, far too friendly with some very undesirable people.' The study door closed with a click, and Claudia pulled a face.

'Darling,' said Aunt Lettice. 'There's no need for that, and Vernon's perfectly right. John Petrus isn't quite the thing, and he's not suitable company for a girl like you.'

'Oh, Mummy, how you do grind on. When did I last see him? Ages ago, do stop fretting. He's just a friend, that's all, I am allowed to choose my own friends, I suppose.'

'Lord, now look what I've let myself in for,' said Claudia, drifting into her room at bedtime. 'Have you got a cigarette? It's all your fault; a whole weekend in Geoffrey's company. He'll love it, just his idea of a good time. Still, I might as well accept, I suppose. I can always tease your swain.'

Alberry Manor, with its riot of red-brick chimneys, knot garden and acres of rolling park was the essence of Englishness. 'God, right out in the middle of nowhere,' sighed Claudia, looking discontentedly out of the window as the car rolled up the long drive. She stubbed out her cigarette in the ashtray and drew her fox more closely around her neck. 'Freezing bedrooms and miles of echoing corridors and family retainers who've been here since Capability Brown did the grounds and planted those endless trees he was so fond of.'

'Ghosts, maybe,' Vee said.

'Oh, spare me the ghosts.'

The motor car drew to a halt, and Piers's chauffeur was round and opening the rear door. Claudia climbed out and sniffed the fragrant, rich country air. 'Fresh air, how I hate it. Do look at the butler, what a gem, he's as wide as he's high.'

Certainly the butler was portly, but then so was Mrs Longthorpe, Piers's aunt, who came tripping out to meet them. They had travelled down from London by train, and Piers's car had met them at the tiny, perfect station, picture-book rural England with the spring sun slanting across the platform, birds singing in the rose bushes and a window box gay with daffodils.

'I do wish Vernon would let me buy a car of my own,' Claudia grumbled as they found an empty first-class compartment. 'He says I don't need one while I'm at Oxford, but it's such a bore dragging down to the country by train.'

'You could have driven with Geoffrey.'

'He won't be down until late, and I hate arriving late, one's whisked into dinner without having a chance to see who's there and what kind of a grim weekend one's let oneself in for.'

Claudia certainly hadn't expected any Mrs Longthorpe to be part of the scenery.

'I do believe she's an ex-gaiety girl or something like that, I'm sure I remember hearing there was a bit of a scandal in that generation.'

'I thought gaiety girls had to be six foot tall and aloof,' Vee whispered back, as Piers came into the hall to greet them.

'Chorus, then.'

'She looks very jolly.'

And jolly she was, eccentrically dressed and full of pep and good humour. She was also a wonderful hostess, as they discovered when the maid led them to the room they were sharing.

'Central heating, what bliss,' Claudia said. 'And our own bathroom. One up to Piers.'

'Not so cold and grim after all, then.' Vee kicked off her shoes and flopped down on the bed. 'Lovely mattress, too.'

'We can't spend the weekend lurking in the bedroom, unfortunately; the company will be grim and cold to make-up for the creature comforts, just you wait and see.'

The mellow house wrapped itself around Vee. Piers wanted to show her every nook and cranny: the library with its dark shelves and worn oak floors, gold shining through black, a fire in the wide fireplace, the smell of old leather and paper. His desk, papers neat, a silver inkstand, a chair that creaked as she sat in it and twirled round. The orangery, with citrus trees in large terracotta pots, and a strangely peaceful room that had once been a chapel and was now a small dining room. The offices downstairs, the still room, the laundry, the stables, where an Arab mare put her head over the stall and turned lustrous eyes on her.

'You don't ride, do you?'

'I can ride, but I tend to fall off, so no, I'm not a great rider.'

'She'd carry you and never put a foot wrong.'

Vee forbore from remarking that it was she, not the horses, who had a tendency to put a foot wrong.

The stable had a clock on a tower, and cobbles smooth with age. A spaniel was slumbering against the wall; he woke and ambled towards Piers, wagging a stubby tail.

Vee was surprised. For all his talk of the country, and Uncle Vernon's approving remarks about his estates, the Piers she knew was essentially a townee, a London man, who belonged to clubs and dined and danced and went to the theatre and opera. Here he was more relaxed, his monocle hung from its ribbon, unused, the well-cut tweeds suited him. There was an aura of kindness about him that was unusual in a man.

He led her across a courtyard and into the evening shadows of the orchard.

'I want to show you the view from here as the sun sets. It catches on the hills over there, and is reflected in the river. Do you see?'

They stood in silence, watching the majestic red sun sink down behind the hill, as the dark greys and purples of twilight crept over the landscape, until it grew too cold to be outside, and Piers pushed open an arched oak doorway that led into a stone-flagged passage at the rear of the house.

'What a wonderful house,' Vee said to Claudia when they gathered for tea. Claudia flipped a long tail of ash from her cigarette into the ashtray just before it collapsed.

'If you're taken with old England. I can't say I am. Too far from London, and such hordes of servants, never a moment to oneself in a place like this, every time you turn a corner there's a maid or a footman. I hope there are cucumber sandwiches for tea, that's all.' Claudia adored cucumber sandwiches, and was a connoisseur of the precise thickness of the bread, the right amount of butter, the perfection of the slices of the cucumber itself.

The arrival of the butler and panoply of the tea trays and all the accompanying ceremony with, indeed, cucumber sandwiches, brought a momentary look of pleasure to Claudia's fretful face. 'Good ones, too,' she said, appropriating the plate, despite the butler's best efforts to retain it.

That evening, the house party were dining and then going on to a dance at a neighbour's house. The dance was being given for the daughter's birthday, this was her first season and Piers had promised to bring a party.

'A country-house dance, oh Lord, is there anything worse?' said Claudia. 'We'll all freeze for one thing, and there'll be dozens of red-faced squire-types and their indistinguishable wives in ghastly dresses with corsets that creak when they move.'

Claudia was quite, quite wrong. The neighbours' house was a dazzling Palladian mansion, creamy-white in the moonlight, and looking, Vee thought, just as it must have done in Jane Austen's day; she could imagine Mr Darcy and Mr Knightley stepping down from their carriages in knee-breeches or pantaloons, and the Bennet and Bertram daughters arriving in high-waisted dresses with toe-roses on their dancing slippers.

This daughter of the house was an enchanting pixie of a girl, happy with her dance, full of laughter, casting her delight over all the guests.

Vee's spirits rose. The house was warm and filled with flowers, their exotic scent drifting across the ballroom. She felt full of life, ecstatic, plunging again into a fairyland and not allowing the images of a harsher world to intrude and cast their shadow across her mind. She longed to dance, to laugh, to drink champagne and go home with the dawn after hours of pure happiness.

These feelings were unusual with her those days, so much so, that she asked herself, why? Was it Piers? Did she find him more attractive than she admitted to herself? Was she falling in love with him? She caught sight of his elegantly tailored back as he bent over the hand of a rakish-looking woman in her fifties. No, not a frisson. She liked him better than almost anyone she knew, and yet she wasn't in the least bit in love with him.

Claudia came to stand beside her. 'Piers might have said. Look at me in this old silver thing – I hadn't realized it was going to be a proper dance.'

'You look lovely,' Vee said, truthfully. 'And since most of these people will be strangers, I don't suppose they'll recognize the dress.'

'Strangers? Don't be silly, Vee, with it being rather grander than one had been led to believe there'll be a good sprinkling of people from London that one knows. It's too bad.'

The little bunch of people standing in front of them drew apart, and Vee and Claudia caught sight of Petrus at exactly the same moment.

For Vee, it was a shock. She'd managed to avoid meeting Petrus in Oxford, and in a perfect world, she'd be happy never to have to see him again.

Claudia's eyes shone with delight. 'He never told me he would be down in this part of the country,' she said, making her way over to his side of the room with an unobtrusive ease born of much practice. Not even the most censorious dowager could have said that Claudia was making a beeline for that rather strange man, not quite one of us, but very dashing, don't they say he's awfully clever . . .

It was, though, exactly what Claudia was doing, Vee thought. Her cousin drifted into Petrus's view, smiled as though in passing and turned her head to toss a greeting and a radiant smile to a stunned young man who worked for her father.

'I say,' he began, coming to her side, but he was too late. Claudia was floating away in Petrus's arms, waltzing like a princess out of a fairy tale.

'They make a handsome couple,' observed a woman standing behind Vee, who was gazing at Claudia and Petrus through her *faces-à-main*. 'That's Lettice's youngest, don't they say she's turned out rather wild?'

Piers was at Vee's side, offering his arm. She gathered up her skirt, and they moved into the dance.

He was a good dancer, fluid and light on his feet, and there was a strength to his back and a firmness to the arm holding her around the waist, a gentle pressure, none of that grabbing quality of those men who were by nature clutchers and grabbers, on the dance floor or in the back of taxis.

He made a remark about some of the other dancers, a clumsy pair who nonetheless seemed to be having a merry time of it. They looked carefree and very young and happy in a way, Vee realized with a pang, that she rarely was. She glanced at Piers's face as they negotiated a tight corner, then quickly looked away, not liking the warmth in his eyes as he looked down at her.

Could she fall in love with him? Was there any decision about it? Wasn't it meant to be a *coup de foudre*, falling in love, a meeting that blinded you, Cupid's darts finding their mark with appalling accuracy and the flutter of wicked wings as the grinning little god went off to wreak more havoc and make more mischief elsewhere?

No. Consider *Emma*, since she'd been thinking about Jane Austen's characters only a little while ago. All that time in company with Mr Knightley, and how long had it taken her to realize that she was in love with him, and had been so for a good long while?

If you hung about waiting for that blinding moment of attraction, then you might wait for ever.

So could you persuade yourself into love? Or was it just a matter of waiting around, until one day, you understood you couldn't do without the other person, that you had, in fact, found your other self, you were complete?

Nonsense. Look at the couples she knew, how few of them were well matched or happily married. If divorce were easier, she was quite sure that half the marriages in London would have fallen apart within a very few years of the ceremony at St Margaret's – the piles of silver sent by friends and relations tarnishing, as the marriage, too, lost its shine. There was no way she wanted to endure the misery of a yoke that had become intolerable.

The beat of the music had quickened, as it wound up to its final moments. Power, that was what love was about. However kind and loving it all was, being in love gave the person you loved power over you.

Then go for an unequal match, the classic of the one who kisses and the one who turns the cheek. Being the cheek-turner would always give you the advantage, but what was the point?

A trumpet blared out the last thundering chords, and Piers swung her round in a flurry of final intricate steps. It was exhilarating, dancing with such a good partner.

Our styles suit, she said to herself and laughed.

'May I share the joke?' asked Piers, as he led her from the floor and raised a hand to summon a glass of champagne for them both.

'I was thinking about Emma, and I remembered the ball at the Crown, and how Mrs Elton wondered whether her and Frank Churchill's styles would suit.'

'One never found out if they did.'

'No, you're quite right.'

'A perpetual delight, Mrs Elton.' A sip of champagne, and then, 'So, do our styles suit, Verity?' He always called her Verity, never Vee.

'Oh, very well,' she said lightly. 'I have to compliment you on your dancing.'

'The right partner is the key,' he said, but also lightly. Too much sense to press any issue, too well-mannered to take a conversation where she didn't want it to go, at least not now, not here in a crowded room.

The music began again, and to her relief her next partner was at her elbow, a round, jolly young man, not the world's greatest dancer, but a man with a lively sense of humour and a chatty tongue.

Her mind drifted away, losing itself in the movement, the colours, the music, the warmth of the room, the mingled scent of perfume and smoke and perspiration, so distinctively the smell of all the dances she had been to since she left Yorkshire.

'That's the trouble,' the jolly young man was saying. 'Our generation has no commitment to anything. All we want to do is dance and have fun and enjoy ourselves.'

'I dare say our parents were just the same at our age.'

Had her sad, austere father and unhappy mother ever danced, light-footed and -hearted through the nights of their youth? Impossible to imagine, yet they'd been young in the nineties, that decade of frivolity.

'My pa was a terrific goer,' the young man said. 'Judging by the way he carries on when he gets a chance now, that is; you should see him dance the Lancers, none of us younger men can keep up with him. And my ma still does a nifty foxtrot.'

'Maybe they danced the nights away, but they hadn't the sheer hedonism of our lot.'

'Yes, it's a gloomy outlook for us, isn't it? The wolf's at the door for half the population, and the other half is buying little boxes in the suburbs and splashing out on a car and holidays by the seaside, while we, the movers and shakers, dance and drink and drug, if we're that way inclined.'

'Are you?'

'I say, don't look at me like that, it's frightening. No, that's not my thing, as it happens, I've seen what it can do to you, and I like to keep tight hold of my senses. I don't even get drunk these days. I'm hoping to stand at the next election, don't you know, and one needs a clean reputation, otherwise the party gets twitchy.'

'Party?'

'I'm a Liberal, same as my father and grandfather.'

'There you are then, it's not all cocktails and dances. You're embarking on a serious career.'

The dance wound to its end, and he escorted her from the floor. He looked around at the other couples. 'Sometimes, I feel we're skating on ice, all of us. And one day, the weather will change, and through into the dark waters we'll all plunge, all of us, high and low, into a monstrous abyss.'

'We've come out of that, that was the war.'

'The war to end wars. Was it?' Then he gave a rueful laugh. 'God, what a way to talk at a dance. I must be tight, I do apologize, really, how very offensive of me.'

'No,' she said. 'It isn't all glitter and trumpets, is it? Or if it is, at the moment, for some, it won't last.'

Piers found her in the library, turning over the pages of a book in a desultory way.

'No partner?'

'I slipped away for a few minutes.'

'I thought that must be the case. They do throng, rather, your prospective partners. You aren't the wallflower kind.'

Piers closed the door behind him and came over to stand beside her.

'Verity.'

She stiffened. There was something in his voice that told her what was coming, and she didn't want him to say the words.

'I think I'd better go back to the dance,' she said, edging away from the table.

He laid a hand on her arm. 'There is something I want to say.'

It was the proposal she had been expecting and half-fearing. She'd received two proposals before – one of them from a sprig of the aristocracy with a title ancient enough to turn even her grandfather's head – but he wasn't even of age, and had been intoxicated at the time. They'd been standing in the flower market in Covent Garden when he'd poured his undying devotion into her ears; she knew that in that frame of mind, he would have proposed to any woman in a pretty frock who'd been with him.

The second proposal had come from an entirely different quarter, from a friend of her uncle's old enough to be her father, rich, successful and not at all her type, if she had any idea what her type was. She'd turned them both down without a second's hesitation, but now she did hesitate.

Had George been right, out there in the dance? Were there dark and troubled times ahead? Dear God, as if the world weren't troubled enough, outside this bubble of an England that existed only for a handful of its most protected, blinkered and comfortable citizens.

In which case, what peace was left to them might be found here, in the heart of England, in a house that reached back into the centuries, and with a man who loved her and who had a mind and character that she admired, whose company she so much enjoyed.

Love. That was the missing ingredient.

'It would be base coin,' she said.

'What?'

'Anything I have to offer you. I don't want to marry, not you, not anyone. And although I like being with you . . .'

'Like? Is that all?'

She nodded, looking down at the floor to avoid seeing the pain in his eyes.

'Is it a question of getting to know me better?'

'How do I love you, or anyone?' she burst out. 'I don't know how to love, that's all. I'm a feral cat, who wasn't stroked when it was little and so can never come indoors for the petting and strokes and the seat beside the fire.'

She could hear the cry of misery in her words; she knew that Piers could hear the anguish, the confession drawn up from some deep place within her, a pain that made his own bitter disappointment no more than a fleeting twinge.

'Hugh loves you,' he said, after a long silence.

'He doesn't. Hugh and I get on well together, but Hugh loves no one except himself at the moment. And perhaps Giles.'

'You know about Hugh and Giles?'

'Yes.'

'Is that why you think you can't love anyone? Because Hugh's chosen another way of love – because Hugh's attachments are to men? Has this thrown you off your balance?'

He was much too perceptive; it was an insight that struck her with the force of a revelation, but even so, it was only half the story.

192

'Claudia loves you.'

She shook her head. 'Not really. I'm sorry, Piers, it wouldn't work. You deserve better, and I need to wait until something, somehow, changes the way I feel about love.'

'I would never want to put any pressure on you. I hope I haven't caused you distress.'

He was drawing away from her now; she watched him with a kind of hopelessness in her soul. This admirable man, this glowing house, this glimpse of a different life, was vanishing before her eyes.

The gaiety and glow had gone out of the dance. She wouldn't let herself look forlorn, she had a smile on her lips and a brightness in her eyes that would have deceived anyone into thinking she was enjoying herself.

A voice at her shoulder; Christ, the very last person she wanted to hear or see. How dare he force his company on her, when he must know how she felt about him?

'Hello, Petrus,' she said, wanting to scream, Go away, don't come near me, I really would much rather never have to see or speak to you again.

And there, radiant suddenly, her discretion shed, how she did give herself away, was Claudia.

Petrus had no choice, and he led Claudia away into the dance, left Vee cursing inwardly, wanting to be somewhere else.

The daughter of the house drifted by, and paused when she saw Vee. 'Are you all right? Can I get you something?'

Her young voice was concerned.

'I'm fine. Just ricked my ankle and it gave me a twinge, it's all right now.'

The girl looked relieved and murmured her sympathy before moving on to another group of guests.

Did she think she was tight? Vee wondered. She leaned down to rub her ankle, as though this act would give veracity to her quick lie. If only this dance were over, but it would go on for hours yet, and when you came in a party you naturally left in a party. She was a prisoner here until such time as Piers saw fit to gather up his guests and take them back to the manor.

She looked across the floor to where Claudia, a vibrant Claudia, was waltzing with Petrus. He danced like a panther, like a coiled spring about to send him flying God knew where. Claudia was too obvious in her passion for him, why didn't she keep some sense of pride, not let him and everyone in the room see how she felt about him?

As if on cue, a pair circling past made a comment. 'Pretty smitten, isn't she?'

'Old Saxony will have something to say about it, you know how that type feels about their womenfolk. There's a touch of the mystery man about Petrus, he won't do for them.'

'Nonsense, Vernon rates him very highly, says he's extremely able.'

'Able is one thing, having the man for a son-in-law is another.'

'No question of that. Petrus has escaped too many matrimonial nooses to fall victim to the charms of Claudia Vere.'

'I don't know what women see in him, but they fall at his feet in droves.'

'Sex appeal, old thing. What you haven't got.'

'I should hope not, that's best left to film stars and foreigners, if you ask me.'

Another dance, with another man, then supper, taken in by Piers, a formal Piers, who kept giving her sidelong looks, worried looks.

'I've upset you,' he said over the salmon.

'No, you haven't. Lovely food.'

'They always put on a good spread here, they keep a first-class chef. That's what being a tycoon does for you.'

'Is that what Mr Urquhart is?'

'Oh, yes. Armaments, plenty of money in blowing people and things to pieces.'

'You don't approve.'

'Of people blowing other people up? Certainly not. Of an armaments manufacturer? What importance is my approval or disapproval? Since ancient man set to shaping the first arrow, there have been such people. And I've known Urquhart all my life, he was at school with my father.'

'So he's not a self-made man?'

'Good Lord, no. He inherited this house, which was almost in ruins, and an honourable name, and a mountain of debts. His father gambled. And he had a mother and three sisters to support somehow. So he left Cambridge and set out to make money. With spectacular success, as you see. Quite restored the family fortunes.'

194

After supper, yet another tune, another partner, another dance. Then a pause, a gap in her partners, the name on her card nowhere to be seen. 'Throwing up in the downstairs lav,' Claudia said. 'Did you see him drinking at supper? He won't be asked again, Urquhart can't stand young men who can't hold their drink.'

In which case, perhaps he should be less liberal with the champagne. Still, Vee was glad to sit the dance out, to slide into a seat in the shadows, and have time to draw breath, to think, to restore herself to some sense of equilibrium.

'No partner?' The voice was mocking. 'My dear Vee, now you really must dance with me.'

Petrus, standing there, his eyes raking her. She reddened, began a disjointed explanation, her partner would be here any moment, her card was full. Then mercifully, out of nowhere, there was Piers. 'Evening, Petrus,' he said, cool and authoritative. 'Verity, this is my dance, I believe.'

'Thank you for coming to my rescue.'

'You looked like a rabbit caught in headlights. Has Petrus been bothering you?'

'No, no, only – well, to tell you the truth, I can't stand him.'

'Then you are remarkable, most women fall for him. As your cousin has so evidently done.'

'She's a fool to wear her heart on her sleeve.'

'With Petrus it will make no difference. Women who try to play hard to get with him usually end up regretting it. He has a very cruel streak.'

'I don't know him that well.' Did going to bed with a man mean you knew him well? 'But I'm willing to grant you the cruelty.'

'Bit of a Janus.'

'Two-faced, do you mean?'

'Not in the usual meaning of the expression, no. Rather that, like the god of the gateway, he faces in two different directions. Impossible to say which one is which, which is the true Petrus and which isn't.'

She was glad to be talking about Petrus. This friendly and slightly distant Piers was easy to be with, and the man who had so recently told her that he loved her, wished to make her his wife, was somehow only a memory. This was the public Piers, courteous and attentive and amusing, the one she could cope with.

Claudia was still starry-eyed when they arrived back at the manor at half past two the next morning. She kicked off her dancing shoes, pulled up her long skirts, unclipped her suspenders, and pulled off her silk stockings. She rolled them into a ball and tossed them across the room. 'I swear I'll never wear those shoes again, I danced like a baboon in them.'

'Can you undo these hooks for me?' Vee said. 'I didn't notice anything ape-like about your steps.'

'That's because I was dancing on air.'

'With Petrus, you mean?'

'Of course.'

How had it happened, Vee asked herself, as she slid between the cold linen sheets, that Claudia, who had been so secretive about her feelings for Petrus, now broadcast them to the world? Did she think that it might force Petrus's hand? In what sense would she want Petrus's hand forced? Marriage? Claudia had never mentioned marriage. Was she still sleeping with Petrus? If so, how was it that she never seemed to know his movements? She hadn't expected to see him at the dance that evening, and Vee didn't know if Petrus had been surprised to find Claudia there.

As long as she didn't have to see the wretched man again in the near or distant future, let Claudia do what she liked. As she would in any case; Claudia asked for advice from no one, and certainly didn't listen to anything that Vee might have to say on the subject of men.

'Darling Vee, it's no good you preaching or saying anything, because you're so heartless, you just don't understand about love.'

That struck home, more than Claudia could have any idea. Vee switched out the light, to lie miserably until a grey cloud of dawn crept in through the windows, and the thoughts of Piers, of abysses and of Petrus and Claudia finally stopped revolving round and round in her tired mind.

THREE

After that weekend, Vee found herself more than usually glad to see Alfred, even though he was beside himself with rage. 'They're cutting the dole,' he said furiously. 'This bloody bunch are cutting the dole by a quarter – families can't exist on what they're getting now, so let's just chop it, shall we, got to balance the books, got to tighten our belts, the country's in a bad way. Are they closing their doors at the Ritz, or putting up shut signs at Lobb's and Locke's because of belt-tightening among the upper classes?'

Used as she was to Alfred's diatribes, Vee didn't respond, nor did she give him the satisfaction of knowing how ashamed she felt when she read the news in the paper. She couldn't begin to imagine what it would be like to live on so little money, not enough to feed a working man, let alone his family.

And who was one of the people responsible for so much poverty and misery? Her grandfather.

She made herself a vow, she was going to spend less time on her own pleasures, such as painting, and put in more hours for the comrades.

'One thing,' said Alfred. 'This will speed up the revolution. Even the most fearful or passive worker is going to explode with anger now.'

Vee didn't think they had the energy to explode, how could you afford anger when you were half-starved and all you could think about was where the next penny was coming from?

But recruitment to the Party was up, the comrades were busier than ever, and she dutifully spent as much time at the office as she could.

Although, as she addressed another stack of envelopes, she found herself wondering if this was truly the stuff of revolution. Would the equality for all that the revolution would bring mean that women stopped addressing envelopes and rose to higher things?

On the last night of the Easter vac, she and Alfred and several of the comrades had a party to celebrate Alfred's birthday. Alfred was in tearing high spirits, 'This will be the year of my life that counts, this coming year is when I start to live, duckie,' he cried, whirling her round and round in an improvised mazurka.

The comrades, who were not by and large a cheery lot, looked on with expressions of disapproval; they had never really been sure what to make of Vee, she knew that perfectly well.

She got back to Rochester Street late, slipping in so that her uncle and aunt wouldn't question her about why she was wearing her daytime clothes. Claudia was home even later, creeping into Vee's room at five to beg an aspirin.

'I drank far too much, and my head is throbbing,' she said.

Vee looked at her flushed skin and the creamy expression on her face. You've been making love with Petrus, she thought.

'Oh, happy days,' said Claudia. 'And off to Oxford tomorrow, no, it's today, now. Let's hope it's the best term yet, full of excitement and wonderful changes to our lives.'

Claudia had stretched herself out on the sofa. She lit a cigarette and blew lazy smoke rings into the air. 'I'm going to Berlin in July. Do you want to come?'

'Berlin? Whatever for?'

'It's the place to be. Sizzling with excitement and wickedness.'

'I thought that now Herr Hitler had taken over, all the wickedness had vanished into the night.'

'It's the state of the future, and I want to experience it for myself.'

'Are you going with Petrus?'

'I am, as it happens. There's a whole crowd of us going, it's at the invitation of the Anglo-German Friendship League. They're paying fares and hotels, we're guests of the German government.'

Lally, staying at Rochester Street for a few days at the end of the vac, was more forthright than Vee in her condemnation of Claudia's plans. 'Fascism is a deadly creed,' she said. 'If it flourishes, it will destroy Europe. Besides, it isn't Germany that appeals to you, it's Petrus.'

'You've never liked Petrus,' Claudia sounded almost petulant.

'I've never felt the inclination to fall at his feet, no.'

Which didn't mean that Lally couldn't feel the attraction of the man. When he turned his attention on to you, and made you feel interesting and clever, and the only person in the world he wanted to talk to, the effect was devastating.

'I wonder how much you really know that man, Claudia. You, or anyone. Is what we see substance, or merely the glittering persona that he wants us to see?'

'That's the source of his lethal attractiveness,' said Claudia. 'He's an enigma. He knows everything about himself, but doesn't choose to reveal it. Full of hidden depths, which is always fascinating.'

'Or hidden shallows,' said Lally, rather sadly. 'I find him reserved.'

'Vee is reserved, and you don't criticize her for it.'

'Vee is self-contained.'

'And, unlike Petrus, she doesn't go in much for self-examination or self-knowledge, for fear of what she might find.' Claudia stubbed out a half-smoked cigarette, grinding it into the ashtray with sudden violence. 'Vee says I shouldn't go to Berlin with the Friendship League.'

'Vee, unlike you, can see beyond the end of her nose.'

'She's practically a commie, you know that. Desperately concerned for the workers. Surely you hate communism more than fascism?'

'They're two sides of the same coin.'

FOUR

'Why the mystery, Claudia? Why won't you say where we're going?' Vee asked.

'Buck up,' Claudia said. 'Or we'll miss the train.'

They caught it by the skin of their teeth, leaping into a first-class compartment as the whistle went.

'I don't want to go to London,' Vee complained, when she'd recovered her breath. She'd got an essay to write, and a ghastly translation for eleven o'clock the next day. 'It's too bad of you.'

She dug into her overnight case, fumbling beneath the evening dress and shoes to find her Racine and a small dictionary. Bother Claudia for dragging her off like this. She could have refused to go, why hadn't she? Because Claudia in this kind of mood was a force of nature, and it was easier in the end just to do what she wanted. Vee knew that if she hadn't, in the end, agreed, Claudia would have hounded her, hunting her down in her room or the library or wherever she was.

'You're like a terrier. No, like a German Shepherd that won't give up on a single stray lamb.'

'Lamb?' Claudia raised her eyes in mock horror. 'Darling Vee, more like pulling a tiger's tail, getting you to do what you don't want to.'

'If you know I don't want to do it – whatever *it* is – then why make such a thing of it?'

'Because you'll be pleased when we get there.'

'Why today? Why not at the weekend when I shan't have a pile of work to do?'

'Because it's happening today, this evening.'

'What is? Why the mystery? Is it a performance or a party? Why the evening dress?'

That was another thing, they were likely to fall straight into the hands of the proctors when they arrived back on the late train, in evening dress. 'It'll be "Name and college?" before you can say a word.'

'No, it won't. You know they always think anyone glam can't be an undergraduate. Besides, we aren't coming back on the train.'

'Aren't we? Why not? Are we walking?'

'Don't be sarky, Vee, not your style. I've fixed with a chum to drive us back. You can change out of your evening frock in the car, and then nip up over the railings.'

'I've still got a bruise from last time.'

'Be more careful.'

Vee opened her book and smoothed down the page. 'I resent it, Claudia, that's all. Now, shut up, and let me do some work.'

They changed at Rochester Street. 'Where are we going? You have to tell me now,' Vee said, as they got into the taxi.

'Olympia,' Claudia told the driver.

He stared at her. 'You don't want to go there, miss. Not this evening. There's an ugly crowd milling around, Jews and communists, and the police have got barriers up – it's going to get nasty. Does your dad know you're out?'

Normally, such a remark from a taxi driver would have brought out all Claudia's hauteur. Not this evening. Her eyes were shining, and she seemed barely to hear what the driver was saying.

'Claudia . . .' Vee began.

'If you can't get to the entrance, driver, then put us down somewhere nearby.'

Olympia. What was happening in Olympia? Vee hadn't even glanced at a paper that week; she rarely bothered to read the news, it all seemed to come from another place when one was at Oxford, that little bubble of a world. Then she remembered.

Mosley. That was it.

'Claudia, you're not taking me to a fascist rally, are you? I told you I didn't want to go to any of your blasted rallies.'

Alfred was scornful about Claudia's growing enthusiasm for the fascist movement. 'She's no idea what mischief she's getting into. Playing with fire is what she's doing, and there'll be hell to pay if your college find out about her going to rallies.'

'She keeps it quiet. She's sworn me to secrecy; never mind Grace, she says her stepfather would be furious if he knew.'

'I'd have thought old Saxony was a bit that way himself, he's very anti-red, and for a man of his class, that's tending more and more to mean pro-fascist – the lesser of two evils.'

'He loathes the Bolshies, but he disapproves of Mosley. Says he's a demagogue, and a lost man.'

'Why does she go? For the phony glamour of the Blackshirts and the stirring speeches? I'd have thought she'd see through all that.'

'She's rather keen on all things German just now.'

'Petrus?' said Alfred, spitting the name out and making Vee jump. 'Do you think that's it?'

'Of course it is. Be your age, Vee. You've seen her when he's with her, or even in the same room. She glows. She's got it quite badly I'd say, what a pest the man is with all his charm and sex appeal.'

'Sex appeal?'

'Women go for him in a big way, haven't you felt it yourself?'

She felt herself redden. 'No, I haven't, actually.'

Dear God, what would Alfred think of her if he knew? 'I rather dislike him, actually. He's arrogant and I don't like his politics.'

Alfred's mind was back on the fascists. 'They're doing a lot of harm, he's gathered a pack of vicious thugs around himself. I wouldn't go with Claudia, Vee, those meetings can get very rough.'

She looked at the bruise fading on Alfred's cheek. 'You went to one,' she said, suddenly enlightened. 'That's where you got all those bruises.'

'There was a bit of a dust-up,' he admitted. 'He sets his bully boys on to anyone who heckles or challenges him.'

'I'd like to see for myself.'

'I can't stop you, duckie, but you'll hate it, that's all. You don't need to go and hear that man in person to understand what's wrong with fascism, you know that already.'

Which she did.

Claudia had become more and more passionate about the British Union of Fascists, going off to every rally she could get to, more than once coming back hoarse with shouting abuse at the communists and socialists who always turned out on such occasions. Vee refused to listen to her ecstatic accounts of what had happened, and what Mosley had said, and she flatly refused to go to the rallies with her.

Claudia had duped her, with the evening clothes. Whoever heard of a political rally that you needed evening dress for?

Claudia was triumphant. 'You see, if I'd told you, you'd never have come. Now you have, and you'll be amazed.'

'I don't hold with men dressing up in black,' said the driver, who had left the glass partition drawn back. 'Not but what this Mosley bloke hasn't got some sense in what he says, the government's ruining this country, and something ought to be done about it. At least Sir Oswald Toffeenose cares about the working man and keeping him in a job and off the dole.'

Vee folded her arms, wondering if she could stop the cab and jump out. 'Will Petrus be there?' she asked. She blamed Petrus for this whole fascist obsession of Claudia's. He'd filled her with enthusiasm for the movement, and then slid away to calmer political waters.

For a moment the glow in Claudia's eyes faded. 'No. I wanted him to come with us, but he's got some do on in Oxford, couldn't get away. He knows Mosley, of course. Goodness, there is rather a crowd. Driver, drop us off here?'

Not in Vee's wildest imaginings could she have foreseen what it would be like. Large, shiny motor cars were drawing up in front of the huge exhibition centre, chauffeurs jumping out to open doors for men and women in evening dress, the women even wearing jewels. Jewels? For a public meeting?

'This isn't your ordinary kind of politics,' Claudia said, with pride. 'This is all about vision, and a new order.'

Vee turned to look at the angry crowd, held back by the police and barriers.

'Who are these people?' she asked Claudia, but Claudia wasn't listening.

'Mob from the East End,' said a man standing beside her. 'Jews and communists, mostly, kicking up a stink. Mosley knows how to deal with them.'

'What's that they're chanting?' Vee asked, straining to catch the words above the shouts and yells.

'Hitler and Mosley, what are they for?
Thuggery, buggery, hunger and war.'

In a momentary lull, the words came clearly across, followed by

203

an outburst of jeering from the Mosleyites who were now swarming around, and chanting their own slogans.

The man beside her made a tut-tutting noise, and urged them to go inside. 'Appalling display, gross language with women present,' he muttered to himself.

They went in, and Vee caught her breath at the sight of the great banners streaming down from the high roof girders, each adorned with a lightning flash. Scores of tough young men, in black uniforms, hair sleeked down, stood to attention, forming a kind of honour guard through which people entered the hall itself.

It was a blaze of light and colour. Loudspeakers were pumping out some tremendous tune, music with a dynamism that sent her pulse racing despite herself. There was a buzz of conversation in the hall, as friends greeted one another; exactly like a night at the opera, she thought, as a stiff young man with a pencil moustache showed them where to sit. 'Go right along,' he advised. 'You'll keep clear of any trouble there.'

'Trouble?'

'Oh, there are always some hecklers,' said Claudia airily. 'Don't worry, Tom's men know exactly how to deal with them.'

'What time does it begin?' Vee asked. The hall was full, there must be thousands of people there. Some of them surprising: she recognized several MPs, and members of the House of Lords. Alfred had told her that Mosley's followers were young men without jobs, and shopkeepers, small tradespeople, the lower classes who felt hard done by. Judging by the people there that night, it looked as though the upper classes were just as keen on the fascist message. There was a mood of expectation, but time went by, and nothing happened. The doors had been closed, shutting out the muted sounds of the crowd outside. More music blared forth.

'He always keeps people waiting,' Claudia whispered. 'It raises the tension.'

It didn't in Vee's case. The music was beginning to irritate her, and she suspected it was having the same effect on other people in the audience, who were shifting in their seats and starting to look restless. The volume of voices grew louder.

Then, as though a whip had been cracked, the men lining the aisle snapped to attention. The doors at the rear of the arena flew open. Heads turned, people stood up to get a better look.

It was operatic, Wagnerian, and, to Vee, terrifying. She pressed back into her seat as if that would protect her from the rhythmic stamp, stamp of soldiers, banging their black boots down with every juddering step. The wave of black passed by the end of their row. The brilliant glare of the spotlights swept over her and Claudia as the beams followed the faithful on their march to the rostrum. The men were larger, glossier, nastier than the ones outside; these were an elite corps, repulsively masculine, cocky and blank-faced as they held aloft Union Jacks and the fascist flag.

A roar was rising – from the crowd? From the Blackshirts? It was difficult to tell. All around her, people were cheering and holding up their arms in the fascist salute. Claudia was bellowing in her ear, shouting Mosley, Mosley, at the top of her voice and punching the air in a kind of ecstasy.

Were these people all mad?

Here, striding along behind the Blackshirts, throwing his legs out in a peculiar way, was the tall, elegant figure of Mosley himself. Then he was through and standing at the rostrum, giving the salute and raising his fists to greet the crowd of enthusiastic supporters.

A gesture, and the din died away. His opening words were a call for an orderly meeting, and at once all hell broke loose. People were shouting from all over the arena, and these weren't shouts of enthusiasm.

'Commie troublemakers,' hissed Claudia. 'Why can't they shut up or drop dead or something and let him speak?'

A scuffle was going on behind them, and Vee turned round to see what was going on. Two Blackshirts had pounced on a man in a shabby mac and were hauling him out of the row. His hand swung round and he lashed out; blood streamed from the cheek of one of the fascists, who staggered back. The spotlights moved from the rostrum and swivelled across the hall to illuminate the scene as the other Blackshirt wrestled the man to the floor and gave him a savage kick in his back.

The violence shocked Vee to the core. She had never in all her life experienced anything like this. 'They're going to kill him,' she shrieked at Claudia.

'Good thing too, he had a razor, did you see? They don't come to listen to Mosley; they just come to make trouble. They call it heckling and free speech, but they bring razors and knuckle-dusters, they're hoodlums.'

Order was restored. Vee could smell the rank scent of sweat and fear and excitement. She took out a handkerchief and pressed it to her mouth. 'I think I'm going to be sick,' she said, when Claudia nudged her.

'Of course you aren't. Listen to Mosley, that'll set you up. Come on, Vee, that's what we're here for.'

It was a nightmare. Every time anyone in the audience interrupted, the spotlight was there, and so were Mosley's men, grinning and demoniac, wielding coshes and kicking with those gruesome boots. A woman was jostled and dragged yelling to the door, a weedy man with dark eyes huge in his pale face had his trousers torn off and held aloft before he was hurled out.

'I've got to get out of here,' Vee said, half out of her seat.

'Don't be stupid, sit down,' said Claudia, hauling her back. 'If you try that, they'll be on to you.'

Vee's dreams that night were filled with the sounds of stamping boots, of bright lights and shouting voices and the screams of the woman who had hurled herself against Mosley's thugs when they began to kick her companion.

'Why didn't the police stop them?' she asked Alfred.

'The police were ordered not to interfere,' he said.

She'd bumped into him as he came out of Schools, looking remarkably kempt in his subfuscs, which suited his tall figure. He was in the throes of his finals, about which he was very relaxed. 'Doesn't make any difference to me what class I get, since I'm going to be a writer,' he said dismissively. 'And, frankly, I'm bored with most of what I've had to write about, it's all so far removed from reality that one can't be bothered to take it seriously.'

Vee was shocked; most of the women undergraduates had a strain of earnestness in their attitude to work, instilled in them by the college and the women who taught them.

'And bear in mind, Vee,' Alfred said, taking off his mortar board and banging it against his leg, 'that the Mosley movement is but a pale imitation of what's happening in Germany. A few thousand turn up for the BUF; tens of thousands go to hear Hitler ranting and raging. Mosley's a good orator, of course he is, or he wouldn't have done as well as he has. But Hitler is in another class altogether when it comes to whipping up mass hysteria.'

As Vee packed her trunk, she felt a sadness about going down. The Trinity term had ended on an uneasy note, far removed from the happiness of her mood at the beginning of the summer. Hugh and Alfred and Giles were going down at the end of their final year; it would all be very different when she came up in October for the start of her last year at Oxford.

FIVE

Claudia was looking pale. In fact, she'd been looking pale for a few days, now Vee came to think about it.

Vee dug the little silver spoon into the jar of Cooper's marmalade and put a heap on her plate. 'Are you feeling all right, Claudia? You look as though you're going down with a cold.'

Her eyes were rather red, as well – had she been crying?

Unlikely. Claudia never cried.

'Hayfever, that's all,' said Claudia.

In September? That didn't seem very likely, either.

'Actually, there is a thing . . .' Claudia's voice trailed off. 'I've got to go into a clinic,' she went on, speaking in a quick, brittle tone, not at all her normal voice. 'For a minor op.'

'Oh, Claudia, what's wrong? Is it tonsils? I had mine out on the kitchen table when I was seven, it was ghastly.'

Claudia shook her head. 'No, I had my tonsils out ages ago. It's just that my monthlies are very heavy, and so they want to do something to sort it out, that's all.'

That explained the pallor. Only why did Claudia, who took everything in her stride, seem so tense about this?

'Is it painful? Do you have to stay in the clinic for long?'

'A day or two,' said Claudia. She got up from the table and wandered restlessly around the room. She took up *The Times*, glancing at the notices, then put it down again. She picked up a knife and turned it over and over in her hands.

'It's a pity you have to have this done now, when Aunt Lettice and Uncle Vernon are abroad.'

Claudia shrugged. 'The doctor wants to get it done quickly. So that it's all over with by the time term starts. I thought it best not to wait. Only, the thing is – would you come with me, to the clinic? I'd like to have a friend. I'd ask Lally, you know how calm and comforting she is, but she left yesterday for Scotland, the American ambassador's taken a house on the moors, and her father says she has to go. So . . .'

Vee knew that Lally would be a much better choice for anyone who wanted reassurance or hand-holding; in fact she was surprised that Claudia had mentioned it to her at all. She wasn't, she felt, really much good at sympathy.

'Of course I'll come with you. When are you going in?'

'Later this morning.'

'Does Bowler know? Has she packed a bag for you?'

'Actually, I've given Bowler a holiday. I thought she'd like to spend a few days at the seaside. Her sister runs a bed and breakfast establishment at Bognor, and she likes to go there and help.'

Which was rather odd, Vee thought, as she polished off the last of her toast. Claudia, she noticed, hadn't eaten any breakfast.

'Shouldn't you have something to eat? Shall I ring for more coffee?'

'I have to fast. Because of the anaesthetic. Otherwise you choke on your vomit.'

'Oh,' Vee said. She wasn't very up on medical procedures, the tonsils operation being her one experience of surgery, and that one she'd rather forget. Her mother took a ghoulish interest in medical matters, and for that reason alone, Vee had always declined to take any interest in the subject, refusing to listen when her mother and her friends discussed an operation that a cousin or an aunt had had, or avidly recounted details of some medical disaster reported in the seedier newspapers; one of which was taken at the Deanery 'for the servants', but which always found its way to her mother's room.

'I'll come and help you pack,' she offered.

Claudia seemed uncertain what she'd need. She had a large suitcase open on her bed.

Vee looked at it doubtfully. 'You're not going to a country house. It'll be more like your overnight case for going back to school, I should think. Pyjamas, dressing gown, slippers, clean underwear, sponge bag.'

'I suppose so,' said Claudia, without enthusiasm.

Claudia was either feeling unwell, or was more nervous about going in to the clinic than she was letting on. It wasn't like her to be so down in the mouth. Vee rang for a footman to take the suitcase downstairs.

'Have you told Jenks you want him?'

'I shall take a taxi,' Claudia said. She took a deep breath. 'Come on, let's get this over with.'

The clinic was in a semi-fashionable part of town, in a street of anonymous terraced houses, each with a set of black railings in front. The taxi rumbled away, and they went up the shallow steps to the black-painted front door. A small brass plaque beneath the bell had 'The Gingell Clinic' engraved on it.

Claudia hesitated, so Vee she reached out and pulled the bell. They could hear it clanging inside, and seconds later, the door was opened by a wary-looking maid in a smart uniform.

'Miss Maxwell,' Claudia said.

Before Vee could say anything, they were inside, and walking down the narrow hall to an inner lobby, where a woman with tight grey curls sat behind a desk. There was an appointment book spread open in front of her.

'Miss Maxwell?' she said. There was no welcoming smile on her tightly-compressed lips. 'Jane Maxwell?'

'Yes,' said Claudia, giving Vee a quelling look.

'For a D and C. Very well. Maria will show you to your room. Is this a relation?'

She looked at Vee as though she were some reptilian form of life.

'Cousin,' Vee said, and picked up the suitcase. 'Which way?'

'I'm afraid visitors are not allowed at this time of day.'

'I'm not a visitor, I've come to help La ... my cousin get settled in and make sure she has everything she needs.'

Vee's cool determination, which surprised her as much as it surprised Claudia, won the day, and the maid led them to a small lift at the back of the house. They got in, while the maid pulled the grille across with a clang and told them that another maid would be waiting for them on the third floor.

'I hate the smell of these places,' said Claudia. 'Disinfectant and disgusting floor polish.'

'Why the false name?' Vee asked.

Claudia looked disconcerted. 'Oh, I don't want the press to find out I'm in a clinic, you know the kind of headline they love: "Peer's sister unwell", and hints that I'm in to have my stomach pumped out for drugs.'

'You don't drug,' Vee pointed out.

'No, of course not, but you know what those ghastly newshounds are like, and it's a quiet time of year, anything will do to fill a few columns. These places all have staff who pass titbits on to the press, when anyone famous or grand comes in. Everyone who has any sense uses an incognito.'

'Your doctor must know who you are.'

'Well, of course, but he's the one who suggested I use another name.'

'Dr Fowler said that?' Vee had encountered the Vere family physician when she'd had a bout of gastric flu, and a more correct, po-faced man it would be difficult to imagine.

Claudia avoided her eye. 'I don't go to Dr Fowler any more, he's so pompous, and he'd go straight to Mummy if there were anything wrong with me. I don't want her to worry and make a fuss about it. Now I'm twenty-one, she doesn't have to sign anything, so it's much less trouble this way. Do drop it, Vee. I'm very grateful for your coming and all that, but I shan't be if you're going to cross-examine me.'

The room they were shown into was pleasant enough, for a nursing home, with flowers on the dressing table. 'And this is your private bathroom,' the maid said, crossing the room and opening the door to a display of gleaming tiles. 'Sister will be along in five minutes, so please can you undress and get into bed.'

She gave Vee a meaningful look, and went out of the room.

'My cue to exit, I think,' Vee said. On an impulse, she gave Claudia a hug. 'Don't worry. It'll soon be over.'

'Yes, it will,' said Claudia in rather a desolate tone.

There were tears in her eyes, Vee noticed; it wasn't at all like Claudia to be emotional about a practical matter. Still, if she weren't feeling well, it would account for it. She'd be back in her usual bounding health and buoyancy as soon as this was over. It must just be that she was, in fact, afraid of the operation.

'When will you be out of here?'

'I'll telephone and let you know.'

'Yes, do, and I'll come and carry you away back to normality in a taxi. We'll have lunch somewhere nice, to celebrate it being over, as soon as you're feeling fit again.'

'To celebrate? Yes,' said Claudia.

It was odd, Vee reflected as she walked down the street. A taxi came past, with its flag up, slowing down as it drew level with her, but she shook her head; she wanted to walk. She needed to clear her head, and indeed to stretch her legs. She had arrived in London only a few days before, after spending a dutiful week in York on her return from France.

London had cast off its August dullness, and the pleasing appearance of a new season was in the air. Leaves were beginning to turn yellow and red. A crocodile of little girls in grey coats and pudding-basin hats went past, all with the shiny look of new clothes for a new school year. The mistress in charge, an energetic young woman in a brown tweed cape had a spring in her step. A footman was walking a dachshund, loitering at the corner and taking the opportunity to have a quick cigarette.

Vee turned into Wigmore Street, where the traffic was busier, and felt her spirits lift at the energy and bustle about her. She loved being in France, for its very tranquillity and the long sleepy hours of a French summer, but she was glad now to be back in London where everything was sharply alive.

Claudia hadn't looked as though she were welcoming a new season. Vee had never seen her cousin look so flat and out of sorts. Might she be really ill? No, it was more oppression of spirits, rather than anything physical. That was unusual for Claudia. And another thing, her cousin hadn't mentioned Petrus once since Vee arrived back in London. The last time Vee came back after being away, Claudia had been full of the wretched man.

Had they fallen out? Split up, as it were, although she wasn't sure how much of a couple they had ever been? Claudia had attached herself to Petrus, that was evident to everyone, but how much of an attachment was it on Petrus's side?

Not much, in Vee's opinion. He liked being seen around with Lady Claudia Vere, that was obvious, but he never took any trouble to seek her out, it was always Claudia who made the running. And Hugh had said that he'd seen Petrus more than once dining in London restaurants, accompanied by a chic dark woman with a foreign accent, and had seen him at a dance paying a great deal of attention to one of London's more fashionable hostesses.

'Claudia's too young for him,' was his opinion. 'He prefers them older and more sophisticated.'

Claudia wouldn't have liked to hear that; Claudia thought of herself as being very sophisticated. Compared to their Oxford contemporaries, she was. Compared to those who moved in Cousin Mildred's circle, she most certainly wasn't. Although she might be, one day when she was older and a married woman.

Was Petrus the marrying kind? Vee doubted it. So much depended on whom someone like Claudia married. One of her brother's kind, and she'd spend her days in some vast pile in the country, growing ever more tweedy and disinclined to come up to town except for hasty shopping sorties. The backbone of England, but would Claudia turn into a dowdy countrywoman? She might marry a fascinating foreigner; Claudia had been very full of some of the dashing Germans she had met in Berlin. That would be an entirely different kind of life – although Vee had a suspicion that the dashing German in Berlin would turn into a formidably dull husband, quite happy for his wife to spend her days at the German country estate. Substitute wild boars for foxes, and life might be very much the same for the Gräfin as it was for the English countess.

Or Claudia might marry an academic, not the glamorous sort, like Petrus, but a more ordinary, less exotic don, with a life in the suburbs of Oxford or Cambridge as her lot. That wasn't a likely future for Lady Claudia Vere, but who could tell?

What of her own future? Vee didn't care to think about that. She would finish at Oxford, and, she supposed, find herself a job of some kind. What kind? She didn't want to teach, and couldn't see herself taking a secretarial job. Time enough to worry about that after her finals, she told herself. Something would come up.

Vee crossed Oxford Street, weaving her way through the cars and omnibuses and finding the lunchtime crowds as much of a challenge as the vehicles. Then into the calmer waters of Bond Street, where there were fewer pedestrians, and those she saw looked quite different from the harassed and cheaply if smartly dressed people in Oxford Street. Here men and women strolled, no cramming in shopping during a lunch hour for them. The women wore autumn outfits and suave velvet hats, and the men well-cut suits.

She idly watched an elegant pair gazing in the window of a jewellers sparkling with brilliants set against a background of black velvet. Were they in love? Engaged? Married, and choosing an anniversary present? They looked happy in one another's company.

For a moment, Vee envied them. Then she shrugged, and quickened her pace. She walked halfway down Bond Street, and on into the heart of fashionable London, through the alley that was the shortcut into Rochester Street.

Where she found Alfred lounging against a lamppost, completely at home, apparently talking to the large ginger cat that lived in the kitchen at number eighteen.

'Hello, Alfred, what are you doing here?'

'I was passing by and thought I'd call in and invite you to lunch at Lyons Corner House. Have you been yet? Fantastic place, worth taking in before it's swept away with all the rest of bourgeois London. I gather from the butler that no one is at home. Is that true, or merely a delightfully Jane Austen way of saying that I'm not a welcome visitor?'

'It's perfectly true, as it happens,' she said. 'And I'd love to come to the Corner House with you, I'm starving. Aunt Lettice and Uncle Vernon are away in Switzerland; the mountains are necessary for Uncle Vernon's lungs, apparently. He was gassed in the war, did you know that?'

'I can't imagine anyone having the temerity to gas old Vernon,' said Alfred. 'Of course, war is a great leveller.'

'Like the revolution. Won't the comrades be allowed to eat at Lyons Corner House?'

'Unfortunately not. Workers co-operative cafeterias will be the order of the day.'

'It does sound a bit dismal. Are we walking to the Corner House?'

'Of course, I'm not one of your capitalists, leaping into taxis at the drop of a hat.'

'I was thinking of taking a bus. I've just walked from the other side of Wigmore Street.'

'Then the short step further to Piccadilly will be as nothing to you. What were you doing in that wasteland of the respectable classes?'

She was about to tell him about Claudia and the clinic, but for some reason she thought better of it. 'Just taking flowers to a friend who's in a nursing home.'

213

'Is Claudia in Switzerland as well?'

'Good heavens, no. She's out of London for a day or two, that's all.'

'And Lally?'

'Scotland.'

'Shooting? Surely not.'

'I don't think actually wielding a gun, but joining a shooting party. Some American friends have taken a moor.'

'That's a relief. I don't care to think of the blissfully beautiful Lally blowing animals to pieces.' Alfred was drawing ahead, as usual; he slowed down to let Vee catch up, then measured his pace to hers. 'After lunch,' said Alfred, with a sidelong glance at her, 'I thought you might care to accompany me to the Party HQ. They're short-handed at the moment. New leaflets to go out, anti-fascist, stirring stuff.'

Not more envelopes. 'Why is it that women's contribution to the revolution and the workers' cause is addressing envelopes?'

'Someone has to do it.'

'Not you, I notice.'

'I shall be attending a committee meeting.'

She had a sudden vision of a future world, a communistic world, where all the women addressed envelopes and all the men spent their days in committee meetings. Who would grow the food or work the machinery or cook the meals? Probably women, in the time they could spare from envelope duties.

'I was thinking about how women's lives change to take on those of their husbands,' she said. 'Whereas men just go on as they are. Your life won't change much, whoever you marry. But Claudia will live one life if she marries a duke and a totally different one if she marries a dustman.'

'Not much chance of that. Anyhow, I thought she had her claws into Petrus.'

'Is Petrus the marrying kind?'

'No, I doubt it. Besides, Vernon wouldn't approve of the connection.'

'Because of his politics?'

'Petrus isn't, at present, sound, in the eyes of the establishment. Too much of a maverick. Too clever, too good with words, too many friends in a surprisingly diverse number of places. However, your premise is correct. Women marry into their husbands' lives, for the most part, unless they choose to spend it teaching mathematics at some girls' school, or to devote themselves to a life of service in a government office. We men make our lives.'

'So much for equality.'

Afterwards, after that day, she was never able to eat steak and kidney pie, which she'd so much enjoyed at the Corner House. She loved the theatrical opulence of the place, and was surprised by how good the food was.

'How can they do it at that price?'

'Ask that waitress how much they pay her. I expect she works six days a week, from eight to six, all for a slave wage.'

'Then why do you come here, if you disapprove so much?' she said, quite crossly. 'Besides, if she didn't work here, she might not earn any money at all, would that be better?'

'Now you sound like your grandfather. Specious logic, my girl.'

She was furious at the reference to her grandfather, and she left the Corner House and walked along beside Alfred in stony silence, tempted to say, Damn the envelopes.

Then Alfred gave her arm a friendly tug, and in a moment, they were running for a bus. They jumped on just as it was pulling away, earning themselves a reproof from the conductor.

'How can we keep to our time if people like you hold the bus up?'

'We didn't,' said Alfred, leading the way up the swaying staircase to the top of the bus. 'We saved you time by leaping aboard when the omnibus was already in motion.'

'Cause an accident, and then there'd be a delay all right,' the conductor said morosely, clipping their tickets. 'Not to mention the danger to life and limb of those passengers who board the vehicle in a proper way.'

'I suppose he'll be on the list come the revolution,' Vee said as the conductor went triumphantly away to harry a flustered woman with several shopping bags.

'Undoubtedly,' said Alfred. 'Move over, Vee, you're taking up far too much room.'

'It's your shoulders that are the problem,'

There was the river, a murky thread stretching into the distance. It was low tide, and the muddy strands looked black and alien, with poles of ancient jetties standing forlornly at the water's edge.

'Funny to think of London's history riding on the river, and how we go everywhere now by car and bus,' Alfred said, looking out at the Thames. 'I'd like to have been a riverman, I think, back in the seventeenth century. There's something noble about working on the water.'

'Not on a freezing February day, with cutthroats longing to leap aboard and steal your takings. At least a taxi driver can make a quick getaway, or sound his horn. Into the inky depths, for a riverman, and that would be that.'

They were driving through meaner streets now, and the people getting on the bus looked tired and underfed. This was the same city in which those people in Bond Street lived, yet you could be on another planet.

They got out at the corner of Wharf Street. The one-time cooper's yard, which had been converted into the Party Headquarters for the area, was further down the street. As they walked along, a ragged child ran round the corner and almost cannoned into them. He tried to dart past, but Alfred shot out an arm and grabbed him.

'What's up?'

'Let me go, I ain't done nuffink, I got to find me mam.'

'Why do you need your mam?' Alfred asked.

Vee put out a hand to comfort the panting boy. He looked terrified.

'Where is she?' she asked.

'She's down Miller's.'

'The tanner's yard?' Alfred said.

The boy nodded.

'Then she won't finish work until six.'

'She's got to come. Our Peggy's bleeding and screaming out, and she needs Mam.'

'Bleeding?' Vee said, appalled. 'Is she hurt? Has there been an accident?'

The boy shook his head. 'No, she was asleep, then she woke up moaning and there's blood all over the floor. Please let me go, mister, I need me mam.'

Alfred had been crouching down beside the boy. He stood up. 'Which house?'

'Down there, number seven, second back.'

'You run and get your mam. We'll see what we can do.' The boy was off. Alfred turned to Vee. His voice was urgent. 'You cut along there, Vee. I'm going to find a doctor.'

'Me? What can I do?'

'Oh for Christ's sake, you're a woman, aren't you? Hold her hand, mop her up, I don't know. She's in trouble, just do what you can.'

As Alfred strode away, she called after him. 'Alfred, what's second back?'

'Second floor, one of the back rooms.'

Number seven had an unkempt, insalubrious air, as did the other houses in the street. Somewhere a baby was crying, a thin, high, unhealthy sound. A dog with ribs showing was nosing a paper bag in the gutter. Vee looked for door bell or knocker, found neither, and gave the door handle a tentative turn.

'Just give it a shove,' came a voice from across the street. A rag-and-bone man, his eyes bright with interest, had brought his cart to a standstill. 'Something up? Are you from the social?'

Vee pushed the door and it swung open. A smell of decay and urine and unwashed bodies hit her, and she recoiled. Then she started resolutely up the rickety stairs. A couple of children, all eyes and elbows, peered out at her from an open doorway on the first, ill-lit landing. Up again, towards the back. She could hear the moaning now, gasping, regular wails.

The door closest to her opened abruptly and a tiny woman, with a witch's nose and suspicious eyes, looked her up and down.

'That's Peggy making all that noise,' she said. 'Got herself knocked up, didn't she, and now look what's happened to her. Serve her right, I say.'

Slam.

Vee knocked on the door at the end of the narrow passage, and when there was no reply, she did the same as she'd done downstairs and pushed it open.

She had very little experience of ill people, but you didn't need a medical degree to see at once that the woman – girl, she could hardly be more than thirteen or fourteen – who was lying on a dirty mattress in a pool of blood, was seriously ill. Her face was white, her lips had a bluish tinge. Her eyes were unfocused, she didn't seem aware that anyone had come into the room. Vee knelt down and took the thin, icy hand in hers. 'Hello,' she said. 'I'm Verity. Can I help you? Where are you hurt?'

217

The girl clutched the meagre blanket that was covering her, and seemed distressed when Vee tried to draw it back. So she went on holding her hand, watching the blood seep out from beneath the blanket, praying that Alfred would come quickly.

Then he was in the room, with a woman, not much older than Vee, who thrust her out of the way, pulled the blanket back from the shivering girl, swore comprehensively, opened a doctor's bag and set to work.

'Shall I call an ambulance?' said Alfred.

The doctor didn't look up. 'They won't come here, not in time. Besides,' she said, 'it's too late.'

Vee couldn't believe it. 'She isn't dying, is she?' she whispered. She knelt down again and held the hand, which seemed even smaller than before. 'You can't let her die. She's only a girl. What's wrong with her? She should be in hospital.'

The girl gave a convulsive shudder, her eyes flew open, looked straight into Vee's, then she gave a gasp, and Vee felt the hand clutching hers lose its grip.

The three of them stared down at the sad figure. Alfred wordlessly drew the blanket up over the girl's face. There was a commotion on the stairs, and a thin woman with grey hair all awry under a shapeless hat came into the room like a whirlwind.

'Peggy? Where's my Peggy?'

'I'm so sorry, Mrs Hurley,' said the doctor, this time speaking in a soft, consoling voice. 'Peggy's gone.'

'We're not wanted here,' said Alfred, taking Vee by the arm. He fished in his pocket as they reached the door, took out his wallet, and slipped a note under a cup with a broken handle that stood on a stool by the door.

They waited for the doctor, who followed them out a few minutes later. In the street, she straightened her hat. 'I need to wash my hands,' she said abruptly.

'Party Headquarters,' Alfred said. 'There's a cloakroom there.'

Vee had to walk quickly to keep up with the two of them; they were talking in subdued voices.

'If I can find out who's doing this, I'll have him or her up for manslaughter and sent down for fifteen years,' said the doctor bitterly. 'I've never seen a worse job. Dear God, what did they use? A poker and a pint of bleach?'

What was the doctor talking about? When they reached the head-quarters, and the doctor had vanished into the tiny ladies' lavatory, Vee took a deep breath. 'What happened to that girl, Alfred?'

'What happened? Oh, it was a botched abortion. Well, that's the normal sort around here. No skill, no hygiene, they might as well throw themselves under a bus and be done with it. It'd be quicker and a lot less painful.'

'Abortion? That girl can't have been more than about thirteen, if that.'

'And so? They go on the game at twelve or thirteen if they have to, and with whole families living in one room, even if they aren't out on the streets, a brother or a father or grandfather can get them pregnant. Don't look at me like that, Vee. Grow up, for heaven's sake. What do you think life is all about? Why do you think I'm so passionate about the revolution? It's what it's all about: girls like Peggy having a chance to have a future. God, it makes me sick. Two miles from here, smart women book themselves into a discreet clinic for a D and C, while a child like Peggy haemorrhages to death.'

'What do you mean?' Vee said, going cold. 'D and C? What are you talking about?'

'D and C, duckie, you know, dilation and curettage, womb scraping, which conveniently removes any unwanted foetus that happens to be there. It's the upper-class euphemism for an abortion.'

She stood and stared at him.

'Don't look at me like that, Vee. You can't be such an innocent as all that, for God's sake, don't you know anything?'

Not really, she thought.

She sat hunched in the bus as it made its slow way back to the other world of the London in which she lived. It was extraordinary that this was the same day that had seemed so full of a new season's promise only hours before. It was a sparkling glass that had shattered and broken into spiky, dangerous shards.

Claudia in the clinic.

A dead girl in the East End.

An ambulance that wouldn't come.

A taxi ride to an anaesthetic and the comfort of a nursing-home room for one, and a bloodstained blanket for the other.

A life, and a death.

She didn't feel any animosity towards Claudia for what she had done. With dreary clarity she knew that the baby was Petrus's, and that he wouldn't marry Claudia. In Claudia's position, might she have done the same?

What about the two unborn babies, two nameless infants whose lives had ended before they ever began? Had they been born, had Claudia married and had the baby, early, but legitimately; had Peggy survived the abortion and the pregnancy, then one would have been born into comfort and easy circumstances, the other into the same grinding poverty as its pathetically young mother.

Christianity, any religion, would say without equivocation, that what Claudia and Peggy had done was wrong. The law would say the same, and inflict heavy penalties on those who brought about the termination of life of the unborn, and on the mothers, wasn't that the case?

Who would say how wrong it was that one woman could have all the medical attention she needed, and that the other must have nothing? The Church? What had the Church ever done for the Peggys of England? The law? A girl like Peggy came from a section of society that was a natural breeding ground for crime.

Who cared?

Alfred did.

That doctor did. She'd been kindly when she came out of the lavatory, drying her hands on a sensible handkerchief that she thrust back into her coat pocket.

'You've had a shock,' she said to Vee. 'Mr Gore, make her a cup of sweet tea.' And then, to Vee. 'Don't take it to heart. There was nothing you could do. Even if I'd got there just after it was done, I couldn't have saved her. No one could.'

'It's hopeless,' Vee said. 'It's all hopeless, a place like that.'

'You're an undergraduate, at Oxford, Mr Gore told me.'

Vee nodded.

'Then make the most of your education, and when you get your degree, take a job that helps people. There's plenty of work for sensible, intelligent young women to do, to make our country a better place for people like Peggy and her family. She should have been at school, being properly educated, with a chance of a job and a decent life. One day, with God's help and with help from people like you, Miss Trenchard, that's exactly what might happen.'

'One day!' Alfred said. 'We can't wait for one day, twenty, fifty, a hundred years from now. That's how long it will take if we go the reasonable way about it. Now do you see why I'm so passionate about the Party, Vee? Now do you see what it's all about?'

Vee simply wanted to get home and have a bath, she thought numbly. Then she was going to send 'Jane Maxwell' some flowers. No wonder Claudia had looked so grim this morning, what a ghastly thing to have to go through; even a smart clinic didn't make what she was doing any easier. Yes, she'd survive, but would she mourn the child she'd lost? Could even Claudia just toss that aside and forget it had ever happened?

She could feel sympathy for Claudia, but there was nothing she could do for her. She'd offered what help she could, and perhaps it was more than she'd been able to do for Peggy.

But if there was nothing she could do for Peggy, there was something she could do for all the other Peggys. Tomorrow, she was going to apply to become a paid-up member of the Communist Party.

SIX

Vee lunched with Hugh the day she went back to Oxford for the start of her third year. He was staying in Giles's flat, which was off Baker Street, and he suggested a restaurant in Marylebone Lane.

'Sorry to be late,' he said. 'I've been doing the rounds of the embassies, arranging visas and permits and all that kind of stuff.'

Hugh was about to set off on his travels, being disinclined to settle down to a job, as Grandfather wanted him to.

'I can last for a year abroad on what I've saved,' he said. 'You can live on next to nothing in a lot of places in Europe.'

He was eager to talk about where he was planning to go; he'd brought maps with him, and talked knowledgeably about cities and mountains and sights until Vee's head was stuffed with undigested information.

'Stop! Enough! Send me postcards, that'll give me time to get the map in my head.'

'There are a couple of mags that are going to look at any travel pieces I send them. That'll bring in some extra cash, keep me going a bit longer.'

'If they take them.'

'They will. I'm a good writer, Vee.'

'Poetry isn't the same as travel writing.'

'Being talented, I can do both.'

'You sound like Marcus.'

'Ah, Marcus is talented indeed; only he dissipates all his talents on playing the fool. Wait until he leaves Oxford, he'll sober up then and surprise us all.'

'What does Giles think of your going off?' Vee asked.

Hugh filled her glass with the white wine they were drinking with the pudding.

'He'd rather I didn't, but he's got plenty to keep him busy.'

Giles had just started at the Foreign Office.

'He's got all those rungs to climb, it's a long haul to his knighthood and the ambassadorship, he's got to concentrate on work. Sir Hector, his chief, has a reputation as a slave driver. That's unusual at the FO; most of the chaps I know there do damn all for most of the time. It's a good section to get for a newcomer, and Giles, who's the keen type, is pleased about that, although . . .'

'Although what?'

'Sir Hector's not necessarily the easiest man for someone like Giles to work for. Never mind, Vee. Drop it. Forget I spoke. You'll be head down this year, I expect. All you girls like to swot for finals.'

Hugh said he'd come to see her off to Oxford. He hailed a taxi, stowed Vee's overnight case by the driver, told him to go to Paddington, and got in beside his sister.

It was the week before full term, but the platform for the Oxford train was swarming with university people, returning after the long summer vacation, some bronzed and fit, some looking tired, and as though they had spent too much of their time away from the university reading and cramming for forthcoming exams.

Hugh and Vee walked down the platform, where the train was already in.

'Hello,' said Hugh. 'Company for you, Vee. A pair of Angels.'

Marcus and Petrus were standing beside the open door of a first-class compartment, waving at Hugh and Vee.

Petrus, looking just as he always did, suave and immaculate. Did he care about Claudia, and what she'd been through? Did he even know? Claudia might have kept it from him, after all. Vee felt a surge of hatred towards him, for being so arrogant, so sure of himself.

'I expect there's room for you with them,' Hugh said, quickening his pace.

'I'm travelling third class.'

Hugh stopped in his tracks and stared at her. 'Whatever for? Are you short of money?'

'No, I'm not, and before you ask, Grandfather has increased my allowance, even though I didn't want him to. I shall give it away.'

'Give it away?'

Vee didn't answer, and they caught up with the others.

Petrus was looking more elegant and successful than ever, in an impeccably cut grey flannel suit.

Marcus, his face pink and his hair blonder and even curlier, no doubt he'd spent the summer weeks basking on some Mediterranean shore. His red mouth was pursed in a moue of disapproval; Vee could see that he resented her breaking into their men's talk.

'Hello, Hugh,' Petrus said. 'Decided to join us for another year?'

'Seeing Vee off. Only,' and he sounded annoyed, 'she's travelling third class for some reason, so won't be with you.'

'Third class?' cried Marcus. 'Dearest Vee, you can't, only think of all the germs.'

'Why, may one ask?' said Petrus.

'Solidarity,' Vee said defiantly. 'Since most people can't afford to travel first class, why should I? Why should some people have to sit eight to a compartment and others four, with carpet on the floor?'

'Way of the world,' said Marcus. 'In fact, in a perfect world, they would have a fourth class, bare wooden seats and no glass in the windows, for the real lower classes to travel in. That would teach them to ape their betters and move about the country. They should stay at home and mind their looms.'

Petrus quelled him with a glance.

'Do we take it that you've lurched to the left, Vee, my dear?' He sounded amused, which irritated her. 'Have you become a socialist?'

'Not socialism, Petrus. That's very milk and water, don't you think? I've applied to join the Party.'

Marcus had been inspecting a scrap of brightly-coloured paper on the platform, shifting it about with the tip of his umbrella ferrule. 'Party?' he said, looking up. 'Oh, goodie, when? Where? Is it fancy dress? Do let it be fancy dress and then I can wear my cherub outfit. You've no idea how adorable I look in it, I'm brown all over, from tip to toe, not a centimetre of white skin to be seen anywhere, even in one's most private spots. I spent blissful weeks with Lord Melville, you know him of course, among utterly like-minded chums, and no nonsense about bathing costumes. Sheer heaven.'

He was impossible. 'The Communist Party, Marcus,' Vee said.

He gave a little scream and stepped back, holding up a hand to avert the evil eye. 'You can't be serious.'

'Vee, you can't,' said Hugh, staring at her with a frown on his face. 'For heaven's sake, do your bit if you want to, give Alfred a hand with his good works, but for God's sake don't become a card-carrying member of the CP. It'll cause you nothing but trouble.'

'Isn't trouble what so many people in this country have to live with, day in, day out? Why should my life be so much easier?'

'Won't it frightfully embarrass your parents?' Marcus said. 'If word gets out, with your pa being such a bigwig in the Church?'

'I can't live my life to please my parents.'

Petrus had a supercilious smile on his face. 'My dears, don't fret. Knowing what I do about the Party – which is mercifully little, the last thing the rest of the world needs is a workers' revolution, I do assure you – you'll find that they don't welcome intellectuals, they regard them with great suspicion. And they don't like members from the upper classes. Unless you have working-class credentials of the right kind, you really aren't welcome. Apply by all means, Vee, get it out of your system, but I doubt if they'll take you. Drawing-room pinks, they call people like you, ballroom communists.'

Vee was scarlet.

'I've already done a lot of work for them as it happens. We're comrades, whatever our background.' And with that she wrenched her suitcase out of Hugh's hand and hurried away down the platform to the third-class compartments, ignoring Hugh's cries for her to wait, come back, no one meant to mock or offend her.

Of course, it was a futile gesture. The compartment was full of other undergraduates, including Sarah, from Grace, who greeted her with enthusiasm and began to talk about a summer spent walking in Switzerland and Austria.

'Things are bad, there, Vee. In Austria, I mean. Vienna in particular.'

Still seething from her encounter at Paddington, Vee grabbed a taxi from under the noses of a group of Oriel hearties at Oxford Station. Worker solidarity could be temporarily laid aside.

'Come on, Sarah. It's too hot to walk.' Then, to the driver, 'Grace College, please.'

●

SEVEN

Vee's third-year room was nearly twice the size of the cell she'd lived in when she first came up. Only two years ago; it seemed like half a lifetime. Yet, as she stopped in front of the brown varnished door, her name written in neat copperplate, time fell away, and she was back for a moment in her old self, naive and dowdy and full of fresh hopes and expectations.

She pulled herself back into the here and now. Her room was one of three on a landing at the end of a long corridor. She went and looked at the names on the other doors. Lady Claudia Vere and Miss Fitzpatrick. They had asked for these rooms at the end of last term.

Vee knocked on each of the other doors in turn, just in case, but there was no reply. She didn't expect there to be; Lally wasn't coming up until tomorrow, and Claudia was driving down from Scotland with Geoffrey, her constant companion these days. She wouldn't be here for hours yet.

Vee put her key in the lock and opened the door. The room was flooded with sunlight, which bounced off the white-painted panelling on the lower part of the room. She went to the window and looked out. She had a distant view of Tom Tower and a closer one of Magdalen. She'd be able to hear the choristers on the first of May without stirring from her room.

What was she thinking of? Here she was, third-class Verity Trenchard, Party member, relishing the creature comforts that privilege brought her. The privilege of wealth and of intellect that had given her this room, this place in Oxford.

The sun dimmed for a moment, then she shook herself, and began to hunt in her handbag for the keys to her trunk. She couldn't be glum, not on a day with such crispness in the air, such promise of the start of the new term. And the start of a whole new era of her life, with a new service and new purpose.

She would unpack later, it was too good a day to waste. She went out through the lodge, into the familiar streets. She stopped to stroke a college cat, sitting nonchalantly on a wall in the sunshine and smiled at the constable on point duty. He was a symbol of oppression, of course, a lackey of the ruling classes, but still a man doing his job.

She paused to look at the bright-red telephone kiosk that had sprouted at the corner of Cornmarket. She'd seen them in London, a novelty still, and attracting a good deal of attention even in a capital used to innovation. She hadn't quite expected to see one here in Oxford.

She would have tea, she decided and then go to a bookshop. Books for her course, and books on Marxism, the ones Alfred had recommended, but which she'd never got around to reading.

She felt reborn, as she had done when she gave up God. And that had been essentially a private apotheosis; this would be a much more public conversion, and one that would infuriate her grandfather much more than her desertion of Christianity would. He was an old pagan and always had been, but he was a capitalist to his bones. The defection of his granddaughter to the communist cause would hurt him more than anything else she could do.

Good.

'Do I get a card, an actual piece of paper with my name on it and a membership number?' she'd asked Alfred.

'You do.' Alfred turned and stopped, taking her arm and looking at her very intently.

Her heart was thumping, damn Alfred for having this effect on her. She shook herself free, and he looked surprised.

'I wanted to say, don't flash it around. Your membership card, I mean.'

'Why ever not? I want to shout it from the rooftops.'

'Yes, well, it doesn't work that way,' said Alfred. He walked away from her, turned and waited for her to catch up. He thrust his hands deep into the pockets of his disreputable mackintosh. 'Vee, this is serious. It's not a gesture. You're becoming part of a long hard struggle. You have to accept that the Party knows what's best, and to do things in the way the Party lays down, not to follow your own wishes and inclinations. That's what it's all about, the good of the majority is much more important than any individual. Party membership is a sign that you've committed yourself to the cause of the revolution, but that's all. The real work is done day in day out, raising the consciousness of the working man in this country until every last docker and miner and industrial worker sees that our way is the only way for a better future for them and their families.'

'Envelopes,' she said.

'What?'

'Oh, nothing.'

Vee knew she shouldn't have made her dramatic announcement at Paddington; never mind, it wouldn't do any harm for Petrus and his acolytes to know. And she told Lally, although not Claudia.

Claudia would argue, try to dissuade her. Her admiration for Mosley had grown into a fervent belief in what the fascists were doing in Nazi Germany, and, as Alfred said, the two great enemies of communism were indifference and fascism.

Lally would understand why she had taken such a step. 'Capitalism will always fight to defend itself, but we can deal with capitalism,' Vee said to her, as she sat on the edge of her bed and watched Lally unpack. It was extraordinary how swiftly and neatly she put everything in its place. What an orderly person she was, how soothing it was to watch her quiet efficiency.

'It's the people who don't care, who think it doesn't matter how the country is run, or who's in charge, and think it's best not to rock the boat,' Vee went on. 'And people like Claudia, who can't see the nose in front of her face, and who has allowed her obsession with Petrus to spill over into worship of all the spurious glitz of the German Nazi Party.'

'You don't have to abuse Claudia.'

'There's no real harm in Claudia, she simply doesn't let herself look deeply into what she's letting herself in for. She isn't cruel, she isn't really anti-Semitic. If you asked her to taunt a Jew in the street or to put Joel in a concentration camp, she'd never be able to do it. It's play-acting with her, but nonetheless she's wrong, and she should grow up and see that she's playing – oh, not with fire – more like sitting on a keg of gunpowder.'

So Vee didn't say anything about her decision to Claudia. Lally took the news in her stride, just as she always did.

'I don't agree with you,' she said in her direct way. 'I think the Communist Party is dangerous, and I believe from the bottom of my heart that what is happening in the Soviet Union is cruel and wicked and is doing nothing to improve the misery of the average working man. But that's my view, and I can see that you think differently. Only, Vee, keep it to yourself. Don't go on any demonstrations or marches where there'll be scuffles and confrontations with the fascists, and photographers and the police. You don't want to be sent down in your final year without a degree. Wait until you've finished here before you get active.'

'In any case, I don't know that they'll accept my application,' Vee said, suddenly morose. 'They turn a lot away, and you can't say my background is working-class. All the commitment in the world doesn't make-up for having a grandfather like mine. Do you think they'll know who he is?'

'I have no idea. If they check people over before taking them on as members, then it won't take them long to find out. However, it might work in your favour, they might think it a coup to have enrolled someone like you.'

'I suppose so. On the other hand, if they want me to just address envelopes and make tea for the comrades, which is what I've been doing in any case, they may feel they don't need me as an official member.'

'Have you really thought this through?' Lally asked, after a difficult silence. 'Are you sure it's conviction and not just cocking that snook you English talk about? Are you doing it to bug your parents and that grandfather who annoys you so much?'

'Something happened in the vac. No, I'm not going to talk about it, but it made me realize that our society is simply too unfair for me not to try and do my part, I know, a small and irrelevant and insignificant part, to make life better for all those people who lead such a hopeless existence.'

'In my country, Roosevelt is desperately concerned to improve the lives of the working man. But he wants them to have freedom, even if you're out of a job and hungry, in America you have the vote, you have choice in your life.'

'That's where I disagree. A starving man, who can't buy food to put on the table or shoes for his children, has no freedom. He fares better in Russia than he does in America, and that's why I'm a Communist.'

The note was in Vee's pigeonhole one blustery early November morning. Late for a lecture, she had snatched up the handful of post from the lodge before going out into the rain sleeting across the cobbles. It was too windy to take her bike, so she walked to Schools.

The lecture was dull, the lecture room warm, and she hadn't been sleeping too well. Her eyelids began to droop, so under the pretence of enthusiastic note-taking, she inspected her post. An invitation to a dramatic reading in French, a cocktail party at the Oronsays, a scribble from Marcus summoning her to tea on Sunday – 'Bring Claudia and Lally, we'll have some music, listen to that pretty first-year boy with the extraordinary voice.'

The last one she opened was a thin white envelope with her name written across it in a foreign and unfamiliar hand. She prised open the envelope, and drew out a single sheet of paper. The words danced and jiggled before her eyes.

'A mutual friend has suggested I look you up while I am in Oxford, for a talk about interests we have in common. May we meet on Thursday at four o'clock by the Sheldonian Theatre, underneath the stone heads? I shall wear a dark coat with a red flower in my button-hole and I shall carry a blue folder.'

EIGHT

Uncertain what to wear – should she strive for a proletarian look? Why had she tossed out all her Yorkshire clothes from her first term? – Vee realized that if she didn't hurry up, she'd be late for the appointment. The man with the red flower might not wait, it might be the end of all her attempts to join the Party, simply because she was so bourgeois that she cared what clothes she had on.

She decided on a grey flannel suit, added a scarlet jumper – red was the colour of the revolution, after all – thrust her feet into the most sensible of her shoes, reached to the back of her door for a raincoat and her gown, seized her notebook and flew out of the room and down the stairs.

She arrived at the Sheldonian just as St Mary the Virgin's bells were sounding four o'clock. Breathless, she looked around. There he was. Unmistakable, and not looking at all like a comrade. His lean, distinguished face had a scholarly air, and his smooth greying hair gave him a touch of gravitas. He could have been a lawyer, or a civil servant or a teacher at one of the older schools. His overcoat, navy, and his dark red muffler were as expensive and well-cut as all the clothes Vee had despaired of. And his shoes were not in the least proletarian or down-at-heel. He didn't hold out his hand, but greeted her with a friendly smile.

'I am told one does not shake hands in Oxford, and of course when in Oxford, one must follow the customs of the university.'

'Do you live in Oxford?'

'I come here four or five times a year. I give lectures, on my special subject.'

'What's that?'

'I am an economist.'

'You aren't English.' Was he Russian? He didn't sound it.

'You will refer to me as Klaus. I am originally from Austria, from Vienna. I have been in England for many years.'

'Klaus . . . ?'

'Just Klaus, I think.'

'Your English is very good.'

'Yes, and so, I understand, is your French. But your German is not so fluent.'

She was surprised. They must be thorough, she hadn't expected that they would go to the trouble of finding out that kind of detail about her.

'I . . .'

'You have a French grandmother, who lives in Broissy. Yes, we know a good deal about you, Miss Trenchard.'

'I suppose you are here because of . . .'

'I think this is not the best place to discuss anything of a serious nature. Ah, here comes Mr Petrus, a fellow economist.' He raised his hat, Petrus acknowledged it and then swept his hat off as he bowed to Vee.

'Do you know Mr Petrus well?'

'I would not say that. I am not sure that anybody on this earth could be said to know Mr Petrus well. We work in the same field, we have crossed swords in the occasional footnote. However, we aren't friends. We disagree profoundly in our politics. I find his distasteful and misguided.'

They reached the High and waited on the kerb for a break in the traffic. 'It is busy today,' Klaus said as he guided her across the road. 'You need these new pedestrian crossings which are appearing in London. They make crossing the road a good deal less hazardous for the pedestrian.'

'I have a friend who disapproves of them. He says they are bourgeois.' She dropped the word into the conversation like a pawn in a game of chess, to see if he would react, would confirm that this unasked-for meeting was to do with her request to join the Party.

Klaus laughed. 'Your friend is, perhaps, an anarchist at heart. Now, let us take a stroll in the botanical gardens.'

The botanical gardens? This wasn't at all how she imagined the

232

Party hierarchy went about things. In fact, this softly-spoken man who had such buckets of charm was quite unlike any comrade she had ever met.

The heat struck them as he opened the door into one of the hothouses. Klaus ducked to avoid a straggling spray of an exotic trailer, bright with red-orange flowers. 'I like the atmosphere in here. They say that heat makes the brain work better, perhaps you should bring your books and study here.'

The water in the pool at the centre of the hothouse was dark green, dank. The pace of life seemed to have slowed abruptly; they were out of time and indeed out of her usual world here. Perhaps that was why he had suggested it, to throw her off balance. She wasn't off balance; in fact she felt preternaturally alert.

She decided on boldness. 'Did you want to meet me to talk about my application to join the Party?'

'Not exactly. See, here is a convenient bench where we may sit and be restful.'

They sat down on a bench, a slightly damp bench, but Vee didn't care.

'I myself have nothing to do with the Communist Party of Great Britain,' Klaus said. 'I am not a member, nor indeed ever could or would belong to such an organization, admirable though its aims and methods are. However, there are those who consider that the revolutionary changes needed in Europe will never be brought about by the unaided efforts of the local parties, however estimable.'

'Those?'

He ignored her interruption. 'It came to my notice that you had applied to join the Party. As is customary, because of the collaboration between us, and given your circumstances, your name was passed to us, and we made some enquiries about you.'

'Klaus, just who are you? Who do you work for?'

'Have you heard of Comintern? Yes, I see you have. We are an international organization of comrades in every country, working together to bring about an end to capitalism and the rise of a new order where the proletariat are the rulers and all men are equal.'

Vee thought fleetingly of the envelopes, then wished she hadn't. Could she ask him about the position of women in Comintern? Perhaps this wasn't the right time.

'My application . . .'

'To join the Communist Party has not and will not be successful. In fact, it hasn't even been considered; all records of your ever having made such an application have been erased. You will learn, when you become one of us, as I hope you will, that written records are dangerous. I trust you don't keep a journal?'

'No, I don't.' Vee was becoming more and more bemused.

'I would like you to tell me exactly what led you to apply for membership of the CP. Then I will tell you why I have approached you in this way, and what will be asked of you. So, if you please, pay very careful attention. Then go away, and think very hard about what I have said, whether you can serve the cause, and Comintern, in this way. Whether you can put aside all personal considerations and do whatever work we ask of you. Meanwhile, you must not, not now nor ever, speak a single word of what has passed in this time here. Not to friends or family or lovers, or in due course to husband or children. Secrecy will become part of your life.'

Vee cut her seminar, and walked for about an hour, unaware of streets or buildings or the weather, her excitement warming her. Her mind darted from one thing Klaus had said to another. She was drawn out of herself, it was as though she were looking at herself from above, detached, watching herself walking along, in a raincoat, a red beret on her head. Looking for all the world like the Miss Verity Trenchard who had left Grace so short a time before. Recognizable to any friend or acquaintance who passed by, and yet, inwardly, so very different. A changed woman.

She found herself walking past St Cross Church, and it struck her as exquisitely amusing that this was the very spot where she had first asserted her independence from her background and upbringing, and had come to realize that her life was full of choices; that nothing need be taken for granted.

She had no doubts. This was her mission, this was another step on the true path towards what she wanted to do with her life, to break down the terrible, stifling tyranny of men like her grandfather and create a new world for all those people whose lives were so grinding and hopeless.

She was brought down-to-earth by the thought that her recruitment to Comintern might mean no more than a lifetime of envelopes, but surely a movement of international communism wasn't going to waste time recruiting women like her merely for that.

She met Klaus again, a week later, and gave him her answer.

He seemed neither surprised nor pleased. He was brisk. The first task that lay ahead of her was to thoroughly lay to rest her left-wing sympathies. 'You must make it clear to all your friends that it was a phase, that you were playing, that you are glad to have a handsome allowance from your family, that your concern for the workers, for the oppressed, for the proletariat, was a whim, a following of fashion.'

'You don't mean that I've got to become an ardent right-winger? Join the fascist movement? I don't think I could.'

'No, not at all. Politics, you now believe, is for men, for other people. Political discussion bores you, those who belong to movements, work for political parties or groups or causes, are dull, there's more to life than that. Cultivate the social circle that your background gives you the entry to.'

'Are you serious? That's not what I want at all; that's why I'm a communist, to break away from all that Society nonsense.'

He was completely serious. 'It isn't my decision. It is Comintern that decides how best to position and use its agents. Consider. We have numerous union members, workers, miners, members of the proletariat, even those of the bourgeoisie who are willing to work openly to convert and help others to see the light. But we need to have a way into the seats of power. That's only possible in a class-ridden society like England if we use those who belong in such circles. Well-bred, well-educated and well-connected young men and women who have seen for themselves the consequences of capitalism, who despair as a national government is formed, who see those around them living in poverty while the bosses and the bureaucrats live self-satisfied, comfortable lives, bolstered by the rule of law, which operates so well for them and kicks the worker in the face.'

Vee was petulant. 'So what do I do in these circles? Rattle the teacups and persuade everyone to vote Labour, to turn socialist?'

He seemed amused, which annoyed her.

'My dear young woman, there is no party in this country worthy of the name socialist. At least none that has any hope of winning more than a handful of votes in any election. Rely on the ballot box, and England will never become Communist. We have to take a different route, and this is where you can help us.'

'By putting on expensive frocks and going to dances.'

'Just so. Remember whom you meet at these dances, whom you sit next to at dinner.'

'Am I supposed to worm secrets out of them?' Vee had visions of herself trying to prise confidential information out of Uncle Vernon. Fat chance.

'For now, you do absolutely nothing. This is the hardest task that could be asked of you, I appreciate this fact. You have to shed your extreme – extreme to the complacent middle classes – views. You must be seen to grow up, to take on the habits and mores and opinions of your class. You become one of them, it is a new persona for Miss Verity Trenchard, one in keeping with your class and circumstances. Then, when the time is right, more, much more will be asked of you.'

'How will you know whether I'm managing to do what you want?' Meaning, although she didn't say it, that Klaus was hardly likely to be on the invitation list for Cousin Mildred's cocktail parties.

'I am happy to say that yours is a world where I don't venture. However, others do.'

She was curious. 'Are there other agents, other people you've recruited, here in Oxford?'

'That's a question you may not ask, but I will tell you, you are indeed one of an elite band, one of the chosen few that Comintern hopes will, in the future, bring about the revolution here in Britain. And across the Channel, too.'

'I can't see there being a revolution in Germany.'

'Should your courage fail you, should you have doubts in the dark hours of the night, remember this one fact: only communism stands against fascism. Your government will dine and play with the fascists if they think it will keep Bolshevism at bay.'

Vee remembered the rally at Olympia. Well, it wasn't in the least what she'd expected, or hoped for, but if that were what she had to do, well then, she would do it.

For a fleeting moment, she heard a voice of warning in her head. How far could she trust Klaus? Who, exactly, was he? And how much use could she really be, what part could she play in this world of power and influence that Comintern wanted to bring down?

NINE

Vee went about her daily round as usual, and if Lally and Claudia noticed that she seemed very up and down, sometimes elated, sometimes subdued, they put it down to the pressures of third-year work.

Vee had other things than her academic work on her mind. Alfred, what could she possibly tell Alfred? What would he think – and say – when she told him that she'd decided she wouldn't, after all, be joining the Party, that she wasn't going to help any more, that she was simply giving up the whole thing?

Was there any chance that Alfred was himself a Comintern recruit? Unlikely; if the idea was to have people moving unnoticed among the movers and shakers, then Alfred, with his vigorous and outspoken support for communism, would be a no-hoper.

She cared, she realized with a pang, very much about her friendship with Alfred. She felt closer to Alfred than to any other human being, now that the childhood closeness to Hugh had evaporated in a world of adult relationships with men like Giles.

What would Hugh say if he knew about her recruitment to Comintern? He had disapproved of the CP, Comintern would be far worse. Well, he wasn't concerned with her and what she was doing. He was off, living his own life. Last heard of in Hungary, she'd had a postcard of Budapest with a drawing on it Hugh had made of a Hungarian policeman, and a line or two saying that he was heading next for the Carpathians.

For the time being, she decided, she'd just keep out of Alfred's way. He visited Oxford, from time to time, well, she'd make sure she was busy with other things.

She saw Giles, though, when he spent a weekend with the Oronsays, in their Oxford house, and she was a guest for dinner. He told her that Alfred had been asking after her.

Giles looked older, less cheerful. Had she heard from Hugh? he wanted to know. He hadn't had a word. Vee confessed to the postcard, but didn't mention the three letters she'd also received, when he was in Belgium and then in Italy.

Giles was missing her brother, but was Hugh missing Giles? Not by the sound of it. She secretly hoped that her brother might have forgotten Giles, or even found himself in love with a woman.

She remembered a conversation she had had with Alfred in the summer. He said it did happen, that men changed in their sexual preferences. Some boys were queer at school, and never afterwards, others carried on with male friendships at university, then gave them up when they began work – marrying and settling down to dutiful, conformist lives.

'Although you never can be quite sure what they get up to under the cover of darkness,' Alfred had added.

'Unfaithful to their wives, you mean?'

'Guardsmen in the park, public lavatories. That kind of unfaithful.'

'Oh,' Vee said.

The thought of Hugh with a guardsman upset her now, as she heard the anguish in Giles's voice, and she resolutely pushed it out of her head. She needn't regret the fact that she'd never been in love; love in whatever form, was the very devil.

She was getting awfully good at pushing things to the back of her mind. Like Alfred, and the way he had lashed out at her with savage mockery when she told him that she'd rather lost interest in the Party.

She'd met him by chance as she came out of the Radcliffe Camera, and he wanted to sweep her off for a pint and a sandwich, despite her protests. 'I've got work to do, Alfred, I really don't have time.'

He stopped, his face pale with cold, a long and shapeless scarf wrapped several times around his neck, his old school coat, too small for him now, barely keeping out the chill wind of winter. His eyes were hawkish, searching her face. 'What's up, Vee? You've been avoiding me. Is it something I said?'

She felt wrong-footed. 'No, it's just that I'm really busy, they pile the work on, you know, anxious that we women should make a good showing in Schools.'

'Balls.' He walked beside her in silence. Then, 'Did they accept you? The Party? No one's mentioned it to me, and I usually get to hear about new members from Oxford.'

'I didn't hear from them – I suppose it went astray, all the bureaucracy, you know what it's like. It was just as well. I thought it over, how my family ... you know. I'm not really cut out for political fervour.'

'What rot!' He glared down at her. 'Someone's got at you, that's what's happened, isn't it? Come on, Vee, I want the truth.'

That was the truth, of course, but not one she could tell him, although she longed to do so, to say, don't judge me, don't condemn me, I'm more committed than ever to the cause and the Party and the revolution. I've been reading Marx, I know in my bones that this is the future, for this country, for the world, the only hope we have of getting out of the terrible mess we're in. She knew a moment of intense frustration, and had to take a deep breath to control herself before she felt she could speak in the right kind of indifferent tone.

'Honestly, Alfred, it was a phase. I thought I really cared, but it would upset Grandfather a lot, I know it would get back to him.'

'And he'd cut off your allowance. Not pay your fees.'

That wasn't the impression she should leave him with. 'No, that's not it, not the money. It's just that I was misguided. I thought a lot of things mattered, and that I could help, to make a better world, you know. All that. Only I can't, and I don't think it's the way to go.'

'Joining Claudia's gang, are you?'

'No, I'm not, and as it happens, my grandfather isn't particularly keen on fascists.'

She didn't add that was because he smelt failure about the Italian variety; he would have supported them like a shot if he'd thought they had any chance of making any headway. Grandfather admired Hitler, was full of praise for what was being achieved in Germany, but was equally loud in his condemnation of Mussolini. 'Nothing but a dangerous, strutting puppet. Oh, he has the right idea, but he carries on like something out of Gilbert and Sullivan, that's no way to run a country. He's drained the swamps and made the trains run on time, good for him, but he's no leader for anyone who wants to succeed in politics in this country to take as an example. Mosley's got his head in the clouds. Germany's the way of the future, mark my words.'

She had wanted to jump and shout out her disagreement, just as she now wanted to shout at Alfred, to tell him to stop looking at her like that, it wasn't what he thought.

He turned from her. 'I don't think I'm hungry any more,' he said, walking away, his shoulders hunched against the wind, his coat flapping around his legs.

Claudia was delighted at Vee's return to the fold, which was how she saw it. 'We'll have you a fascist yet,' she declared.

'No thanks,' Vee said. 'I'm simply not interested. Politics are a bore. All I want to do is get a decent class in Schools and then go to London and have a good time.'

Lally kept her counsel, never being one to thrust her opinions on her friends or judge their actions. Yet Vee had a suspicion that Lally alone among her friends sensed her secret, knew that what she was proclaiming to the world was but a façade, a deceit.

It made her uneasy.

Marcus was full of curiosity, she never knew anyone who had such a nose for secrets and gossip. She ran into him in the High, and he cajoled her into going into a second-hand bookshop with him, 'To look at such a delightful little volume, utter wickedness,' he said, his eager eyes flickering over her face. 'What's this I hear about you dumping the comrades? My dear, I'm so pleased, one true soul has seen the light. What a pity you aren't a man, then I'd tap you for the Angels, and you could come and persuade some of our errant feathery brothers of a left-wing persuasion that their views are hopelessly jejune and misguided.'

The delightful little volume was pornography, and Vee turned away in disgust. How extraordinary that a respectable Oxford bookseller should stock such stuff; she'd never noticed that kind of book when she'd been browsing in there.

'He keeps them for special customers, like me,' said Marcus happily. 'Only I have to be quick and get in first, for there are so many of us in Oxford with similar tastes.'

She felt the same mixture of emotions about Marcus as she always did when she was with him. Out of his company, she knew that she disliked him intensely, and would be glad never to see him again. With him, however, his charm got the better of her instincts, and she found herself responding to his gaiety and warmth and unabashed, mirthful amorality.

1935

ONE

Oxford lost some of its charm for her that last year. She was on tenterhooks, waiting for she knew not what. The spires and the gracious quadrangles, the gowned figures, the university ritual, she saw all these as through a veil. This world was unreal, the world of substance lay beyond its gates, but as yet out of reach.

She only saw Klaus twice during that time. Once in each of the Christmas and Easter vacs, and once in each term, she was sent a letter, or a note in her pigeonhole, which gave her a number to telephone. Then she was directed to spend a weekend in a house in north London, the kind of place where she had never been, genteel rows of identical houses, with tiny forlorn squares of garden inside neat fences or railings, and gates that swung open at eight in the morning to let the bowler-hatted men of the house out and off on the first part of their journeys to work in banks, insurance offices, in the more obscure realms of the Civil Service. They returned on the six nineteen or the ten past seven, when lights were on behind closed curtains in the cold spring evenings, the drear of February heavy on the long, badly-lit streets.

Number forty-three Magnolia Avenue was a house just like all the others, with a bowler hat whom she never met, and a wife, whom she knew as Mrs Granger. She had her hair in a bun and looked like all the other anxious housewives, striving to make a small income go further than it could.

Vee wondered if her unsuspecting neighbours ever noticed the cold intelligence of the grey eyes hidden behind Mrs Granger's round spectacles.

Vee learned to use a small camera, how to photograph documents. Documents; where in the world of the Cousin Mildreds and the balls and dances of Mayfair would she ever need to photograph documents?

Mrs Granger taught her the essentials of tradecraft, letter drops, how to be aware of anyone following, how to shake off a tail. There were telephone numbers to recognize, passwords without resonance such as the Dankworth Laundry or Wilton Bicycles, and a procedure for ringing off and redialling; dates that meant other dates, meeting places that had code letters, letters that were embedded in addresses or innocuous greetings.

Vee was a quick learner, absorbing it all. The trouble that was being taken with her was reassuring, but the purpose of it all eluded her.

Mrs Granger gave nothing away, and reproved Vee for her curiosity. They were there to serve as best they could. As women, it was little enough they could do, and it was wrong to question any instructions that came through for them. Obedience was the first rule, and the strongest. Fail in obeying orders, and you were no use to anyone, least of all to Comintern and the revolution.

Did her husband know about her? Was he another one of them, beavering away in some dingy office, garnering secret information that somehow would make sense to Comintern?

Those times in the Granger household were in stark contrast to the weeks in London. Lally came to London for the Christmas festivities and the New Year, and they had a tacit agreement that Claudia wouldn't preach fascism, and Vee wouldn't express her boredom at all things political.

'I sometimes think,' Vee said to Lally as they helped decorate the hallway with boughs of greenery brought from Kepesake, 'that you're the only really politically savvy one of us.'

'I was raised in a politician's family,' Lally said, inspecting a branch of holly and discarding various withered leaves. 'The berries are very pretty, what a lot there are this year.'

'Cold winter, it's supposed to mean,' said Claudia. She was wearing slacks and had climbed to the top of a ladder, where she was perched perilously as she tried to attach some mistletoe to the chandelier.

Kimber brought mince pies and cocktails, a combination that made Aunt Lettice raise her eyes to heaven and predict endless digestive trouble for them in middle age.

As usual, Vee's aunt and uncle and Claudia had been invited to spend Christmas at Kepesake, and to take Vee with them; as usual, they had declined the invitation. Uncle Vernon disliked Kepesake and regarded his stepson with the kind of loathing Gabriel might have felt for Satan. Besides, he hated Christmas, considering it a tiresome distraction from work, and the extra spending the season brought as being thriftless and unnecessary. Claudia called him Scrooge behind his back and always put herself out to buy him the most expensive present she could find.

'Lucius is a lunatic,' Vernon Saxony said. 'He takes after his grandfather, and it's a mercy that Jerry and the girls seem to have escaped that particular inheritance.'

He was referring, Vee knew, to the present earl's grandfather, whose eccentricities had overcome even the reluctance of the English to shut away their aristocrats. He had been removed from the west wing at Kepesake in a straitjacket, babbling in tongues, and incarcerated in a lunatic asylum in the north of England.

'One that had the reputation of being a very humane establishment,' Aunt Lettice assured Lally, who looked shocked when Claudia had regaled her with this story.

'And the late earl, Gustavus, Claudia's father, was utterly sane,' said Aunt Lettice. 'Otherwise I would never have married him.'

'He took after his mother,' said Uncle Vernon crossly. 'A born fool, but such wits as he possessed were perfectly normal. Obsessed with hunting; well, that was the death of him.'

'And also perfectly normal,' Claudia remarked, when she filled Lally in with the details of her rather peculiar family. 'He went over the hedge and his horse didn't, and that was that.'

Lally was always amused to hear about the oddities of the English aristocracy. 'I believe in republicanism and democracy,' she said, 'but your upper classes are simply fascinating.'

She met Cousin Mildred, and quickly took her measure. 'She won't make old bones,' she observed to Vee as they watched Mildred dance a dizzy foxtrot in the arms of a tall man with a small head and extraordinarily long legs. 'Look at her eyes, however much does she take?'

Vee was surprised at how worldly Lally was. Lally laughed at her. 'I may not be very wild myself, but I keep my eyes and ears open, and I didn't fall off a potato cart. I'm more used to people taking too much alcohol, there aren't many who drug in my circle.'

245

'Where do you Americans get your Christmas hooch from?' Claudia called down from the stepladder. 'Don't tell me you all drink lemonade and water with your Christmas dinner.'

'We make more of Thanksgiving, you know. Christmas for us is special because it's the birth of Christ. And on both festivals, we drink wine, only don't ask how it arrived in Pa's cellars in those days, because I have no idea.'

'Would it have damaged his political career, if he'd been caught drinking bootlegged liquor?' Vee asked, twirling a glass bauble so that it sparkled in the light.

'He was in good company, I bet there weren't more than a handful of senators in the House who didn't have bottles of Scotch whisky and French wine stashed away in their houses. We're good at keeping secrets, us in the New World.'

So am I, Vee said to herself. She opened a box of crystal decorations and held them up for Claudia to see. 'Where do you want these?'

There was a power to having a secret, and she pitied those Americans with their hidden stocks of alcohol; how small and unimportant a secret compared to hers.

TWO

It was over. The last papers had been written, and Claudia and Lally and Vee emerged heavy-eyed and drained from Schools to drink champagne in the High and celebrate the end of exams, the end of their time at Oxford, the beginning of a new life.

'What will you do when you go down?' Vee asked Marcus, when they were having coffee in Fuller's in those leisurely days after finals, days spent on the river and evenings and nights partying and dancing.

'I'm glad you show some interest in what little me is doing, since I have to work for a living, unlike Alfred, you used to have a *tendre* for Alfred, no, don't go pink and lie to me, sweetie, I can always tell.'

He ran the spoon around the saucer of his cup, looking sulky. 'Actually, who cares about Alfred? He's got money, pots of it, his people are rolling. He doesn't have to work, he can carry on cherishing his comrades as much as he likes.'

'That isn't fair, he's a writer.'

'A reporter, hardly an artist, admit it. And they'll pay him peanuts, that's why he gets the work, because he can afford to work for next to nothing. Now, I have to earn a living, if I'm to live the life of luxury that's going to suit me best.'

'How?' she asked.

'I intend to take the BBC by storm. How can they refuse me? I'm simply bursting with ideas, and I relate to the younger audience, that's important these days.'

A man sitting at the next table in an Oriel scarf, clearly

eavesdropping, swung his chair round. 'Really, Sebert? What are the BBC going to take you on as? A tea lady?'

He and his friends laughed uproariously. Marcus sighed. 'This place is becoming positively uncouth. It will be so pleasing to my delicate soul to find myself among kindred spirits.'

'I thought you despised the BBC,' Vee said. 'And that's my cake, and I'd like to finish it.'

'No, best not,' said Marcus, deftly forking the last morsel into his rosebud mouth. 'You girls have to watch your figures, if you're going to be secretary to some frightfully important person, he'll want you to look svelte. So that when you sit on his knee to take shorthand, you don't crush the life out of him.'

Vee was annoyed. 'I'm not going to be that kind of secretary, as it happens.'

'Now you're in a huff. Let's order more coffee, thank goodness those dreadful hearties have cleared out. I want to hear all about what you and the others are wearing to the ball, every last detail, please.'

She wasn't inclined to humour Marcus. 'I can tell you what I'm wearing, which is white and red, but how should I know what the others are wearing? Which others, anyhow?'

'Don't get grumpy with me, darling,' said Marcus. 'I mean what you and the divine Lady C and ravishing Lally are wearing, of course. Down to the shoes and bags and jewels, miss nothing out. I don't care about any other Graces who happen to be going to the ball, although I hardly think that's likely, they're such a bunch of frights with their lisle stockings and serious expressions. A perfect reason for not letting women into the university, admit.'

'I admit no such thing.'

'And I know perfectly well that you've all been running in and out of each other's rooms in your delicious lacy undies, trying on one another's dresses and trying out hairdos and make-up, such fun, how I wish I could be at Grace instead of Balliol.'

She gave up. 'Oh, all right. My dress is white with tiny red roses. A little white satin bag with a flower clasp, and a pendant my grand-mother gave me of white gold and cornelians.'

'Not clunky stones, I do hope.'

'More flowers, I'm afraid. Lally is wearing sea-green chiffon, and looks like a nymph. Claudia's dress is dark-blue silk, with satin bag

248

and shoes. Lally is wearing a pearl choker, Claudia has sapphire eardrops. Is that enough for you?'

'I can't wait,' said Marcus. 'I can never get over the unfairness of living in times when men are confined to black and white, unless one happens to be a Scot, and not even the prospect of heavenly black velvet and tartan would make-up for that kind of a misfortune. I belong in the eighteenth century, embroidered waistcoats and pink velvet coats, what bliss it must have been.'

Christ Church was *en fête* for the Commem, and in Jubilee mood. The King had celebrated twenty-five years on the throne only the month before, when London had been lit up for the Silver Jubilee festivities, and the college was continuing the theme, with red, white and blue lights and streamers and balloons.

They arrived at the college after having dinner at the Oronsays, a glittering occasion and one of joy for Vee when Hugh miraculously appeared, only just back in England. And Alfred was there, in perfectly correct tails, looking very striking and somehow older, more grown-up.

And when she'd torn her attention away from Hugh and Alfred, there had been the sight of Lally and an army officer, Harry Messenger, clearly smitten with one another, deep in conversation over the superb food which Ruth always served.

A convoy of motor cars delivered their party to Tom Gate and they went through into the great quad, transformed from its cloistral calm into a fairyland of mediaeval tents, with red, white and blue pennants streaming from each coned top.

Hugh was beside Vee. 'Shall we dance?' she said.

'What, no line of eager swains waiting for your hand?' he said mockingly.

'Dozens, but they'll have to wait. I want to hear all about your travels, and everything you've been doing.'

'Very well, and then you can tell me what you're going to do, now that your varsity days are over, and sober reality strikes. I hear from Daddy that you plan to train at some secretarial college, can this really be so?'

'You first, and then I'll tell you what I'm up to, which won't take long, because it's all very dull.'

They walked through to Peckwater, where a marquee had been set up, with a dance floor and a band from London.

'There's jazz in Meadows,' said Hugh, swinging her into a brisk foxtrot. Her spirits rose. She was so happy to see Hugh, a thinner, somehow harder Hugh, but still the same brother of their salad days. He was talking about Spain and the Falangists.

'Who are the Falangists?' she asked, not really caring, just enjoying the music and the rhythm of the dance and the sense of ease that came from being in the arms of a brother, a man who had no designs on her, and for whom she had no feelings beyond warmth and affection, and the ties of childhood and family.

'Right-wing. Interesting people.'

'I thought Spain had gone left.'

'It has, but the military and the church and the landowners grumble about it. No, don't ask me to explain, I don't understand it, and I don't want to, politics aren't my thing.'

'You used to be rather pink yourself.'

'No more. The older you get, the more you realize that nothing is as clear-cut as you think it is when you're eighteen and burning to reform the world and right its wrongs. There are no absolute rights or wrongs. So now I don't trouble myself much about political labels. Instead, I observe with a poet's eye; I focus on personalities and passions and the sense of watching a drama unfold before my eyes, with no indication of how the final act is going to end.'

'Is it a comedy or a tragedy, do you suppose?'

'Oh, the air you breathe in Spain at the moment is heavy with tragedy.'

'Then it ends with bloodshed and everyone strewn across the stage, that's what tragedy is about.'

'Not according to Aristotle, I would remind you.'

'Oh, I know, bad times to good times is equally tragic, as long as there's the change. No one remembers that, it's all black and white, gloom and doom and unhappy ending, tragedy. Laughter and good times and happy ever after, comedy.'

'There are no happy endings in Spain, nor for any of us, I don't suppose, Vee. How's your work for the Party?'

She nearly jumped out of her skin. Her mind had been floating, she'd responded to Hugh's remarks with light-hearted indifference. Now she came back to earth. Did Hugh know about her work for Comintern? Sense reasserted itself. Of course he didn't. He was talking about her days in the East End. 'Oh, I've rather given that up. Politics

250

aren't for me, either. Nothing I can do will make the slightest difference, so I might as well not bother. I'm going to concentrate on having
as good a time as I possibly can, before the balloon goes up again.'

'Do you mean war?'

'Isn't it inevitable? This year, next year, some time, but never never.
That's what everyone says. Within the next ten years, we'll have to
tackle Hitler.'

'Warmongering,' said Hugh firmly. 'Don't you believe a word of
it. These crises build up and then make a noise like a hoop and roll
away. The dictators will wear themselves out; people will get fed up
with them, that's what happens. No one wants a war, we're all still
war-weary from the last one. Don't worry about that, Vee. But why
the secretarial business? Is that really necessary?'

The dance had ended, and applauding the band, they strolled off
the floor. They went outside and Hugh lit cigarettes for both of them.
He propped himself against a rope and glanced back inside the
marquee. 'There's Claudia dancing with Petrus. Is she still keen on
him?'

'I don't think she's been seeing him recently,' Vee said.

'Good thing, too. I'm not sure I trust Petrus.'

'Why not?'

'Too glib, too smooth, too ready with all the right answers. Look
how he's drifted from being mildly pink to full-blooded fascist and
back to a kind of neutral English liberalism – which just happens to
suit the present lot. Doesn't he do a lot of work for the government?'

'I really couldn't say. I hardly ever see him.'

'Uncle Vernon was talking about him. Yes, I dropped in to change
and leave some of my belongings, and Uncle Vernon took me out for
lunch. We had a chat.'

'About Petrus?'

'Among other things. We talked about your plans. Vernon said
Grandfather wasn't too keen on the secretary lark, but that he and
Lettice persuaded him it was just the thing, learning to keep accounts
and organize the servants and so forth, so useful for when you're
married. Is that what it's all about?'

'No, it's about learning shorthand and typing and getting a job. I
can't drift around month after month. One needs a purpose in life.'

'So no prospective husband in the offing?'

'Now you sound like Grandfather. No.'

There was no point in saying any more. Even if she hadn't been under instructions from Klaus not to become romantically involved with anyone – her dedication to the cause, he had said, with that grave authority she found so comforting, would be weakened if she were to become entangled with a man, want to marry; that was the price she must pay for serving the revolution – there was no chance of that. She simply wasn't romantically inclined, and that was that.

Look at Piers. Could any man have been better husband material? And she'd rejected him, with hardly a moment's hesitation. No, the truth was that her capacity for love lay in the cold Yorkshire soil, alongside Daisy. Such love as her mother had for Vee had died that day, and for Vee, marriage meant the Deanery and unhappiness, an unhappiness that still haunted her, even at this distance, and one that she had no wish to impose upon herself through her own marriage.

She wished Hugh wouldn't question her like this. She felt uncomfortable, lying to him about her political commitment and not being able to say that secretarial work was the last thing she would have chosen, that it had been chosen for her. Her own brother, and everything she said was obfuscation and half-truths. That was the cost of idealism.

There was a silence. Hugh blew some elegant circles of smoke into the June night. 'What's up, Vee?'

'Up? Nothing. Why would anything be up?'

'There's something about you that isn't quite right.'

'Of course there is. End of term, coming down for the last time, out into the big bad world.' She could see Giles making his way purposefully towards them, and was relieved. 'Here comes Giles.'

'Oh, God, spare me,' Hugh muttered under his breath.

Then Giles was standing in front of them. 'Here you are,' he said accusingly to Hugh. 'I've been looking for you.'

'And you've found me. How are you, Giles?'

'All these months, and not so much as a postcard. I've written you a dozen letters – no, more – and never a word.'

'I've been in the kind of places where postal services are a message carried in a bag on a donkey, no one's had a line from me since Christmas.'

Hugh was lying. Vee had had several scrawled postcards from him, and she knew that he'd written to their parents at least twice.

'Why didn't you let me know you were arriving back in England? I would have driven down and collected you at the port.'

'What, haven't you a job and a desk any more? I came home on a sudden impulse, Giles. No one knew I was coming, I hardly knew I was myself until I saw the white cliffs rising up from the waves. How's life at the Foreign Office treating you?'

'Hugh, we must talk.' Giles was deathly pale, and clearly having trouble containing his emotions.

'I'll just go and . . .' Vee began, wanting to get away, but Hugh held her arm. 'Not now, Giles. This is neither the time nor the place. Let's meet in town for lunch one day, catch up on each other's news.'

'News? Hugh . . .'

'Ah,' said Hugh, releasing Vee. 'Claudia's off the floor, the next dance is mine.'

He removed himself with remarkable swiftness, leaving Vee and Giles staring at one another. Then Giles swore and strode away, brushing through a little knot of people coming into the quad.

'Hey, Hotspur, what's biting you?' said one of the group, but Giles ignored him.

'Moody fellow,' the man said.

Hugh, clasping a bottle of champagne and two glasses, found Claudia sitting on a gilt chair in the marquee. She had a pensive expression on her face. He looked down at her. 'A wallflower? I don't believe it.'

'I have a partner, but I'm hiding from him, he's tall and thin with a face like a horse. Come to think of it, he has a voice that sounds like a neigh.'

'If it looks like a horse, and sounds like a horse . . .'

'So I'm hiding this one out.'

'I don't like to disillusion you, but a young man of unquestionably equine appearance is at this very moment making his way hither. However, if we were to widen the gap in the canvas behind you, he would search in vain.'

No sooner said than done, and in a moment they were standing outside the marquee in the quad. Behind them was the great Wren library; above, beyond the strands of lights, hung an enormous full moon.

'He'll be out looking for me any second now,' said Claudia philosophically. 'He's that kind of a man.'

'Then we'll thwart him,' said Hugh, seizing her hand and setting off for the entrance to one of the Peckwater staircases.

'This is your old staircase,' said Claudia.

'Can't go in there, sir,' said a melancholy voice. 'Ladies' rooms is on the ground floor on the south side.'

'Good Lord,' said Hugh, pulling Claudia into the shadow of the doorway. 'It's Tewson.'

'Why, Mr Trenchard, sir, I didn't recognize you at first.' He removed his bowler hat. 'And her ladyship, a very good evening to you, my lady.'

'Who's got my rooms this year, Tewson?' Hugh asked.

'Young Mr Rutherford, you wouldn't remember him, I don't suppose.'

'Oh, yes, I would, he was my fag at school for one memorable term.'

'Wild in his ways, very wild,' said Tewson, shaking his head. 'Rusticated twice, and now he's been sent down for good.'

'So there's no one in residence now.'

'No, sir, but if . . .'

There was a clink of coins, and a key was passed over. 'I'll thank you to sport the oak up there, though, Mr Trenchard, and to leave the inner door open, the college is very particular on such matters, as you know.'

'It's all right, Tewson. We aren't getting up to any kind of mischief. My cousin here simply wants to look over the college from an upstairs room.'

'That's all right, then, sir.'

Hugh led the way up the worn wooden staircase, past the door of his old set on the second floor and on up a narrower flight of stairs to the top floor.

'Where are we going?' said Claudia.

'You'll see.'

There were two dark-blue doors on the top landing. Between them was a white sink and a tap, and above that a small sash window.

'There's a trick to this,' said Hugh, wrestling with the catch on the window. 'Let's see if I can remember how to do it.' There was a click, and he pushed the window right up. 'Here, I'll give you a hand getting over the sink. Are you all right in that dress?'

Claudia gathered her skirt above her knees, and with an athletic twist, raised herself on to the sink and then slipped out of the window.

They were standing on the narrow strip of leading behind the carved stone balustrade that ran right round the quad. Behind them, the dark shadow of the roof was silhouetted against the starry sky.

Hugh reached back in through the open window and retrieved the champagne and the glasses. He deftly removed the cork, and tossed it over the balustrade. An indignant cry wafted up, and Claudia, peering down into the quad, began to laugh. 'You hit the horse.'

'Most unsporting of me,' said Hugh, handing her a glass. 'I drink to your blue eyes, Coz.'

Claudia looked up at the radiant moon. 'I think I shall drink to the moon goddess.'

'In that case,' said Hugh, 'we need to make a libation.' He flicked bubbles out of his glass above Claudia's head.

'I say, watch out!'

'That's to the gods of the upper world, now to the earthier gods, and,' with a final scattering of wine over the balustrade, 'to the gods below. The moon goddess is, of course, Selene, one of those triple-aspect deities, with Artemis and Hecate making up her terrestrial and underworld counterparts.'

'To Selene, then,' said Claudia, and raised her glass.

Hugh could see tears shining in her eyes.

'What's amiss, Claudia?'

'Nothing in particular. Just end of termish, I suppose; well, the end of Oxford. Isn't one supposed to feel sad that it's all over?'

'I didn't.'

'For a man, going down is freedom. It isn't for me. It's London, and more dances and parties, and when am I going to get married?'

'Are you? Going to get married.'

'No. The only man I want to marry doesn't want to marry me.'

Still Petrus, then, thought Hugh. 'You could do a job.'

'Tedious. Have you got a cigarette, Hugh?'

He opened his case and she took a cigarette. He pulled out a silver lighter from his pocket and lit her cigarette and then one for himself. She leaned her elbows on the stone parapet. 'Oxford's magical by starlight. And with the moon. The spires and the roofs. We're like a pair of angelic beings up here, looking down on scurrying mortals. We can see them, and they can't see us. There's Giles, I'd know that sleek blond head anywhere. Who's he with?'

'Joel, I think,' said Hugh.

'Lally was dancing with that man in regimentals, what was his name?'

'Harry Messenger.'

'He seemed rather smitten.'

'Aren't men always, by Lally?'

'What's she going to do?'

'Go back to the States. That's why she was so keen to gather everyone together for this ball. A farewell.'

'You'll miss her.'

'We all shall. She'll go back to Chicago or Washington or wherever it is she lives, both places I suppose, with her father in the Senate. She'll marry a doctor, like her father was before he took to politics, or a politician.'

'I can see Lally as a political hostess.'

'Yes, perhaps she'd be wasted on a doctor. Although she might be happier out of the political rough and tumble. One gathers that American politics can be tough.'

'And ours aren't? Do you still support the fascists?'

'Not Mosley, no, that's all rather petered out. Too much Mussolini and adore the leader, and not enough policy. Do I support National Socialism? Yes, I do. I believe Hitler is the man to save the world, it's as simple as that. Germany's amazing now, he's put the heart back into the Germans. Full employment, and a belief in themselves; we could do with that.'

'People are saying we'll have to come to terms with Hitler, sooner or later.'

'Sooner, then, before all the types like Churchill hustle this country into rearming and causing trouble. Hitler has no quarrel with us, and most people in this country realize that he's the only one who can make a stand against communism.'

'Vee wouldn't agree with you.'

Claudia turned her back on the scene below and looked at Hugh. She blew out a languorous stream of smoke, which hung in the air before drifting away. 'Vee's given up, she doesn't support the left any more. Nor the right, she simply says she isn't interested. You can't argue with her about it, she just shrugs and says it's all a bore, and changes the subject.'

'How infuriating.' Hugh was amused. 'I'm surprised, though. Vee's always struck me as the type to abandon herself totally to a cause.'

'I dare say, perhaps she just hasn't found the right cause yet. It doesn't have to be politics, does it?'

'Maybe, these days, it does.'

Hugh stirred a feather with his shoe, and it floated up to be caught by a sudden breeze that bore it out between the stone pilasters and down, in lazy circles, towards the ground. He watched it go. Then he took Claudia's hand and turned it over to look at the palm. 'They say that your future is written here, in these lines. If I were a gypsy, what would I say? Where will you and I, all of us, be in, say, ten years from now?'

'That's easy,' said Claudia with some bitterness. 'We're talking about 1945; doesn't it sound ages away? Only it'll come in a flash, as years do. I'll be married to the horse, or his twin. Vee will be married as well, to a man about town who'll take her to the theatre and France in the summer. Lally, well, we've said what Lally's fate will be. In ten years? She'll marry a good Catholic, of course, so that'll mean a quiverful of children. Alfred will be a successful writer, brilliant young essayist and so forth. Joel will be winning all the mathematical prizes, and being offered fellowships all over the place. Lord knows where Marcus will be, Hollywood or in prison, probably. And you, Hugh, will be the most promising poet of your generation, with several slim vols to your name.'

'And a fascist government in England, and Hitler a happy Chancellor of a wider Germany, is that what you foresee?'

Claudia shook her head, the tears now blinding her. She stood bathed in moonlight, which drained the colour out of her dress, her hair, her eyes.

She looked, Hugh thought, like a sibyl.

'It isn't going to be like that at all. At night, I dream of gunfire and explosions and vast crowds of people without eyes. They have their mouths open to scream, only no sound comes out. I see London in flames, and flickering figures everywhere, in uniform. Oh, Hugh, it's terrible.'

She clung to him, and he wrapped his arms around her taut body. 'Those are nightmares, Claudia. We all have nightmares.'

Her voice was muffled, her face pressed into his shoulder. 'Other people don't dream the future, and I do. I always have done.'

She pulled away from him and looked him straight in the eyes. 'Do you think I'm mad, like Lucius?'

'Because you see into the future? I doubt it. Grandmère has the second sight, after all, I expect you've inherited it from her.

'Why not you, or Vee, or my sisters? Or Mummy, or Aunt Anne? Why me?'

Hugh took her glass, and filled it. Claudia made to push it away. 'I must be drunk, to carry on like this,' she said. 'What an exhibition I'm making of myself. Have you a hankie?'

He passed her his handkerchief, and she dabbed at her eyes and blew her nose. 'I must look a perfect fright.'

'Nothing that a dab of powder won't fix. We'll go down and give the key back to the obliging Tewson, then you can tidy yourself up. After that, we'll have a dance.'

'I don't feel like dancing.'

'It's customary at a ball.'

Claudia went down the stairs behind Hugh. 'Are you and Giles still . . . I mean . . .'

'I haven't really seen much of Giles since we came down,' Hugh said, in the kind of voice that didn't invite further questions.

Giles and Joel were sitting side by side at the bottom of the steps that led down to Meadows Building. Giles had an arm draped round Joel, who was waving a bottle of champagne in the air. Giles looked raffish, with his blond hair in disorder and his tie undone.

'Let's drink to the abolition of love,' Joel said. 'Let's pass a law banning it. They ban everything in Germany, why can't love be banned as well? Take the pain away from fools like you and me.'

Giles struggled into a more upright position and made a swipe at the champagne bottle. He tipped some of the dregs into his mouth. 'Find a waiter, get another bottle,' he said. 'Lally giving you hell?'

'Dancing and smooching with that man in the ridiculous uniform. He's old enough to be her father, what does she think she's doing?'

'Fallen for him, I expect,' said Giles. 'That's what women do. That's why I never go near them.'

Joel thought about that, then ran both hands through his hair, making it stand upright. 'No, it isn't. You don't like women. You're in love with Hugh.'

Giles hurled the bottle against the wall; it didn't smash, but bounced off and rolled back towards them.

'Hugh isn't in love with me, that's the point. Lally doesn't love you, Hugh doesn't love me. It's all over, Joel. To hell with them both. To hell with everyone.'

258

THREE

Vee loathed the secretarial course and disliked the instructor, a Miss Duchet, who was a woman with a thin moustache and a large behind. She also had a disagreeable London accent, which grated on Vee's nerves, as did Miss Duchet's BO and the thick lisle stockings she wore. Then Vee felt guilty for being a snob and letting her class prejudice get in the way of comradely feelings.

Miss Duchet was a whizz with the typewriter, though, Vee had to admit, as she herself struggled to find the letters on the huge, heavy black machine, with a cloth spread across her fingers so that she couldn't look at the keys.

'If you look, you slow down,' pronounced Miss Duchet. 'There are no jobs for women who approach typing with look and peck.'

Shorthand had an initial fascination, like learning a new language, but quite soon the skills and pothooks began to pall. Vee dutifully did her exercises, but began to look so depressed that Aunt Lettice ordered a tonic from her doctor and forced Vee to drink it every morning, a vile black liquid with a bitter aftertaste. Vee tried to look more cheerful and her spirits improved as a result.

She was missing Oxford, that was part of the trouble. She was missing it more than she had thought possible. The camaraderie of Grace, the intellectual companionship – how different it was from the hours she spent among the solemn students at the Secretarial Academy. And she was missing her friends.

At least, Vee reminded herself, Lally was in England and not in America.

*　　　*　　　*

Lally's wedding to Harry Messenger in August after a whirlwind romance had been a joyful affair, against all the odds. The couple themselves were so much in love that the opposition from both families and the obstacles presented by Lally's Catholicism had somehow been overcome.

The Messengers, county and army and Protestant, had risen as one to proclaim their hostility to the match and to make Harry see what a fool he was making of himself.

Harry was a widower, his first wife having died in childbirth, and they had wanted him to marry again for years; his little boy, Peter, was nearly seven, he needed a mother. His mother and aunts and sisters had paraded any number of suitable girls under his nose: debutantes, country girls, daughters of generals, and he had smiled a knowing smile and ignored all their attempts to ensnare him.

And now, he had to go and choose a girl half his age, who had been to Oxford of all ridiculous things. A foreigner! At least as an American she spoke English – of a sort – but she was of Irish ancestry. A papist, a Roman Catholic, and from Chicago! They said her father was a politician, a gangster more likely. A senator? That was something, but even so . . . And was he rich? No, he was not. He had been a physician before he'd gone into the Senate, for heaven's sake.

Lally's father was even more forceful. He forbade the marriage, that was that. Lally was to return to America, immediately, the tickets would be in her hand the next morning. When the *Mauretania* docked, with no daughter on board, he at once set sail for England himself, accompanied, rather against his will, by his formidable mother-in-law. As soon as he was in England, he made the Ambassador's life a misery by his insistence that Lally be made a Ward of Court, whatever archaic arrangement that was, so that she couldn't run off with this Messenger man. An adventurer, he was certain. Old enough to be Lally's father.

In vain did the Ambassador point out that Lally, at twenty-one, could marry whom she pleased. And that the Messengers weren't the kind of people to run away with anyone.

'Stuffy, old English family, all that out-of-date nonsense?' said Mr Fitzpatrick. 'I won't allow it, and that's my final word. What are my constituents going to say when my daughter rolls up on the arm of an English army officer? The British Army isn't too popular in Chicago, let me tell you. Besides, she's Catholic, and she can't marry a Protestant.'

The Ambassador sighed. 'As a serving officer, I doubt if Colonel Messenger will have much time to visit Chicago.'

'There you are, he's taking my girl away from her family. I knew I should have forbidden her to come to England, I knew college at Oxford was a mistake. Never educate a woman, it causes nothing but trouble.'

Lally's grandmother listened to his fulminations, then sought out her granddaughter to see for herself what was going on, and to meet this Harry Messenger. One look at the two of them, and she set about planning the wedding. Nothing, she saw at that first glance, was going to separate these two.

In the end, with Lally so unhappy at the prospect of a Register Office ceremony, although she would have done that if she'd had to, they were married in the private chapel of a great house belonging to a friend of the Oronsays.

Ruth had understood just what Lally was going through. 'It was the same for us, we had to be married in a civil ceremony, with me being Jewish and Sir Iain a Catholic, although not, I must say, a practising one. Now, Gervase and Emily are delighted to help you out of this mess, because he's Catholic, and she isn't, and they're perfectly relaxed about it. Their chapel is still consecrated, apparently it serves quite a large Catholic community, and she knows a priest who is prepared to conduct the ceremony.'

The in-laws to be sat stonily on separate sides of the small chapel, the feathers on Agnes Messenger's hat quivering ominously as the couple exchanged their vows. Lally's mother, who looked, Vee thought, just like Lally would in twenty years' time, wept, but Claudia remarked that she had seen her eyeing Harry and would bet that she knew just why Lally had wanted to marry him.

'He's a sweetheart, and has bags of sex appeal, apart from being very good-looking. I can't think how he's escaped a second marriage all these years!'

Once the older generation had rolled away in their various cars, Lally and Harry and their friends danced the night away at Stoke Park. It was, Vee and Claudia agreed, a wonderful end to their time at Oxford.

'There we've been, seeing one another every day, and now Lally's married, and you're going to start that dire secretarial course and get a job, and I suppose I'll have to find something to do as well,' Claudia said. 'At least you're staying at Rochester Street for the time being, it'll make being without Lally less hard.'

Lally settled happily into married life, living mostly in the country, although she did come up to town for shopping and hair and shows. She said she was blissfully happy, and she certainly looked it.

'No problems at all?' cynical Claudia asked when the three of them met for tea at the Ritz.

Lally thought for a moment. 'Only on Sundays, when I miss the Oxford services, or the ones in America,' she said. 'I get up at the crack of dawn and go to Mass at a neighbouring village, to hear a decrepit priest rattle through the service.'

'Not the priest who officiated at your wedding?' Vee asked. 'He looked to be about a hundred years old.'

'I think he was one of the original recusants,' Lally said. 'I mean, he looks like he could have been hidden in a priest hole since your civil war. Wasn't that what Catholic priests had to do? He looks as though they just let him out, kind of cobwebby.'

'I thought it was bad form ever to utter a word of criticism about any of your priests,' Vee said. She was feeling ratty that afternoon, although a delicious tea at the Ritz was restoring her to a better mood.

Lally laughed. 'Only converts mind what they say.'

'How do you get on with your Harry's little boy?' Claudia asked.

'Peter's a pet,' Lally said. She summoned a stately waiter and asked for more tea. 'So full of fun, and do you know, I think he's kind of glad to have me around.'

'Why shouldn't he be?' Vee looked at Lally with affection. 'Wouldn't anyone be?'

'Wicked stepmothers, all the legends and fairy stories give women like me a bad press.'

'He never knew his mother, so you're hardly supplanting her in his affections.'

Lally's face clouded. 'The only trouble is, he has to go away to school.'

'Isn't he a little young for that?'

'Next year, when he's eight. It's bizarre, the way you English send your kids away from home when they're hardly out of the nursery.'

'Girls don't usually go off then, although some do,' Claudia said.

'It's to toughen them up. Get them ready for army life and ruling the Empire. I don't know that it does them any harm.'

'Hugh went off at about that age to his prep school,' Vee said. 'I remember I cried when he went, but he didn't seem to mind, and he survived all right. They all do, don't they?'

'Peter's a sensitive child. With a vivid imagination. And babyish for his age. Harry says that's just why school will be so good for him, but I reckon it's better to let children grow up at their own pace, not try to make a man of a boy who's still happiest at home.'

'A word of advice, Lally,' Claudia said. She sat back with a sigh of satisfaction. 'I never grow tired of afternoon tea. It's the one thing I miss when I'm in Germany, the moment I get back, I always order an enormous English tea.'

'Is that the advice? Tea?'

'No, the advice is that you don't under any circs question the Englishman's wish to send his son away to school. It's like threatening his masculinity, it won't do.'

'Harry doesn't take any notice of what I say, anyhow,' Lally said. 'He just laughs at me and says not to fret about it, that I don't understand, that Peter will love school.'

'He won't, actually,' Vee said. 'That's the lie parents always tell you when they send you off to boarding school. You don't love it, but it's OK. I was quite glad when Mummy sent me off, even though I knew she'd done it to get rid of me, not for the sake of my character or education.'

'Vee!'

'Oh, Lally, it's all a long time ago. And I had a good education at my school, and Peter will from his. Where's he going?'

'Somewhere called Halliburts.'

'Army family school,' said Claudia. 'Don't worry, he'll be fine. And won't you be having one of your own?'

She eyed Lally's slim form. Lally's cheeks went pink. 'I hope so.'

Vee wished she could meet Klaus at the Ritz for tea, instead of their clandestine encounters in St James's Park or Green Park, where they walked and sat on benches, and on wet wintry days, grew colder and colder.

'First principles,' he told her. 'Out of reach of spying eyes and microphones.'

'Where could I possibly be where there'd be microphones? Secret ones, you mean?'

'In the telephone is a usual place, or embedded in a wall behind a picture. At the moment, you aren't in the kind of surroundings where this is likely; I don't suppose the public rooms at the Ritz are bugged.'

That startled Vee. 'How did you know I was thinking about the Ritz?'

'Because you go there, to take tea and dine with friends.'

She stiffened. 'How much of what I do do you know about? And how do you know what I'm doing in my private life?'

'You have no private life. Don't misunderstand, we don't disapprove of your going to the Ritz and other such haunts of the rich and the privileged, it's what we instructed you to do. However, your life has no privacy, not now. So we keep an eye on you, for your own protection, to make sure that no one has any suspicions of you.'

A surge of resentment came over Vee. She didn't like the way they were keeping tabs on her, as though they didn't trust her.

'Why should anyone be suspicious? I don't do anything except learn shorthand typing, and go out to dine and dance and go to cocktail parties. With weekends in the country, which, by the way, make Miss Duchet furious, as I miss Monday morning lessons. A life like that is hardly going to raise any eyebrows or send any alarm bells ringing.'

'Not yet. Never, we trust. You are a long-term agent; one we hope will be in place for many years.'

'I thought the revolution was going to happen soon, not in many years.'

'Don't be impatient. Like turning a great liner around, things take time. To change the political structure of a nation is no small thing. It doesn't happen overnight.'

'Didn't it in Russia?'

'You are woefully ignorant about the Russian revolution. You must go and read more about it.'

As so often with Klaus, Vee felt at a disadvantage. He treated her with a kind of avuncularity, which was in a way comforting, but did he treat the men he had recruited in the same way? She was becoming dependent on him, hoping for a word of approval. She wanted him to think well of her, yet sometimes she resented the fact that she was so much under his thumb.

*   *   *

And she often came away from these meetings with a sense of dissatisfaction, of nothing being achieved. There was Alfred, more committed than ever, tirelessly working for the revolution and actually helping people to have better lives while he was about it, bullying officials, taking sick children to clinics, raising money for the cause and the poor in whatever way he could.

They had long-term plans for her, Klaus said. Well, her course would finish at the end of the month, and she'd have a certificate proclaiming her competent in shorthand and typing, ready to go out and get a job. She asked Klaus about that. Comintern would decide what position she was to apply for and he would pass this on. All in due course. Meanwhile, there was another course she could do at the Secretarial Academy, more general administration duties.

So she enrolled for another few weeks of learning how to be the perfect secretary, how to arrange her boss's desk, how to keep his diary, how to file his papers – always a him, she thought angrily, as she banged her knee against the filing cabinet.

A dippy blonde beside her whispered that she'd jolly well file the lot under L for letters. She was only doing this course so as to get a good job and marry the boss.

'If you put them all in L, the cabinet will fall over and squash you,' Vee pointed out. 'Or flatten the boss, and then there won't be anything left to marry, nor a job. Besides, he'll be bound to have a wife and four children, isn't that what bosses do, while they play around with their secretaries under cover of darkness?'

The blonde giggled. 'Don't depress me. I want my marriage lines, I don't believe in being a kept woman, there's no security.'

'More choice, though, and you can move on when you grow tired of the man.'

Vee acquired another certificate, and to her surprise felt a sense of pride in her Distinction in Office Work. Miss Duchet was anxious to place her, as she put it. 'We must place you somewhere where you can use your qualifications in a proper way,' she said.

Place, just like moving a chesspiece on to a particular square on the board. The chesspiece had no say, of course. And she would be placed, of that she was sure, but not by Miss Duchet.

Klaus had a gleam in his eye. This time when she met him, she took a bag of stale bread to feed the ducks.

'Bread for birds, when people are starving.'

'I'm not sure that my stale bread can help anyone,' she said. 'I could gather it all up and take it to the East End, but someone would notice, and they'd know I was back to my old ways.'

Klaus laughed. 'I think the ducks may have their day.'

'Come the revolution, we'll probably be eating them,' she said gloomily. 'I've been reading like mad, and I can see that when everything grinds to a halt, as it will have to, and the sources of supply are taken over but aren't working properly, and the rich are holed up in their castles, then no duck nor cat nor even dogs will have a hope.'

'I don't think anything would allow an English person to eat his dog.'

'No, most Englishmen would probably rather devour their children.'

'Still,' Klaus said, 'I think you take an unnecessarily gloomy view. Russia is a very different country, vast, with a huge population made up of many different ethnic tribes. Also they had serfs, so terribly oppressed, and the landowners were rich beyond imagining. It won't be the same in England. Revolution is never the same, that is why it is always revolutionary.'

Vee thought back to the French Revolution, how gloriously and with what high hopes it had begun, and into what a bloodbath it had descended. 'Napoleon,' she said aloud.

'What?'

'Napoleon. The French Revolution gave the world Napoleon. He was a dictator, and look at the damage he did. To France, to the whole of Europe. Do you think that will happen in Russia?'

Klaus had gone quite pale. He stopped and gave her a very searching look. 'That is not an idea that must ever enter your head. It is, it is – like sacrilege to a religious person to suggest such a thing.'

'You aren't suggesting that revolution and religion have anything in common, are you?'

'Religion is totally and always mischievous, and always serves the ruling classes.' Klaus had anger in his voice. 'Dear Vee, I urge you not to trouble yourself with these thoughts. They are ideas too big for you to grasp. Your role is to play the part that you can, that is all any one person may do.'

Vee was silent. Klaus was never patronizing, but he had come close to it with those words.

'We would like you to apply for a position at the Foreign Office,' Klaus said, his voice brisk and normal now. 'This is the telephone number that you call, or you may write, and ask for an application form. We think there should be no difficulty, with your family connections. They like girls from good families, as they put it, for this kind of job.'

'What is it, filing clerk?'

Klaus brightened. 'That would be very good, very useful, in some circumstances, but that is not quite the role we have in mind for you. A secretarial position, using your shorthand and typing, would be best.'

For a moment, her heart had leaped. If Klaus and his masters wanted her in the Foreign Office, then at last she might use the skills she had learned on those weekends in north London.

'You have no qualms, about handling secret material?'

'No,' she said.

She was lying, she had serious qualms, but she wasn't going to tell Klaus that. How could you not have qualms about betraying your country? Only she wasn't betraying her country, except in official eyes. What she was betraying was her class, about which she didn't give a damn, and the entrenched attitudes of capitalists like her grandfather, whose greed blinded them to the real good of the country they professed to love.

It would be odd to work in the Foreign Office, in the typing pool or for some sober-suited man, when she had so many friends there. One law for men and one for women; she was probably as clever as many of them, but there were two sides to each desk, and women were on one side and men on the other.

FOUR

Uncle Vernon was pleased, when she told them in Rochester Street what her plans were.

'You'll find the work stimulating, and you'll be amongst your own kind of people. I don't think you'd be happy working in some commercial organization, Vee.' He wiped his mouth with one of the huge white linen napkins that Aunt Lettice favoured. 'I'll put in a word for you in the right quarters, I can't see that there'll be any trouble in your getting a suitable position.'

'Oiling the wheels,' Claudia called it.

Claudia was back on a visit from Berlin, still starry-eyed about Germany. 'It's a matter of cleansing,' she said. They were sitting in the big drawing room, waiting for Claudia's parents to come down; they were going to a show and dining afterwards. Claudia was smoking a strange-smelling cigarette that she'd brought back from the continent, and Vee hoped Uncle Vernon wouldn't make a row about it when he came down.

'That's an awful stink, whatever it is you're smoking. Is that what they like in the new Germany? It smells like old socks mixed with cabbages.'

'French,' said Claudia, vaguely flapping the odorous smoke towards the fireplace. 'Very exhilarating. Anyhow, as I said, you have to be brutal and tough to clear away all the old ideas and rubbish from the country, and begin with everything fresh and wholesome.'

'Wholesome? Hitler?'

'He's a vegetarian, you know. Terribly fussy about what he puts into his body.'

'Then it's a shame he isn't more particular about what comes out of his mouth,'

'You don't understand what it's like. You've got to come over and see for yourself. People are working, unlike in this country, and everyone is putting one hundred and ten per cent effort into their work, because they know they're building for the future, a better world for them and their children.'

'Unless you happen to be a Jew or a Bolshevik or an intellectual with views that aren't the same as Hitler's.'

'You're relying on propaganda. I'm there, I see the truth with my own eyes. You've got to come over, and listen to Hitler giving a speech. I swear to you, Vee, it'll change your mind.'

'Going to hear Mosley didn't.'

'Oh, Mosley. He was nothing in comparison. Truly, it's glorious, Vee. It makes you glad to be alive and in on a movement that's so momentous and grand.'

Vee got up as she heard voices in the hall.

'What's that dreadful pong?' demanded Vernon as he put his head round the door to tell them the car was there.

'Chimney needs attention,' Claudia said. She reached for her fur wrap and sauntered out, giving Vee a broad wink.

Vee duly filled out her application form, and was called for interviews. She took tests in shorthand and typing, administered by Mrs Jaspar, the Head of Services. Then she was led along a series of wide and elegant corridors to a big, polished wooden door. Mrs Jaspar knocked on it and waited.

'Come,' said a deep male voice.

Inside the room sat a portly man with a walrus moustache and world-weary eyes.

'You're Vernon Saxony's niece,' he said. 'Sit down. Let me see, Oxford, hmm, all the right skills. Can't you find anything better to do than secretarial work, eh? I thought all you educated young women wanted to do men's jobs.'

'I don't,' she said.

'Give us a year or so before you go off and marry some young fella, is that it? Are you engaged to be married? I didn't notice any announcement in *The Times*, but I miss things.'

'No, I'm not engaged.'

269

'Good, good. This isn't a marriage mart, by the way. You won't mix much with our young men, except on a strictly professional basis. We don't encourage mingling. However, I dare say you know many of them socially, eh?'

'I have some friends who work here.'

'Good, good. We're keen to get the right sort of young woman working here, we can't let just anyone in, can we, Mrs J? You'll handle confidential material, in due course, and we want women we can trust. Women from your kind of background.'

Vee looked straight into his eyes, and nodded fervently. What had her headmistress said about her acting ability? She felt weak at the knees, what was she letting herself in for? In theory, she had no doubts. But in practice . . .

'Over to you, Mrs J.' He picked up the paper Mrs Jaspar had laid on his desk when she came in and scrawled a signature on it. 'All tickety-boo.'

'You'll start in the New Year,' Mrs Jaspar told her.

Vee went shopping for office clothes, accompanied by Claudia and Lally, who was in town for Christmas shopping.

'Let's get you what you need, and lunch at Fortnum's and then go to Hamleys,' Lally said.

'Hamleys?' said Claudia. 'What a heavenly idea. I haven't been there for ages, I adore toys. I can shop for all my nephews and nieces.'

'How many, now?' Lally asked as they climbed into the taxi. 'Bond Street,' Vee told the driver.

Claudia was counting. 'Geraldine has three little girls. Olivia has two sons and a daughter, and Henrietta has twins, baby girls, such darlings, if you like that kind of thing, and two older boys.'

'What about Lucius?'

Claudia's face took on a witchy look. 'Oh, well, there's the heir, and a spare, all just as it should be, and a little girl. Monica says that's it, she's had enough of child-bearing.'

Lally sighed. 'I'd love to have about half a dozen children.'

'No luck?' said Claudia, after a pause.

'Not yet.'

'Have you seen a doctor?'

'There's no reason why I shouldn't get pregnant, it just hasn't happened yet, that's all.'

'Does Harry want children?'

'Very much. He'd like another son; I hope for girls, because then they don't get sent away to school.'

'Yes, but they grow up to be like us,' said Claudia with sudden bitterness. 'Clever and full of energy and ideas, and all anyone wants to know is when we're going to meet Mr Right and get married. Boys have much more choice, and get all the fun.'

1936

ONE

Vee's shopping was in vain, her skirts and blouses and jackets lay shrouded with tissue paper in drawers, for in January, the King died, and the country, which had the year before thrown itself into a frenzy of monarchist fervour, now put on black clothes and prepared to mourn a king who was neither witty nor wise.

Claudia was full of hope for the future under Edward VIII. 'He's young, he's quite a sweetie pie, and he really cares about the country waking up to what's wrong with it.'

Vee wasn't so sure. Apart from the fact that the monarchy was a doomed institution, she too, had seen Edward enjoying the social life of a young royal, and she hadn't been impressed. Marcus would descend on Rochester Street and bear her off in a taxi to the latest fashionable nightclub, where she often saw the prince and his ultra-smart circle of friends.

'He's a lightweight,' she told Klaus. 'And rather pro-fascist, if anything. Despite all that stuff about how something must be done for the unemployed. It's all just words, he doesn't actually give a damn.'

'The words of kings have never counted for much in the way of truth,' Klaus said. 'Didn't Shakespeare say, "Put not your trust in princes"?'

'It's the *Book of Common Prayer*,' Vee said automatically. 'From the Psalms.'

'Ah, one forgets what a religious upbringing you had. But no remarks unfavourable to the new king to anyone but me, please. We expect you to show all the proper feeling for the death of the King, wear the correct clothes and behave as would be expected of you. These details can turn out to be very important.'

'You're wearing a black tie and armband for him, and you aren't even English.'

'Of course I wear black, the symbols of woe. This is my adopted country, and so I exchange words with the milkman and the grocer about how sad it is, and what a good king Edward will make.' He patted Vee's hand. 'This is our job, my dear Vee, do it with a glad heart.'

The girls at the Foreign Office were intrigued by Vee, and frankly envious of her smart London address. Most of them lived in rooms or tiny flats or girls' hostels.

'It's awful,' said a willowy brunette called Felicity. 'You have to be in by ten o'clock at night, and the old bag who runs the place snoops through your underwear drawers. And there's no proper heating, a couple of lumps of coal are all she gives you, you have to beg for more, and pay extra. I always bring some back with me when I go home to Suffolk.'

Vee was grateful to have been spared that experience, although surely it was closer to the workers than her comfortable room at Aunt Lettice's. 'It's my aunt's house, I shan't stay there, I shall look for a room, soon.'

The other girls stared at her. They were crowded into a cubbyhole down in the bowels of the earth, where they met for coffee and tea and biscuits during the ten minutes they were allowed off morning and afternoon. That was in addition to three-quarters of an hour for lunch.

'It really isn't fair,' said Felicity, biting into an iced bun. 'Our lords and masters swan out of the office whenever they like, hours for lunch, no one minds a bit. I was two minutes late back yesterday, two minutes, mind you, and got hauled over the carpet by Mrs J. Honestly, it's worse than being at school.'

'If you were a miner down the mines, you'd not have long lunch breaks, nor be able to sit in a cosy room drinking tea,' said Megwyn. She was a clergyman's daughter from Wales, and held serious views on the plight of the workers.

Vee longed to be able to say, yes, you're right, but Christian sympathy isn't the answer, that's anodyne stuff. If you care about the miners, then join the Party, do some work that will be of real benefit to them. Megwyn cared about the poor overseas as well, saving money each week from her wages to send to missions in Africa and China.

'Isn't your aunt a countess?' said Felicity. 'Aren't you related to an earl?'

The aristocracy were a source of endless fascination to the secretaries and clerks.

'My aunt is plain Mrs Saxony now,' Vee said. 'She was married to an earl, but he died.'

'Her son is the Earl of Sake. He lives in a huge castle, Kepesake, I saw lots of pictures of it in a magazine,' said Megwyn. 'He's awfully handsome.'

'So he's your cousin?' Felicity said.

Vee had to admit that he was.

'What's he like?'

'I haven't seen him since we were children. He's something of a recluse, and seldom leaves the castle.'

According to Claudia, he wasn't often allowed to leave the castle, and on the rare occasions when he went into the nearby village, at least two members of staff went with him.

'Isn't he nuts?' Felicity asked.

'Eccentric,' Vee said.

'Inbreeding,' said Megwyn, nodding her head sagely. 'That's the trouble with lots of these old families.'

'It must be nice, to be related to an earl, though.'

Vee shrugged. 'My aunt happened to fall in love with an earl. My mother married a clergyman, like your mother did. Different worlds, you know.'

'Girls, girls, here you are, gossiping, high time you were back on duty,' said a senior clerk who was bustling by with an armful of buff files. 'Miss Trenchard, please take these up with you and spare my legs.'

Vee picked up oddments of information from the other girls, about the men they worked for and what A had said to B. She passed these dutifully on to Klaus, who was always interested, and told her that Moscow were pleased with what she was doing.

'How can it be of any use to anyone?' she said, dissatisfied with the dullness of the job and her sense of not playing any real role in the class struggle or the victory of the proletariat. Yet when she was sitting there with Klaus, with his kind eyes and grave smile, he made it all seem worthwhile, and she felt appreciated and valued.

'It's like a jigsaw puzzle, information,' said Klaus soothingly. 'A piece here, a piece there, and it all adds up to give a clear picture. Besides, it's early days yet. Your time will come when you can be of much greater service to the comrades. Be patient.'

One day they were spotted in the park by Felicity, who was all eagerness to ask who she'd been with. 'Is he a beau?' she asked. 'Isn't he rather old for you? And he looks foreign.'

Vee turned it off with a laugh. 'He is foreign, he met my brother Hugh, who's in Yugoslavia, and brought me a letter from him.'

'You seemed very deep in conversation.'

'I don't often hear from Hugh, and he's not been well.'

She told Klaus that they had been seen together, and after that there were no more lunchtime meetings; instead, he sent her tickets to concerts of classical music, where she passed him the notes she had made. If they needed to talk, they met at weekends, when her fellow workers wouldn't be in central London, and St James's Park was given over to tourists and the geese.

Claudia was delighted when the new king, in March of that year, expressed his opinion that England shouldn't intervene when Hitler reoccupied the Rhineland. 'You see, he's mostly German himself,' she said to Vee. 'I think he'd like to rule properly, to put his country in order, it's a pity he's hamstrung by Parliament and all his officials.'

Thank God he was, was Vee's view. Edward as dictator didn't appeal to her at all, although maybe that would help to hasten the revolution.

Klaus told Vee not to worry about Edward and his closeness to the Germans and his evident enthusiasm for the Nazis. 'He can't last, this business with Mrs Simpson will bring about his downfall, and one of his brothers will take his place on the throne.'

She realized that Klaus despised Edward as much for not doing his duty as he did for the mere fact of his being a king, that outdated constitutional symbol of everything that Russia had overthrown in 1917.

Thanks to Klaus, she was a great deal better informed about the King's infatuation with Mrs Simpson and his determination to marry her than most of her fellow citizens. British papers were heavily censored, but American and European ones followed every twist and turn of Mrs Simpson's divorce and of the royal courtship.

The abdication came as a shock to Claudia, but not to Lally or to Vee. Lally also knew all about the Simpson affair, through her American family, who wrote her long letters quoting all the reports in the American papers.

'It would be odd to have an American queen,' she said.

'Queen Wallis!' said Claudia in disgust. 'How could he ever think it possible? Oh, it infuriates me. He could have done so much to cement relations between our country and Germany, and he's thrown it all away for that stick insect of a woman and a life in exile.'

'She's very glamorous and chic,' said Lally. They were lunching together; Claudia was over from Germany to attend a wedding, and Lally was in town to see another doctor.

'Honestly, Lally,' Claudia said. 'Give it time.'

'Didn't it take four or five years for your sister-in-law Monica to start a family?' she asked.

Claudia paused and looked at Vee. 'Yes, but . . .'

'But what?' said Lally.

'Oh, but nothing. Yes, it was ages before Alcuin was born. Then two more in quick succession, it'll happen to you, Lally. You'll see.'

'My mother had my brother ten months after she and my father were married.'

'Good for her, but you aren't your mother. If Harry's doing his duty in bed, then you've nothing to worry about.'

'Claudia! Duty, indeed.'

'Well, I hope it's a pleasure as well,' said Claudia. 'Otherwise, where's the fun in being married? Lots of lovely bed, and all perfectly respectable and legal, no sneaking in and out of bedrooms and all that. Not that you ever did or would, of course, Lally, but for us lesser mortals, marriage does have its attractions in that department.'

Lally and Vee steered the conversation away from marriage. They both knew that Claudia had been seeing Petrus again; he was involved in Government discussion on behalf of the Treasury with the German government, and so had been spending quite a lot of time in Berlin.

'And in Claudia's bed, from what I hear,' said Lally, when Claudia had waved them goodbye and gone off for a fitting.

Vee laughed. 'Nothing shocks you, does it Lally? Even though you'd never behave that way yourself, you take other people's misdemeanours and immorality in your stride.'

'I believe it's up to each individual to decide what they will and won't do. It's not for me to draw a moral line and say, over that you shouldn't step.'

'What about your Catholicism? Doesn't that lay down right and wrong very strictly?'

'It does, but I'm a Catholic, and Claudia isn't. I'd be very happy if she converted and found a faith and was bound by the same beliefs that I am, but until that happens, which I don't suppose it ever will, then she has to make her own decisions. Just as you do.'

'Don't look at me like that, Lally. I shan't ever convert. I've had years of Christianity, remember, and that's it as far as I'm concerned.'

'If you got married, would you marry in church?'

Vee thought about it. 'I'd say, Register Office every time. Only that would hurt Daddy and please my grandfather, who's completely irreligious, so I dare say it would be white roses and the Minster. Only it isn't going to happen, because I have no plans to marry.'

'Alfred?' asked Lally.

'Alfred? What about Alfred?'

'I always thought you and he might make a match of it.'

'I'm not in love with Alfred and never have been, and he certainly isn't in love with me, he disapproves of me. Besides, he's going around with that Vincent girl. Who has thick ankles, by the way, which is bad taste on Alfred's part.'

Vee's voice was light; she wasn't going to show even her oldest friend how much she minded about Alfred and Marjorie Vincent; how bitter a stab of envy she'd felt when she'd seen the two of them dining together at Boulestin's, and heard from gossipy friends that Marjorie spent a lot of time on social work in the East End. She'd gone over to their table and said hello; she hadn't seen Alfred since then, but she heard rumours.

'It looks as though Alfred's going to settle down,' Uncle Vernon told her aunt. 'Good thing, too, knock all that Commie rubbish out of his head.'

'The Vincent girl?'

'Yes. Good family, and she'll have a bit of money.'

'I thought she shared Alfred's leftie views,' Vee said.

'Oh, that will all stop when they're married and she's got a family to think about,' said Aunt Lettice with certainty. 'It always does. Not that I'm sure she's right for Alfred. Too much of a lightweight if you ask me, and very little sense of humour. Alfred will get bored with her within a year.'

'Nonsense,' said Uncle Vernon. 'A man doesn't want humour in a wife. She's a thoroughly sensible young lady; she'll do very well for him.'

Vee treasured her aunt's judgement, but it looked as though Uncle Vernon would be proved right; at a cocktail party not long afterwards, she overheard Mrs Vincent telling a friend with great satisfaction how they were expecting an engagement any day, and an autumn wedding. 'Chrysanthemums and St Margaret's, I think.'

How vulgar, Vee said to herself. And not at all Alfred's kind of thing. He'd taken leave of his senses if he were really planning to marry Marjorie, and in St Margaret's of all places.

She saw him, by coincidence, only a few days after she'd heard that conversation. It was at the Wigmore Hall, where she'd been meeting Klaus. She didn't see Alfred until after the concert, and she jumped when she heard his voice.

'Vee? I didn't know you cared for Brahms.'

He wasn't with Marjorie; he appeared to be on his own. Klaus had melted away, as was his habit.

'Where's your friend gone?' Alfred asked.

'Friend?'

'The man you were with. I saw you talking to him.'

'Oh, he's a stranger, I have no idea who he is. A foreigner. They talk, you know, where no English person would.' She gave him a bright smile, and resolved to tell Klaus that the Wigmore Hall was another venue that must be crossed off the list.

'I've seen him here before, he obviously likes music.'

'Again, how very un-English.'

They stood awkwardly together outside the hall as concertgoers hurried away, anxious to catch Tubes and buses, talking about the quartet that had been playing.

'Let's go and have a drink,' Alfred said, when he'd asked her how the job was going, and how his godmother was.

Out of the corner of her eye, she saw the Homburg Klaus always wore. 'I don't think I can, Alfred,' she said. 'I promised Aunt Lettice I'd come straight home, she wants me to help with some invitations she's got to do.'

A look of amusement crossed Alfred's face. 'What a lame excuse.' He raised his hat, bidding her goodbye, then strode swiftly away up Wigmore Street.

Damn, she said softly to herself. No sign of Klaus now. Did he know who Alfred was? Did it matter?

She decided to walk.

Alfred's voice again. 'If you're needed at home, hadn't you better buck up a bit? Won't your aunt be gnawing at her pen and eyeing the cards even now?'

'Why have you come back?'

'Because I decided it was all baloney, the invitations, and so, if you don't want to have a jar, I'll walk back with you through the quiet streets of London.'

'Quiet?' she said, as a taxi honked its horn not two feet from where they were standing, making her jump. A lorry rumbled by, and from a window above them came the sound of a baby crying and adult voices, perhaps its parents, raised in a shouting match.

'I wanted to talk to you,' Alfred said as they walked. 'About Hugh.'

'Hugh? What about Hugh?'

'I saw him in France. About a week ago. He didn't look frightfully well. He's got very thin.'

'He was ill not long ago. I don't expect he's completely fit.' She tried not to seem anxious. 'What's he doing in France?'

'He's just come back from Spain. He admitted he wasn't feeling a hundred per cent, I gather he's planning a trip to the country. You have a grandmother over there, don't you?'

Relief flooded over her. 'He'll be all right if he goes to Grandmère, she'll look after him.'

'He says he's going back to Spain as soon as he can. He wants to live in Andalucia for a year, and write a long poem about the Moors and the Christians.'

'How very mediaeval.'

'Ambitious, anyhow.'

The old feeling of ease at being in Alfred's company was stealing over her again, and for some reason a vivid memory of that time in the punt, and his kiss, came into her mind. The only man who had ever sent a tingle racing through her. Clever Lally to have spotted it. And, of course, a man that, for all kinds of reasons, she couldn't let herself feel more than friendship for. The dance, the river, the kiss. It was another Vee who had been there that night, not the Vee she was now.

Despite his passion for the Party, she knew that Alfred would not approve of the decision she'd made. He wouldn't forgive her working for the Soviet Union – for she was no longer so naive as not to admit that Comintern was little more than a front for Moscow – in however humble a capacity; Alfred was, at heart, a patriot. He admired the Russians for their patriotism; he would despise and reject her for her lack of that very quality. Yes, comradely solidarity was to workers everywhere, not to one's own country or family and friends. Yet she knew, with total certainty, that he would not have anything to do with Klaus or with instructions for covert work for Comintern. There was nothing secretive about Alfred.

'Here we are. Shall I disturb my godmother? I think not. Best not to enquire about those invitations, I look forward to receiving mine.' He smiled at her, kissed her lightly on her cheek and then was off again. This time, there was no voice out of the darkness, coming back to say more.

Kimber opened the door for her. 'Is my aunt in?'

He relieved her of her coat and gloves. 'Mrs Saxony has retired for the night. She had a headache coming on. Mr Saxony is working in his study.'

Aunt Lettice was prone to migraines.

'I want to make a telephone call. Is the telephone switched through to the drawing room?'

'I'll see to it, miss.'

She would call Grandmère, who was an owl and never went to bed before the early hours of the morning. Hugh might be there, and she could find out how he was.

'My dear, he's gone back to Spain, says he wants to write. Some of my friends in Madrid say the country is a tinderbox, liable to go up in smoke at any moment.'

What was Grandmère on about? Forest fires?

'Fighting. Civil war, Vee.' Grandmère's voice sounded tinny and distant down the line. 'Republicans and the church, left- and right-wing, don't you read the international news? All very tiresome and quite unnecessary, fighting only makes everything worse for everyone. Spain is such a complex country, I don't think Hugh should be there just now.'

'Did you tell him?'

'He laughed and said I was seeing bogles under the bed.'

She could hear him saying that, mocking Grandmère with affection, but resolute in what he planned to do. Obstinate was Hugh's middle name.

'Does Hugh support either side? I mean, is the part of Spain where he's going to be a place where he'll argue with everyone?'

'He says it's all a mess, and that this man Franco is the one he'd go for in a struggle. Only he thinks nothing will happen this year or next year, and by the time it does, his poem will be finished.'

Vee put the receiver down with a sensation of profound unease. She would ask Klaus about Spain.

'Not the best place to be,' said Klaus succinctly. 'The church and the army hate the republican government. It will end in tears, as your English nannies say.'

'As long as it isn't tears for Hugh, I don't mind what the Spaniards do. I know nothing about Spanish politics, and I don't want to. Are the Republicans comrades?'

'Indeed they are.'

'Will Moscow help them?'

'Ah, that all depends.'

TWO

'Joel, you can't possibly go.' Vee was horrified. 'Not to Berlin, not now.'

'Because I'm Jewish?'

'Well, yes, but also – well, should anyone go? It's showing support for a fascist regime, for Hitler. Even apart from what he's doing to the Jews, taking their jobs and livelihoods away, turning them into second-class citizens, no, into non-citizens, un-people, the whole of Nazism will be on display in Berlin. Triumphalist flags, ghastly in every way.'

They were at Marcus's flat, in Worcester Square. It was outrageously decorated with flags of every country in the Empire; Empire was Marcus's big theme at the moment. He was intensely patriotic, and stirring songs and marches were blaring out from the gramophone in the corner.

'My dear Vee, so vehement?'

A smooth voice, and coming from a smooth person. Petrus was standing beside them. The years were adding gravitas, even though he was still a young man. The leading economist of his generation, people were starting to say. A crony of John Maynard Keynes, travelling to and fro, to America, to the Far East, all over Europe, to advise on currencies and gold and all the part and parcel of that dismal science.

Only Petrus didn't look dismal at all. Sleek and happy, if a trifle wary.

'I thought you'd abandoned your political ideals, Vee, left all that behind you with your student days, and here you are, passionate against Hitler.'

Vee flushed. Damn it, she had almost given herself away.

'I don't have any involvement in politics, no. What use is all that protest and talk? But I still find Hitler repulsive, and his anti-Semitism is disgusting.'

'You don't have to go to Germany to find anti-Semitism,' said Joel, his voice bitter.

This was a party for Marcus's Oxford friends, Angels and others, he had told Vee. 'A get-together, to remind ourselves of our comradeship, I use the word in its purest sense, not as referring to the communist sort, how political movements do appropriate perfectly good words, so that none of the rest of us can ever use them. I make a point of using them, so we can take them back. A language cannot afford to lose a single word, or it will in due course become extinct.'

Every time Vee went to one of Marcus's parties, she swore it would be the last, and yet she always relented when his invitations arrived: never in the ordinary style, but scribbled on the back of grocery packets, or on a label attached to a plastic flower. On this occasion, an errand boy had delivered a tiny Christmas angel, with straw hair, clutching a slip of paper with the time written on it.

Klaus disapproved of Marcus.

'He'd be a good recruit for you, so brilliant, he knows so many people,' Vee said. 'It's a pity he's become so right-wing, he used to be quite pink.'

Klaus shook his head. 'He's openly homosexual,' he said austerely. 'Those proclivities and his delight in shocking people will get him into serious trouble one day. Whatever his politics, he would be too risky for us.'

Marcus certainly had the knack of pulling together an extraordinary collection of people. A cabinet minister, two or three top people from the BBC, a well-known actor, the head of a huge industrial concern, two or three men in the services, his charlady, wearing an absurd hat and chatting away in the corner to her host.

The charlady was a refugee, and Austrian. Marcus was talking to her in German; it seemed an animated conversation, and it was unusual to see him arguing so intently with a woman. He invited few women to his parties, and was inclined to take a pet if friends, however heterosexual, turned up with a girl.

Vee was one of the few who were sometimes invited. Lally, too, when she was in London, and Claudia, who wasn't there yet, although she'd said she might look in.

'I'm dining with some dull people who are big in Anglo-German relations,' she said. 'I think they want me to act as interpreter, which is a bit of a cheek, you pay a fortune for a professional. Only they say such people aren't trustworthy, and I am; I don't know why they think that.'

Claudia was trustworthy, oddly enough. She never gave anything away about her work for a Berlin export agency or the meetings and dinners she was summoned to. The tables had certainly turned, now Vee's cousin was the one with facts and figures and arguments at her fingertips, and Vee was, apparently, the one who neither knew nor cared much what was going on in the wider world.

Of course she did care, very deeply. Her hatred and fear of fascism grew by the day, and she was more than ever convinced that communism was the only bulwark against a tide of right-wing fanaticism and oppression. She and Claudia had a tacit agreement not to talk about politics, since they could never agree; Vee found herself almost praying – to whom? she rebuked herself – that Claudia would see the error of her ways.

Would she still be so committed to communism if it weren't for the fight against fascism? What had happened to her all-consuming passion to improve the lot of people like Peggy and the barefoot children playing in the street? They mattered, of course they did, but, as Klaus said, in his solemn and reassuring way, nothing mattered as much as ensuring that fascists did not take over Europe.

Claudia might swear that Hitler wasn't as bad as he was painted, that he was really working for the German people, who'd had a rotten deal. Under Hitler, men had jobs, women and children had enough to eat, the economy was going from strength to strength; what a pity England didn't take a leaf out of his book. Vee knew that it was all lies. England didn't need a dose of Hitler, rather it needed to shake itself out of its torpor and moral weakness, and to oppose the threat of fascism.

She came out of her reverie to find Joel at her elbow, looking fit from his head to his toes; he was running faster than ever, she'd heard from Lally who still found time to follow his form. He was planning, actually planning, to take part in the Berlin Olympics.

'I've been selected, I must go,' he said. 'Dear God, Vee, even Harold Abrahams wants us Jews to go. He says there's so much hostile feeling against the Jews just now in England that it will do great harm if we don't participate. It'll just give the Jew-haters more ammunition, they'll call us unpatriotic.'

'Why care what people like that call you?'

'Oh, Vee, you don't understand, do you?'

'Can't you see what's happening?' she cried.

Vee knew that she'd drunk too much of the excellent champagne that flowed so freely at Marcus's parties; where did he get the money?

'Rich admirers,' he'd told her, with a smirk and a wink.

The Austrian char seemed to be very interested in what Vee was saying, and Joel was looking at her with some surprise. She must stop this; she was letting the mask slip.

'I just think everyone ought to stand up for something, Joel.'

'I am. I'm standing up for sport, and youth, and the internationalism that sport brings; we sports people are *supra* national.'

Tell that to Hitler, Vee thought, draining her glass and holding it out for Marcus to refill. 'When the swastika flies above the stadium, and Aryan youth wins against the lesser races, how will you feel then?' She herself felt quite sick; not sure whether from the champagne or the hatred that welled up inside her when she thought of Hitler and everything he stood for.

Then Petrus was speaking again, soothing words dropping from his lips. 'I can tell you that Joel has been clocking in some remarkable times. Of course, his college is delighted, always an honour to have one of their men selected for the Olympics.'

'For these Olympics?'

'Hitler's politics can't touch the sporting efforts and achievements of a generation of young people, Vee. Once every four years, they have a chance to show what they can do, to race against the best in the world, in front of the world. That's an honour and spur to ever greater speed and endurance. Do you want them to be robbed of that? Surely the Olympic ideal is greater than Hitler and his posturing.'

'Posturing? Is that what you call it?'

'That's what all the show and the rallies are. Effective, yes, but no more than that. If Joel misses these games, he won't be running as fast in another four years.'

Klaus's warning words, not to let her mask of indifference slip, ever, echoed once more in her ears. She made an effort to smile. 'Oh, I dare say you're right. Hitler's just such an ogre, in his uniform, and all the storm troopers and the rest of it. In four years Joel himself will probably be in uniform, biffing a former fellow athlete who happens to be wearing a German uniform.'

An MP whom she knew slightly, a friend of Vernon's, was laughing at her. 'My dear lady, how very melodramatic. Hitler will caper all over his part of Europe, this is true. But it will amount to no more than that. You've been listening to warmongers. This country doesn't want war, isn't ready for war, won't fight a war. Has no need to fight a war. We have problems enough of our own in this country without looking overseas for trouble. No, Britain will mind its own affairs, and keep its young men occupied in running the Empire, thank God, not fighting the Nazis.'

Several other people had been listening to the MP. The Austrian char broke in first, shaking her head, and saying in loud, indignant German that this idiot was an ostrich, his head in the sand, he had no idea of the reality of the situation in Germany, in Austria.

Marcus grabbed her by the arm, and hustled her away, spitting uncomplimentary remarks at the MP over her shoulder. He pushed her down into a chair and handed her a glass of champagne. 'Drink this and shut up. Don't harangue my guests, it isn't polite.'

'Harangue, is it? You harangue all the time.'

'That's my way of annoying people, but why should you want to annoy Petrus or anyone else?'

'Because I'm a refugee, I have no feeling, no opinions, no voice?'

'Don't be silly, dear. He knows perfectly well what's going on in Germany, he's in Parliament. What he also knows is that this country will do anything to avoid a confrontation with Hitler. Why? Because it's a fight we couldn't win. So just be thankful that you're here in England, and not still in that very dangerous part of the world from which you've fortunately escaped.'

Marcus shouldn't talk to the woman like that, Vee thought. But his approach seemed to work.

'My magic touch,' said Marcus, coming up to her with a sly grin and clinking her glass gently with his own. 'Don't rip up at Joel, Vee, he has the right to go if he wants.'

'Would you go?'

'You know, I'm so glad to see the old Vee is still with us. I thought all the fire had gone out of your belly.'

'It has, except when I've had too much to drink. I must go.'

'Kiss, kiss, then,' said Marcus, popping his mouth an inch from Vee's cheek.

THREE

The train pulled into the Zoological Gardens station in Berlin. A strange monster of a train, huge and powerful and bull-nosed, a far cry from the gleaming, puffing dragons they were used to in England.

It was Vee's first trip to Germany since she was a schoolgirl, and she was amazed at the change. Everywhere was clean, not a scrap of litter to be seen. Martial music blared out from loudspeakers, interspersed with crisp, barked announcements about train arrivals and departures, and words of welcome to visitors who were in Berlin for the historic games.

She noticed with a certain wry amusement, as she listened to the announcements, that the train from Rome had arrived exactly on time. That was what everybody said about Mussolini, he had made the trains in Italy run on time.

No one had ever doubted the ability of the Germans to ensure their trains ran on time.

It was a glorious morning, blue skies with high wisps of mare's tail clouds. Lally sighed as she looked up. 'Seems like God's on their side,' she said.

'Nonsense,' Vee said. 'Claudia, is that all the luggage?'

Despite herself, despite the fact she was bristling with wary rage and dislike of the very large number of men in some kind of uniform around them, Vee was fascinated. She had come to the lion's den, well, she was going to notice everything, to take in every tiny detail, imprint it on her mind.

It had been Klaus who had informed her that she was to take the opportunity offered to go to the Games. 'You have a friend running, and I think you know some of the other athletes, from your university days.'

Vee was aghast. 'Go to Berlin! To the Olympics? I'm doing no such thing.'

Klaus went on as though she hadn't spoken. 'Your cousin, Lady Claudia is going . . .'

'My cousin is a fascist.'

Klaus shook his head at her. 'Why don't you believe me when I tell you that fascism for your cousin is a temporary obsession?'

'Temporary? It's lasted for years, well, more than two years, anyhow.'

'It may last another two, but she is not deep down a person who can maintain an allegiance or a belief in such a cause. She welcomes the rigidity and order that fascism presents, and she has the ability to screen out all the most unpleasant aspects of what is going on. She is too intelligent not to know that fascism is the great threat of our time, but too afraid not to understand that when there is a great danger, you stand against it, you don't side with it. Communism in England has no glory, no glamour, it is often very dull, solemn young men make earnest speeches, the communists do not seem to know how to enjoy life. Lady Claudia is a young woman who very much likes to enjoy life, to be stimulated, to have drama in her life. Otherwise she might just as well have become an ardent communist.'

'Claudia? Never.'

'No, now she won't ever be, you are quite right, she will grow out of the desire to be part of any such movement, left or right. She longs to live at the extreme, it is her nature. In another age, she might have become a religious zealot, ardent for God. As it is, the fascists have the most dramatic appeal at present, so she goes to Berlin, to revel in the ceremony and show and spectacle they will present.'

'She can go alone, then.'

'She won't be alone. Your very good friend Lally Messenger is going.'

'Lally? How do you know that?'

'I hear these things. She has a great warmth for Joel, who has long nurtured a hopeless passion for her, is that not so? And they still make music together, he comes to her house for weekends, with other musicians. Her husband encourages the music, because it makes Lally happy, but he does not want her to go to Berlin. However, her husband will be away then, at a training camp, as army officers are from time to time. So she is going to Berlin.'

'It makes no difference, Klaus.'

'I have my instructions. There is no better way of showing how far you have removed yourself from your days of red enthusiasm. And the appeal the Party had for you is not completely forgotten in some quarters. Also, at a party not so long ago, you . . .'

'How do you know about that? Who told you? Is someone watching me?'

He was very amused. 'I have many friends, many contacts.'

'Other agents?'

'No, no, you are a very select band. But I hear many things, especially about the wild parties that your friend Marcus gives, and what has been said. Snippets, but enough to worry me. So, the decision is made.'

'I can just refuse to go. You can't make me.'

'Oh, my dear Vee. Only think of the consequences of such disobedience. You would no longer be trusted, and perhaps a word would have to be dropped in someone's ear about your reliability for the job you do. Would you really want that?'

Vee was beginning to realize that there was an iron fist in Klaus's velvet glove.

'You have no choice, Vee. Orders are orders. You will go to the Olympics, with your friends. I shall be very interested to hear what you have to say on your return, particularly about how such Jews as your friend Joel fare.'

'There was a girl at Oxford, at my college, a Jewish girl. She married a German doctor last year. Will she be safe in Germany?'

Klaus frowned. 'Is her husband, the doctor, also a Jew? If so, then definitely not. If he is gentile, an Aryan, then he will be in trouble for marrying the wrong kind of girl.'

'She looks more Aryan than he does, blonde, blue eyes. Rather like Claudia.'

'Then, if she can change her papers, disguise her inheritance . . .'

'I don't think she'd want to. She's very honest, very brave. And a believer in the revolution, incidentally.'

'Then her future is bleak, at least, it will be if she stays in Germany. The Reich has no place for such people; Bolshevik and Jewish is doubly dangerous.'

'Klaus, you're Jewish, aren't you?' She had never asked him this before; she knew that one of the rules was, No questions.

'I am half Jewish. My mother is a Jew.'

'Would you take part in the Games?'

Now Klaus was laughing out loud. 'I? My dear Vee, I can hardly run three yards. I am a – what is the word? – a clumsy fellow. Sport was never my field of achievement or ambition.'

'What was?'

'Music. Music is the passion of my life, after my work for the revolution.'

That was all she was going to get out of him. He stood up, signalling that the meeting was over. 'Consult with Claudia, and she will make the necessary arrangements for your journey. Remember, you must talk with pleasure at work and in your family about the trip.'

'Perhaps the office won't let me have the time off.'

'You are due for some leave. You will find that there is no problem.'

The streets they drove through on their way to their hotel were another shock. Flags, swastikas alternating with the Olympic rings, flew from thousands of masts and from windows, not carelessly hung out, but each one in line with that flying from the adjacent window.

Traffic moved with precision, and on every corner there were policemen in uniforms and long boots, directing the traffic and answering tourists' requests for directions. It was a city in festive mood, bursting with a horrible energy and glory. Banners hung across the streets, welcoming the youth of the world to Germany and to the Games. There were thousands of pictures of Adolf Hitler, with that ridiculous moustache and the far-away look in his eyes, the eyes of a madman, a swastika armband on his arm raised in the Nazi salute.

Vee hated the troops who marched up and down, showing off, goose-stepping. 'Blond beasts,' she said to Lally, who smiled, and said that she was glad to have come, glad to see for herself what people talked and wrote about in the newspapers.

'I don't care for the regimentation,' she commented.

Regimented clothes, regimented peculiar marching steps, regimented minds, regimented beliefs.

Of course Lally cared very much about the Nazis' attitude to religion, especially Christianity. The Pope and the Nazis had long been at loggerheads; there was no room in the modern Germany for the gentler virtues laid down by the Church.

The official opening of the Games was on August 1st, a day that dawned overcast and wet; perhaps God wasn't smiling on the Nazis after all. For weeks before, there had been pictures of a relay of runners bearing the Olympic torch from Greece; there seemed to be no end to the German knack of twisting anything to conform to its own present predilection for flashy ceremony and glorification of the Aryan ideal.

'Look at this Olympic stadium!' Claudia said with almost proprietorial pride, as they joined the huge crowd streaming in for the opening ceremonial. 'It seats a hundred thousand people, imagine! And none of your concrete rubbish, this is all marble and stone from all over Germany.'

Stone quarried by people in concentration camps, Vee wanted to say, for Klaus had told her how the Germans had sited their camps in places convenient for quarries, such as Silesia. But she held her tongue, and took her seat between Lally and Claudia. At least you could count on the whole ghastly thing starting on time, it would run like clockwork, Claudia had assured them, like everything else in Nazi Germany. 'Couldn't we just do with some of their efficiency in England?'

'No,' Lally said, opening the huge programme they had been handed as they came in. 'I like the way the English muddle through. And in the end, it works out perfectly well.'

True, in minor matters, Vee thought, but the vast armies now assembling in Germany filled her with dread. In her mind's eye she could see waves of them advancing with that chilling goose-step, mowing down everything that stood in their way. How could the English muddlers hope to defend themselves if it came to war?

There was a murmur and a burst of applause from the crowd; everyone was looking up into the grey skies, where, like a giant and comfortable silver bird, came the Hindenburg. The airship had a huge swastika emblazoned on its tail fin; behind it streamed a pennant with the Olympic symbol.

With the airship hovering overhead, an air of expectancy filled the huge audience. 'Any minute now,' said Claudia.

To the accompaniment of musical fanfares – composed specially for the occasion by Richard Strauss, the programme said – the brown-uniformed dictator came into the stadium. The crowds erupted in a roar of delight, Nazi salutes, and demonic chants of *Heil Hitler*.

The Führer himself was so far away that Vee couldn't make out any details; she borrowed Lally's excellent binoculars and trained them on Hitler's face, his moustache, those chilling eyes made familiar by thousands of photographs and posters. There was a jubilant look to him, she thought, beneath his severe expression.

'If you give the Nazi salute, I'll never speak to you again,' Vee yelled in Claudia's ear.

Startled, Claudia glanced at her cousin, perhaps seeing something in Vee's eye that made her pause. 'It's very rude not to.'

'Oh, no, it isn't,' said Lally. 'You aren't German. You don't have to salute their dictator, even if you do admire him.'

'I bet the athletes will give the Nazi salute,' said Claudia.

'Not the Americans,' said Lally confidently.

She was right. They swept off their hats and held them against their left breasts as they marched past the stand where Hitler stood, but the flag bearer held the Stars and Stripes aloft.

'We don't dip our flag to anyone,' murmured Lally.

'Look, there's Joel!' Claudia cried.

She waved, but the figures far beyond them were turning their eyes right towards the stand of dignitaries; no Nazi salute from the English team, Vee was glad to see.

Speeches, inaudible for the most part, and then Hitler declared the Games open. They jumped as a cannonade thundered through the arena and a cloud of pigeons rose into the air; for a moment, Vee thought they were shooting at the birds.

Doves of peace, how ironic.

The athletes were drawn up in silent squads, as a lone runner – blond, naturally – entered the stadium, bearing the Olympic torch. He was dressed in white, visible from every part of the arena against the red cinder track. Up on the marble dais, he thrust the torch into the brazier; the flame flared into a huge plume of fire, and a collective sigh rose from the spectators.

'Thank God that's all over,' Vee whispered to Lally.

'It's very effective,' Lally replied. 'All this theatre.'

FOUR

'The best moment was when Jesse Owens won his gold medals,' Vee reported to Klaus.

Klaus wasn't interested in black American athletes. He wanted to know whom Vee had met at the various parties and receptions she had attended, what gossip she had picked up.

'I heard that the soldiers and everyone else had to pretend they weren't anti-Semitic,' she said. 'Only they say that in Potemkin, soldiers were dashing about and shouting that when the fortnight of the Games was over, they'd gas all the Jews.'

'They took down all the notices forbidding Jews and insulting them,' Klaus said. 'Bear in mind, though, that the anti-Semitism is no stronger than their virulent anti-communism. The stone for that stadium, the porphyry and marble and granite, was hewn out of the earth by as many communists as Jews; our comrades in Germany pay a very heavy price for their commitment to the revolution.'

Uncle Vernon wanted to hear all about the trip, as well. 'It's amazing what Herr Hitler has done to the German economy, truly astonishing. I was discussing this with that fellow Petrus only the other day. Did you run across him in Berlin?'

'No,' said Claudia, a shade too casually. 'Was he there?'

'I understood he was flying over to Germany for some talks during the Games.'

'We didn't see him, in any event,' said Lally, who was spending a couple of nights with Claudia to do some shopping before she went back to Wiltshire to be reunited with Harry and little Peter.

'How did that friend of yours, Joel, do?' Vernon went on.

'He won a bronze medal.'

'Good show. Isn't he a Jew?'

'Yes,' said Lally. 'It was brave of him to go.'

'The Germans had Jews on their Olympic team, look at that blonde girl who fences. I saw her picture in the papers. It shows that a lot of what they say about Hitler is so much exaggeration.'

'The Nuremburg Laws are hardly an exaggeration,' Vee began. Then a raised eyebrow from Uncle Vernon reminded her of Klaus's words. 'Joel said he had no trouble from the German athletes, even though he made no secret of being a Jew.'

'There you are, then.'

'Alfred was in Berlin,' Claudia said. She reached for the salt and tapped a spoonful on to the side of her plate.

'As a reporter? Pity he's such a red, he's a good writer, could make something of himself if he weren't so blinkered in his politics.'

'He's going to Spain next week,' Lally said.

Vee put down her spoon. 'How do you know that?'

'He told me. Off to write about the war for the *News Chronicle*.'

'Any news from Hugh?' Vernon asked her. 'I know your father was in London while you were away, trying to get some sense out of the Foreign Office. He wants him to come home.'

'Knowing Hugh, he's probably unaware that there is a war,' said Claudia. 'Let alone that it might be dangerous out there, not if he's in the middle of a poem.'

'It won't be dangerous for him if he doesn't fight, and why should he? It's not our war.'

'They say people are flocking from all over to fight for the Popular Front,' Vee said.

She had avidly, but discreetly, devoured all the newspaper reports she could find on the situation in Spain. She must ask Klaus for more information; surely the USSR would support the Republicans. 'Even Germans are going to fight against the rebels.'

'They won't be welcomed back to the fatherland with open arms,' Vernon said drily. 'More likely to be shot, if they survive the war in Spain.'

There was talk at the office about Spain when Vee went back to work. She had been promoted, and was now working directly for Sir Hector Paget, and Spain was one of his departmental responsibilities.

'Spain, Hitler, the King playing about with that Wallis woman –

what kind of a Christian name is Wallis, I ask you? – and this at a time of year when all one wants to do is take off for the moors. Glad to see you back, Verity, there's a heap of papers for you to sort out for me.'

Papers whose contents she scanned and made notes on, to be passed on to Klaus at their next meeting. Contents that might help in the fight against fascism.

Klaus was gloomy about Spain. 'Victory for the Republicans? I wouldn't be too sure, Vee. Germany is gearing up to pour tanks and guns and aeroplanes in on Franco's side. It's good training for the war that's coming.'

His words sent a trickle of fear down her spine. 'My brother's there.'

'Fighting?'

'Oh, no, I don't think so. He's a writer.'

'It's the writers who plunge into a war without any idea of what they're doing, all *dulce et decorum est*.'

'Except that it isn't *pro* his *patria* that he'd be fighting for.'

'He'd be fighting for a cause, that's the way it is with intellectuals. He might join the International Brigade. I suppose he'd fight on the Republican side?'

She thought about that. 'I'm not sure,' she said, thinking aloud. 'You never know with Hugh. Last time I saw him, he said that the issue in Spain wasn't left against right, that it was more complicated than that, and that Spain is different.'

Even as she spoke, she had a feeling that she shouldn't be talking about Hugh to Klaus. She wished she'd never mentioned him, although, with the way Klaus seemed to know so much about her and her family, he probably knew where Hugh was anyway.

Besides, she trusted Klaus, and what was it to him if Hugh fought or didn't fight, or on which side he threw his lot? Could she have fought, there wouldn't have been a second's hesitation, the popular front were the goodies and the Francoists unutterably wrong.

She hoped Alfred wouldn't end up somewhere where he might get shot at. She hoped that Hugh would come to his senses, and get out of Spain as soon as he could. She wished she hadn't been born then, at that time in the twentieth century. She wished Hitler had never been born at all.

*   *   *

'Show trials in Moscow: nine men condemned,' the headline screamed at her as she reached the Tube station to catch the underground home.

Vee hoped they were all guilty. They must be guilty.

A voice inside her head whispered that they probably weren't.

She didn't want to think of Alfred's parting words to her and Claudia and Lally: 'Wake up, you three. Have a long hard look at the world you live in. You think fascism's the answer, Claudia? It isn't; it's one of the most destructive forces ever unleashed in Europe.'

'No worse than Stalin and communism,' Claudia had lashed back.

Then Alfred had said the oddest thing: 'You might be right about that, Claudia.'

'No words of advice for me?' asked Lally, ever the peacemaker and not liking the tension in the air.

'Persuade your father and his cronies that if it comes to war, America can't be isolationist.'

'Come on, Alfred. Why should America get involved in a war in Europe thousands of miles away? We saved your bacon in the Great War, isn't that enough?'

'No. It's never enough, Lally. That's the price you pay for being top dog. We were, but our time is over. Hitler thinks he's going to be, and he has to be stopped. You think America can stand back and do nothing? That isn't the way it works, Lally.'

FIVE

'We have a very important job for you.'

Vee's heart missed a beat. At last. Months of doing her work dutifully and conscientiously, and every time she saw Klaus, he'd say, 'Be
patient, the time will come. For now you earn yourself a reputation
as a good, solid, utterly reliable worker. This is important.'

What were they going to ask her to do? Watch someone? Steal
papers, and hand them over? Whatever it was, she would do it,
because then, at last, maybe, she would be doing real work for the
cause of communism and anti-fascism, not merely passing on oddments
of information which were, she was convinced, of no real use or
interest to Moscow. Klaus rarely made any comment, simply told her
not to be selective, not to use her own judgement, just to look for
the names or topics that he mentioned to her.

'We want you to marry Giles Hotspur.'

Vee was so stunned that the breath rushed out of her, and she began
to hiccup.

'Marry?' she said, when she'd recovered. 'Marry Giles? Are you
all mad?'

She was under no circumstances to call Comintern mad, Klaus said
severely. If orders came, then they came for a reason. It wasn't up to
agents to question them or make comments; a good agent merely
agreed and waited for further instructions.

'It's unexpected,' she said, after a long, long pause. 'I thought that
it would be to do with papers, information. That could be useful, I
can see that. But this!'

Marry Giles? Her reason told her that they had, somehow, made a ridiculous mistake. If ever there was a man who wasn't the marrying kind, it was Giles.

'There are many different ways of serving the Party and the revolution,' Klaus said. 'It is not just a question of from each according to his means, to each according to his needs. It is also a question of each comrade serving in the way he or she best can. For some, the services are intellectual. As you say, information, papers. For others, there are physical ways of serving.'

Because I'm a woman, she thought, she served with her body. Male comrades served with their minds. Just as it was in Party headquarters. You women lick stamps and run errands, while we masculine minds plan the revolution and make things happen.

'You don't completely understand about Giles,' she began.

Klaus was patient. 'That he is a man's man? That he has sexual relationships with his own sex, not with women? I understand this perfectly well, and so does Moscow. Such men are valuable to us, for their feelings, shall we call them, place them outside the world in which they have grown up.'

'That's nonsense,' she said. 'In Giles's world, it's taken for granted. About men and other men.'

'Yes, because they begin at school, and it's all part of the game, stiff upper lip and beat the fags, isn't that so? However, when these beautiful young men venture into the world of, say, the Foreign Office, then perhaps the world is not so understanding. If a young official, a promising young man, such as Giles Hotspur, has as his senior a man who is of the same kind, then there is no problem, no conflict. All is tolerance and turning a blind eye. Only, as it happens, this is not the case with Giles. Giles works in Sir Hector Paget's department, and Sir Hector is not full of warm understanding about men who love other men. He is, you might say, an ardent heterosexualist. He is rational about it: he wants men in his section who are normal, who have wives and children and the right kind of home life.'

That was true. A lot of gossip went on in the ladies' cloakroom and over coffee and tea, morning and afternoon. Sir Hector's austere ways were no secret. A devoutly religious man, he had a clear sense of right and wrong when it came to sex.

'Nonetheless, it doesn't alter the fact that Giles doesn't like women. He never has.'

'He likes, if you want to use that word, your brother.'

'My brother has nothing to do with this.'

'He has,' said Klaus. 'Cigarette?' He offered a packet, and she, more for something to stop the trembling in her fingers than because she wanted to smoke, took one. Klaus smiled into her eyes as he lit it.

'You're troubled, Vee. I see this. However, it is not so hard. Giles must marry, or lose his job.'

'He can move to another department.'

'Not with a bad report from Sir Hector, who has the ear of everyone who counts, both in the Foreign Office and in the Government. No, if Sir Hector blacklists Giles, that's his career in the Foreign Office finished. Which would be a pity, don't you think? Such promise! Such a brain. Such a waste, if he has to go into the City, or something even more mundane. How upset your brother would be to hear of this.'

'Hugh and Giles were a long time ago. Hugh isn't even in the country, I told you, leave Hugh out of this.'

'My dear, Hugh is the crux. You are very like your brother. You are a boyish type, very gamine, very chic, of course, because you are not a boy. Still, the physical type is the same. If Giles has to find a wife, you would do least violence to his feelings, for you are almost Hugh.'

'Am I to marry Giles simply so that he can stay in the Foreign Office? Is that the deal?'

'My dear Vee, there is no deal. This is your job; it is not a matter of deal or negotiations. Once you are married to Giles, there will be further work for you to do. Responsible work. Work that only you will be in a position to undertake.'

'Giles isn't at all left-wing,' she said. 'I don't think he ever was, even when it was the fashion, at Oxford.'

'Giles's political stance is of no importance. What is of importance is the job he now does. Through you, we can ensure that he continues to do it.'

Klaus got up, and stubbed his cigarette out with his shoe. 'It is ten to two. You will be late back to work. You must hurry.'

It's all right, Vee told herself, over and over, as she stood on the Tube, her hand holding the strap so tightly that it became numb. They've misjudged, Giles won't want to marry me, or anyone. It just isn't going to happen.

302

SIX

She had racked her brains to think of a way she could approach Giles, but in the end it was simple. Had Klaus known that Giles had, reluctantly, decided he must marry?

She heard the rumours in the office, the quiet whispers about whether Giles was 'one of them'; the reports of Sir Hector's remarks. 'Young diplomats need to be married,' he'd said, forcibly, when the matter of a posting for Giles had been raised. 'I don't trust a man who doesn't have a wife.'

His proposal was down to earth. 'I have to get married, Vee. For reasons of state, you might say. You know how I am; well, it won't do, not with Sir Hector. You aren't still going about with Piers, are you? He wanted to marry you and he was awfully cut up when you turned him down. Or so I hear, I don't know him that well.'

'I was sorry about Piers.'

'Why didn't you marry him?'

'I didn't love him enough.'

'So you're waiting for Mr Right to come along. A man that you can fall in love with.'

They were sitting in a pub, in the smoky, dark almost dingy back room of The Sedan Chair. All around them was a buzz of smoke and conversation, the winding down of midday Saturday, the end of the working week.

These people would be going home, on foot, or by train, to houses in the suburbs or blocks of mansion flats. Meals would be cooked in dinky little kitchens, or sent up from the restaurant, or served in a trim dining room. These people lived open lives.

Or so she supposed, but how could one possibly tell? Was another Russian agent watching them, even now? Was that man over there with a deep scar above one eyebrow not an official or a clerk but also a fascist, was he secretly sending information to Italy or Germany?

Or were the secrets within each besuited breast of a more personal kind, adultery, perversions, a tendency to lie or to cheat, an over fondness for the bottle, an inclination to waste the week's pay on the horses. Vices large and small.

Her secret wasn't a vice. It was not a personal failing, a lapse. She was doing what she did because she wanted a better future, a world where everyone counted, where the whole shabby façade of England, with its classes and its pettiness would be swept away.

'I doubt if I'll ever find a man to love, actually, Giles,' she said. 'I'm not the sort. Too cold, too rational for the usual kind of marriage.'

'And the unusual kind?'

'Of course,' he said, a little later, when he was on his third large whisky, 'it would mean you'd have to give up your job.'

She frowned. How absurd, that was a thought that simply hadn't occurred to her.

'Does every woman employee, when they get married?'

'Oh, yes. So what will you do with yourself all day? Keep house?'

'I expect I'll find something to pass the time. I'll have to. Where shall we live? Isn't your flat very small?'

'It is. It won't do. But I like it there, and there's another one available. Two floors up. Bigger. I'll make some enquiries.' Another swig of whisky. 'Do you mind if we do the deed at the Register Office?'

'You forget, my father is the Dean of York. People would think it odd if I married at the Register Office. I think it's better if everything is as conventional as possible, don't you?'

'Better wedding presents, as well,' said Giles, with an attempt at a smile. 'Lord, I wish it hadn't had to come to this. What do you think Hugh will say when he hears about us?'

'I dare say he won't for a while. He's out in the wilds of the Sierra Nevada, I don't suppose he reads *The Times*.'

'I'll have to go north and meet your people.'

'Don't worry, the one that counts is my grandfather. He has the money. He'll love you.'

'It seems wrong to deceive so many people. And to take those vows, in a church.'

'Not a church, in the Minster, and only think of all the mismatches that have been made there over the centuries, all those noble northern families marrying their sons and daughters off. Or are you afraid that the hand of God may reach down and smite you as you kneel at the altar?'

'Don't you believe in God?'

'No.'

'The funny thing is, I do.'

Vee still considered a quiet wedding, perhaps in the crypt of the Minster, with only close family and friends in attendance would be best.

Giles would have none of it: 'If it's to be the Minster, then we'll do it properly.'

And, when she broke the news to her parents, they agreed with Giles. In particular, her mother was adamant.

'Are you ashamed? You don't have to get married, do you?' she added, with an anxious glance at her daughter's waistline. She'd come up to London as soon as she'd heard the news, to start buying a trousseau for Vee, with her sister's help. Aunt Lettice, with three daughters married, knew all about trousseau buying.

'No, Mummy, I'm not pregnant. It's just that Giles wants to get married before Christmas, there's a chance of a posting some time next year, and . . .'

'Posting?'

'Abroad. He is a diplomat, remember, it's his job to work abroad.'

'I hope nowhere too hot. Or too foreign. Africa, for instance. It's bad enough Hugh being in Spain, with everything so uncertain there, and if you were to be in Africa. Or China, even . . .'

What difference would it make? Vee asked herself. The number of times she saw her parents these days, it wouldn't matter greatly if Giles were to be posted to Mars.

Vee and her mother were lunching at Gunters, or rather, waiting for Aunt Lettice to join them, before embarking on an afternoon's preliminary sortie to the shops.

'Lettice gets no more punctual with the years,' her mother said. 'Darling, do you really want another of those cocktail things? In the middle of the day? Aren't they dreadfully strong?'

'No,' Vee said mendaciously. 'Hardly more than fruit juice, I promise you.'

Alcohol was the only thing that was going to get her through this lunch and the afternoon and the days to come. Mummy was pressing her to give up work at once. 'They must understand that an engaged girl needs to prepare for her wedding.'

Vee minded giving up her job; she minded it very much indeed. Not because it was an interesting one, but it was hers and it gave her a kind of status and a sense of purpose, and she'd made friends with some of the other girls. Moreover, why was it necessary to give it up? If she were expecting a baby, that would be different, but why should she be any less capable of doing her job simply because she had taken a trip to the altar? They weren't making Giles give up his job, of course not.

'Don't be ridiculous, Vee. It's quite different for a woman,' her mother said, horrified at her outburst against the Foreign Office. 'Of course a woman gives up her job when she marries, it's an understood thing. It's not just the Foreign Office, no firm or institution wants to employ a young married woman, that would be shocking. Your job from now on is to make a home for Giles. You'll be busier than you have any idea of, you have no notion of how much work it takes to run a household.'

Vee didn't think a service flat in London was exactly a household, but there was never any point in arguing with her mother about that kind of thing.

'Ah, here's Lettice at last.'

The sisters exchanged a frugal kiss, a hovering waiter appeared at the table, and they ordered.

Her mother drew out a neat leather notebook, and opened it. 'Notice for the papers, it hasn't been put in yet, has it?'

'Vernon's seeing to that, it will be in *The Times* on Thursday,' Aunt Lettice said, between greedy sips of her soup. 'This is delicious, it's ages since I've lunched here, I'd forgotten how good their lobster soup is. Don't worry, Anne, Vernon will have it exactly right, you know how precise he is about that kind of thing.'

The talk went on, drifting in and out of Vee's mind. She responded with a dutiful yes, or no, when asked, and although Mummy rebuked her for not attending, she felt she was putting on a pretty good show.

Invitations, wedding lists, guest lists, motor cars, flowers, music . . . What a bore it all was. What a sham, a mockery.

'Very different from poor Lally's wedding,' Aunt Lettice said. She adored organizing weddings, and although she would have preferred to be planning Claudia's nuptials, Vee's was next best. 'With her family and his glaring at each other, it was awful, Vee, wasn't it? No flowers, no choir, such a hurried, unsatisfactory kind of ceremony.'

Maybe, Vee thought, but the bride and groom were in love and didn't give a toss for all the flummery. Even Lally, whose conscience had stung her at marrying a Protestant, had taken her vows without a second's hesitation. And when the disapproving elders of both families had gone their separate ways, Lally and her friends had mingled with Harry's friends, nearly all army men and their wives, and had had a splendid party, dancing the night away.

Aunt Lettice was telling her mother more about Lally's wedding.

Her mother had her disapproving face on. 'Mixed marriages like that never work. The Dean won't have it. He says a couple must decide to be one thing or the other. Best if the Catholic converts to Anglicanism, of course, so much more satisfactory and sensible in every way. But perhaps your friend ...' she looked reprovingly at Vee '. . . being an American, and of Irish extraction – isn't that so? – well, perhaps she had a stubborn streak. The Celts are a very stubborn people, I've often observed it. Look at the Synod of Whitby.'

Vee wasn't in the least bit interested in the Synod of Whitby, all she wanted was to get away from these plans and details, and try to forget that in a few short weeks she would be a married woman, Mrs Giles Hotspur, without a name or a job of her own.

'Giles wants all the Angels to come,' she said suddenly, thinking out loud.

Her mother and aunt broke off their conversation and stared at Vee, as though she were suggesting that Messrs Gabriel, Michael and Raphael should be sent elegantly inscribed cards of invitation.

'Sorry. It's an Oxford society. A men's dining club, sort of. Lots of people belong.'

She was floundering now. 'Like Hugh, and Giles. And Harry, when he was up, he was an Angel, too, so Lally says.'

'As long as they don't come wearing wings,' said Aunt Lettice, laughing at her own joke. 'Your Uncle Vernon was an Apostle when he was at Cambridge, I dare say it's much the same kind of thing, only possibly more frivolous at Oxford. Cambridge men tend to be more serious, I've noticed.'

'The Dean was at Cambridge,' her mother said.

307

'Of course he was.'

'Make sure their names are on Giles's list, please, Vee, if he wants them invited. And you have to draw up a list of your own friends. Not too many, the wedding will be held in the choir rather than the nave, that's what Daddy says.'

'The choir?' said Aunt Lettice, surprised. 'Isn't that rather hugger-mugger?'

'Not at the Minster, Letty. All the guests would freeze to death in the nave in December. You forget how enormous the Minster is; we can easily seat three hundred in the choir, it won't be a problem.'

'Reception in the Deanery? Can you cope with all the guests?'

'The Dean wouldn't countenance an hotel.'

'You can hire winter marquees, with heating; at least you can in London, I expect it's possible in Yorkshire. No trouble with booking, either, at that time of year, you're not competing with the season, as we were with Hetty's wedding, that was a perfect nightmare to organize.'

'Henrietta looked quite lovely, a fairy princess,' her mother said. 'And that brings us to the most important question: who will make the dress?'

They both looked intently at Vee.

'Worth,' said Lettice. 'Her measurements must be sent over to Paris, and one of Giles's friends can bring it back in the diplomatic bag, that way you avoid all that stupid duty. Only don't tell Vernon, you know what a fusspot he is.'

Duty, in comparison to the huge sums of money that her mother and aunt were preparing to spend, seemed a drop in the ocean.

'Mummy, can you afford such an extravagant wedding?' Vee asked abruptly. 'A dress from Paris and so many people? Is it all really necessary?'

Mummy reddened, vexed with this outspokenness. 'It's very vulgar to talk about money, Vee, as I've always told you. As it happens, your grandfather – who is delighted with the match by the way, he'll be writing to you – has offered to pay for the wedding. Indeed, he insists upon doing so. He's looked into the Hotspur family and thinks you've done very well for yourself, Vee. He couldn't be more pleased. I expect he'll come up with a very handsome wedding present.'

Now who was being vulgar? Vee thought.

SEVEN

The wind was bitter. It sent flurries of snow whipping off the tiled roofs. A forlorn pigeon sat huddled and fluffed out behind a grotesque grinning down from the north side of York Minster.

Vee was at the Deanery for her wedding. She had escaped from the frenzy of wedding preparations and the growing list of thank-you letters she had to write for the mound of presents, and had come across to the Minster for a few moments on her own.

'Where are you going?' her mother called after her. 'Don't be long, more presents have arrived this morning, and there's so much to do.'

'Just Christmas shopping,' she lied. 'I haven't found just what I want for Giles yet.'

That was a masterstroke. It was becoming for a bride to choose the perfect present for her groom. Vee's mother, the Dean's secretary, the typist from the Minster office who had been drafted in to help, the butler and several maids all beamed their approval. Such a handsome man, Mr Hotspur, such a nice young couple. And a Christmas wedding was always nice, adding an extra touch of celebration to the festivities.

Inside the Minster, it was cold, the centuries-old icy coldness of stone floors and walls. There was a school service going on; looking down the nave, Vee could see rows of girls in a familiar grey and purple uniform. Behind them were rows of parents, warmly dressed, pleased members of the northern English upper-middle classes, there to celebrate the end of term with carols and the traditional Christmas lessons.

A senior girl was reading the lesson. 'And when they were come into the house, they saw the young child . . .'

309

Five years ago, that had been Vee, climbing up into the pulpit and speaking in the clear voice of one who had been taught elocution. She could still remember the words, and she mouthed them silently now, as the girl spoke them:

'. . . with Mary his mother, and fell down and worshipped him, and when they had opened their treasures, they presented unto him gifts; gold, and frankincense, and myrrh.'

Vee even recognized the girl. It was Georgina Williams, when last seen a pale, scrub-faced first-year, all ginger hair and narrow feet. Here she was, in the upper sixth, poised and confident. On the brink of her adult life. Perhaps this time next year, she'd be at Oxford, a student at Grace, eager and happy and keen and relishing her independence from school and family.

Just as Vee had.

Five years! Dear God, what a change those five years had wrought. If she, that ghost of her former self, standing on that very same spot, reading those identical words, could have looked forward and seen the Vee standing there in the shadows, about to be married to a man she cared nothing for, deeply caught up in a movement that would shake the foundations of the world of Yorkshire Ladies', of the Minster, of everything that Georgina and she had ever known – then what? Would she have felt daunted, excited, fearful? Would she have looked clearly at that future Vee, and said, I want none of her. That is a path I do not choose to take?

Did one ever have the choice, in fact, or was it just one little step after another? And there you were, at the edge of a precipice, or down a deep hole. Or treading the rightful path to revolution and a new future, not only for these daughters of the rich and comfortable, but for every unprivileged and downtrodden woman in the country.

That was a future with no religious services, no school uniforms, no Yorkshire Ladies' College. No stiff headmistress with a grim expression and a pince-nez, no clergy. No Minster, as she knew it; religious buildings in the Soviet Union had been appropriated for more suitable uses. What could any official do with the Minster? Tear it down, stone by ancient stone, down to its Roman roots. Use the stone and lead to build houses for workers, level the site and let time forget the centuries of authority and corruption that had existed there.

The choir was singing again, and the words rang in her head: 'Rejoice, rejoice, Emmanuel.'

310

Once a favourite carol, now a symbol of everything she hated about the church, the Minster, her family. Rejoice! At what?

A voice, an irritating voice, whispered in her ear, Isn't it better to rejoice than to be miserable?

To which the answer was, we have no right to rejoice when there is so much oppression and misery in the world.

When had she become so joyless?

When she had realized how short-sighted and self-centred her life had been. Before she had heard the call, had seen a way to diminish and destroy Grandfather and all he stood for, that was what following a cause did for you. It filled the void in your life that brought you unhappiness, and in payment, it took away joy, of a carol, of Christmas, of friendship.

She shivered and got up from the stone seat she'd been sitting on. A kind of desolation crept over her. She frowned. It was the music, playing on her emotions and memory, wasn't that what carols were for? She was on edge, it was a difficult time, she had a difficult task ahead of her. Had brides before her stood and shivered at the prospect of the union she and Giles were entering into?

Giles had been open with her, would that she could have been as open with him, but of course that was impossible. She didn't know what plans Klaus had; he refused to discuss them with her.

'You have cold feet,' he said. 'Because Giles is a friend and a decent sort, as you would say. All very well. But he is also a representative of all that is rotten in England.'

That was true enough. Giles's family, as she had swiftly discovered on her ceremonial visit, were dyed-in-the-wool conservatives, with a large and a small c, who disliked Jews and pinkos and socialists of any and every description, who admired the new Germany, and were eager for England to come to an accord with Hitler.

'We're all on the same side,' Giles's firmly-corseted mother informed Vee. 'Of course all that strutting and saluting isn't the English way, but our principles are the same. I'm so glad to see Giles is marrying a thoroughly English girl.'

The daughter of the Dean of York, and cousin to an earl, even a deranged one, was proof to the Hotspurs that Vee was 'one of us', unquestionably a right-thinker.

'Vee used to be quite pink herself,' Giles said in a thoughtless moment.

Stiff disapproval all round the dining table, where they were gathered in chilly discomfort for one of those interminable meals of too much not very good food that Vee had come to loathe. She looked down at the plate of solid meat and toughly roasted potatoes, knew that a sugary, floury crumble would follow, Giles's favourite – she must make sure their cook understood about cooking roasts and fruit pies and crumbles – and then Stilton, her least favourite cheese.

'It was rather a fashion,' she said, with a bright smile. 'It only lasted a few weeks, dreadfully dull and earnest, all those left-wing people. Didn't you think so, Giles?'

'Young women shouldn't meddle with politics,' said a gruff uncle. 'They don't understand what's going on, time enough to have political opinions when you've raised a family and know what makes the world tick.'

Which is money and influence and power, Vee said inwardly. Another smile, the tension slackened. An evil spirit prompted her to say, 'I'm not entirely English. My grandmother on my mother's side is French.'

Giles frowned at her.

'So I'm a quarter French.'

'The French can't be trusted,' said the gruff uncle, predictably. 'Look at that terrible crowd they've voted in. Won't last, of course, that's the thing about the French, change their minds every two minutes.'

Giles's mother was working out that the French grandmother must also be the grandmother of the earl. Which no doubt made it all right. She sighed as a plump maid took her plate away, and the pudding appeared.

'Jolly good,' said Giles.

Vee had a premonition that there were going to be a lot of 'jolly good's in her life from now on, although Giles with his family was a different man from the Giles she'd known at Oxford, and the Giles making a career for himself at the Foreign Office. She suspected the politics were the same, but that the London Giles was a more sophisticated character than this son of the squire she was seeing here. She hoped so.

'Of course, Vee's French will be a great help when we're in Paris,' said Giles, keen for her to make-up lost ground. 'The FO do appreciate wives who can talk to the French. They don't expect it or encourage it for some postings, Africa, for instance, or the Far East, but they like it in Europe.'

'Good, good,' said Giles's father. He was a taciturn man, a retired general who had been badly gassed in the war and left a gaunt skeleton for whom every breath was a struggle.

Vee felt a touch of pity for him. He had fought with enormous bravery, and had paid a high price for his war, yet at the same time, he was a representative of a class that had no place in the world as it should be. He was the least philistine of Giles's large and mostly disagreeable family. He had a real love of music, his tired, thin face lit up when he spoke of Mozart. That was where Giles had got his appreciation of music and literature and paintings, she supposed; Giles himself was no philistine. She sighed as she pushed the apple and crumble about her plate with the heavy silver spoon. That, too, might make her married life easier than it might otherwise have been.

Did Klaus have any idea of what he was letting her in for? Apart from the emotional quicksand of Giles's feelings for Hugh, what of the practicalities of living as man and wife when the reasons for their marriage were so far removed from any normal ones? Would Giles want to make love to her? That was an area she preferred not to think about. Giles had implied that he wouldn't. Her instinct was that he was entirely a man's man, that it would indeed be that most out-dated of unions, a marriage of convenience.

She had heard that such couples weren't uncommon in America, in Hollywood; Hugh had once told her that many of the most famous male film stars were queer. 'It would be fatal to their careers and the prestige of the studio if any hint of such sexual preferences got out. Therefore wives are found, or husbands in some cases, there are rumours about some of the most glamorous of the screen goddesses.'

So she was in good company with her life of pretence. Film actors and actresses deceived their fans for the sake of fame and fortune, she was deceiving her family and friends and colleagues for a far more worthy reason. So why did she feel so depressed about it?

Mrs Hotspur noticed her future daughter-in-law's subdued spirits, and spoke about it to Vee's mother when they met for a lunch at the Women's Club in York to discuss wedding arrangements.

Mrs Trenchard was surprised. She hadn't noticed that Vee was out of sorts, or in low spirits. She hadn't paid much attention to how her daughter might be looking or feeling for years and years, ever since Daisy died, in fact, although Mrs Hotspur wasn't to know that.

'Girls are always a bit nervous coming up to their wedding day,' she said.

'As long as she isn't going to bolt at the altar or throw a fit the night before the wedding,' said Mrs Hotspur, severely. 'With so many guests coming, many from very long distances, that would be unforgivable.'

'Verity wouldn't do that,' said her mother. One thing she did know about her daughter was her staying power. 'Once Verity has made up her mind to do something, nothing deflects her.'

The triumphant sounds of 'Hark the Herald Angels' signalled the end of the carol service, and brought Vee back to the present moment. The congregation stood as the procession wound its way out, then knelt, then stood up again, talking and waving and looking around.

The girls, boisterous at the thought of holidays were chatting and calling to each other as they filed out, despite the efforts of the mistresses to quell them. A tall young man who was ahead of the rush was in the crossing, looking for one particular girl. A sister, Vee supposed, he was too young to be a father.

Then everyone had gone, the Minster was restored to its cold quietness, the chill and darkness of ages creeping over the stone flags and the marble memorials.

Giles appeared at her side, spruce and cheerful, what had he to be so cheerful about? Here was a troop of little bridesmaids and two tiny pages, looking bewildered. And her mother, notebook in hand, conferring with one of the minor clergy as she came purposefully down the central aisle.

EIGHT

The choir of the Minster seemed bleak and even desolate, the boys' voices thin and with a purity that had nothing to do with nuptials and passion and bedding and all the other things that went with a wedding. Beneath the soaring roof, fading away into shadows, Vee looked small and remote in her close-fitting white dress; she had become very thin lately. Giles was pale, handsome and courteous, but his bride could tell that every word of his vows was an effort.

'I never saw an unhappier-looking couple,' a burly Hotspur guest said to his wife as the congregation came out of the Minster and stood about while photographs were taken.

Claudia and Lally, both chilled despite their fur coats, exchanged glances of agreement with this remark.

'A good catch,' said a stranger in a shabby morning coat. 'Giles Hotspur is worth a bob or two, I suppose she's marrying him for his money, can't say they look as though they're in love.'

Vee was smiling; smiling until she felt her face must crack. Smiling for the camera, smiling for her parents, smiling for the guests.

Hugh wasn't there. Vee wasn't sure whether to be glad or sorry; she felt that Hugh would have seen the wedding as the phoney business it was. But she was worried about him; he was still in Spain, although not involved in any fighting, according to the messages that came through from various of his friends who were back in England. Alfred, sending daily reports for the *News Chronicle*, had seen him several times, and sent word via his newspaper office.

Alfred had come, wearing his customary shabby clothes. He arrived after the beginning of the ceremony and slipped in unnoticed after a brief skirmish with a verger. Marcus, an usher, spotted him and waved the verger aside.

'You could have managed a morning coat, Alfred, honestly you are the limit.'

'Only just got off the boat last night, came straight up,' said Alfred, smothering an enormous yawn. 'Had to see Vee turned off; why on earth is she marrying Giles? I couldn't believe it when I heard.'

Marcus shrugged. 'Vagaries of women, they feel the need to put on Hymen's saffron robe, and grab any poor sod who happens to be passing. Literally in this case,' he added, laughing at his own joke and causing a great aunt to turn round and shrivel him with a glance.

'Oops,' he said, putting a finger to his lips.

Alfred settled himself as comfortably as he could. 'Wake me up when the shouting's over. I hope they've plenty to eat at the reception, I'm starving.'

'Bound to have,' said Marcus. 'Yorkshire, you know, northerners are all hearty eaters. Lots of Angels here, I'm glad to say.'

'I can hear the rustle of wings,' said Alfred.

'Including Petrus.'

Alfred's eyebrows shot up. 'Petrus? Vee invited Petrus? She can't stand him.'

'No, he's on the groom's side. He and Giles always were close. Politically and in other ways.' He gave a lewd chuckle and watched Alfred lapse into slumber.

'Verity acquired some very odd friends at Oxford,' Vee heard her mother remark to Grandfather when she caught sight of Alfred.

Good for him, she thought.

The honeymoon was to be spent in France. The newly-weds went by train to London after the ceremony, where they spent the night at the Ritz. Giles got drunk, and passed out, snoring loudly, on the large bed. Vee read a book and slept like a log; exhausted by the preparations and the nightmare wedding day, she was beyond wakefulness.

The next day they made the crossing from Dover; a choppy, uncomfortable journey, with scudding clouds and a biting wind. Giles stayed on deck, his cheeks burning from the cold, while Vee took refuge in a cabin. Then they caught the train to Paris.

'Since I've got to take up my duties in the New Year, we might as well get there early, enjoy Paris a bit,' Giles had said.

Which, surprisingly, Vee had. The violent weather of the previous few days vanished overnight, giving way to brilliant skies and sparkling air. At lunchtime, it was mild enough to be able to sit outside the cafés and watch the world go by. Giles was in his element showing her around the art galleries. If only he wouldn't talk about Hugh all the time.

'It was Hugh who taught me how to look at paintings,' he said. 'From my first term at school. How did he know so much?'

She had no idea; paintings had never been part of the landscape at the Deanery, unless you counted the portraits of former Deans hanging in gloomy lines along the corridors, or the paintings of windswept moors with stags, which had belonged to her grandfather on her mother's side.

Her father knew a good deal about art, it was part of his gentle cultivation, but he had little rapport with his children; she had never heard him and Hugh discussing painters. Besides, painting to her father stopped at about the time of Raphael, while Hugh was keen on the Impressionists and the moderns.

'One is tempted to believe they all have something amiss with their eyesight,' her father had ventured, spotting an article in a magazine that Hugh was reading. 'One cannot imagine why they wish to distort the world in such a way.'

Hugh had merely glanced up and smiled at his father; it wasn't a discussion that held any promise for either of them, and they both knew it.

'Hugh's one of the most artistic people I've ever known,' Giles said, as they wandered through the Louvre. 'It's astonishing how much he knows.' His voice was bitter. 'I always thought we'd do Europe together after we came down. Visit all the galleries and museums, and go round the ancient sites.'

'I thought you and he did go off together in the vacs,' Vee said, wishing Giles wouldn't brood so.

'I counted the time up, I keep a diary, you know, and it barely amounted to more than a few weeks *in toto*,' Giles said. 'He'd say, let's go here or there, and then, when we got there, he'd vanish. I'd get a phone call or a postcard, some whim had taken him off to quite a different place, different country even. He never said, Let's both go. I suppose I should have realized then . . .'

She had had enough of these ruminations on Giles's relationship with Hugh. 'Look at this Greek vase here, what energy, don't you agree?'

It was an unfortunate choice, she realized, as soon as the words were out of her mouth. Giles stared glumly at the portrayal of two Greek men, one bearded, one a youth, reaching out for each other in a very erotic way.

'Oh, look, that must be the goddess Athene,' she said, even more brightly. And then, 'My feet ache, Giles. Let's go and have a coffee and sit down.'

It was a relief when the New Year came. They saw it in at a party thrown by a cousin of Vee's who had a huge apartment in Paris and flamboyant tastes. Philippe had encouraged her to invite some friends from England, smart English guests would add chic to the occasion, he said.

'None of your tweedy types, however,' he warned. 'What about the lovely Lady Claudia? We see her pictures in *Tatler*. She is your cousin also, so a connection of mine.'

Recklessly, but not expecting any of them to come, she invited a clutch of friends from England: Claudia and Marcus among them, and to her surprise the two of them turned up, brimming with festive spirits, shrieking with delight at Philippe's apartment, demanding to know every detail of the honeymoon.

'Such an interesting couple as you are,' Marcus remarked in his usual malicious way. 'One wonders how it is in bed, one really does.'

'Shut up, Marcus,' Claudia said. 'Heavenly dress, Vee, where did you get it?'

1937

ONE

Vee and Giles took an apartment in the Quai d'Orfèvres, overlooking a triangle of greenery. They had the top two floors: a huge drawing room, with a tiny balcony and a little dining room off it. Beyond that was a small kitchen and an even smaller broom-cupboard of a room, for the maid. Upstairs on the top floor, there were two bedrooms, a large one, flooded with light, which Vee immediately fell in love with. Giles took the smaller room. 'What use is a bedroom with a view?' he said prosaically.

Vee loved the fact that she could open the window and sit outside, on the narrow ledge behind the parapet, overlooking the roofs of Paris. She could see the Seine in all its moods, brown and turbid, grey, sleek and sulky, and on some days, almost blue, a gentle, smiling river.

She adored living in Paris. She had been there, of course, many times, but always as a visitor, mostly going to and from Grandmère's house. Now it was different, now she lived there, and she relished the city in all its splendour and steaminess.

As the winter drew into spring, she set out every day to explore. Giles rose early to go to the Embassy, and after he'd left, Vee would walk down the steps, out into the little square that wasn't a square, and cross over to the little café on the other side. The proprietor would greet her with a nod and a 'Bonjour, Madame,' and she would sip a *café au lait* and dunk her buttery croissant in it.

Then it was off, without a map, walking through Paris. Over this bridge on to the Île de France, back over that bridge, along the Right Bank and the Left Bank, into Notre Dame, how gloomy it was; she didn't linger, into the Pantheon and Les Invalides. She went to the Louvre and to modern art exhibitions, she lunched in tiny restaurants near Les Halles, or outside in a café on the Champs-Elysées. She wandered among the second-hand bookstalls and the print shops, and then, when she was tired, and her feet would carry her no more, she would curl up outside her bedroom window, like a cat in the sun, and read. There was actually a cat, a neighbour's cat, a sinuous creature with great yellow eyes, who would drop from the chimney pots to sit just a few inches away from her; she liked its company.

Then she shopped for clothes, revelling in the fascination the Parisians had for precisely the right cut, the right style, the perfect fit. She had never been so happy. Coming to Paris was a liberation for her, and it showed in her looks and her bearing.

She was much admired within the diplomatic community, for her allure, her charm, her good manners, her lovely clothes, her excellent French.

So much so, that the Ambassador's wife thought to give her a hint of warning. 'It doesn't always do for the wife of a very junior diplomat to shine too brightly, my dear. Perhaps not quite such elegance in what you wear, and we do encourage embassy staff to wear English clothes, we must fly the flag, you do understand.'

Vee smiled and was courteous and took no notice. Let Giles fly the flag, with his Savile Row suits and clean-cut English looks. She would please herself.

Best of all, there were no park benches in Paris with Klaus sitting upon them. She could stroll in the parks, in the Bois de Boulogne or in the Tuileries, just for the pleasure of it. No assignations. No duties.

Her relationship with Giles was polite and companionable. He was delighted with the good impression she made and told her not to worry about the Ambassadress, 'She always looks a perfect fright in those English dresses of hers, I do believe she buys them in Leeds or somewhere. The French admire her for it, they think she's formidable, but there's no reason you should go around looking like that.'

They kept strictly to separate bedrooms. Vee was quite sure that Giles had his adventures; there were evenings when he came home late and with a luxurious, gleaming look to him. She asked no questions, he saw no need to confide in her; they told one another no lies.

Giles did touch, with slight embarrassment, on the subject of her sex life. 'I can't condemn you to celibacy, Vee. Just be discreet, that's all, you know what a sea of gossip Paris is, and the diplomatic crowd are the worst of the lot.'

Vee didn't want a lover. She was self-contained and happy, and saw no way in which the complication of a lover would improve her sense of wellbeing. Freud might say differently, but lovers didn't mean goodbye to repression; to her the word brought up visions of Petrus, a thought to make her flesh creep and not likely to send her scudding off for new adventures.

Besides, although her life was so blessedly free of comradely instructions just at present, she was still under orders not to become involved with any man. 'Your duty to the Party and to Comintern overrides everything,' Klaus said more than once. 'Pillow talk is dangerous, our comrades would not be very happy at any suggestion of a liaison, unless it were with another comrade.'

Since she had no idea who else Klaus's – clients, she supposed she might call them – were, that was hardly an option.

Her idyll lasted until April, when she found a letter in their postbox at the foot of the stairs, purporting to be from an old school friend in Paris, but using the code words that meant Klaus had come back into her life.

She crumpled the letter in her hand, and dropped it into the litter basket outside the café. Her coffee and croissant were ashes in her mouth that morning; damn Klaus. Damn all of them, although she had known all along that these days of freedom and happiness were too good to last.

It was appropriate that it wasn't one of Paris's more amiable days, with a biting wind and scurrying, gloomy clouds sending sudden downpours of rain to set the gutters gurgling and shoppers hurrying into nearby doorways and shops.

The bench where Klaus was sitting was damp, and she wrapped her mackintosh around her as best she could. She tried to keep her umbrella open, but the wind whipped it inside out, and she had to give up and just sit there in the rain, fortunately now no more than a drizzle, as Klaus greeted her with his customary friendliness, and proceeded to give her instructions.

'I can't be any use to you at present,' she said, knowing that she sounded aggressive.

Klaus took no notice, continuing in his calm, authoritative way,

'News from the diplomatic circuit, for instance, you must have come across the German Ambassador.'

Vee had come across most of the Ambassadors in Paris, and many of them were very happy to chat and flirt with so attractive a young wife. 'They're hardly likely to say anything that would be of the slightest use to you or anyone else,' she said crossly. 'It's just idle conversation.'

'Then you must have some gossip, there is always a lot of gossip connected with embassies and so on.'

'I don't care for gossip.'

That was the wrong answer. Klaus frowned. She must make more effort. She must get together with other embassy wives; he had heard that she was leading a very independent life in Paris, that had to stop.

She was appalled. 'They meet and drink horrible coffee, which they are frightfully complacent about, thin, milky stuff, not like the horrid continental coffee that the Parisians drink, is what they say. With English biscuits, and they talk about babies and dogs.'

'And their husbands, and about what's going on in other embassies,' said Klaus shrewdly.

'I wouldn't know.'

'I'm afraid you must swallow your dislike of such company and cultivate these circles. That, my dear Vee, is an order. Then, presently, Giles may begin to bring documents home. He has a heavy work-load, and a busy social life, so he will find sometimes that he needs to catch up with his work at weekends.'

'He already does; he goes into his office.'

'Then you must discourage him. Say he can bring his work home, that you are lonely without him.'

'Our relationship is hardly of a kind to make that plausible,' she said.

'You are a clever woman, you will find a way. Then, when he is asleep, you can go through the papers, and photograph them.'

There it was. Finally, the techniques so painstakingly taught in the house in north London were going to come into their own. Klaus had a tiny camera for her, with a folding stand. 'You must find an extremely secure place for this, where neither Giles nor the servant will ever find it.'

Vee sighed, and took the camera. 'Even if he does bring papers home, he stays up later than I do, and is off very early in the morning.'

A small round chemist's box of pills was handed over. 'Half, a quarter, even, of one of these, in his after-dinner brandy, and he will feel much sleepier. They are perfectly harmless, a mild bromide, nothing more. He will feel no ill effects, he will wake bright-eyed and refreshed after a good night's sleep, and you will only need to use them when you wish to get at the papers, they are not to be taken every night, of course.'

'Of course,' she echoed, looking down at the round white box. Perhaps she'd swallow them all, and put an end to this. Then rationality reasserted itself. She was being childish. This was her work, her real work. She had made the commitment, and if the joys of Paris had led her away from that commitment, then it was good that Klaus had reappeared to remind her what she was doing and why; there was enough poverty and misery in Paris to make anyone wish for the revolution.

She had taken some weeks out of time, out of real life; now it was time to come down to earth, and to do what she could for the cause. Where had her idealism gone, where was that vitalizing surge of energy that she had felt when Peggy died and when Klaus had summoned her to the service of Comintern? The cause of International Communism? Which sounded so much better than, we want you to work for the Soviet Union.

As it turned out, she had no need of suggestion or cajolery to get Giles to bring papers home; he began to do so of his own accord. And, what was more, there was no need of secret rummagings. 'Your French is better than mine, Vee,' he would say. 'What does this phrase here mean, exactly?'

And she would explain and translate and discuss the precise meaning of a word or a sentence, meanwhile noticing what the papers were about, planning for the small hours when Giles lay in a deep pill-induced slumber and she could open his briefcase – the lock was child's play after Mrs Granger's lessons – and extract those that would interest Klaus.

She laid the papers flat on the table in the kitchen, where the light was brightest. Then she set up the tiny camera, and took picture after picture. Then the papers were replaced in exactly the right order, the briefcase locked and set where Giles had left it. The camera and its stand went into a jewel box she had bought especially for it, beneath a layer of rings and earrings.

Giles had noticed the jewel box. 'Locking your stuff away, Vee?'

He might well comment, for she had a habit of leaving her jewels wherever she'd taken them off, and Giles was quite used to finding them under the cushion on the sofa, or beside the basin in the bathroom.

'I've got one or two rather good pieces, and I thought that I must be a little more careful. If I lost anything, then we'd suspect Cécile, which is hardly fair, for I'm sure she's honest. So I bought this, and I lock everything away.'

Giles thoroughly approved.

Then, in the morning, when Giles had gone off remarking on how well he had slept, she would tuck the rolls of film into her handbag, inside a brown envelope, and set off for wherever Klaus had told her to leave them, in a bag on a bench, tucked behind a branch of a tree, under a seat in a church.

She was rather impatient with this side of her secret life. It was too cloak and dagger for her taste, and hardly necessary. Why couldn't she simply post the film to Klaus?

He drew in a sharp breath when she suggested that.

'No postal service is ever safe. The intelligence services here in Paris have no scruple about opening mail, as indeed is the case in England.'

'Why ever should they? If I post it in a letter box across town, why should they bother?'

'One can never be sure. The correct delivery of all such secret material is the first rule of our trade, Vee. It's not for you to question it in any way.'

No questions, ever.

TWO

Giles's behaviour began to change. At first, Vee was reluctant to admit it to herself, but he was less at ease, more drawn about the face. He frequently asked if she'd heard from Hugh, and she always shook her head, although she had had two letters from him; letters that she took from the box and quickly hid away, thankful that they hadn't come on days when Giles was at home and opened the post himself.

Hugh's letters were brief enough, mostly descriptions of his life in Portugal – well away from the fighting, he said; Vee was thankful that he seemed to have no desire to become involved in Spain's civil war. It never occurred to her that he wouldn't tell either her or his parents just how much time he spent across the border in Spain. He never mentioned Giles, or asked her about her life in Paris, although once there was a French book he wanted sent, c/o the embassy in Lisbon. 'I'm sure you can fix that through diplomatic channels.'

Vee could, but it was difficult without Giles finding out. After that, she took a post office box, and told Hugh it was easier for him to send correspondence there, it was unreliable at home.

Together with Giles's tetchiness over the apparent silence from Hugh, she noticed that her husband was drinking more. The couple of glasses of wine with dinner became a bottle, and that was often after he'd had more than enough cocktails at the receptions and parties they went to nearly every evening. Giles held his drink well, and formerly, she probably wouldn't have noticed it, but living at close quarters with him had made her aware of his moods and his degree of inebriation.

She taxed him with it, and then wished she hadn't.

'Oh, for God's sake, do you feel so much a wife that you have to nag? I'll drink what I want, when and where I want. Besides, I don't drink too much, you're turning into some kind of a Puritan, it's that churchy upbringing coming out.'

The maid took exception to clearing up the mess in the bathroom, and gave in her notice. Vee put up her wages; the girl stayed, but she knew she would have to look around for another maid, one less knowing, someone up from the country maybe, who wouldn't be so good at her job, but would be less inclined to notice and comment on what she wanted to keep hidden.

She told Klaus that Giles hit her, when he was drunk. He looked into the sandy area in front of the bench, where a couple of pigeons were strutting around each other. Then he shrugged his shoulders.

'A few bruises, only think of the suffering that our comrades have endured since the revolution.'

'I don't know why he hits me.'

'It is because you are not Hugh,' Klaus said. He folded up his newspaper, tipped his hat to her, and walked away.

She felt she was spying on France, and this caused her more unease than she had felt since she had been recruited. 'How can information about France be of interest to Moscow?'

'It is not for you to question your orders or to give a moment's thought to what Moscow wants.'

'I'm a quarter French,' she said, apropos of nothing in particular.

'We know, and therefore you will be glad to see the revolution in France, a country ripe for revolution.'

'The last one didn't work out so well.'

'The French Revolution was a great success, but they forgot or never knew that revolution is continuous, that there never is a moment when you say, this is it, the revolution is finished, we have accomplished this much, now we rest. For when the people rest, then the tyrants return.'

'Tyrants! I begin to wonder just who the tyrants are.'

'Unquestioning obedience is what we ask of loyal comrades,' Klaus said gravely. 'You are a woman, we take on very few women, you have a special role to play. And remember that with the freeing of race from the oppression of a tyrannical government comes sexual liberation, so that between men and women and men and men and even women and women all things are possible.'

What was possible between her and Giles was painful and had taken her by surprise. She locked her bedroom door, now, and often lay awake as Giles banged on her door and swore at her.

'From the back, you could be a boy,' he'd said to her, in one of his drunken fits. Sober, he was reasonable, agreed with her that their marriage was a sham, that they had known it was to be a sham, and that part of the bargain was that they would demand nothing from each other.

Drunk, no holds were barred.

Giles had fallen into a routine. From Monday to Thursday, he behaved beautifully. He was a good companion, courteous, sober and dutiful. 'Friday and Saturday nights God has given me for mine,' he told her. 'And I intend to enjoy them in my own way. Stay, or go, I don't care. Only not a word of criticism.'

That was when he started bringing men home. Young men, hardly more than boys sometimes, who more than once left on Saturday or Sunday morning with the bruises that she had become accustomed to. It was a relief; they had the bruises, not her. They got paid for their trouble; she'd seen the notes stuffed in a trouser or jacket pocket. If she were there, he insisted that she treat them as honoured guests, then encouraged the visitors to join him in teasing and taunting Vee, before he and the boy – or boys – would vanish into Giles's bedroom.

He wanted to take over her room. 'After all, I'm paying the rent, and when I have friends to stay, we could do with a bit more room.'

'Friends! What kind of friends are they?'

'My friends,' said Giles, 'which should be enough for you.'

THREE

Claudia came to see Vee when she was in Paris for a few days, on her way to Germany.

'You're in *Tatler* this week,' Claudia said as Vee opened the door. 'Goodness, you do look awful. I can't say that marriage suits you.'

'I've got a hangover,' Vee said.

'You didn't use to drink.'

'I didn't use to be married to Giles.'

'Is he a drinker? You surprise me.'

'He was drowning his sorrows last night.'

'Vee, did he hit you?'

Vee put up a hand to cover the bruise on her cheek. 'This? No, of course not. I fell over. While under the influence.'

More lies, her life was nothing but lies these days, from the continuous lie of her marriage to the other lies; lies to cover up the kind of man Giles had become, the small daily lies, told to prevent anyone finding out where she'd been or what she'd done, not Giles, not anyone. Not because there was anything to hide, but simply because lies were now part of her life and nature. The only person she didn't lie to was Klaus, and she hadn't seen him now for five weeks.

Vee took the copy of *Tatler* that Claudia was holding out. The photograph looked formal and unnatural. Mr and Mrs Hotspur, one of Paris's smartest young English couples.

She looked so poised, as did Giles, immaculate, elegant, assured, smiles, the happiness of a young married couple.

How was it possible that the agony of their marriage and the misery of their life together didn't show? No one would know, from that photograph, that they weren't exactly what they seemed to be. She drew her wrap more closely about her, anxious lest she reveal more of her bruises.

The maid was out shopping, so Claudia went into the kitchen to make coffee. She set the gas on a low flame and rattled cups about, taking longer than she needed, while she thought about Vee. She looked dreadful, and, for some reason, scared. In all the time she had known Vee, she had never seen her afraid. Nervous, apprehensive, anxious, worried, moody, but never afraid. And there were those bruises, swiftly hidden, but not swiftly enough.

'Are you pregnant?' she asked, when she went back into the drawing room with two cups of coffee. 'You've got that ghastly look that some women get when they're in pig.'

'It's the throwing up that does it, I expect,' Vee said. 'I threw up because I had too much to drink, I told you.'

Claudia knew about Vee and throwing up. Vee vomited when there was something in her life that she couldn't stomach.

'You appear such a perfect couple,' Claudia said. 'Harry Messenger thought, too perfect. He said you didn't argue like a married couple, and you had no real rapport. That you were playing at being married and the reality hadn't come home to you.'

'Reality? Honestly, what's reality to do with being married? Drop it Claudia, everything's fine, I'm loving Paris, and it's just I've not been too well lately. Giles is working very hard, we keep late hours, which doesn't suit me. Tell me what you're doing, what brings you to Paris?'

'I'm on my way back to Germany,' Claudia said. Which was true, but what had brought her to Paris was Vee. She'd met Lally in London, and they agreed that the letters they'd had from Vee, few enough of them, were strained. She wasn't happy, Lally said, and how could she be, married to Giles? And then they'd asked one another, as they did whenever they met, why had Vee married him?

'Still obsessed with fascism?' said Vee, with a flash of her old spirit.

'It works,' Claudia said briefly. She had a life of sorts, in Berlin. She had a flat there, lovers, she drank rather too much and partied rather too wildly, and lived for the rare, rare occasions when she saw Petrus – only once in the last six months, and then he had been disapproving of her enthusiasm for Germany.

'It might have worked, Claudia, but it hasn't. Don't hitch your star to that particular wagon, or you'll come to grief.'

'Don't tell me you're a warmonger!'

He'd given her a supercilious look. 'Recognizing the threat that Hitler poses is hardly warmongering, it's sense. And if you thought with your brains instead of some other fuzzy part of yourself, you'd see through all the humbug to the menace beneath, and you wouldn't spend another five minutes in Berlin.'

He had left her morose and unhappy, and determined to prove him wrong. But she wasn't really looking forward to going back to Germany, not this time.

FOUR

Vee sent a message to Klaus, saying she had to see him.

'I can't stay with Giles, you know,' she said to Klaus, when she met him.

He was not best pleased at having to come to Paris 'to discuss your emotional problems,' as he put it. 'I had thought it was a serious matter, for you to send such a message. An operational hitch, not Giles's behaviour.'

Vee couldn't believe what Klaus was saying. Operational hitch; he sounded as though he were talking about a machine.

'I can't put up with this. Once or twice, maybe, but he's become too hostile for me to live with him any longer.'

'Does he treat you badly in front of other people?' asked Klaus, his voice more sympathetic now, low and comforting; but Vee no longer found a sense of security from Klaus's presence or his soothing voice and seeming concern for her.

'No.'

'Would anyone else have any idea of how things are between you?'

'No, he always behaves perfectly well when we're out, or have guests – other than his horrible friends.'

'Then, Vee, you must grin and bear it, as the saying is. Have you seen the news from Germany this morning? Or, indeed, from France? Do you know that there is a strong fascist undercurrent here in Paris, that many key people feel that Germany is the way of the future, that even the milk-and-water socialism of the present government must be cleansed out of the political system of the country?'

'Klaus, I know that, but it's not possible for me to go on with Giles. You don't understand . . .'

'No, and I don't want to understand, and you must understand that this serves our purposes very well. Giles holds now a key position, he has access to many vital papers and secrets that would be of inestimable value to the comrades. So it is your duty to manage as best you can, and to say nothing.'

She tried, but one morning, after a particularly appalling display by Giles and a leering Algerian sailor he'd brought home, she told him that she was going to leave him.

Giles was horrified. Not, as she knew, that he cared a button for her, but because of the threat her departure would pose to his position. Young, promising diplomats whose wives walked out on them had a large black mark against their names. A successful and stable marriage was a sine qua non for the job, however much it was all on the surface, while in private the young couple hated each other. Appearances were everything; wives walking out were far too obvious to be ignored.

He pleaded with her, promised to mend his ways, to be more considerate of her.

Vee didn't tell Klaus what she had threatened, but merely said that things were a little easier for the moment between her and her husband. She knew it wouldn't last.

Klaus seemed to sense this. 'It is time we brought a little more pressure to bear on Mr Giles Hotspur,' he said, with a foxy smile. 'Now, I need the keys to your apartment, and for you to be not at home between the hours of nine and eleven tomorrow morning. Tell your maid that electricians are coming to do some job connected with the wiring, that it may be messy – let her be out shopping, or send her on an errand.'

'What . . .' Vee began.

'It is a precaution we take, a kind of alarm system for your own good. Do not worry about it, you will not be bothered in any way.'

Alarm system? she thought, as she hurried away the next morning. That sounded unlikely. When she came back to the apartment after lunch, everything seemed exactly as it had been. The maid commented that if the electricians had been you'd never know it, they were usually thoughtless, untidy fellows who left everything for the poor servants to clean up after them.

Perhaps they hadn't come, Vee thought, retrieving the key from her box downstairs. She, too, could see no signs of any work. She had vague ideas of hidden microphones; well, they could listen in to her conversations if they wanted to, and Giles rarely used the telephone in the apartment; he did all his telephoning at the Embassy.

She was looking forward to some leave they had planned to take in London. They had kept up their flat there; as Giles said, with a posting only just across the Channel, it would be handy to have a London base. She had only been back once, to shop and do some theatres and meet Lally, up from the country. Lally had seemed a little subdued, still worrying about Peter going off to boarding school in the autumn. 'He's such a little boy. Being brought up without a mother has affected him. His nurse is a kindly woman, but it isn't the same.'

'I'm surprised Harry didn't send him to live with his mother, doesn't she live in some vast pile fairly near you?'

'I'm glad he didn't, for I'd never see him. I don't think she could be bothered with bringing up another child. She said as much, four of her own was more than any woman could be expected to cope with, and I don't suppose she ever had much to do with them, it seems you English families don't care to have children around you.'

'Under your feet is what they'd say. No, you're right, the nursery world and the world of the grown-ups are two very separate places.'

'Harry wanted to see as much of Peter as possible, he's a good father, very loving for an Englishman, but even so, he thinks nothing of sending the boy away for twelve or thirteen weeks at a time, and you know, they don't get to come home at all, most terms.'

'There's usually a weekend off in the middle of term,' Vee said. 'I never went home then. Sometimes I went to stay with a friend, or I stayed at school with the girls whose parents were abroad. We had a lot of those, fathers serving in the army or diplomatic families, or working in the Far East.'

'Why didn't you want to go home?'

'My parents . . . oh, it was just easier to stay at school,' she said. Lally saw the blinds come down and pried no further; she never did.

Claudia would be in England this time, back from what sounded like a frenetic life in Berlin. 'Having a wild time, your cousin,' Giles told her, half laughing, half disapproving. 'Quite a wow with all the Nazi top brass, one gathers. The Ambassador asked me about her, thought she might be useful to us. I told him, not a hope, pure fascist, and as dotty as her brother. H. E. doesn't think so badly of the Nazis, anyhow, he's a Halifax man, thinks we should come to some accommodation with Hitler.'

'Appeasement is the word, I think,' Vee said, forgetting herself. Then seeing the look of surprise on Giles's face, 'Isn't that what Halifax wants? Not to go to war? I'm sure that's what the whole world is keen on, no war.'

'It'll come to a fight in the end,' said Giles gloomily. 'Somehow it always does, with the Germans.'

FIVE

They crossed on a clear, sunny August day, with the Channel a millpond, and both of them in tearing high spirits. Giles was spending some time in London before going north for the shooting. Soon Vee was wishing she'd gone to the Deanery or anywhere, since after his initial good humour, Giles flung himself into the London life that he had in mind with a terrible vigour.

She met Klaus again. Sitting beside him on the bench in Green Park with a terrible sense of *déjà vu*. 'Giles is getting worse,' she told him. 'I've done my best, but I really don't think I can stand it much longer.'

'You won't have to,' said Klaus. 'We have arranged for certain things to happen while you are in England, and I think from now on, your life will become easier with regard to him.'

There was no point in asking Klaus what he meant, for she knew he wouldn't say. Were the comrades going to bring some pressure to bear on Giles? That was hardly possible, given his views.

Thankfully, they were due to go down to the Messengers from Saturday to Monday; Giles would behave impeccably there, even if he did drink too much it wouldn't be noticed among the several guests that she knew had been invited. Lally's house parties were always tremendous fun; for at least those days, she would have a respite from Giles's brutal habits and bad temper, not to mention the guardsmen he had brought back to the flat on more than one occasion, huge, burly young men; she found the very thought of them and Giles made her feel ill.

Giles cancelled at the last moment. 'Something's come up, bit of a flap on in Paris, got to go in and give a briefing.'

'On a Saturday, in August?' She didn't believe a word of it. 'I'll go, just the same,' she said.

'Of course,' he said, surprised that she would have thought of doing anything else.

Naturally, he wanted her out of the way. No doubt he had some gathering planned, days and nights with his ghastly companions.

Vee went to Wiltshire with a heavy heart. The train trundled through a basking English countryside, beautiful with its dark-green foliage and glowing cornfields. An English heaven under an English sun. It looked so peaceful, so content, and yet what seething emotions and tensions lay beneath that serene surface. Personal lives as warped as her own, and the wider misery of inequality and oppression.

She had met Grandfather for lunch in London, bowing to pressure from Aunt Lettice. He was very full of himself, rubbing his hands at the money he was making, he'd gone in for armaments, he told her, and had bought up two textile mills in the north, there'd be a huge demand for uniforms come the war.

'At least it's work for the unemployed,' she said, trying to look pleased.

'I reckon that men who've been out of work aren't worth employing,' her grandfather said. 'I only take on hands who are in work in any case. I offer them a slightly higher wage, and then, once they're in, I cut them. They can't go back to their old jobs, and I don't have anyone who's got out of the habit of working.'

Vee wanted to shout at him, to rant and protest at his disregard for the humanity of his workers, but she bit her tongue and dug her fork into the meat with an energy that nearly caused the piece of food to shoot off her plate.

'You're not looking well, Vee,' said her grandfather hopefully. 'Are we to expect the patter of tiny feet?'

'No.'

'Well, early days, early days. Don't like to see you looking peaky, however. Get up to Yorkshire, get some good Yorkshire air into your system, that'll bring back the roses to your cheeks.'

Had her grandfather never noticed that hers wasn't the kind of complexion that ever had rosy cheeks? Daisy, now, if Daisy had lived, she would always have had pink cheeks. And at least in the end, her grandfather's schemes were providing more work for the unemployed, lucky them, really, not to be working for him.

The thought of armaments and uniforms sent a chill through her, maybe Grandfather would turn out to have made a wrong investment for once, and he'd find himself with useless concerns on his hands.

Armaments, useless? She wished it might be so, and knew that it was a childish wish, and one not likely to be fulfilled in her lifetime.

The last part of the journey took place along a slow country line, with the train stopping at every country station and halt. Roses bloomed in each station garden. A large cat sunned itself on one platform, on another, pigeons cooed and strutted in the sun. There were cows and sheep in the fields, boys fishing near old arched bridges over lazy rivers, an old man digging his vegetables in a cottage garden. Utterly normal, utterly tranquil.

Daydreaming, she nearly missed her station, unaware that the train was there until she saw Lally, at the window of her compartment, laughing and gesticulating to her to get out.

Lally and Harry were living in an enchanting manor house, which belonged to his mother, Agnes Messenger. Lally didn't share her mother-in-law's tastes, and it had taken a mixture of determination and tact to make the house the way she wanted it. Harry wouldn't get involved, 'My mother gets very het up about that kind of thing, much easier to do what she wants, I find.'

Since what she wanted was musty colours and old – and to Lally's eyes, ugly – furniture, most of which, she discovered, had been dumped in the Manor simply because no one else in the family had any desire for it, Lally couldn't agree with her husband.

So she smiled, and set about removing the largest and grimmest pieces of furniture to a dry barn at the back of the house and replacing them with antiques. Marcus, who adored doing houses up, would descend on the house and sweep Lally off to sales, and with his help and many pots of paint, the Manor had been transformed into a vision of light and colour.

Harry loved it, and told Lally she was a witch. He even had a few sharpish words with his mother, when she tracked the missing furniture to the barn, telling her that it would come to no harm there, and it was time for her to back off. He was married to Lally, she was mistress of the house now, and that was that. If she was going to make a fuss, then they'd simply move out and rent another house.

Friends came down from London for the Messenger weekends, the livelier among Harry's colleagues, and the intellectuals and artists from Lally's circle. Lally was a superb hostess, and her odd mixture of guests were swept up into the gaiety of her house; playing tennis and swimming in the lake in the summer, sitting in front of huge log fires and discussing politics and the latest scientific discovery on winter evenings. Summer meals, when the weather permitted, were eaten outside on the terrace, lit with strings of electric lights. In winter, guests sat until the small hours in the oak-panelled dining room, talking and eating by glowing candlelight.

Vee settled down to enjoy herself, having long chats with Lally, although never mentioning Giles or her marriage, flirting with Harry, who was as handsome and attractive and civilized as ever, and delighting in the company of her fellow guests and the amusing and intelligent talk of theatre and music and books.

SIX

Vee travelled back up to town with some of the other guests, relaxed and less unhappy than she had been for months. She was regretting the fact that she couldn't stay longer, as Lally and Harry had pressed her to do, but she had invited Marcus to come round for drinks, and both she and Lally knew he would sulk if she cancelled.

She took a taxi from the station, paid the cabbie, and looked up automatically to the first-floor window of their flat. Odd, the curtains were still drawn. Could Giles still be asleep? At four in the afternoon?

Perhaps he'd decided to leave for his shooting a day or two earlier; she hoped so, then she'd have a whole glorious week to herself in London.

She ran up the stairs, ignoring the cranky lift. She fumbled for her latchkey and let herself in.

There was an odd, stuffy smell, and the hall was dark, with all the doors leading off it closed. She wrinkled her nose and frowned. She switched on the hall light, put down her suitcase and took off her hat. Then she opened the door into the sitting room. It was untidy, and empty. She closed it and went into the bedroom, calling out to Giles as she did so, although she could tell there was no one in the flat. There was an atmosphere there, though, and it made her shiver. A Claudia feeling, she called those moments. Giles's bedroom was empty, and it looked as though his bed hadn't been slept in. Then he probably had gone north.

She went back into the hall and opened the door to the small room that Giles used as a study.

Vee went back into the hall, the door slammed behind her. She leaned against it, her head ringing. She felt as though all the air had been sucked from her lungs and that she would never breathe again. Her eyes were blind to everything except the image seared on her retina, the image of what she'd seen in that room, she would never be rid of the tiny picture, blotting out everything else that existed.

A jolt to her stomach, and with a flash of clarity, her mind and eyes were sharp and clear, quite unnaturally so. She was immediately certain, without any need to think about it, of what she had to do. Without a second's hesitation, she went to the telephone, lifted the receiver off the hook, and waited, earpiece held in a vice grip, for the operator to reply.

Hours and weeks and years went by.

The operator's voice quacked in her ear. In a completely calm and ordinary voice, she requested the number of the doctor who attended Giles. She was through to his receptionist, then to the man himself. There had been an accident, she explained. A very bad accident, she feared that Giles was seriously hurt, if alive.

Of course Giles wasn't alive. She hadn't taken two steps into the room, taken more than a millisecond's glance at the chair where he sat, his head slumped over the desk, not to know he was dead. No need to take a pulse, or to look more closely, even if she could have brought herself to do so.

'Yes, Dr Yardley, please come round immediately.'

The doctor only lived a couple of streets away. He would be there in minutes, the time it took him to pick up his medical bag, leave the house and walk the short distance to the flat.

Vee's mind was working with astonishing rapidity, what did she need to do in the few minutes before he arrived? In a case of sudden death, might the police come? Yes, they would. Might they search the flat? It was possible. Then she'd have a look first, she said to herself, feeling a need to somehow protect Giles's secret life from prying eyes.

The photographs were hidden under his mattress, in a plain brown envelope. She stood looking down at them with an odd feeling of detachment. They were grainy, but Giles's face was clear enough, as were the activities he was engaged in. They had been taken in the flat in Paris, that was the work Klaus's men had done, installing a secret camera in the bedroom.

Blackmail was an ugly word.

Vee forced herself to think clearly. She would not have expected Giles to submit meekly to blackmail. Those photos sent to his superiors would have spelled the end of his career, that was true, but,

342

knowing Giles, he might have told his blackmailers to do just that rather than deciding to do away with himself.

Well, at least she could protect his reputation, for his and for his parents' sake. For her own? She was past caring.

Ten minutes later, there was a ring on the doorbell. She opened the door, and there was Dr Yardley, as expected, but behind him, wholly unexpected, two other people.

'Alfred!' she exclaimed. 'Oh, you're with Marcus.'

'We were lunching,' said Alfred, following Dr Yardley into the hall. 'Marcus said he was coming on here, so I decided to accompany him. Is something up?'

'He's in there, Doctor,' Vee said, pointing at the door. 'If you don't mind . . .'

The doctor hurried forward, opened the door, let out a little puff of astonishment and closed it behind him.

'Is Giles all right?' Marcus asked.

'You're white, Vee,' Alfred said. 'In fact, I think you're going to faint. Marcus, hunt around and find some brandy. Sit down, Vee. Put your head between your knees.'

'I don't feel faint,' she said, but she sat down, and accepted the brandy which Marcus found in the cupboard. 'It's Giles. It's dreadful. He's in there – an accident with a gun, I think. I've just got back from the country, I've been staying with Lally and Harry. Giles didn't come, he had some urgent work, he said. He was leaving tomorrow or the day after, to go north, for the shooting, in Yorkshire, his uncle has a moor.'

She was talking too much and too fast. Alfred sat down beside her, and took her hand. His grasp was warm and firm and infinitely comforting.

'Have you telephoned the police?' Marcus asked, and at that very moment, the doctor appeared, shocked out of his customary professional urbanity.

'I've dialled 999,' he said to Alfred and Marcus. 'You must steel yourself, Mrs Hotspur. I have to tell you that your husband is dead.'

Vee sank her face into her hands. The doctor took it for a sign of distress; and distress there was, although not the desperate grief of a loving wife that the doctor saw.

Vee was grieving for the beautiful, laughing Giles who had sat at the window seat in his set at Oxford, who had loved, and been loved by Hugh, his childhood friend; for a lonely and desperate man with whom she had shared her life for a brief time; for the man full of promise whose life had ended so abruptly and so tragically young; for his parents; for the waste of a life.

And she grieved for what she had done to him. Shame and guilt spilled out into tears. Some, at least, of Giles's unhappiness could be laid at her door. She had agreed to marry him for reasons that had nothing to do with friendship or helping him out of a tricky situation, and her into a comfortable position as a wife. His reasons had been as mixed: his persisting love for Hugh, the need for the appearance of a respectable marriage and a normal home and sexual life. His were more honourable reasons than hers.

The strain of living a lie had been too much for him, hence the drink, hence the savagery, hence the desperate attempts to find solace in the company of those dreadful men he brought home.

She had no doubt that Giles had shot himself. Didn't it happen, sometimes, after a drinking binge, that depression set in, a sense of worthlessness, and in that frame of mind, suicide seemed the only happy ending?

If only he had come to the Messengers for the weekend. If only she hadn't gone on her own and left him there in the flat. Yet that was what he'd wanted, he didn't wish for her company, her presence irked and irritated and restricted him.

'Did you know he kept a gun in the flat?' the doctor was asking.

She raised her tear-stained face. 'A pair of guns. He had them here because he was going shooting.'

'I see.'

'Usually he left them at home, at his family home in Yorkshire, but he said they needed an overhaul; he was worried about something to do with the bore on one of them. So he'd brought them down to London before we went to Paris, and left them with Purdy's. He must have collected them on Saturday, or Friday – they weren't here when I left to catch the train, at least I didn't see them.'

'When did you get back, Mrs Hotspur?'

Vee stared at him. What had time to do with this? She pulled herself together.

Concentrate.

'My train got into Paddington just after four and I took a taxi. It must have been about half past four when I got back here.'

She looked down at her wristwatch. Five past five. How could it

344

only be an hour since her train had come steaming to a halt at Paddington Station? Outside, trees rustled in a slight breeze, and a bee buzzed at the window. The room was stuffy. As though sensing her thoughts, Alfred rose and went over to the window and opened it fully. Warm air and the sounds of London came in, restoring a sort of normality, but the smell was still there.

'When . . . ?' she began, not finishing the question as she looked at the doctor.

'This morning, about eight hours ago, I should estimate. Of course there'll have to be . . .' he paused '. . . a proper examination. The police surgeon will see to all that.'

'Why does it need to be a police surgeon? Why not you?'

'In cases of sudden and violent death, the police have to be called, and they have to go through the necessary investigations.'

'But it was an accident.'

'I'm sure that's exactly what it will turn out to be,' the doctor said in his most unctuous and soothing tones, with a flicker of a glance at Alfred and Marcus. 'My dear, is there someone we could telephone to come to you? A mother, a sister, perhaps, or a friend?'

She shook her head. 'Alfred and Marcus are friends. My family's in York. My aunt and cousin live in London, but my aunt and uncle are abroad and my cousin's in the country.'

Shut up, she told herself. She was talking too much.

Marcus's forehead was puckered into a frown; how odd, Vee thought, Marcus never frowns. 'Vee, who's your solicitor?' he was saying.

She blinked. Solicitor? What was he talking about? Thoughts of wills and inheritance whipped through her mind.

'A man in York,' she said. 'Giles's people are Thornton & Roget.'

'Ah, King's Bench Walk, I know the firm. I think I'll just give them a call and put them in the picture.'

The doctor nodded his head approvingly, and he drew Marcus aside.

'A young woman – a young widow, as she is now, poor creature, can't have too much professional support at a time like this. She's suffering from shock, although she's bearing up remarkably well under the circumstances. We call them the weaker sex, but in my experience, women often cope extraordinarily well in such tragic situations. At least, they do so at first. Soon, the horror of her discovery and her grief for her husband – good heavens, they've only been

345

married a few months – will hit her. I'll prescribe a bromide, and arrange for a nurse to attend.'

'She can't possibly stay in this flat,' Marcus said.

'No, no, of course not. In any case, the police . . .'

Dr Yardley stepped over to the window as the clangour of a police-car bell and the roar of a powerful engine came through into the drawing room, 'The police have arrived,' he said. The doorbell rang. 'I'll go to the door, if you don't mind, Mrs Hotspur.'

Marcus went out with the doctor, Alfred stayed with Vee.

'Here's a thing,' he said. 'Did Giles commit suicide?'

Vee took a deep breath. 'Oh, I think so. I can't imagine him making a mistake with a gun, he was always very careful and precise, he's had guns since he was a boy, he wouldn't do anything stupid. And why would the gun be loaded here in the flat?'

'Not been a success, your marriage?'

'That's not why he's killed himself.'

'Do you know why?'

'Alfred, he's been leading the most desperate kind of life. Men, you know. And getting drunk.'

'And hitting out at you,' Alfred said drily, running his finger over a bruise that just showed at the side of her neck. 'No, don't pretend. I've known Giles a long while, he always had a violent streak in him. And you weren't Hugh, and it was very hard to lead a double life, he's not the kind of man who copes with deception and secrecy. Giles was meant to be open and happy and at ease with himself, but the way things turned out, because of his nature, and because of the society he lived in, it wasn't possible. Poor man.'

For a moment, Vee was tempted to pour out the whole story to Alfred, to tell him there was more to it than self-disgust, that there was the matter of exposure, of public shame and humiliation, which was, perhaps, more than he could bear.

In the hall, the doctor was talking to the police.

'Poor Mrs Hotspur, married less than a year. I can't think what could have driven her husband to do such a thing. Although I had wondered, in the past. As a medical man with many years' experience, I've known of cases . . . Naturally, Mrs Hotspur, an innocent young woman, would have no idea of that side of her husband's life.'

'Could we see . . .'

'Of course. In here.' Dr Yardley opened the door into the study.

346

SEVEN

The police inspector was a pleasant soft-spoken man with a Welsh lilt to his voice, kind but firm. 'I'm Inspector Pritchard,' he said, showing Vee a card that might have been written in hieroglyphs for all she knew; there was a ringing in her head and she wanted to be sick.

'Special Branch,' Alfred said under his breath, after one swift look at the man in his grey suit and plain tie. 'The doctor must have mentioned the words Foreign Office. Bear up, duckie, this isn't the time to throw up.'

Inspector Pritchard was expressing his sympathy in formal words. 'I'm afraid I have to ask you some questions, Mrs Hotspur. A police-woman will be arriving shortly, so if you prefer to wait until she is here, then we can do so.'

'No,' Vee said. She looked around for her handbag, retrieved it from the back of the sofa and took out a handkerchief. She dabbed at her eyes and blew her nose.

'It is very distressing that you should have been the one to find your husband,' the inspector began. 'Did he know you would be back today?'

She sought for the right words. 'I told him it would be today or tomorrow. I usually come back to London on a Monday after the weekend, of course, but I had considered staying on for an extra day and motoring up to London with Lally. With Mrs Messenger. I was staying with the Messengers.'

The inspector took their name and address. 'Just a formality,' he said.

Did he suspect her of murdering Giles? Alfred put a reassuring hand on her shoulder. 'Just routine, Vee.'

The inspector held out a sheet of notepaper, clasping it carefully in his gloved hand. 'Is this your husband's handwriting, Mrs Hotspur?'

Vee stared at the familiar, elegant script. Giles had exquisite hand-writing and took a pride in it. Had taken a pride in it. 'Yes, that's my husband's writing,' she said, with a tremor in her voice. 'It's very distinctive.'

'A beautiful hand,' the inspector said. 'Did you see this on the blotter on the desk when you found your husband?'

'I didn't see anything,' she lied. 'I took one look and . . .'

'Of course. Very understandable.' He looked at the note, making a tut-tutting noise. 'Dear Vee,' he read out. 'I can't go on. G.'

She swallowed, and turned her head away. She ran her tongue over her lips. 'That was in front of him?'

'I'm afraid it was.'

'Do you mean he committed suicide?'

'It seems to us that it is possible that Mr Hotspur took his own life.' The inspector paused. 'I regret having to ask you, but had your husband appeared troubled in any way recently? Were there finan-cial pressures, anything you knew about?'

The minutes passed, turning into an hour and then two hours. A policewoman came, stout and compassionate, and made tea, over-sweet tea, which she insisted that Vee drink. Men in uniform, with apologetic but eager expressions went through the flat, room by room. 'Just routine,' the inspector said. Then Sir Hector arrived, ashen-faced, horrified, full of the right words of dismay and condolence. Mr Thornton, the solicitor, was there, patting her hand and telling her not to worry, everything was going to be taken care of.

She wished they'd finish and go. She just wanted to be left alone. Here was Inspector Pritchard again. 'You had separate bedrooms, Mrs Hotspur.'

'Sometimes,' she said, thinking quickly. 'Giles sometimes slept in the dressing room. When he was working late, and he didn't want to disturb me, or if he had to leave early in the morning. He was a most considerate man.'

Men in sombre suiting, with professionally grave faces, appeared and took Giles away. Then the policewoman was in Vee's room, pulling down a suitcase and asking her what she should pack.

Alfred came in, and said that Claudia would be in London within the hour, and he was going to take Mrs Hotspur round to Rochester Street in a taxi.

Inspector Pritchard asked for the address and telephone number, and gave a click of recognition with his tongue as Alfred mentioned Uncle Vernon's name. 'They'll have to be informed, of course. Do you know how to reach them?'

'Vee, where are Vernon and Lettice?' Alfred asked.

'Switzerland,' she said. 'Claudia will have their address, or Kimber. The butler,' she added, for the inspector's benefit.

'I'll see to all that,' said Sir Hector. 'Poor Giles, poor young man. To think that he was in such a state of mind . . . we had no notion, all the reports of his work were excellent, a first-rate mind, one of our most promising young diplomats. Devoted to the service. It's a tragedy, a tragedy. Perhaps there's some instability in his family?' He looked questioningly at Vee.

'I don't think so,' she said. 'Not that he ever mentioned to me, at any event. He was tired, and he'd been a bit under the weather.'

'It happens like that, sometimes,' the doctor said.

Inspector Pritchard was warning Alfred, whose name he recognized, not to write a word of what had happened or pass on the information to any newspaper.

Alfred took the warning in good part. 'Not I, Inspector. I'm not that kind of a writer, and even if I were, Mr and Mrs Hotspur are very dear friends. I shan't breathe a word to anyone.'

'Good, good.'

'It will be best . . .' began Sir Hector, and went out of the room with the inspector.

'It'll all be hushed up, duckie,' Alfred said to Vee. 'Won't it, Marcus?'

'Bound to be,' said Marcus, who had been deep in conversation with Mr Thornton.

The solicitor, a precise, long-legged man with half spectacles, pursed his lips. 'Mr Gore, I don't think the phrase "hushed up" is perhaps one we should be using. There must be a degree of uncertainty as to exactly what happened here, and until the exact truth is established, it would be wise not to come to any premature conclusions.'

'What did you mean by all that hushed-up business?' Vee asked Alfred as the taxi trundled towards Rochester Street.

'Oh, they'll bring it in as accidental death. There'll be an inquest, of course, and you may have to give evidence. You'll say Giles was fine and well and contented and looking forward to his shooting holiday, and how idyllically happy you both were, and the doctor will say that his hand slipped and the coroner will utter some pompous words of how dangerous it is to have guns in the house, and how even the most experienced man can make a tiny error and as a result blow his brains out.'

'It wasn't an accident,' she said flatly.

'No, it wasn't, but it's the kindest thing for his family to think so, and best for the Foreign Office, too. They've had long practice at cover-ups, Vee, it'll all be most expertly done.'

She stared out of the window. 'It's all rather ghastly, isn't it? The dishonesty of it,'

'It's what Giles would want.'

'He hated scandal of any kind. That was what he was so afraid of. Oh, God, Alfred, why ever did I marry him?'

'I did wonder,' said Alfred, putting a comforting arm around her shoulders. 'I dare say it seemed like a good idea.'

'Only it wasn't. Not then, not ever.'

'That's what life is about, duckie. One mistake after another. Do we learn from them? If we're lucky. Otherwise we just go out and make the same mistakes all over again.' He dropped a kiss on her neck. 'Next time you feel an urge to get married, Vee, do come and talk it over with me.'

'That's one mistake I certainly shan't be making again,' she said. 'Lord, are we here already?' Her heart had stood still at the affection in Alfred's voice and the gentle kiss; now she withdrew once more behind her veil of reserve and secrecy.

'I'll come in,' said Alfred. 'I'll stay with you until Claudia gets back.'

'She's already here,' Vee said, for the front door had opened, and Claudia was dashing down the steps towards the taxi.

EIGHT

Several Angels came to Giles's funeral, although Hugh wasn't among them. Vee didn't know if he'd even heard about Giles; she'd written to him at the last address, and Alfred, on his way back to Spain after the funeral, promised he would try to contact him. 'If he's still in Spain. He may have come to his senses and be in Portugal or France.'

'He's in Portugal,' Vee said, not really taking in what Alfred was saying.

She felt a fraud at the funeral. The young wife, tragically widowed, came in for so much sympathy; what right had she to any of it, with his parents there at the graveside, bleak and haunted and old? She hated herself, and hated Klaus and all he stood for. Well, with Giles's death, her part in the revolution had come to its end. She could no longer summon the passion of being right, of being the one who understood and fought for the workers. Let Grandfather and his mills triumph, let the country appease Hitler, she simply didn't care any more, not if the price of supporting Moscow was the death of a man like Giles.

Klaus had tried to contact her; she resisted all his approaches for a while and then reluctantly arranged to meet him for one last time. She ranted at him, pouring out her rage at Giles's death, at the way she had been manipulated by Moscow, telling him that his bloody, beloved Comintern had been responsible for the death of a young, healthy, good man.

Klaus came out with his old, and to her, now pitiful, arguments that the end justified the means, that serving the revolution wasn't something where you could pick and choose; the individual didn't matter.

'I can see that,' she said, getting up from the bench. 'Giles didn't matter. Well, I don't matter any more, either.'

'They won't let you go, Vee.'

'They will. I'm no further use to them. I don't care if fascism wins in the end, can it be any more heartless than your lot?'

'You're emotional, this is an emotional reaction, it has all been very distressing for you. Give it time, get over what has happened, and then, once more, you will find that your loyalties lie with us.'

I wish you were here, Klaus, she said to herself, as earth rattled on to the lid of Giles's coffin. I wish you could see what your lot have done. What she'd done, she corrected herself, the chill wind that blew in the Yorkshire graveyard even in the height of summer sending the tears scudding across her cheeks behind her black veil.

Giles's father came to stand beside her. He looked more than usually remote, but his voice was kind. 'Don't blame yourself, Verity.'

'Blame?'

'His mother prefers to consider Giles's death an accident, but it wasn't, of course. Oddly enough, an uncle of mine died in exactly the same way, at much the same age. Possibly for the same reasons. We were so very happy that Giles married you, and I did hope that it might bring him some peace of mind, and joy to his heart; children might have been the making of him. I now see that it was never a possibility, that, given his nature, his life was bound to end in tragedy, one way or the other.'

Before an astonished Vee could reply, General Hotspur had moved away to join and comfort his wife.

Vee found herself a rich woman, a state of affairs which she could hardly bear. What could she do? Give her money to the poor? That would upset General Hotspur, who was one of her trustees; the trust would be wound up when it was clear that there was no possibility of Giles leaving an heir of his body; Mr Thornton had explained it all to her in dry, impersonal, legal language.

'I'm not pregnant,' she'd said at once. 'There's no possibility of that.'

'The law must be allowed to take its proper course, Mrs Hotspur. After the due period of time has elapsed, then the other clauses in his will come into force. Either way, you stand to inherit a considerable fortune, and I would recommend that you take proper advice on how best to manage it.'

Grandfather, sympathetic at her loss, was jubilant at her inheritance. He would send round a cracking good chap, just the man to advise her. With skilful investments, she could hope to double her capital within a decade, especially if there were a war.

'I shall use the money to do something in Giles's memory,' she said. 'Scholarships, that kind of thing. Hugh will know what he'd have liked, Hugh knew him very well.'

'Hugh! If you wait to ask Hugh, you may have to wait a very long time,' Grandfather said. 'You've still no word from him?'

'Nothing.'

Which alarmed her, and added to her misery. Guilt and shame and worry were a rich recipe for unhappiness. Weeks had gone past without any news of him before now, but this was the longest silence yet, and she hadn't heard from Alfred, either. She read all his reports avidly, and gradually formed the conclusion that the civil war in Spain was a mess, a complicated mess, and that she hardly began to understand the intricate network of beliefs and prejudice and personalities that underlay the brutal combat.

Hugh had always warned her not to look at international affairs in a simplistic way, unfortunately, she hadn't listened to him.

It also seemed to her that Alfred had a new view of the world; she wondered if the passionate search for justice which had found its home in communism had wavered in the light of the war in Spain.

Nearly everyone she knew who'd gone out to fight for the International Brigade on the Republican side was dead, wounded or disillusioned. She prayed that Hugh might merely be disillusioned, and, for the first time since she had her spiritual crisis at St Cross in Oxford, found herself in a church, literally praying. It was a Catholic church, and a middle-aged priest with world-weary eyes enquired whether he could help.

'No, thank you,' she said bleakly, noticing the candles in front of the statue of the Virgin Mary for the first time. She felt rather as though she were trespassing. 'I didn't realize . . . I mean, I thought it was an Anglican church.'

'God has many houses,' the priest said.

She told Lally about it, when she was next in London. 'Perhaps it wasn't an accident that you went in there,' Lally said in her placid way. 'I'm coming to think that very little of what we do is purposeless.'

'Don't raise your hopes, I've done with the Church in all its forms, you'll never make a Catholic of me.'

'Why should I want to?'

'Don't you all have a mission to convert?'

'Not that I ever heard. I didn't try to influence you about religion when we were at Oxford, why should I do so now?'

1938

ONE

Vee was back for the time being in Rochester Street, with her aunt and uncle, and Claudia, who was now spending more time in England, with sorties to her beloved Berlin. She worked as an assistant to a politician who had a strident belief in Britain's indissoluble ties with the Germanic peoples; a dreadful man, Vee thought, never mind his politics.

Claudia turned out to have a gift for catching the attention of the press.

'They call it propaganda in the Reich, they devote a lot of energy to it. Actually, it's the Americans who are really brilliant at it; it's all about persuading people without their realizing that they're being guided rather than making a free choice.'

'You want to influence them?'

'Of course. Isn't that what politics is all about?'

Vee was bored. She was still numb from Giles's death, and her old friends and haunts held few attractions for her. Even if she'd wanted to join in the social life of London, it wouldn't have been appropriate for so recent a widow.

Her interest in art resurfaced, and she began to go to classes. She spent hours in the National Gallery and other collections, grateful for the dozy quiet of the great galleries, the haunting beauty of the pictures. She gazed at the faces in the portraits, wondering about the lives of these men and women, frozen in paint and time.

When Alfred came back to London for a visit to his newspaper, he took her out to dine in a dimly-lit, unfashionable restaurant where the food was superb, and the waiters Italian and courteous. He hadn't managed to contact Hugh, although he did have reason to believe he was alive and well, he'd heard this through hemi-semi-demi official channels.

'Why shouldn't he be alive and well? He's in Portugal.'

'Off and on, Vee. He spends quite a lot of time in Spain. He isn't a prisoner, he's not been reported as wounded, and Marcus swears he saw him in Valencia three weeks ago.'

'Marcus! Don't tell me Marcus is fighting there.'

'No, merely visiting, his idea of a jolly outing, he told me. He managed to get temporary accreditation for *The Times*, believe it or not, he's done one or two pieces for them.'

'I thought he was a producer at the BBC, nothing to do with the news.'

'Marcus tends to be whatever he wishes to be at any particular moment.'

'I haven't seen him since the funeral.' She hadn't had the heart to go around to Marcus's messy flat with its startling wall decorations and his outrageous friends, part of the old times, when Giles was still alive, and she still believed in something.

'Perhaps you should. Some social life would jolt you out of yourself. A solitary existence isn't really going to suit you.'

'Who says I'm solitary?'

'Claudia. I bumped into her in Piccadilly Circus yesterday, and I took her for tea at Fortnum's.'

'Oh,' she said, vaguely resentful that Claudia should have had Alfred to herself.

'Has she got over Petrus yet?'

'I don't suppose she ever will do; he's the kind of man that gets under your skin. I don't think she sees him very often, but he seems to have had a lasting influence on her love life.'

And on hers, Vee thought, wondering if the tart she was eating tasted bitter because of its fruit or from bile in her mouth. 'Are you going back to Spain, Alfred?'

'Of course.'

'Do you like it there? No, that isn't the right word, how could anyone like it?'

'It's the only place to be just now, for a journalist.'

'Not in Berlin?'

'Oh, Berlin has come to Spain, duckie, as has Moscow. They're fighting it out in the plains and mountains of Iberia, just as they soon will be across the face of Europe.'

Claudia was worried about her, and through a mixture of cajoling and bullying succeeded in persuading her to spend Easter at Kepesake. 'You've never been, and although Lucius is odd, the castle is wonderful; Monica is a marvellous hostess. They're having a large house party; heaps of interesting people. Otherwise, what are you going to do? Mummy and Vernon are going to Scotland, and you'll hardly want to go to Yorkshire.'

Yorkshire was the last place she wanted to go, at Easter or any other time of year. In the end, she gave in to Claudia's nagging, simply because she didn't have the energy to resist any longer. 'If it's going to be charades and shrieks of jolly games and all that kind of thing, I'll be rather a Banquo's ghost at the festive table.'

'Kepesake is never vulgar. Peculiar, yes, like anyone else's home, no. If the worst comes to the worst, there's an enormous library, crammed full of fascinating vols, you can curl up in front of the vast fireplace in there and read to your heart's content.'

'Do I need to bring layers of woolly clothes?' Vee knew all too well how cold an English spring could be, and castles, although outside her direct experience, were notorious for the chill of centuries that was lodged in their stones.

'Naturally, for there's no way to keep the main rooms warm, but I promise you the bedrooms are cosy and there's always lashings of hot water, trust my sister-in-law for that.'

Kepesake was one of the glories of English architecture, exemplifying several styles of historical interest. It was built in 1210 by Ranulf de Vere, one of King John's rebellious barons, and since then had been battered in every civil war and skirmish over the succeeding centuries. What bombardment and besiegers hadn't done, keen earls had: the original keep was attached to a Tudor pile, with an unreasonable number of chimneys, while the south side was a riot of Gothic revival.

'There's nothing like it,' Claudia said, looking out at her ancestral home without enthusiasm as they drove up the mile-long drive and rounded a bend which gave them a magnificent view of the façade – done in the Palladian style by an eighteenth-century earl.

Vee hadn't seen Lucius, the eighteenth earl, since she was a little girl. She remembered him as a fair, lanky youth. Nothing had prepared her for the adult man with his extraordinary beauty of feature and his brilliant, dazzling blue eyes through which he viewed a world entirely different to the one observed by his fellow men.

'What you have to bear in mind,' Claudia said as the butler, two footmen and a maid stepped forward to greet them and relieve them of coats and hats and gloves, 'is that Lucius suffers from certain delusions. He believes that all the servants are ancestors, alive and well and living in the castle. Lowker, there, for instance, the butler, is the fourth earl, who fought and died at Agincourt, while the boot boy is the eleventh earl who died at twelve from an arrow shot in his direction by his brother, who became the twelfth earl.'

'Playing bows and arrows, or were they fighting in some civil war?' Vee asked, as they tramped along an endless, draughty corridor.

'Archery practice,' said Claudia. 'Ah, here's Monica.' She greeted her sister-in-law – a tall, dark woman with a vampish air to her – with great affection. 'I was just explaining to Vee about Lucius.'

'The ancestors?' said Monica.

'Yes.'

'What happens when a servant leaves?' Vee asked, intrigued by this insight into her cousin's delusions. Her mother had always been rather tight-lipped about the exact nature of Lucius's loopiness, as had Claudia.

'They rarely do, but when they retire or a maid does leave to get married, I replace him or her with one who resembles the original as closely as possible,' said Monica serenely. 'Otherwise Lucius frets. The other thing you must remember is that all guests are ghosts.'

'What?'

'Lucius believes that all strangers to the castle are, in fact, the ghosts of his ancestors, or of other people associated with the castle over the centuries. He's perfectly polite to them, but they don't really exist, they aren't of this world, as far as he's concerned.'

Lucius should not be living in this castle, Vee told herself. He should be locked away in a padded cell.

'It's not his fault,' Claudia said. 'It's inbreeding, he can't help it. The strain started as dottiness, and then too many first cousins married first cousins, and in his case it's simply gone over the edge.'

'Is he safe?'

'He mostly stays within castle grounds,' said Monica. 'Because he

360

gets confused when he goes out; he thinks the villagers are villeins or serfs or some such thing, and they tend to resent it.'

'Has he never been to London?'

'Not since childhood,' Claudia said.

Why, Vee wanted to ask, had Monica married him? And wasn't she also some kind of cousin, albeit a distant one, a descendant of the fifteenth earl, Aunt Lettice had told her? 'So what on earth are his children like?' she couldn't help asking.

Claudia waited until Monica was out of earshot, and then said with a wink, 'Fortunately, the children are perfectly normal. Trust Monica to make sure of that.'

'What do you mean?'

'They aren't his, that's all.'

Vee had a vast room, hung about with tapestries and, as a centre-piece, a four-poster bed complete with hangings.

'I'm next door,' said Claudia. 'We share a bathroom across the passage.'

'I hope you'll be comfortable,' Monica said, looking round with a housewifely eye. 'Hislop will be looking after you both.'

Hislop was standing by the window, and she bobbed as Monica said her name.

'Odd maid's uniform,' Vee whispered to Claudia, as Hislop took her keys. 'Are the long skirts to do with Lucius's fantasies?'

'Not really. It's the way at Kepesake. Practical, actually, in winter; the long skirts keep them warm.'

'And servants stay?'

'Monica pays them well and takes a great interest in them all, and Lucius is really extremely sweet and good-natured. And although it's such a pile, there is an enormous number of servants, so none of them have too much to do.'

Vee didn't need to question where the money for all this came from. She knew that the Veres were as rich as Croesus, from land and rents – they owned several squares and streets in the choicest part of London as well as in other towns. They had income from mineral rights, and investments across the Empire, as well as land and oil holdings in America.

Looking around her, and feeling the familiar anger at the unfairness of a world where some could live like this and others eke out an existence on twenty shillings a week for an entire family, Vee knew in her heart that the revolution that she had believed in, and Alfred had been so certain was coming, and Klaus was working for, was not, after all, ever going to happen. Nothing was going to take away the wealth and therefore power that all this represented, whether Kepesake stood or not.

'If there's a war,' she said to Claudia when they went down to take tea in the baronial hall that passed for a drawing room, 'this will all be taken over for a hospital or government building. Then what will happen to Lucius?'

'There isn't going to be a war,' Claudia said. 'That's what this weekend is all about, that's what we're all working for: peace.'

Vee was amazed at the luminaries among the guests who assembled before dinner that evening. Claudia had said that they were all members of a movement called Party for Peace, but what a broad church that turned out to be, encompassing the extreme right wing, anti-communism, anti-Semitism and fascism.

What was Vee doing there? Why ever had she agreed to come? She couldn't blame Claudia, for her efforts at appearing to eschew politics in whatever form at Klaus's instructions had been all too successful, and her cousin now felt Vee was ripe for conversion to the greater cause of fascism and peace. And, since Giles had become more openly right-wing in his views, no doubt she might also be considered sympathetic to the Let's Appease Hitler group.

Vee didn't want to sit down to dine with the likes of Oswald Mosley. The last time she'd seen him had been at the rally at Olympia, and then he'd been a distant figure in a black uniform. Now he was dressed in ordinary evening clothes, very tall, very dark, with a thin moustache and a limp. He was talking to Lord Halifax; what would the Nazis, with their drive for physical perfection of the species, make of those two, one with a wonky leg and the other with a withered arm? Lord Halifax was obviously self-conscious about his arm, even here, at a private dinner, he kept his hand tucked inside the sleeve of his coat.

There was nothing deformed about Mosley's second wife, however. Diana Mosley was stunning as always; Vee had seen her about in London, well, you couldn't not, even if you weren't in the very centre of the smartest social set. It was a glacial beauty, unreal. People often said she was aptly named, for the goddess; Marcus, who knew the Mosleys, had remarked that the huntress part was possible, but not the rest of the attributes.

362

There were no close friends of Vee's there, and she felt uncomfortable and out of it.

Then, to her astonishment and dismay, she saw two men she knew very well indeed. One was Petrus, standing beside a large aspidistra, talking to a dark, stocky man with thick spectacles.

The other was Klaus.

Klaus? What was Klaus doing here, in this nest of Nazis? Klaus, the man who hated fascism more than he loved life. Or so she thought.

Vee had never met Klaus socially. All their meetings were arranged by him, took place in the open air, come rain or shine, and among indifferent strangers.

He shot her a quick glance, and she could tell that he was surprised to see her, only the merest flicker of an eye gave him away, but yes, he hadn't known she was going to be there.

Of course, she hadn't known herself until the last minute, what with her shilly-shallying; only when Bowler came to her room to attend to her packing did she give in to Claudia's urgings. Now, more than ever, she wished she hadn't. Petrus was bad enough – his presence still gave her gooseflesh, that was one incident from her past that hadn't faded into a sepia memory. But Klaus, of all people.

At dinner, she was seated next to Petrus. The old glamour was still there, and she could see, from the way his other neighbour was eyeing him up, that he had lost none of that magnetism that had been Claudia's undoing – and hers, for God's sake, although somehow, in her case, the attraction hadn't lasted beyond their single night together. He wasn't offensively masculine, he wasn't especially good-looking, despite that pale hair and those searching eyes, but there was a charismatic quality to him, and a personality that crept over you and left you with only a remnant of your own sense of self.

They talked on neutral matters; she felt that he was mocking her, and she knew, quite suddenly, that he was a dangerous man.

On Easter Sunday, most of the house party went to church in the village. Some of them donned stout shoes and walked across the fields, the rest climbed into shiny motor cars and rolled away down the drive.

Vee went out for a walk with Klaus. She didn't want to, but he insisted.

'Doesn't this break your rules?' she asked, when he came and found her in the library. 'Our being seen together?'

'We are fellow guests, fellow non-attendees at church. Who will notice us? Who will care?'

'Who else is in the house?'

Klaus shrugged. 'Our hostess. One or two guests who drank too much last night and are taking time to recover.'

They scrunched along a gravel path that branched off the drive and led to a pleasant-looking walled garden. It was warm, even though the spring sunshine was weak and there was a wind with a bitter touch to it. From the trees espaliered against the wall, she judged that this was part of the fruit garden, and in due course the branches would be heavy with peaches and apricots, and other non-English fruits. They were walking up and down, no benches here; she felt better on her feet and moving, less like a rabbit in the headlights.

'So why are you not the dutiful guest and attending church?' Klaus asked.

'I don't go to church because I am not a Christian any more. Communism and religion have nothing to do with each other, isn't that what you've always said?'

'It is what Marx and Lenin and now Stalin all say.'

She stood still for a moment, grateful for the warming rays of the sun on her face. Her eyes were shut.

'What are you doing here, Klaus, among these dreadful people?'

'Know your enemy. Do you think I'm the only person here under false pretences?'

No, she thought, there's me, for a start. But Klaus wasn't thinking of her. She had, yet again, the feeling that she didn't count, not in the sense that men did.

'There will be at least one member of the intelligence services here. Watching and taking note of what is said, and who is saying it.'

'Do you really think so? Does this wretched government give a button about the activities of appeasers? I thought they were all on the same side.'

'Politicians may be, but the intelligence services outlast the careers of politicians. They know that whatever the outcome of gatherings like this, war is more likely than not, and that war will be against the fascists. In which case, they will move in and round up anyone they suspect of having greater loyalties to that cause than to their country.'

What about her? Wasn't that the case with her? Or had once been;

if she'd been pushed to an honest answer, she thought that by now her loyalty to her country would have won.

'I can't see them putting Lord Halifax in a cell.'

Which was where she should be.

'Lord Halifax is misguided, secure in his beliefs, even if wrong-headed, but he isn't a traitor. If it comes to war, he will serve his country with faith and commitment. I can't say the same for all of the others who are present here.'

'What if Lord Halifax were to become Prime Minister? My uncle says it's likely.'

'He's in the Lords, he'll decide that it isn't possible at a time of national crisis for the Prime Minister to sit in the House of Lords; the Prime Minister must come from the Commons.'

'Churchill, then,' she said. 'He won't kow-tow to Hitler.'

'Churchill is a pragmatist, but also he hates communism. It is contrary to everything he stands for. He'll need the support of Russia to win any war against Germany, and that will stick in his gullet. Ah, little Vee, we live in interesting times.'

She didn't like the edge to his voice. 'The churchgoers will soon be back. We'd better go our separate ways.'

'Just one minute. I have instructions for you. And a message: Comintern is not happy that you haven't responded to my requests for a meeting.'

'Klaus, I told you. I'm having nothing more to do with you or Moscow, let's drop the Comintern bit shall we? I want out.'

'We appreciate that you were upset after Giles's death, and not capable of thinking clearly. You needed time to come to terms with what happened to him, and also to come to terms with yourself. But your beliefs haven't changed, why should you think differently about our cause now, why this change of heart?'

'Haven't you seen what's going on in the Soviet Union? Haven't you read the accounts of the show trials? I've been a fool. I believed I was working for a better England, a better world, for the sake of all the downtrodden workers who slave away for a pittance in my grandfather's factories. Well, I realize I was wrong. Moscow isn't going to liberate the workers of England, given half a chance, it wants to oppress them and enslave them the way Stalin is doing in Russia. And the way the Communist Party will in France, if it comes to power.'

There was a long silence after her outburst.

'I think you have been listening to some strange people,' Klaus said finally. 'This is propaganda I'm hearing from you, not the truth.'

'Truth! There is no truth. No, Klaus. Because of what I did, Giles killed himself. I find it hard to live with that.'

'Oh, I assure you that Giles did not kill himself on account of anything you did.'

There was an underlying irony to Klaus's voice that made Vee wary.

'All right, what your goons did caused him to kill himself, those photographs you took of him with men, and sent to him, was what made him shoot himself – only none of it would have happened if I hadn't done what I was asked to do. I betrayed Giles, it might as well have been me who pulled the trigger.'

'One man, against the welfare of millions?'

'Now you're the fool, Klaus. If you – and they – don't care about an individual life – or death – then how can you care for the millions? It's all words; it's all vague for the greater good, omelettes and eggs. I've heard it all, and it simply isn't true. It isn't true and it isn't right.'

Tears were blinding her eyes, and, furious at this sign of weakness, she made to leave the garden. Klaus caught her arm, holding her back. For the first time, she was afraid of him. He had a strength she hadn't suspected, and those sympathetic grey eyes held nothing but contempt and hardness.

'Let me persuade you. Let me tell you something that may help you to change your mind. It concerns your brother, Hugh.'

Vee listened, as the spring stopped, the birds were silent, the clouds were pinned in the sky and Klaus laid out her choice.

'It won't work. He won't do that.'

'You have always found him an attractive man, even if you won't admit it to yourself. You have a problem with men, we're aware of this, it has made you especially valuable in the work we have asked of you. This is less than you did when you married Giles.'

'It means betraying my friend.'

'What is that, set against the life of a beloved brother?'

'Why? Why me? Why him?'

'You have his trust. He likes you, he finds you attractive also. He will be of great value to us, but we need to have a hold on him.'

'It won't be enough, an affair.'

'Oh, I think it will, taken in conjunction with a few words in the right places. His career, his good name, his marriage? It has worked before, it will work again.'

'Why don't you use people who believe in what you're doing, instead of resorting to blackmail?'

'There is nothing I and my masters will not do to further the cause of communism and to protect the revolution. Nothing. Individuals matter to you, that is because you're still what you always were: a bourgeoise, a little girl making gestures against your grandfather who made you angry.'

Klaus was moving towards the doorway, and she had no means of stopping him. His hand on the latch, he turned back to her. 'It is a little thing we ask of you, a seduction; who knows, it may even give you some pleasure. I say goodbye to you now, Verity. I leave here this evening for London, and tomorrow I leave the country.'

At first, she didn't understand. Why should he leave the country?

'I have been recalled to Moscow.'

'What will happen to you?'

He shrugged. 'I don't know. I merely obey orders, as I have done ever since I committed myself to the party. Moscow will send someone to take my place. He will be in touch with you.'

And so Klaus walked out of her life.

Would that she had never met him.

PART THREE

1938

ONE

As the *Gloriana* steamed on its way and left the Bay of Biscay behind, the relentless pitching eased, the waves subsided, the sun shone. Wan passengers, not seen since the first night out, appeared on deck, sitting languidly on deck chairs, sipping the beef tea and crackers that the white-coated stewards served to passengers every morning at eleven.

The quoit slithered along the planking of the deck and just over the edge of the numbered square. Peter let out a yell of delight. 'I've won again.'

'You always do,' said Perdita. She retrieved the quoits. 'As long as we don't count all the quoits that go overboard.'

'Only two this morning.'

Lally was stretched out on a deck chair, watching Peter and Perdita. 'That's enough, now, Peter,' she called out. 'Run along, Miss Tyrell will be waiting for you in the library.'

'Must I?'

'You must.'

'No one else has to do lessons on board a ship. And Miss Tyrell doesn't have a clue about what I'm doing, much better if I can just work through the exercises by myself.'

'I dare say, but, no, Peter. You've missed a lot of school and you need to catch up, otherwise your grades will fall and you'll have to repeat a year.'

'We don't have grades at my school.'

'Marks, then. And look at Perdita, here, she works hard every single day, even at weekends. Isn't that so, Perdita?'

'Oh, music,' said Peter, a world of young scorn in his voice. 'Music's easy. Arithmetic and all that is much harder.'

A look from Lally quelled the rebellion, and he sauntered off, hands provocatively in his pockets and whistling, a new and shaky accomplishment.

'You're very good with him. Have you younger brothers and sisters of your own?'

'No, I'm the youngest,' said Perdita. 'Oh, good, here's the steward with heavenly beef tea. I should go and do some more practice before lunch, but . . .'

'We have it on Peter's authority that it's only music. Not so hard as sums.'

Perdita laughed and thumped down next to Lally. She was wearing grey flannel shorts and canvas shoes, and she let her long legs drop on either side of the chair.

'It isn't hard, not for me, although I'm good at sums, too. But it's the hours that count.'

'Are you going to be a professional?'

'I hope so,' Perdita dunked a cracker into her soup and rescued it just before it began to dissolve. 'That's my plan, only with the war . . .' Her voice trailed off, a minor key of the unexpressed.

'War,' said Lally, almost to herself.

'Please don't say, maybe there isn't going to be a war,' said Perdita. 'I'm sure there will be, and everyone else thinks so really, even if they try to pretend it's not going to happen.'

'You don't think the British Government will make peace with Hitler?'

'They may, but what peace is Hitler going to make? Fascists don't know the meaning of the word. They're right and everybody else is wrong, and there's an end to the argument.'

'Tell me something about yourself,' said Lally. She'd taken a liking to this lanky English girl with her clear mind and frank ways. 'Didn't I hear you say you come from the north of England?'

'Westmoreland. The Lake District. Do you know it?'

'I've been to Yorkshire and Scotland, and that's my experience of the north.'

'I went to school in Yorkshire. So did Mrs Hotspur. You know her, don't you? We were at the same school, only I was a first-former when she left.'

Yes, Lally and Vee were friends, although she'd hardly seen anything of her so far. She'd been ill, and then Vee was keeping to her cabin, putting out a Do Not Disturb sign. She had asked the stewardess if Vee were unwell, but no.

'Writing,' said Pigeon, in tones of strong disapproval. Her ladies should have better things to do than shut themselves away in a cabin and scribble, scribble all day long.

Peter said that it was probably better for her to be in her cabin. 'Mrs Hotspur is terribly jumpy, won't go near the rails in case she falls overboard. I've told her practically no one ever does. What's the point in coming on a boat if you're afraid of falling off? Much better to stay put on dry land.'

'Mrs Hotspur seemed preoccupied,' said Perdita. 'We had a chat about school, though.'

'Was it a boarding school? Did you hate it?'

Perdita looked surprised. 'It was pretty ghastly, but one can get used to anything. And home wasn't . . .' A wary look came over her face. She leaned down to put the empty bowl on the deck. 'It's all in the past now. Where does Peter go to school? I know he's been ill, but he'll have to go back, won't he?'

'Not if I have anything to do with it.'

'You're American, aren't you? You don't have that thing about sending children away to boarding school.'

'Some do. It's never been the way in my family.'

'Everyone in England does it, well, not everyone, most people can't afford it, but those who can, do.'

'Do you agree with it?'

'No, I don't, actually. I don't like doing something just because that's the way it is and the way it's always been, and I went and survived, so you can just get on with it, and not thinking about whether it's right for you or the children. My sister-in-law says she won't send her children away to school. She's a foreigner.'

'Won't her husband insist?'

Perdita laughed. 'Edwin's a bit of a bohemian. He wasn't especially happy at school, so I don't think he'll mind too much, if there's a good day school locally. He says everything will be different, in any case. After . . .'

'The war,' Lally finished, with a sigh.

'If we lose, no one will have any choice about anything, the Germans will tell us all what to do. And Lidia will be dragged off to some camp, because she's a Jew, and Edwin will probably be hauled off with her. I don't want to think about it. And if we beat Hitler, then things will be different anyhow. Everyone goes on about how much things changed after the last war. Women getting the vote and skirts getting shorter, and jazz, and new ideas. This time around, we'll all be communists, I expect. So there won't be any boarding schools, not like there are now.'

Lally was taken aback by these forthright views. 'How old are you?'

Perdita grinned. 'Seventeen. And you're thinking, what does she know about it? It's my generation that's going to have to pick up the pieces, so I'm entitled to my views.'

Lally's heart went out to the gawky girl beside her. She might only be seventeen, but she was setting off bravely into an unknown and hideously complicated world. It was impressive how matter-of-fact she was, talking about the terrible things that might happen to her family.

'You have to look facts and fears in the face,' Perdita remarked. Her eyes were on the gently-swaying horizon. 'It does no good to pretend that awful things don't happen. I despise people who go around in a woolly cloud, saying one must never think or say the worst. For if the worst is going to happen, it's much better to see it coming. And if it has happened, then you just have to buck up and live with it.'

There was a strained note to Perdita's voice as she said the last words. Lally wondered just what awful things this child – for she was really little more than a child – had had to face up to in her short and no doubt privileged life.

'When the war starts, will you go back to America?' Perdita asked.

Lally was taken aback. 'I don't think so. Peter might be safer there, but my husband would say it was running away. And I expect he – my husband – will be in the thick of it, and I would want to be there when he came home.'

'He's Henry Messenger, isn't he? Colonel Messenger, I should say.'

'Yes. Why, do you know him?'

'I think I met him, once, in London. At a cocktail party. Tall and thin and handsome in a heroic kind of way.'

Lally laughed. 'That sounds like Henry, all right.'

'I didn't see you at the party.'

There was a pause. Then Lally said, 'Henry was in London on his own for a while. When Peter was ill. I had to stay at home with him. It was better for him to be in the country, for the air and the peace and quiet. It was the kind of illness that needs a lot of rest and looking after. Henry was working at Headquarters at the time.'

'Is he in India now? Is that why you're going out there?'

'Yes, he's adjutant to the Viceroy.'

'It'll all be parties and protocol out there,' said Perdita wisely. 'I expect he'll be glad when he gets the chance to biff away at the enemy. Here's the steward for the empties.' She scooped hers up, took Lally's coffee cup and handed them to him. Then she scrambled ungracefully to her feet. 'Back to the scales.'

TWO

Marcus and Joel both spent quite a lot of time in the library, listening to Perdita practising. Marcus because he was sketching her, loving her lean body, the intensity of her concentration and the way her hands moved over the keyboard; Joel because he was himself something of a musician, and he liked to listen. She played Bach every day, and to him that was akin to listening to a prayer. He told her so, and she agreed.

'My teacher says, you can play Bach every day for a lifetime and you'll never get bored with it, and never stop finding new things in the music.'

'I'd love to design a dress for her,' Marcus said. His stalk of charcoal scratched rhythmically on the cartridge paper. 'Do you remember the dress I made for Lally, when she was Queen of the May?'

He gave a sidelong glance at Joel, to see if the remark had gone home. Joel's expression didn't alter.

Marcus tried again. 'Still carrying a torch for Lally? She's been married for three years now, isn't it time you found a new object for your adoration?'

'Shut up, Marcus,' Joel said, amiably.

'You looked as sick as a parrot at her wedding.'

'You looked drunk, which you were. And most of the guests looked as sick as parrots, if you remember anything about it.'

'I passed out under the table with the cake on it. I came to just as Henry was lifting his sabre to slice down into the iced perfection, very alarming from where I was lying. His family still haven't forgiven him for marrying Lally, the fools. He could scour the Empire and not bring home a nicer woman, nor a more beautiful or kinder one, and all they do is carp because she's, "American, from Chicago, of all dreadful places, my dear",' Marcus said in cruel mimicry. '"Of Irish origin, squeal, gasp. And a Roman Catholic!" I wonder where they dredged that old priest up to do the ceremony. Perhaps he wasn't a real one, but an actor in costume. Perhaps Lally isn't really and truly married and there's a chance for you yet, Joel.'

'Oh, pack it in, Marcus. He was a priest. He volunteered to marry them, Lally told me, because he said he was too old for the Church to be able to do him any harm for conducting a marriage between a Catholic and a non-Catholic.'

'I don't know why Harry didn't convert. I would have, all those juicy young priests in soutanes and that wonderful colour cardinals wear.'

Joel frowned. Perdita was playing very quietly and could probably hear what they were saying.

'Why are you glaring at me like that?' Marcus asked. 'Oh, I see, *pas devant les enfants*. Let us change the subject then, and turn away from the divine Lally to you, Perdy. I may call you Perdy, mayn't I? Come over and join us, and tell us why you're here on board this ghastly ship instead of putting in the hours at the conservatoire.'

Perdita shut her music and plonked herself down in an overstuffed leather armchair. 'I think these chairs are meant for gorillas, not for human beings,' she observed. 'You are nosy, aren't you, Mr Sebert?'

'You may call me Marcus, everyone does. Come along, spill the beans.'

'It isn't very interesting. I had measles, quite badly, and the doctors thought a voyage somewhere warm would help me get better more quickly. So it's out to India for a while, while winter does its worst at home, and then back again for the spring. And if war breaks out before then, I'm going straight back on the next boat, and never mind torpedoes and all that.'

'Good for you,' said Marcus. 'Now, as a reward for your speaking up so nicely to the grown-ups, I'll tell you that I'm also on board for my health.'

'Rubbish,' said Joel. 'There's nothing wrong with your health, bar a pickled liver.'

'I have a piece of paper to prove it,' said Marcus. 'From one of Harley Street's finest. I'm only going as far as Port Said, however. I shall sample the delights that Cairo has to offer.'

'Goats, perhaps,' said Joel under his breath.

'And then return to the loving arms of the BBC. And if war breaks out I may decide to stay put, although I'm sure war will be waged all over the globe, and I shan't be able to escape.'

'There's always Switzerland,' said Perdita.

'Do you think so? Don't you think the Germans will be over those snowy mountains in a trice? Besides, could I bear to see the war out in the company of six million Swiss? I think not.'

'No plans for war work, Marcus?' Joel asked.

'Propaganda, my dear Joel. Propaganda is going to be the key to this war. And there's bound to be a slot for me in Intelligence, in MI one or two or twenty, don't you think?'

Marcus had objected vehemently at being directed to sail to Egypt on the *Gloriana*, with orders to watch Mrs Hotspur's back. They were walking in Kensington Gardens, he and Michael, the Lithuanian-born businessman who had looked after Marcus since his recruitment in 1932.

'She's a lost cause, you do realize that,' Marcus said.

'I hope you are not allowing your friendship with her to cloud your judgement.'

Marcus thrust his hands into his pockets and kicked a pebble to the side of the path. 'She's at the end of her tether. You can't do much with a woman when she gets like that.'

'The stakes are very high for her; she believes that her brother's life depends on her doing what we want.'

'Does it? All right, none of my business, and you won't say. What do you mean by watch her back?'

'Make sure she isn't saying or doing anything she shouldn't. Anything that might be compromising for us.'

'If she is?'

'There will be someone else on board to deal with her if she becomes a threat. I'll give you details of how to keep in touch with him.'

'I can't just leave the BBC and bugger off to Egypt, you know.'

'That's been arranged. Go to see this doctor, he will say you have a problem with your lungs. Sea air, a few weeks in a warmer climate. Your superior at the BBC won't question it.'

'And what if war breaks out while I'm away?'

'It won't. We will get you back to England in time, don't concern yourself about that. Then, as you say, it will be time for you to find yourself work in the intelligence services.'

*   *   *

380

'Are you going to Egypt or India?' Perdita asked Joel.

'India,' he said. Then feeling this was too terse, he amplified. 'I'm a mathematician. I'm going to work for a few months with an Indian mathematician in Delhi.'

It sounded thin to his ears, even as he said it. Marcus had a knowing look on his face, and the girl looked surprised and yes, doubtful.

His college hadn't taken too kindly to his sudden announcement that he was setting sail for India.

'Good God,' the Warden said. They were in the Warden's room, a large, panelled room, with the evening sun making the polished wood glow. He poured Joel a glass of pale sherry. 'What's wrong with the post? And if anyone's got to sail halfway around the world, why not Amar Singh, why do you have to be the one to go?'

'He won't leave India.'

'He left it to study at Cambridge.'

'He says, never again. He can't bear the climate. And he's involved in setting up a new department, it's difficult for him to leave his students. I don't have any, so . . .'

'The purpose of a fellowship is to be a member of the college. It's not as though you were an archaeologist who needs to be on site or anything like that.'

'Mathematicians often go to conferences and congresses.'

'Well, yes. Paris, or Berlin, although perhaps not Berlin these days. Or America, that's quite far enough, and five days out and five days back is much more practical.'

'Only Amar Singh doesn't live in America.'

The Warden pursed his lips. 'It's no secret that war's a strong possibility, Joel.'

'A probability, I would say, Warden.'

'Yes, very well. In which case, a man of your particular abilities is likely to be needed . . .'

Joel listened politely, his mind far away. He had already been approached, and invited to go on a course to cover the basics necessary to work as a cryptographer.

'You're doing first-class work. In the coming months and years, a mind like yours will be invaluable. You will be called on, I would think, to do work of the highest national importance.'

That was true. Important to whom?

Joel had a sleepless night, and was up at the crack of dawn, tossing things into a suitcase. He didn't have a second case, so he took his golf clubs out of their bag and filled it with various items. He thrust his sponge bag, snatched up at the last moment, into a shopping bag he'd wrested from the cleaner on his way out. She stood looking down at him, a stout, indignant figure in a shapeless hat, her hands on her hips.

His scout was waiting further down the staircase.

'A shopping bag, sir?'

'Have a heart, Phipps, I have to carry my shaving tackle in something.'

'And why not in a suitcase, like a Christian traveller, I'd like to know? And where are you off to in such a tearing hurry, sir, and no breakfast eaten?'

'India,' he said, brushing past the disapproving scout. 'Look after my things for me while I've gone. I don't know when I'll be back. There's an envelope for you on the mantelpiece. Christmas box.'

Almost, he hoped there wouldn't be a berth. But, 'Yes, sir, we have a cabin available, the gentleman cancelled this morning.' So here he was, sailing to a country he didn't have the least wish to visit, keeping up a cheerful front before the other passengers. He was on the *Gloriana* because Lally was going to be on board. He wanted to see her, he wanted to be near her, he wanted to be able to talk to her, because she would advise him better than anyone he knew on what he should do.

So far, the voyage had been a disaster. He'd been seasick, Lally had been seasick, and then, when she came on deck, pale but beautiful, the hopelessness of the situation flooded over him with new anguish. She and Harry weren't getting on too well, he'd heard. Harry was in Delhi, she had stayed behind with the boy. The boy was better, convalescent, Harry had read the riot act, Lally was to join him in India.

He would never have this chance again, of Lally on her own. But Lally wasn't on her own. She was with Peter, and a sharp-looking woman, whose eyes missed nothing. It would have been agony to stay in England, knowing that every day carried her further from him; it was agony to be on board the same ship as her.

'Aren't you good at running?' Perdita asked him.

Joel jumped, dragging his mind back to the conversation.

'Running?'

'Didn't you compete in the Olympic Games? I saw your name in the papers.'

'Oh. Yes.' That sort of running.

'Now he's running away,' Marcus said, with glee in his voice. 'Fast and far, Joel, isn't that it, so that you're elsewhere if there's a war?'

He was running away, but he wasn't going to say so, nor what he was running away from.

'Come the war, I'll be in there, Marcus,' he said, keeping his voice light. To his mind, there was no question of If. War was imminent. This month, next month, the spring, next summer. It was coming as certainly as Christmas and the next full moon. His father had been of the same opinion when he'd last seen him.

'Here we go again, Joel. You'd think we'd had enough of it to last us a century or more, but no, here we go again, with the dead of the last go still not mouldered away in their graves. At least you won't be in the trenches like I was. There won't be any trenches this time, but in any case, your war won't be frontline. That's what brains do for you.'

It was clear to everyone but him where his duty lay in the coming conflict. The powers that be, the British Government in its official shape, and the Warden, had no doubts, as they had told him. A mathematician of his ability . . .

An opportunity to be at the centre of a secret world.

Safe, as safe as anyone could be in war.

He didn't want to be safe. If there were a war coming, he wanted to be part of it, as his father had been. Anything would be better than spending the war in a desk job; he would rather volunteer for the navy, serve in the abominable closeness of a submarine. Only the authorities would laugh at him; what use to them was a brilliant mathematician at the bottom of the sea? He could lie about his degree, enlist as a private in some infantry regiment to be sent overseas as cannon fodder.

That had an appeal, the anonymity, all decisions taken away from him. He would be a number, not a person. Under orders, no responsibilities, no torn loyalties.

'I don't suppose we'll be given much choice,' Perdita said, her face serious. 'In the last war, you got sent off to the front if you were a man and to the munitions factory if you were a woman and that was that. That's what duty's all about, I expect.'

'My advice to you,' Marcus said, 'is to sign up for the WRNS as soon as you're back in England. Much the most chic of the uniforms, and there'll be a queue around the block once the fun begins.'

THREE

Pigeon wasn't having it. She gave three efficient taps on Vee's cabin door, and used her pass key to let herself in.

Vee was hunched over the table and her notebook. 'How the devil did you get in here?' she asked, not looking up. 'Whoever you are, just go away.'

'It's Pigeon, madam, and I've come to lay out your clothes for dinner.'

'I'm not dining.'

'That's what you said yesterday. Your friends are enquiring after you. Miss Richardson, and that nice Mrs Messenger, the one with the little boy, just down the passage here, she's been along several times.'

Vee looked up. Her eyes were red with fatigue, and there was a dull throbbing inside her skull. Too much writing, too little sleep, too little air, too many cigarettes.

'You can open the window,' she said.

'I should think so. It's not very fresh in here, if you don't mind my saying so.' Then, in a cajoling voice. 'You'll feel much better for going out on deck for a breath of sea air before dinner. And then dancing, dancing always makes one feel more cheerful.'

Dancing? Vee sighed, and put down her pen. 'Just get me some coffee and a plate of sandwiches, please. And tell people – oh, tell them I'm seasick.'

'That's not very likely, now, is it, with the sea millpond flat, and even the worst sufferers back on their feet and enjoying shipboard life.'

'Oh, for God's sake. Say it's a migraine, that should keep them at bay. I don't want to see anyone, anyone at all.'

'You do look as though your head is hurting you. Shall I ask the nurse for some aspirin?'

Vee wasn't listening. 'What? If you want to.' Why didn't the wretched woman take herself off? Then her conscience smote her; the woman was only doing her job.

'We'll be arriving at Lisbon tomorrow. You'll want to go ashore. All my ladies enjoy Lisbon.'

'Lisbon? Already? Yes, yes, I'll go ashore.' She'd be finished by tomorrow, in any case, if she could just be left alone to get on with her writing. 'Get me those sandwiches, please, and lock the door behind you.'

Vee finished writing at half past three the next morning. Drained, exhausted, yet with a sense of catharsis, she closed the fat leather notebook and tied the leather thongs in a neat loop. She opened the drawer and dropped it in.

Then, still in her clothes, she lay down on her berth, weary to her bones. Pigeon was right, there was no movement, just the vibration of the engines, and the very slightest creaking as the liner moved through the water.

She had no sense of her physical body, but words and images floated into her mind. Marcus, drunk, at his flat. Putting his arm around her, an intimacy that was rare with Marcus, who never liked to be too close to any woman. Whispering in her ear, How are the comrades, darling Vee? And Klaus, all is well with Klaus? Be careful, Vee, don't put a foot wrong, always do what our masters say, they haven't an ounce of forgiveness in their souls, because they don't have souls, do you see? You don't want to end up like Giles, a gory end.'

Then Lally, tea at the Ritz. 'I don't know what's come over Henry. He's suddenly at home as often as he can be, and he even listens to me when I talk about Peter. He doesn't pay any attention, he simply takes it for granted that the boy must go back to school, do him good. And it's just what all the Messengers say. I wonder if he's been having an affair.'

The words were spoken so calmly, in such a matter-of-fact way.

'Henry?' was all Vee could say.

'It's possible. Men do.'

There had been a long silence. Then Vee spoke, quite normally. 'What would you do? If he had. Been having an affair, I mean. Would you divorce him?'

'Catholics don't.'

'Take a lover? Jump into bed with Joel?'

'Tempting, but no.'

'Tempting?'

'If I hadn't met Henry and fallen for him as I did, I dare say I would have married Joel. We had quite an understanding.'

'But you never went to bed with him?'

'Catholics don't do that either. Fornication is a sin. Or, if they do, they never talk about it. Except to their father confessors.'

Giles, strained, bad-tempered and unhappy. And drunk. 'The only person I ever loved was Hugh. I still love him. I don't think life without him is worth living.'

FOUR

Even before the *Gloriana* had sailed up the Tagus to her anchor, the news had flashed around the ship.

'Peace!'

'It's peace.'

'There isn't going to be a war, after all.'

'Chamberlain's back from Munich, it's peace in our time, that's what he says.'

There was general jubilation, a rush of good spirits and camaraderie as people flocked to be among the first on the launches to go ashore and find out more.

On the bridge, the first officer read the radio report and handed it to the captain. 'Do you believe it, sir?'

'Chamberlain is a weak man. This'll buy us time, no more. Enjoy this voyage, Martin. It may be the last one you'll make in peacetime.'

Lally and Vee walked sedately off the launch, while Peter jumped on to dry land. He burst out laughing to find himself staggering. 'My sea legs,' he said with pride.

At any other time, Vee would have loved Lisbon: the warmth, the colours, the vitality. Even the presence of so many men in uniform – for Salazar had a tight grip on his country – couldn't remove the feeling of holiday.

'They say Lisbon's full of spies and Germans,' Lally said.

Vee winced. 'Where's Spain from here?'

They'd taken a guide, and he was eager with information. 'Over there, senhora, not so far to the border from here. But you do not want to go to Spain, it is all desolation now, war and prisoners and dead peoples and horses everywhere. Portugal is much, much better. Portugal is a peaceful country, like England.'

Vee looked in the direction the man was pointing. That was where Hugh was, somewhere in the devastated country that lay on the other side of the border. Was Hugh, in fact, one of the dead peoples, not a prisoner at all? Were the Soviets dealing in base coinage? It was perfectly possible. She looked at Lally, cool under a wide-brimmed hat, straightening the collar of Peter's shirt.

Disloyalty, betrayal, cowardice. The words that had begun to be whispered about Chamberlain as the details of his contemptible deal became known echoed in her head. If they applied to Chamberlain, who was no doubt doing what he thought was in the best interests of his country, how much more did they describe her? Only the best interests of her country had never come into the equation; she'd swallowed the old lie about wider loyalties, about a common idealism that knew no national boundaries.

'Look,' shouted Peter, taking his handkerchief from his pocket and waving it furiously. 'Hello, Lady Claudia! Mummy, it's Lady Claudia.'

Claudia, Claudia of all people. In Lisbon. Looking quite dreadfully thin, and with dark shadows under her eyes; Vee had never seen her look so unlike her normal self.

Lally was direct. 'Claudia, you look just awful. Are you ill?'

Claudia's eyes looked huge in her haggard face. 'No. Just had rather a time of it, that's all. I'm so glad I caught up with you, you must have got off the boat very quickly, and had gone by the time I got there.'

Lally laughed. 'That was Peter, wanting to be first ashore. I am glad to see you, Claudia.'

'I thought you were in Berlin,' Vee said. 'Have you heard the news?'

'About Munich?' Claudia nodded. 'It's the most worthless piece of paper in the history of the world,' she said bitterly. 'All lies. Hitler will bide his time and then move in and take whatever he wants. And God help the men, women and children who fall prey to him and his armies.'

This was a change of tune. Lally and Vee exchanged puzzled glances. Claudia tried for a brighter tone, with an obvious effort. 'I gather you're on your way to India, Lally. You too, Vee?'

'For a change of scene,' Vee said. 'I wanted to go somewhere I'd never been, where there's no connection with Giles.'

There was a pause; since Giles died, Vee never mentioned her marriage normally.

'What are you doing in Lisbon?' Lally asked Claudia.

'Waiting for you, actually, Lally. Your ma-in-law, who is a dragon of the most flaming kind, told me you were on the *Gloriana*, off to join Harry. With Peter, which seems to make her even more wild. Anyhow, I needed to get away from England for various reasons which I won't bore you with just at present, so, here I am, watching out for you. I thought, Lally, that if I come on to Delhi, I could stay with you and Harry for a while.'

Lally was delighted. 'Of course, how lovely.'

Vee was horrified. Claudia, with her keen eyes and curiosity and uncomfortable sixth sense, in Delhi? She'd spot in a trice what Vee was up to, and she'd be protective of Lally, of course she would, and feel obliged to speak her mind to Harry; it would wreck her plans.

Yet she felt a kind of relief. She saw no way she could carry out Moscow's orders. They were living in an unreal world; they had little idea of how people behaved. She had seduced Henry at a time when he was lonely and hurt and jealous of the attention Lally was lavishing on his sick son.

Henry in Delhi would be a very different man.

Only, might there be photographs? Such as the ones she had found of Giles? Would they be enough to ruin a man, when the woman he'd been with arrived on his doorstep, a glamorous widow and the long-time friend of his wife? Would Henry do as they wanted, to save his name and his marriage?

She didn't know him well enough to say, but she doubted it. Moscow might despise men like Henry, but they would be unwise to underestimate them. Henry might have all the faults of his class and upbringing, but he had its virtues as well. Virtues that in the coming war would be the saving of her country.

Claudia went off with a wave, and a cheery, 'See you on board.'

'Perhaps there won't be a cabin,' said Vee.

'There will always be a cabin for a Lady Claudia.' Lally's tone was dry. 'I hope she does get a berth, I want to know what's made her change her views like that. Did you notice what she said about Hitler?'

FIVE

Lally was right. When they went back on board, it was to find Claudia installed in a cabin only a few doors away from Lally and Vee.

Pigeon was all approval. 'You're a friend of Lady Claudia Vere's, are you, Mrs Hotspur?'

'She's my cousin,' said Vee, and went up several notches in Pigeon's estimation.

'Now, no nonsense about not dining tonight, madam.' Pigeon was firm. 'Otherwise the ship's doctor will be along to see you. You've caught the sun today, you should have worn a hat with more brim to it.'

Vee obediently put on the long dress that Pigeon laid out for her. 'We'll take our cocktails to the library for a good natter before dinner,' Claudia had said. 'No one will be there at that time of day, we'll have it to ourselves.'

It wasn't like Claudia to want to be out of whatever liveliness was going. And Vee doubted if they'd have the library to themselves, she was prepared to bet that Perdita would be in there.

She was. Claudia gave her a startled and not altogether friendly look when she arrived and found Perdita rippling up and down the keyboard. 'We can ask her to buzz off,' she suggested to Vee and Lally.

'Leave her be,' Lally said. 'She gets lost in the music, she won't listen to anything we say, and we aren't going to talk secrets are we?'

'Not exactly, no, but . . . Doesn't she play tunes at all?'

'She will,' Lally said. 'Beethoven, usually and always Bach.'

'Oh, Bach, twiddle, twiddle, twiddle.'

'She's like a creature from a pagan land,' Lally said softly. 'Clear-eyed and clear-headed. A twice-born, William James would call her. Young in years but like one of the old ones.'

'Don't you get fey,' Claudia said. 'Look at my famous sixth sense, what good did that do me?'

Lally tucked a cushion behind her back. 'OK, Claudia, spit it out. Why were you in Lisbon? Why do you look like a ghost? How come you've not got a good word to say for the fascists?'

Claudia knocked back her cocktail, and summoned a steward to bring her another one. 'Do you remember Sarah Blumenthal?'

'From Grace?' said Vee. 'Of course.'

'She married a German,' Lally said. Then realizing what that meant, her hand flew to her mouth. 'A doctor. A Jewish doctor.'

'Who was dragged from his house, taken to a camp and shot,' said Claudia, with another gulp of cocktail. 'Sarah told me about it. And other things, too.'

'It's been happening a lot,' Vee said. 'We did try to tell you.'

'Don't,' said Claudia. 'Don't say, we told you so. There's nothing you can say that can make me any more aware of how stupid I was. As though I'd been hypnotized. How could I not see what fascism really was? How could I swallow all that . . . ? Well, I'm not the only one. But I've come to my senses.'

'Because of Sarah's husband?'

'Because they wanted to arrest Sarah, too. She and her husband had been working for the communists, the Gestapo knew all about it, and she was high on their hit list. I mean, she simply didn't have a chance.'

Sarah, their friend from college days, letting them in through the window, playing the oboe with Lally and Joel, making them jump with her caustic wit; Sarah, in the hands of the Gestapo?

SIX

Claudia looked round the Berlin apartment, wondering where her stockings had ended up. She retrieved one from under a cushion and found the other peeping out from beneath the bed. The bedclothes were in tumbled disarray, a testament to an active evening. What a bore that Josh had to leave.

'A cocktail party, I'm already late for that, then a dinner and on to a dance,' Josh said, lifting his chin to knot his tie. 'Perils of the diplomatic life.'

Claudia could go to one of half a dozen cocktail parties, lifting the telephone would bring half a dozen invitations to dine out, to go to a show, to go dancing.

She pulled on her stockings, and attended to her face. Then she lit a cigarette and wandered over to the wireless. Martial music, announcements, a replay of a recent speech by the Führer, a snatch of Wagner. A French station, then a faint thread of jazz.

She considered the possibilities for the rest of the evening. First, she'd get a taxi back to her own flat. Next, a bath and dress. By then she'd have decided what she felt like doing, whom she would telephone.

She put on her hat and thrust a pin in place, then tossed her fox fur around her shoulders. She let herself out of the apartment, and tucked the key in her handbag. The lift wasn't at her floor, so she clattered down the stairs. Josh had deliberately chosen to live in a building without a concierge, 'I prefer not to have some nosy besom watching my comings and goings.'

No, thought Claudia, but what's the difference, with the secret police watching your every step? She didn't go through the main door, but went on down the next flight of stairs to the basement and let herself out through the back entrance. The main door led on to a brightly-lit street; this door opened on to a cobbled alley, the dustbins and detritus of the apartment buildings and the shops neatly stacked against the walls for collection in the early hours of the morning.

Claudia began to walk towards the street, then paused at the sound of hurrying feet. Not quite running, but with a sound of urgency about them. A figure stopped at the end of the alley, then ducked into it. Claudia drew back into the shadows. There was the familiar, raucous sound of sirens, harsh voices, the sharp clatter of boots on pavements.

Whoever this person was, he or she was in trouble, and nipping down this alley wasn't going to help. She stepped out, not wanting to get caught up in anything awkward, and cannoned into the fugitive. A swift curse, a gasp, an apology. It was a woman, for God's sake.

A young woman, who sounded familiar. Claudia peered at her in the dim light from the single streetlamp. 'Sarah!'

The young woman drew away, was starting to run. Claudia leaped forward and siezed her. 'You'll never make it,' she said. 'This way.'

The basement door that she'd come through hadn't closed completely, thank goodness, that was time saved. Claudia pushed Sarah through the door and closed it firmly behind them. 'Come on,' she said. 'Up the stairs, to the second floor, as quick as you can and don't make a noise.'

Inside the apartment once more, Sarah, breathless, was staring at Claudia with huge, alarmed eyes.

'We've got to get a move on,' Claudia said.

'If they come, they'll search and find me, and then you'll be in trouble, too.'

'Diplomatic flat, they won't search it, and they won't want to. Let me think. Wardrobe, plenty of room, you can sit down in there. Don't sneeze, that's all.'

She thrust Sarah into the huge mahogany double-doored wardrobe, shut the door and turned the key. Then she tore off her hat, slung her fur over the back of a chair, removed her jacket and smoothed her shirt into her skirt. She heaved the bedclothes into some kind of order, no point in arousing disapproval, you never knew with Germans how moral they might be, and switched the wireless on. Wagner would do nicely. Then a dive into the kitchen, to mix herself a drink, and by the time the thunder of knocks sounded at her door, she was settled down for a peaceful evening, waiting for her boyfriend to come home.

Her heart was thudding, but her face was a mask of surprised enquiry as she opened the door, holding it on the chain.

Of course they could come in. Here were her papers, everything in order, yes, it was Mr Sanger's apartment, an official at the American Embassy, a good friend of hers, he wouldn't be in for a while yet.

Had she heard anything, seen anyone, had she been in the flat long?

Several hours, and no, bar the noise in the street that they'd made, she hadn't seen or heard anything since Josh Sanger left about an hour ago. They were welcome to look round.

Hard-faced men in hateful dark uniforms, suspicious, but they were suspicious of everyone. They were impressed by her fluent German, by her title, and she heard one of them mutter to another that she was friends with some very influential government people. Their inspection of the apartment was rapid and cursory, then, with bows and clicking of heels, they apologized for disturbing her and left.

She sat down in the nearest chair and took a good swig of her cocktail. She heard them moving to the next apartment. She wasn't going to let Sarah out until she was sure they'd left the building, and even then, they'd probably leave someone on guard.

'It's safe to come out now, Sarah,' she said, swinging open the door. 'Were you suffocating in there?'

'I've been in worse hiding places,' Sarah said.

How thin she was, and dark rings under her eyes spoke of fear and exhaustion.

'Have a drink,' Claudia said. 'Then I'll fix something to eat, and we'll make a plan to get you out of here.'

Sarah sat down abruptly. 'It's awfully kind of you, Claudia, but actually, there's no point. Oh, I'll take myself away, but I've nowhere to go. It's a miracle I've kept out of the Gestapo's clutches for as long as I have, but it's no good kidding myself, I might just as well give myself up and be done with it.' She sat up, her eyes narrowing. 'Come to think of it, why didn't you give me up? Why are you helping me? You're one of them.'

'I'm English, first and foremost. You're a friend, we were at Grace together, remember? Grace girls help one another out. So shut up, there's no question of my handing you over. I wouldn't hand over my worst enemy to the Gestapo, as it happens. Drink this.'

While they ate, Sarah talked. About her marriage, about her dangerous involvement in left-wing activities, about her husband's arrest: 'They shot him, I didn't know for a week, then a member who works at Headquarters came and told me.'

'Do they know you're Jewish?' Claudia asked; she had noticed that Sarah wasn't wearing a yellow star.

Sarah nodded. 'Yes, but I pretend not to be, I look more Aryan than most non-Jewish Germans, so as long as I have false papers, I can get away with it.'

'Where are your papers?'

'Someone betrayed me. That's how they got on to me, and why I made a run for it.'

Claudia was frowning. 'You need to get out. Out of Berlin, out of Germany.'

Sarah raised her eyes to heaven. 'Yes, me and every other Jew who's still here and not in prison or a concentration camp. Only, they aren't letting any of us out, and if one does manage to escape, no one wants to give us refuge.'

Claudia was thinking aloud. 'I'm due to leave for England in the morning. On a train leaving at a quarter past eleven.'

'Lucky you.'

Claudia was examining Sarah's pale face and hair, tied back in an unflattering bun.

'Your hair is longer than mine,' she said, speaking to herself rather than to Sarah. 'A bit lighter, needs a wave . . .'

'What are you talking about?'

Claudia sprang to her feet. 'Come on, hurry up, we haven't got long, you'll have to be out of here before Josh gets back, I can't get him mixed up in this.'

'Who's Josh?' said Sarah, turning round as she was propelled towards the bathroom. 'No. I don't want to know, but they'll be waiting for me whenever I go. There's no point in putting it off.'

'Every point. Wash your hair, go on, just do as I say.'

Sarah protested, argued, couldn't believe what Claudia was planning.

Guts, thought Claudia, she's living and no doubt had been living for months on pure courage. Shame swept over her, for all the things she'd refused to see, but there was no time for remorse now; she had things to do.

At half past ten, a tall woman with fashionably-waved fair hair pinned under a smart hat, her face exquisitely made up, an expensive fur over the shoulders of her elegant suit, walked confidently out of the main door of the apartment building.

'Thank God we have much the same size feet,' Claudia had said. 'Now, timing's all important. At ten o'clock, the woman who looks after my apartment building shuts up shop, so there's no problem getting in. The morning's more tricky, but she always leaves her box to have a coffee and cake at half past ten. That's when you leave, wearing the clothes I've written down for you. Don't make any mistakes, gloves, shoes, suitcase, everything has to be just as I've said. Hail a taxi, there are always taxis there at that time of the morning, and go straight to the station, and catch that train.'

Sarah was still in a state of bewilderment as she went out on to the street. A glance from the shadowy figure waiting in the street, then he nodded and went back to persuading his cigarette to stay alight.

In her handbag were the most precious things in the world: a British passport, an international railway ticket, and up-to-date, perfectly in order papers for Lady Claudia Vere.

Josh was surprised to find Claudia still there when he got back soon after midnight, but pleased to have her company for the night. She left with him in the morning, deliberately dressed as differently as possible from the previous evening. Thank goodness she kept so many clothes at the apartment. Another style of hat, lower shoes, her hair pinned back, no fur.

'A new look,' Josh said. 'I think I prefer the old you. When will you be back from England?'

'I'll let you know,' she said aloud, and inwardly, Never.

Now she needed to keep out of sight for twenty-four hours, enough time for Sarah to be over the border to Holland and across the Channel. A boring day in her flat, telling friends who rang that she had a dreadful sore throat and had postponed her return to England, no, couldn't dine or dance.

And then, the next day, the short walk to the British Embassy. 'To see James Merton,' she said. 'No, he isn't expecting me. Yes, I'll wait.'

James was livid. 'You've lost the lot? Passport, ticket, papers? Claudia, this doesn't make sense. How did you lose them? Have you reported it to the police? No? For Christ's sake, that was the first thing you should have done. Anyone could be out there using them.'

'Give me a cigarette, and stop squawking like an old hen,' Claudia said. 'There are hardly going to be many women who could use my papers. Too, too conspicuous, a Lady Claudia, don't you think?'

'Even so . . .'

'The less fuss made about this, the better, James my pet. I want to get out of Germany, and I give you my word I'm not coming back.'

'That's rather changing your tune, isn't it?'

'Never mind that. What I want is for you to arrange for me to slip out to Switzerland, preferably incognito. From there I can get back to England.'

'It's out of the question.'

'Best, though, James, for all sorts of reasons.'

'It's impossible. I know what you've done, you've . . .'

Claudia held up a warning hand. 'Walls have ears, you know.'

'Sarah would have problems in England, she couldn't go on pretending to be you,' said Vee. She was astonished at Claudia's courage and quick-wittedness and at the generosity of what she'd done.

'I told her to go to Monica at Kepesake, and tell her the truth. I knew Monica would take her in. I suppose she'll be interned when war starts, being a foreigner. Meanwhile, she's working on the family archives, very happy, Monica says. Lucius has decided she's the second wife of the second earl, one Mathilde of Anjou, and talks to her in French.'

'What about her papers?'

'Vernon fixed it. I said if he didn't, I'd go to the newspapers with the whole story. Scandal! Senior government official's stepdaughter breaking all the rules. He made it a condition, though, that I leave the country for a while. He wanted me to go to Grandmère, but Sandy Buchanan, do you remember him? was off on his yacht and said I could go with him. So I did, and we ended up in Lisbon, after sailing through a vile storm, I may say. We weren't on the best of terms after that. Sailors are dreadful bores, do this, do that, pull on

397

this, out of bed at unspeakable hours to do things to the sails. Lord, it was exhausting. He'll be pleased to see the back of me. Like everyone else, it seems.'

There was a tremor in her voice, despite the flippancy of her words.

'I'm glad about Sarah,' Vee said. 'I know she's only one saved out of thousands who aren't, but even so.'

'Grace girls together,' said Lally. 'Dr Margerison would be proud of you, Claudia.'

The steward was tinkling the bells to announce dinner. Lally got up. 'Come on, Claudia, wonderful food on board, and you look as though you need a proper meal.'

Claudia grimaced. 'I told them not on any account to put me at the Captain's table. I'd much rather be with you. Marcus and Joel are on board, too, aren't they? And guess what? Alfred Gore's down as a passenger, travelling from Lisbon to Port Said.'

'All the old gang,' Lally said, draping her shawl around her bare shoulders.

'Except for Giles and Hugh, of course,' said Claudia. 'Any news of Hugh, Vee?'

SEVEN

Vee hadn't worn the dress since Paris. It was a favourite of hers, she loved the way the bias cut made the fabric hug her body and swirl about her ankles. It wasn't a light, floating frock, but a dress that enveloped her, became part of her, protected her with its weight and fluidity. The silver insets caught the light as she moved, as though the dress itself were alive.

Alfred was at her table. She'd known he would be, that was what Fate was dealing out to her at the moment. Hugh had been fascinated by Fate. 'Read the Greeks, Vee. They knew everything there is to know about what really shapes our lives and how little we can do about it. When we think we're taking a decision, we mostly aren't, it's taken for us by forces and powers beyond our sight or understanding.'

That was the poetic mind at work. Sadness swept over her at the memory of Hugh, his moods, his witty drawings, his tolerance, his hatred of injustice and his disinclination to accept the ideas and convictions of those around him. 'Work it out for yourself, Vee, don't fall into the habit of portmanteau thought.'

'Portmanteau?'

'Yes, all in a Gladstone bag. Tell me a man's views on – oh, let's say traffic lights. I'll tell you how he voted at the last election, how he'll vote at the next one, what he thinks about India, his opinions about marriage, the position of women, religion. Nine times out of ten, you could probably say what he eats for breakfast. Incapable of radical thought, do you see, of taking each subject or issue and looking at it for itself, free of mental clutter.

There are very few people in this country who can think for them-selves.'

Hugh was one of them. She wasn't. He'd hoped she would be; she'd paid no attention, walking instead straight into the trap of her time and the illusionary security of being part of a greater cause.

'Stunning dress, Vee,' Alfred said. 'Shimmers as you move. It suits you.'

Never since she'd known him had Alfred commented on what she was wearing, or made any kind of complimentary remark.

'Bags.'

'What?'

'Your Oxford nickname. And here you are, dressed just as you ought to be.'

'My steward was very firm about that.'

Alfred looked striking in his evening clothes. Different. Then Vee realized it had nothing to do with the clothes. It was the man himself. Older, with a new shrewdness in his eyes, leaner, with a more deter-mined set to his mouth and jaw and a wariness to his carriage.

'Why Lisbon?' she asked.

'I crossed over from Spain. The rag wants me to do some articles on Egypt.'

She wanted to ask him about Spain, was longing to find out if he knew anything of what had happened to Hugh, but this was neither the time nor the place, not with the others at the table starting to look curiously at them.

'Old friends?' said the colonial type on her left.

'What? Oh, yes, Mr Gore and I are old friends.'

They danced, after dinner. Under the stars of a balmy evening, with the whispering sea all around them, and the deck moving slightly beneath their feet. Alfred was courteous, friendly, pleasant, grown-up. There was a barrier between them as wide and high as though they were on either side of a prison wall.

'It was a surprise to see Claudia on board, quite a reformed char-acter, I understand. And the ever-delightful Lally. She's been having a tough time of it, I gather.'

'Claudia?'

Alfred laughed. 'Not Claudia. She's simply had her comeuppance, the scales have finally fallen from her eyes, and it hurts to look out at the world as it is, instead of through a fog of wishful thinking.

No, I meant Lally. She's worried, desperately worried about how Henry is going to react to Peter going out to India with her.'

'Doesn't Henry know?' Lally hadn't told her that.

'He said the boy was to go back to school. Lally disagreed.'

'It's difficult, when he's only her stepson. Was he very ill?'

They danced in silence for a few minutes. 'You're very close to Lally. Couldn't you be bothered to find out what was happening, when Henry was in London and she was in the country?'

Vee looked at him, her spine stiffening, so that the dancing became an ordeal, not a pleasure. Alfred could feel the tension, of course he could. And he knew about her and Henry, she was certain of it. How? Alfred had barely been in London at that time, only on fleeting visits from Spain. When she'd seen him, he'd been tired to the bone, lines around his eyes, telling her more than she could bear of the horror and futility of what he'd witnessed in Spain, then abruptly stopping. 'It's an indulgence to talk about it, I'm like the ancient mariner, compelled to tell my story to those who don't want to hear it, and don't care.'

'Your readers want to have the truth.'

'Do they, Vee? I doubt it. Not this truth.'

'Must you go back? If it's so awful?'

'It's my job. And someone has to be there, to report what's really going on, even if no one wants to hear or read about it.'

She'd changed the subject, not wanting to hear any more.

The music stopped. Alfred took her arm and led her to the rail. She leaned on it, looking down into the foam and the phosphorescent gleam of the sea.

'Lally drove down to the school as soon as she heard Peter was ill,' Alfred said, in a conversational tone. 'She probably saved his life. He had a high fever and was in great pain. The matron was furious that Lally had arrived, late in the evening, unannounced, certainly unwelcome. Peter was malingering, the matron said, in order to get out of games. He was a difficult boy who'd been mollycoddled and found it hard to adjust to school life. She would give him an aspirin, and a tonic, and he'd be out of the san in no time.'

'I had no idea. What was wrong with him?'

'Rheumatic fever. Lally took no notice of the matron, nor of the master on duty, nor of the headmaster who was summoned to remonstrate with her. She simply wrapped the boy in blankets, carried him out to the car and took him home. He was ill for weeks and weeks, but she nursed him devotedly. Poor little devil, he's still skin and bones.'

Dear God, Lally, her friend, had been going through all that, alone. She'd no idea Peter had been so ill, Harry had made light of his son's illness, and had left Lally in the country, while he sought solace in the time-honoured fashion. With Vee, because she was there and willing, and because he could talk about Lally with her. He'd wanted to lash out at Lally, for putting Peter before him; he was ashamed of himself for feeling such jealousy, and his pent-up frustration and self-hatred found its release in Vee's arms.

Vee moved away from the rail. 'Let's go in,' she said. 'I'd like to look for the others.'

'Claudia's sitting in the Winthrop Bar with Joel and a tall girl I don't know.'

'Perdita,' Vee said.

'Joel was very anxious about Sarah. He'd lost touch with her and feared the worst. He'll be pleased with what Claudia did for her.'

'Amazed, too.'

'Is one automatically amazed when a leopard changes its spots?'

'When the leopard's Claudia, yes, one is.'

Without asking, he put his arm round her waist and drew her closer, moving once more into the dance.

Vee held back, she didn't want to be in any man's arms, least of all Alfred's.

'Are you still a fervent communist?' she asked.

He didn't reply at once, humming several bars of the music instead. 'No, since you ask. No one who saw what was done in Spain could remain a communist.'

'A lot have. And I thought General Franco's mob were far worse, fascists are, isn't that the rule?'

'Left, right, communist, fascist, right, wrong; that's not what the war in Spain was about. The dewy-eyed types who piled in to join the International Brigade and fight for the Republicans had no idea why there was a war in the first place, nor that the war would turn into a Tom Tiddler's ground for the Soviets and the Germans. Nor did noncombatants like me, naive to my bones as far as the realities of the political situation there were concerned.'

'Guernica, how can there be right or wrong about that?'

'There can't, but there have been atrocities on both sides, take my word for it. And the Spanish gold that's now in Moscow vaults, what will be the consequences of that for Spain, with the war over? No, before you ask, I'm not a communist any more, Vee. How about you? As committed as ever, still working for Comintern, making yourself believe it's for the universal good of mankind?'

Vee pulled away from Alfred; she felt as though he had punched her in the solar plexus.

How did he know?

'You and I need to have a talk,' he said. 'Perhaps not on the dance floor.'

They found a place away from the music and people, down a gangway, where sunbathers lounged in the daytime, but which was deserted at night. Alfred put up a couple of deck chairs.

Vee waited for him to speak, but he sat still and silent, looking out at the reflection of the rising moon on the calm surface of the water.

'How do you know?' she said at last.

'About Comintern? Hugh told me.'

'Hugh?'

How could Hugh have told Alfred? She had never spoken to him about it, never given him the slightest hint about Klaus or any of it. He had been abroad for most of the time after she'd been recruited, how could he have known?

'He'd guessed. He knows you better than you know yourself. He was sure that your sudden abandonment of the Party meant that you'd moved on to higher things, that the delight in the social round, the new, frivolous Vee, was no more than a pretence. And then Giles wrote to him.'

'Giles was always writing to him.'

'This letter was written the day Giles died. He told Hugh what he'd been told by the Soviets who were putting the screws on him, that you were working for their side.'

Vee felt cold. 'Giles knew?'

Alfred took out a cigarette case. 'Want one?'

'Are they Woodbines?'

'They are not.' He lit two, with a lighter, not a match, and handed one to Vee; she noticed that her fingers were trembling.

'I was fooled, I must admit,' Alfred said. 'I was hurt and angry. You avoided me, I supposed it was because I was associated with the

Party and you'd done with all that. Actually, I was more than angry, I was blind with rage, that you could have the compassion you had for a barefoot boy or a Peggy, and then just walk away from it all. If I hadn't been so furious, I might have used my mind, as Hugh would tell me to do, and I would have realized for myself that you'd been recruited as an agent.'

'Did they never approach you?' Vee was talking without really paying attention, anything not to have to think what Giles's letter to Hugh meant.

'No. I was too loud in my opinions, too vocal about my support for the Party, too concerned about what I could do here and now. A paid-up member? What use would I be to the Soviets and their under-cover world when the intelligence services in London knew I was a card-carrying Red? Moscow likes secrecy, and it takes a long view. I've given it a lot of thought over the last couple of years, watching how they operate on the ground was an eye-opener.'

'Not a pleasant one, I gather.'

'No. Don't make any mistake, Vee. We live in an unfair, unjust world, where the haves win every time over the have-nots, and it's got to change. Only I don't any longer think that a communist revo-lution is the way to change it. Moreover, I shouldn't like it if it did. Life under a Soviet-style regime would be far worse for your average worker than life on the dole is at the moment.'

'That can't be true.'

'No? What about what they did to Giles?'

Vee had no reply to that.

'That was another thing that made Hugh suspicious, your marrying Giles. He knew that it had to be a fraud, and he couldn't think why you'd let yourself in for such a marriage unless you had another, secret reason. Your life's been full of secrets, hasn't it?'

Alfred's face was in shadow, and Vee couldn't tell from his voice whether there was sympathy, or pity, or contempt in what he said.

'Why don't you tell me about it? Get it off your chest.'

Vee's temper flared out. 'Because I don't trust you, I don't trust anyone. They've sent me to do a job I can't do and certainly don't want to do; no, they haven't sent me, they've blackmailed me into going. And I can't not do it. I'm sure there's someone on board, one of them, watching me. What if it isn't a stranger in a Homburg, but one of my friends? What if Marcus or Joel, or Lally even, is waiting for signs that I'm not sound, that I might give myself in to the authorities? With instructions to tip me overboard? What if what you've just said is a pack of lies, and you're the one who'll see to it that I don't slip out of their clutches except into a watery grave? You, or Claudia. They recruited me, who else did they sign up for a life of treachery? Who can I trust? I don't even trust myself.'

Alfred sat up and reached for her hand, but she snatched it away. 'You are in a state,' he said equably. 'And frightened, you really are frightened.'

'Wouldn't you be, after what they did to Giles?' And what they were doing to Hugh.

'They said it was an accident, but of course he shot himself. Didn't he?'

'You tell me. You were there, that day. Did he shoot himself, or did someone force him to pull the trigger? The suicide note was phoney, I can tell you that much. Oh, he wrote it all right, but not for that reason, it was a note to me, to say he wasn't going to make it to a dinner party that Thursday.'

'You saw it on the desk.'

'I did, but I didn't realize until later what it meant; I truly thought he had committed suicide. I hid all the photos he'd been sent. Later, when the police had gone, I burned them.'

'That, I didn't know. Oh, I knew about the photos, but not what you'd done with them.'

Vee got up from her deck chair and looked down at Alfred, her face and body taut. 'How could you know about the photos?'

Alfred got up to stand beside her. 'Hugh told me. It was all in that letter from Giles.'

'When did Hugh show you the letter?'

'A couple of weeks ago. It took months to reach him.'

A couple of weeks ago? A fortnight ago? How was it possible? 'You're lying, you can't have seen Hugh so recently. He's . . .'

'A Republican prisoner? He was, but he escaped weeks ago, in all the confusion there was in the summer. Long before the Ebro.'

'Escaped? Where is he? Is he safe?'

'By now, I imagine he's with your grandmother in France.'

Vee felt the blood drain out of her face. 'I'm going to be sick,' she said.

'Not all over me, if you don't mind. I don't have any other evening clothes with me. And, when you've finished throwing up, which does seem to be a habit of yours, you can tell me the whole story. You need help, duckie.'

Vee lunged for the rail.

Alfred waited, and then handed her a handkerchief. 'Stay here, I'll be back.'

Vee sank back into the deck chair, and closed her eyes, her mind a whirl of disbelief and hope. Would Alfred lie to her, about Hugh? Could he be such a monster of deviousness and deceit?

No, was the answer. He wasn't and couldn't. And with that realization, Vee felt a load slide from her spirit, as real as though she had just put down a physical burden too heavy to bear.

Then Alfred was back, with a glass of water in one hand and a bottle of champagne with two glasses in the other one. 'First, a glass of water, swill your mouth out over the side, if you please. Then champagne. And after that, I'm going to kiss you.'

'Again?' said Vee, spitting out the water.

'Again?'

'You kissed me after the Trinity dance. When we'd been in a punt. You were very drunk.'

'Lord, was I? Did I? God, what a fool, to do that and not to remember. What a fool to go around ranting communism at you when what I really wanted to do was make love with you.'

Vee stared at him. 'You what?'

'You heard.'

'You never made the slightest pass at me. Except for the punt, and, as you say, you don't remember that. So, you wanted to go to bed with me, that was it, was it?'

Alfred sighed. 'If you want the truth, Vee, I fell in love with you the first time I saw you, at Fresher's Fair, I do remember that. But I didn't want to be in love with anyone, I didn't want my important political work to be complicated by a heap of messy emotion.'

'Messy emotion?'

'Don't open your eyes at me like that. You, of all people, should know about messy emotions. Shut up and let me kiss you.'

Later, he murmured in her ear, 'We have to make a plan, Vee. They'll guess that you'll know about Hugh, and then your life will be in even more danger.'

'Danger?' said Vee, rolling on her back and looking up at the stars.

'Oh, I'll worry about that tomorrow, some other time. Why are we in a lifeboat?'

'Safer, don't you think, in case of shipwreck.'

'I'd like to be shipwrecked,' said Vee, closing her eyes. 'To float away on a spar until we're thrown by a foamy wave on to the strand of a desert island. Away from everyone and everything. I don't think I'd want to leave.'

Alfred raised himself on one elbow and looked down at her with infinite tenderness. Her lashes were damp, and he wiped the tears away with a gentle gesture. 'I don't think P & O boats have spars any more. Besides, I believe desert islands are liable to be full of scorpions, or furious inhabitants.'

'And one can't run away from life.'

He drew her towards him again. 'Come here, dear heart.'

'The present moment,' she said, as she pulled his head down to kiss him. 'In the end, it's all we ever have.'

A steward came round in the early hours, as they lay hidden, fast asleep in each other's arms, propped against a couple of lifebuoys. He tut-tutted and bent to remove the glasses from beside the deck chairs. The empty bottle of champagne rolled across the deck, and he put out a foot to stop it, then stooped to retrieve it. He knew just what had been going on. Passengers!

EIGHT

The SS *Gloriana* arrived at Port Said at dawn. Vee had woken before the sun made its swift and sudden appearance, so unlike the gradual sunrise of England, this dramatic arrival of light taking only a few minutes to bring the world from darkness to light.

'Even swifter in India,' Alfred told her. 'And in a blaze of colour.'

'When were you in India?'

'As a little boy. My father did a tour of duty there.'

Alfred. The very name brought a warmth to her heart and a peace to her soul, as she lay there, the very slight motion of the boat, hardly more than the rumble of its engines, lulling her into a tranquillity and a happiness which she had never known.

It wouldn't, couldn't last. The problems and worries would come crowding back into her mind soon enough; nothing was solved or resolved, except that everything was changed. She loved Alfred and was loved in return, and after years of not loving, of not knowing how to love, her reserves and barriers had come crashing down, annihilated by the strength of her feelings for Alfred.

She shut her eyes, relaxed for once, after a night when she had slept undisturbed by memories or dreams, and thought about Alfred. His voice, the swift intelligence of his eyes beneath those heavy lids, his energy, the vibrant, loving kindness of him, the strength of his arms and the power of his mouth and hands to overwhelm her with a shared passion that almost frightened her by its intensity.

A tug hooted. Someone was shouting out in a strange tongue. Bumps and a change in the pitch of the ship's engines.

Now there were voices in the corridor outside her cabin. Vee looked at her watch. Half past five. Why should anyone be up this early?

Of course, it would be the passengers who were making the Cairo trip, which included a tour of the pyramids and a ride on a camel.

One day she'd come back to Eygpt, and wander among the marvels of the ancient kingdoms. She'd always wanted to see the sphinx and found it ironic that now she was here, within reach of it, she might as well be in London for all the opportunity there was of her being a tourist. Then a cloud came over her happiness; how long would the coming war, which Alfred and so many others now spoke of as a certainty, last? Four years for the Great War. This time, nobody would be saying it would all be over by Christmas. By the time liners once again sailed on peaceful voyages across the face of the earth, the world might have changed for ever.

She shivered, and slipped out of bed. It was too early to be up and about, but there was too much in her mind for her to lie in bed. Besides, she wanted to see Port Said.

Unobtrusive clothes, Alfred had said. Look as much like everyone else as you can, no bright colours, no ultra-smart suit that other women would automatically notice. So she put on a cream linen skirt, a white short-sleeved blouse and beige shoes. She wouldn't need a hat yet; when she did wear one, later on, to go ashore, then that, too, should look as ordinary as possible. Many of the women on board had taken to wearing cotton hats with semi-stiff brims, a grown-up version of the sun hats she'd worn as a girl. She'd go down to the shop and buy one of those.

Alfred was on deck, in shirtsleeves, leaning on the rail. He didn't greet her with words; he didn't need to, his smile was enough.

The heat and the brilliant light, dancing on the water made her blink. 'That's Port Said?'

'It is. The gate of the East.'

Vee stared at the teeming dockside, where shabby old buildings stood side by side with hideous newer ones. Voices came to her across the grey-green water, with its patches of oily debris moving to and fro. Car horns honked, the sound mingling with the hoots of tugs and the loud braying of a donkey standing by a rusty vessel, the animal laden with a burden almost the size of itself. Chains and winches rattled and clattered and the roar of a lorry starting up ended in a cracking back-fire. Then the smell hit her: petrol and brine and fish and tar, and underneath it all, an indefinable scent, spicy and exotic.

'The smell of the East,' Alfred said. 'We've had a bit of luck; apparently there's a spot of trouble with one of the ship's engines, and we won't be going through the canal until tomorrow. So the Cairo party

409

are getting an extended trip, if they want it, there'll be more confusion about passengers embarking and disembarking, and we'll have more time in Port Said to do what we need to.'

Bumboats were hovering alongside the ship, with men in galabiehs and tarbooshes standing in them, holding up fezes and topis and beads and gesturing to leather pouf covers stacked in perilous piles.

Alfred approved of Vee's appearance when she came back on deck after breakfast. The ship had moored alongside the pontoon bridge – the water being too shallow for the *Gloriana* to anchor off the jetty. A gully-gully man was on the deck, with a crowd of children around him as he extracted fluffy yellow chicks from behind their ears and did dazzling things with cards, all the time keeping up a stream of patter. He addressed Alfred as Mr Macpherson, and invited him to play dice; there was a beaming smile for Vee, 'Madam Melba, join in the game,' he said in beguiling tones.

Vee would have been content simply to sit and watch the constantly shifting scene and the tricks of the gully-gully man, but there was no time for that. She and Alfred were among the first ashore, mixing with a throng of people planning a visit to Simon Artz's famous emporium to buy souvenirs.

Alfred headed for the customs shed. 'I haven't got much stuff, this shouldn't take long.' He edged his way through the passengers who were waiting to complete all the disembarkation formalities and approached the bored-looking official standing at the head. A smile, a flash of a press card, a crackle of notes changing hands, and then Alfred was picking up a large brown leather portmanteau and waving at a porter to take his two strapped suitcases to await collection later.

'Come on, bustle about, Vee, we've got a lot to do. A photograph of you, first; we'll need those for the passport. Oh, God, there's Marcus; quick Vee, along here.'

'Marcus?' she said, puzzled.

'He's disembarking, remember. Heading for Cairo, planning to camp out at Shepheard's Hotel and go on the rampage, I expect.'

They left Marcus, looking hungover and cross, haranguing a customs officer about a missing item of luggage.

Vee was stunned by the half-world that Alfred led her into, with swift, confident steps. He deposited her in a hairdressers, where the woman in a white overall seemed startled but resigned when Vee insisted she wanted her hair bleached as fair as possible and waved.

'Maybe your hair will all fall out,' the woman said. 'Maybe it won't.'

Alfred laughed when he came back to get her. 'It does make you look common. We'll have to buy you a bright-red lipstick, I think.'

'I think not, thank you,' Vee said. 'Altering my appearance is one thing, looking like a tart is another.'

'Photo, now, and then you can buy clothes and whatever bits and pieces you'll need while the pictures are developed.'

'How often have you been to Port Said?' Vee asked, as he held aside a grubby bead curtain into a shop that was little more than a hole in the wall.

'Once,' he said. 'We newspapermen learn to find our way around, if you don't, you don't get the contacts or the stories.'

An Egyptian in an ancient cream jacket and cotton trousers came through a door at the back and beamed a welcome at Alfred. A camera appeared, a backcloth was rigged, and Vee was photographed looking forwards, not smiling, not moving a muscle.

'Good,' said Alfred. 'That will ensure the typical passport photograph look, as of an escaped convict. Ready by three o'clock?' he said to the bowing Egyptian photographer. 'We'll be back.'

'Don't buy anything that you would normally,' Alfred warned her, as Vee headed into a shop promisingly called Madame Chic. 'Different styles, different colours, you're a different person now, Mrs Gore. I think I'll put your name down as Veronica, then if I call you Vee, no one will think anything of it.'

'I still don't know how you plan to get me put on your passport.'

'Money. Money will do anything in Port Said, and it couldn't be simpler, just adding a wife to a single man's passport; the man I'm going to use will sneer at the ease of it.'

Vee was struck by an alarming thought. 'You're taking it for granted that there will be a cabin.'

'You have to have faith, Vee.'

The cabin, for two of them, was smaller than her first-class cabin. 'What a start to our married life,' Alfred said, as he dumped his portmanteau on the floor and swung Vee into a passionate embrace. 'Separate bunks, I ask you. It'll be a dreadful squeeze, in that bottom bunk.'

'We aren't married.'

'We are according to my passport, and we will be as soon as we arrive and find an obliging clergyman.'

'Do you realize you haven't asked me to marry you?'

He looked at her in surprise. 'Do I need to?'

411

NINE

They stood side by side at the rail, enjoying the warmth, which was tempered by a slight breeze. The *Gloriana* was moving through the Suez Canal at hardly more than a walking pace. It was strangely quiet, only the dull throb of the engine disturbing the silence.

The light was still painfully bright, intensified by the glare from the sand, and Vee had her sunglasses on. She waved to a group of children splashing close to the bank, and exclaimed at the sight of a group of camels clustered under some palm trees.

It was odd, Alfred thought, watching her as she drank in the sights and sounds of Egypt and the vast expanse of desert that lay beyond the thread of activity, how the fair hair and the sunglasses changed her. She was thinner than he remembered her, too, and her face had a finer, more grown-up look to it. He turned away for a moment, the curve of her arm and the hairs on the nape of her neck sending a tide of emotion through him that was almost more than he could bear.

She was absorbed in the present moment, able to forget her nightmares as she pointed out a sandy hillock that had a mirage lake at its foot, and the sudden greenness of an oasis.

She didn't want to miss a minute of it, and they were still there as night descended and the stars began to shine with their astonishing brilliance in a velvet sky. A searchlight at the bow of the ship sent its powerful beam across the water, and made the surrounding darkness darker still, until they reached the end of the canal and were into the Gulf of Suez, with the lights of the harbour and the town adding to the feeling that they were caught up in a voyage from the *Arabian Nights*.

They watched the Cairo party, grubby and tired after their extended trip, come aboard, together with a handful of new passengers. Then the *Gloriana* weighed anchor and set sail into the Red Sea.

Their steward disapproved of them. 'A ramshackle pair,' he said to his colleagues in the staff dining room. 'Out of place on my corridor. The way they speak, they should be in first class, no question.'

'Passengers travelling from Port Said to India are always a shifty lot, in my opinion,' said Mrs Tolkin, who was in charge of the linen. 'Why would anybody respectable be travelling from Egypt to India, tell me that? Unless they're in the army or government service, which from what you say isn't very likely.'

'And she dyes her hair,' the steward added. 'Very poorly done, makes her look common, which she isn't.'

'Maybe they're actors,' Mrs Tolkin suggested. 'They can speak any way they want. They may speak like first-class passengers, but there's more to it than that.'

'He's got a typewriter with him. Perhaps he's a reporter, working undercover. After a scoop.'

'What scoop is there on the *Gloriana*?'

'Writers are always hard-up, perhaps that's why he isn't travelling first class.'

'They're very free and easy in their ways. I'm not too sure they're man and wife, so lovey-dovey as they are. Maybe that's what's bugging her, you can see she's got something on her mind. Guilty conscience, that's what she's got. Now, he's a gent, you can tell from his shoes. Even if he has come down in the world.'

'Callous, too. When I told them one of the first-class passengers was lost overboard, they just looked at one another. She seemed a bit upset, but he said, "They won't find her."'

'Which is true, but even so . . .'

Vee found release and happiness in making love with Alfred, but her nights were still times of darkness and despair. Alfred would wake and draw her close, tell her how much he loved her.

For a while, she'd be comforted, but then the guilt would flood back. 'I don't deserve to be loved. I've done nothing but lie and betray and be disloyal and utterly destructive. How can I live with that?'

'First, you don't deserve or earn love. It happens. Second, you can't go back and expunge those years. What you did, you did. I won't say, you did it for reasons that seemed right to you, because you know that.'

'I did it because I was a fool and I wanted revenge on my grandfather, I wanted to tear down everything he stands for. Under the name of world peace and justice for the workers. I killed Giles, as surely as if I'd pulled the trigger.'

'Look, Vee, stop lashing yourself. Growing up means you take responsibility for what you've done, but it doesn't help to wallow in self-pity.'

'Self-pity!'

'Guilt is a kind of self-pity.'

'I've made up my mind. As soon as I get back to England, or even while we're in India, I'm going to go to whoever's responsible for this kind of thing, and make a clean breast of it.'

Alfred, exasperated, took her by the shoulders. 'Look at me, Vee. No, look at me, don't dodge away. I'll tell you what will happen if you go to anyone in authority with your story. You think you'll be helping to undo some of the harm your espionage has done. It won't.'

'They can find out who's behind this, who passed my name to the Soviets . . .'

'They can, but they won't. One of two things will happen. First, they may believe you. Unlikely, but it's possible. You'd be tried, and imprisoned for a number of years. Your family would be disgraced, as would your college and school, if that counts for anything with you.'

'It does, actually, but . . .'

He swept on. 'They might even hang you, I'm not up on the penalties for treason. And then you'd have wreaked more destruction, including breaking my heart.'

Vee looked at him, then lowered her eyes, which were brimming with hot, unhappy tears.

'Second, they won't believe you, which is much more likely. A woman, the daughter of the Dean of York, working as a Soviet agent? Impossible. Ergo, you're off your rocker. Solution: shut you away in an asylum and lose the key.'

'You're just saying that, so that I won't confess.'

'As I see it, the only chance you've got of making any amends is to keep your mouth shut. Don't you see that in the war that's coming

414

there'll be opportunities for you to serve your country, to do your duty and repair some of the damage you've done?'

'Oh, God,' she said, the words wrung out of her. 'If only one could stop the clock and wind the hands back, to there and there, and say, "At that moment I made a wrong choice, I took a bad decision, did a stupid thing", and change it all. If only I could bring Giles back. But I can't. I started all this from emotion, and then I continued from reason, and the end of it is, I betrayed everyone, including myself.'

There was compassion in Alfred's eyes, which was almost more than she could bear.

'That's what you have to live with for the rest of your life, your betrayal and its consequences.'

'Alfred, don't you understand? What I did was criminal. Giles is the worst of it, but think of the harm I've done, with all that stuff I passed to Klaus.'

Alfred sat on the edge of the bunk, gazing down at the floor. For the first time, it occurred to Vee that he was exhausted. Then he looked up at her.

'I think that, in practice, you probably did very little harm. Those papers you photographed, from what you tell me, there was nothing there the Soviets wouldn't know in any case. They were using you to get Giles, Vee. That's all. What you passed to them was chickenfeed. I'm not saying you weren't wrong to do it, we've been through all that. Just that, in the end, it's not that important.'

'They won't leave me alone. As soon as they find out I'm still alive, they'll come after me.'

'Quite likely. Which is why what you need to do, is put everything you've told me about your recruitment and work for Comintern on paper. We'll make sure your solicitor gets it, and then you can tell your Russian comrades that if you meet with an accident, your lawyers will pass all the information on to the right quarters. Here's a type-writer, and paper, everything you need.'

He looked at her, exasperated. 'Now what have I said?'

Vee's hand had flown to her mouth. 'Alfred, I did write it all down. In a journal. And I forgot to bring it, when we left the boat at Port Said.'

'Oh, for Christ's sake, Vee, you didn't!'

She nodded.

415

'Where is it?'

'In a drawer, in my cabin.'

'Watch where you're going,' said Alfred, swinging the boy up and standing him on his feet. 'You nearly knocked me over.'

The boy grinned, and then his expression changed. He looked pleased. 'Hello, Mr Gore. What are you doing here? Did you come through the laundry, too?' Then he looked puzzled. 'I say, I thought you left the boat at Port Said, that's what Mummy told me.'

'How is Mummy?'

'A bit weepy. I'm glad now that Miss Tyrell came, although I was jolly cross at first. She's looking after Mummy. Perdita practically doesn't play the piano any more, and the others all go round looking glum, except for that Lady Claudia. She's quite cheerful and she keeps on telling Mummy not to worry, that Mrs Hotspur is still alive. Miss Tyrell says that Lady Claudia always was able to see around a corner further than anyone else.'

'Now, Peter, you're just the man I need. I've got a job for you to do. Do you often come through from first-class?'

'I like exploring the whole ship. I know passengers aren't allowed to go into the other class, but nobody notices me.'

'I want you to take a note to Perdita. If she asks any questions, when she's read the note, tell her that I'll explain at a later date.'

Peter thought about that. 'Perdita's awfully sensible for a girl. I don't think she will ask any questions. Is it important?'

'I'll tell you what it is, and then you won't want to ask any questions or talk about it. It's about rather a special document, that belonged to Mrs Hotspur, and it's got to be given to a particular person.'

'OK,' Peter said.

'One other thing. You are not to tell anyone that I'm on board.'

'Why not?'

'It's a bit shaming, having to travel tourist class.'

Understanding spread over Peter's face. 'Are you hard-up? OK, I won't split on you.'

'Wait here, while I write the note.'

'Wouldn't it be better for Peter to bring the journal to you here?' Vee said, when Alfred reported his encounter with the boy.

'No. A note, and that's it. I don't want to involve him more than I have to.' He hesitated. 'He does live in rather a fantasy world, which, from what you say, Perdita doesn't.'

'Fantasy world?'

'Yes. Luckily for us. He told an officer about you being afraid of going overboard, and he said that he saw you on deck, standing by the rail, the night we sailed from Port Said. That was one of the things that convinced them you'd been lost at sea.'

'He probably did see me, Alfred, only when he was looking down from the first-class section on to the lower deck here. He wouldn't expect me to be there, and so afterwards, he'd think he must have seen me elsewhere.' She sighed. 'It does seem dreadful, not to be able to let the others know that I'm all right.'

'Perhaps Claudia will manage to convince them. I'm sorry, Vee, it is hard, and it'll be hard on your family, but it's better than the alternative, which really would be you inside a shark.'

'I should like to have seen something of Eygpt.'

'You shall, one day. Only I don't think there'll be any foreign holidays for any of us, not for many years. Make the most of these days between here and Bombay, my love, days out of time and away from worry.'

He knew that wasn't true; the worry and guilt and, even now, fear, were never far from the surface of Vee's mind, but, once word came from Perdita that she had the journal, she made an effort and threw herself into shipboard life.

Alfred held snapshots in his mind: Vee laughing, her canvas shoes slipping on the deck as she hauled at the rope in the tug-of-war; absorbed in a game of Housie, and throwing her arms around his neck when she won twenty shillings; laughing at him when he took part in the dog races, sitting with his back to the table, furiously winding a handle to propel his wooden dog along its groove to victory; Vee flushed and happy in a crazy outfit she'd contrived for the fancy-dress dinner and dance: 'I'm a teapot,' she announced when he tried to guess what she was going as.

'There's more camaraderie here in tourist class,' she said.

'Except for the minor government officials and their wives, who so desperately long to have the rank to go first class.'

'Terrific snobs, aren't they? But some of them are sweet when they let their hair down and talk about their children and homes in England.'

She let out a long sigh. 'What's going to happen to them, Alfred? To all of us?'

'They may be the lucky ones, who see the war out in comparative peace and comfort, who knows? We won't, though. As soon as we get to Bombay and know that your journal is in safe hands, then back you come to life, amid general rejoicing, I feel sure, and back we sail to England, and our uncertain future.'

'The Soviets won't rejoice if I rise from the waves, as it were.'

'Good.'

And, after a pause, 'It isn't such an uncertain future, you know. Not as long as you're alive. Will you enlist?'

'I don't know, I'll do whatever they want me to. One can't pick and choose in wartime. Perhaps I'll stay as a war correspondent.'

'In the thick of things?'

'That's where we'll both be.'

AFTERMATH

THE TIMES
July 1942
Colonel Henry Messenger has been awarded a posthumous VC.

THE DAILY TELEGRAPH
June 1946

Earl's daughter weds
The wedding of Lady Claudia Vere and Piers Forster, MP, at St Margaret's, Westminster, yesterday brought a touch of glamour to lighten the austerity of post-war London. Lady Claudia, sister of the Earl of Sake, wore an ivory silk dress designed by her friend, Marcus Sebert. She was attended by six bridesmaids . . .

THE OBSERVER
March 1946
In an impressive recital at the Wigmore Hall, Miss Perdita Richardson gave a superb performance of the Beethoven Sonata Op. 110 . . .

THE TIMES LITERARY SUPPLEMENT
January 1947

War Essays by Alfred Gore
Used as we are to the exquisite brilliance of Alfred Gore's prose, this outstanding collection . . .

THE DAILY TELEGRAPH
June 1949

Permafrost is a searing indictment of Soviet Russia by long-time socialist writer and journalist Alfred Gore. This fable in the form of a novel has become the most talked-about title of the year. Mr Gore's left-wing publisher, Victor Gollancz, rejected the title, because of its 'anti-Soviet bias', but the house of Faber took it on, and now have a world-wide bestseller on their hands. Allen Lane are to bring out a paperback edition under their Penguin imprint.

—◆■▶—

THE DAILY MAIL
February 1951

All Paris is abuzz with talk of the dazzling new collection by the English fashion designer Marcus Sebert. His summer frocks . . .

—◆■▶—

THE TIMES
October 1951

French honour for Englishwoman

Mrs Verity Gore, one of the heroines of SOE, was yesterday awarded the Croix de Guerre in a ceremony in Paris. Between 1942 and 1944, she was twice parachuted into occupied territory in France, and was captured and tortured by the Gestapo. She escaped while en route to Ravensbruck concentration camp, returned to England, then was once again sent back into France to work with the French Resistance during the last days of the war.

—◆■▶—

THE NEW YORK TIMES
August 1964

Princeton mathematician wins Nobel

The Nobel Prize for Economics has been awarded to British-born Joel Ibbotson, Professor of Mathematics at Princeton

University, for his work on the Theoretical Analysis of Waves and their Effect on Financial Markets.

THE TIMES
May 1966

Mrs Verity Gore, MA, has been appointed Mistress of Grace College, Oxford. She will take up her position in the autumn. She is a graduate of the college, and after serving with outstanding bravery in SOE during the war, helped to set up Unesco in Paris.

THE SUNDAY TIMES Bestseller list
September 1970

Charmed Circle by Claudia Vere
Scintillating insider's account of life in the Thirties; a heady mix of sex, drugs and politics.

THE CHICAGO SUN
November 1974

Daughter follows in father's footsteps to take Senate seat
Mrs Lally Messenger, the daughter of the late John Fitzgerald, who sat in the Senate for twenty-seven years and retired last year, has won her father's seat, beating the strongly-favoured Republican candidate in a hotly-contested election. Senator Messenger . . .

THE GUARDIAN
April 1985

Famous fashion designer Marcus Sebert has died of AIDS in Paris. His long-time friend . . .

Obituary

Sir John Petrus

Sir John Petrus, former Master of Balliol and one of the leading economists of his generation, died yesterday at his home in Burford at the age of 78. Educated at Charterhouse, he went up as a scholar to Balliol College, Oxford in 1926. Awarded a first in 1929, he became a Fellow of his college and embarked on his distinguished career as teacher, writer and adviser to every government from 1932 until his retirement in 1977. A fluent German-speaker, he put his knowledge of Germany to good use during an outstanding war career in MI6, and he was instrumental in the restructuring of the intelligence services in the post-war period.

After the war he returned to Oxford, and became Master of his college in 1967. Generations of undergraduates owe a debt to his inspired teaching and widely-read papers and books, and remember him with affection and respect. A notable host, his parties were a feature of Oxford life for many years. Sir John never married; his only sister, Lily von und zu Dornbach-Waldstein, survives him.

THE SUNDAY TIMES
3rd September 1985

Oxford Don was Soviet spy

By Nigel Henley

Sir John Petrus, ex-Master of Balliol, worked as a Soviet agent for more than forty years, I can now reveal. There have long been rumours of an Oxford spy ring, and Sir John was at the heart of it. Privy to the most confidential secrets in his role as government economic adviser, he used his position at Oxford to have anti-communist colleagues removed from their posts, and to recruit from among the most promising of the undergraduates he came into contact with. During the war, this traitor worked at the heart of MI6, and continued to serve in

Intelligence after the war, passing top-secret material to his Soviet control. John Petrus was probably recruited when . . .

THE DAILY MAIL
10th September 1985

Posthumous betrayal

Dozens of people are under scrutiny by MI5 now that it has been revealed that the late John Petrus, one-time Master of an Oxford college, left a detailed record of all the students and colleagues he recruited for Moscow, with 'poison pill' instructions that it should be made public if, and only if, his own spying activities became known after his death. The list has come into my hands, and among those named are the late Marcus Sebert, the world-famous fashion designer, and his lifelong friends, Mrs Verity Gore, who was Mistress of Grace College at Oxford, and the Nobel laureate, Joel Ibbotson. It has long been assumed that the Thirties generation at Oxford spent their time writing witty detective novels, while their contemporaries at Cambridge were busy betraying their country. Now it seems that perhaps the Oxford spies were simply cleverer at escaping detection.

THE GUARDIAN
15th September 1985

Joel Ibbotson: 'I was never a spy'

In a statement yesterday issued from Princeton, Manchester-born Professor Ibbotson said that, although approached by an 'unknown person' in 1936 to work for the cause of International Communism, he did not at that time, nor afterwards, ever work or pass information to Comintern, or any other communist organization.

THE DAILY EXPRESS
17th September 1985

Keep it in the family

425

It seems that treachery is catching. The story is flying round London that Mrs Verity Gore's first husband, diplomat Giles Hotspur, who died of an 'accident' in 1937, was himself a Soviet agent.

———◀━▶———

THE DAILY MAIL
21st September 1985

Paris

While the press besieged the apartment in the fashionable Seventh Arrondissement where the Gores now live, Mrs Verity Gore, named as a soviet spy in the Petrus scandal, was hiding away in the country. It is believed that she has taken refuge in a convent; Mrs Gore was received into the Catholic Church in 1959. Mr Alfred Gore refused to comment on the spying allegations, his wife's whereabouts, or the rumour that both he and his wife declined honours.

———◀━▶———

STOP PRESS

Statement from Mrs Verity Gore

'I became a communist at Oxford, and was recruited to work for Comintern in 1934. By 1938 I no longer supported the communist movement either internationally or in England. I did not know that John Petrus had anything to do with my recruitment. I was unaware until shortly before his death that Marcus Sebert had been a Soviet agent. My late husband, Giles Hotspur, was never a Soviet agent; I believe he was murdered by the Russians. I informed the British Intelligence Services of my activities during those years in the 1930s before taking up my appointment as Mistress of Grace College. They were satisfied that nothing I had done in any way helped the Soviets. Although in my own mind I am guilty of having betrayed my country and my family, and that guilt can never be absolved by any reparation made in the course of my life, I have always loved my country, then as now.'